"WHATE...   ENT
DO...
...IT

Sawyer ... the calm ... suppose ... before. ... stone into a pond and that was the end of it.

"So you see," Nyere smiled wanly, "what it is is our having a long, considered look at the aliens and reporting our findings to Command. Command then decides if Earth is ready—for the first time and for an absolute certainty—to know such aliens exist."

"And if Command decides not?"

"Then it falls upon us to make certain that they—and any witnesses to their arrival"—he shook his head, unbelieving—"cease to exist."

STAR TREK

STRANGERS FROM THE SKY

MARGARET WANDER BONNANO

BASED UPON STAR TREK CREATED BY GENE RODDENBERRY

POCKET BOOKS
New York   London   Toronto   Sydney   M-155

POCKET BOOKS, a division of Simon & Schuster, Inc.
1230 Avenue of the Americas, New York, NY 10020

This book is published by Pocket Books, a division of Simon & Schuster, Inc., under exclusive license from CBS Studios Inc.

Originally published in 1987 by Pocket Books

ISBN-13: 978-1-4165-2463-2
ISBN-10:   1-4165-2463-0

This Pocket Books paperback edition August 2006

10 9 8 7 6 5 4 3 2 1

POCKET and colophon are registered trademarks of Simon & Schuster, Inc.

Manufactured in the United States of America

Cover art by Jerry Vanderstelt

For information regarding special discounts for bulk purchases, please contact Simon & Schuster Special Sales at 1-800-456-6798 or business@simonandschuster.com.

Author's Introduction

BEING THE FIRST to do anything has its risks. It's especially dangerous to be assigned to tell the first version of a particular story in an ever-expanding universe. This is not to say it isn't exhilarating to take that one small step for a writer, but only if you're willing to accept the likelihood that the story you've told might become outdated and/or preempted by a later story.

Strangers from the Sky was written some nine years before the release of *Star Trek: First Contact*. The discrepancies between the two stories are obvious from the very first pages, but that's not necessarily a bad thing. I'll explain why in a bit. To begin, though, let me tell you how *Strangers* came to be written.

Following the release of my first *Star Trek* novel, *Dwellers in the Crucible*, in 1985, there was a new editor, Dave Stern, in charge of *Star Trek* novels at Pocket Books. Now, no one's ever accused me of being shy. I immediately called Dave to congratulate him on his assignment, and just sorta kinda hinted that I was ready to write my next *Star Trek* novel, thank you very much.

One of Dave's goals as *Star Trek* editor was to launch a series of "Giant" novels, somewhat larger both in page-count and in concept than the standard *Star Trek* novel of that era, in the hope of appealing to a broader audience and drawing in a larger readership. These Giant novels were also intended to do something that I love best about *Star Trek* novels, i.e., fill in some of the gaps before and between the Original Series episodes with the kinds of stories that there was simply no time to fit in onscreen.

Dave had already contracted Vonda McIntyre to write *Enterprise: The First Adventure,* about Kirk's first mission as the ship's captain. He was looking for a concept that would fit into the chronology just before the events of "Where No Man Has Gone Before."

I, meanwhile, wanted to write a Vulcan story. And I had a specific—much earlier—era in mind.

Some years before, I'd been loitering in Forbidden Planet, then the quintessential SF bookstore in Lower Manhattan, when I came across a big ol' trade paperback entitled *The Star Trek Space Flight Chronology,* written by Stanley and Fred Goldstein, and illustrated by Rick Sternbach, in the same era as those indispensable volumes for the serious *Star Trek* fan, Bjo Trimble's *Star Trek Concordance,* Franz Joseph's *Star Fleet Technical Manual, The Star Fleet Medical Reference Manual* (Eileen Palestine, editor), and my particular favorite, Allan Asherman's *Star Trek Compendium.* One entry in the *Chronology* grabbed my attention. It was about the crew of an Earth ship helping to repair a disabled Vulcan scoutcraft trapped in the Sol system and sending it on its way home in the year 2045, even though the official First Contact between Earth and Vulcan—according to the *Chronology*—did not take place until twenty years later.

That was the story I wanted to tell.

I ran the idea past Dave. He asked if I could work it into a frame story about Kirk, Spock, and Gary Mitchell on *Enterprise* not long after Kirk takes command. Obviously the only solution, we agreed, was a time travel story. And because I'm an English major who's been faking my way through physics for my entire adult life, I made the culprit responsible for the glitch in the time line not a mad scientist or a wormhole or a rogue star or a temporal anomaly, but a hapless Egyptian sorcerer who, like T.H. White's Merlin, had the dubious fortune of having been born backwards in time.

And, to further complicate matters (let me never be accused of writing a simple, straightforward narrative), I wrapped the Kirk/Spock/Mitchell frame story—which was already wrapped around the Vulcan First Contact with Earth story—in yet another frame story, that of a historical novel that Dr. McCoy happened to be reading in his off hours just prior to the events of *The Wrath of Khan*.

So if you're looking for a simple action/adventure novel—exploding starships and great battle scenes on every fifth page—this may not be the book for you. But if you're up for a story within a story within a story within a story featuring our favorite characters in both the TV-Trek and movie-Trek eras, confronting one of those forks in the cosmic road in *Star Trek* history where Everything Is About to Go Horribly Wrong Unless the Crew of the *Enterprise* Can Fix It, you've come to the right place.

And if you're still ready to argue that *Star Trek: First Contact* renders this story outdated and no longer interesting, hold that thought for a moment.

Yes, in the strictest sense, the time line in *Strangers from the Sky* is no longer precisely correct. It's been refuted by what was established in the first season of *Star Trek: The Next Generation*. In addition, according to *First Contact*, Zefram Cochrane is originally from Earth, not Alpha Centauri.

But given the sheer magnitude of *Star Trek* lore—onscreen, in print, and in the collective consciousness of its fans—it's little short of miraculous that ultimately so much of it tracks so well. Because if you look at it closely, *First Contact* has Cochrane meeting the Vulcans in 2063. The *Star Trek Space Flight Chronology*, from which I took my cue in *Strangers*, gives the year as 2065.

Given the fact that, according to the revised Gregorian Calendar, Jesus was born in 4 BC, maybe we can allow for a little leeway.

As for Cochrane's being from Earth, he does eventually emigrate to Alpha Centauri (before ending up, apparently in an entirely different body, on Gamma Canaris N in the episode "Metamorphosis"). If we can accept Cochrane's complete physical transformation without saying "Yeah, but—" what's a little change of venue among friends?

Ultimately, once you've gotten to the end of *Strangers from the Sky,* I think you may find that it does not so much contradict *First Contact* as complement it.

Because, really, isn't the goal just to suspend one's disbelief and enjoy a good story? You the reader are the final arbiter of whether or not what you're holding in your hands has achieved that goal.

Meanwhile, speaking of time travel, I'm still trying to wrap my brain around the notion that *Strangers from the Sky* was first published almost twenty years ago. As with all of my best experiences in writing for *Star Trek,* it was a serendipitous confluence of the skills of both writer and editor and, from the feedback I've gotten over these— Holy timewarp, Batman!—nearly two decades, it seems to be high on the list of reader favorites.

It was, and is, an honor to have been given the opportunity to write the "first" First Contact story in the *Star Trek* universe, and it's the essence of cool to see it reissued for *Star Trek*'s fortieth Anniversary. I hope you'll find as much joy in the reading of it as I did in the writing.

Margaret Wander Bonanno
September, 2005

Dedicated to my "crew":

For Russell, Danielle and Michaelangelo
("For nowhere am I so desperately needed
as among a shipload of illogical humans . . . ")

~~~~

My special thanks to:

Mimi Panitch, for saying "yes" to *Dwellers* so long ago

Karen Haas, for her two-fisted editing of same

Messrs. Harve Bennett and Jack B. Sowards, whom I have come to know only in legend, for understanding what it was we loved about *Star Trek* and giving us more of it, and for writing dialogue that rings not only true but also eternal. Mr. Bennett has been quoted as advising writers to "steal from the best." With all due respect—I believe I have.

Dave Stern, whose name means "Star," *alias* the Guardian of Forever, for offering me a variation on the no-win scenario. I accept the challenge . . .

Historian's Note:

Strangers from the Sky encompasses two different eras in the lives of Kirk and Spock.

Book I begins in those nebulous years between the *Enterprise*'s encounter with V'ger in *Star Trek: The Motion Picture*, and the death of Spock in *The Wrath of Khan*.

Book II focuses on a younger Captain James T. Kirk, newly in command, and his Vulcan first officer, not yet quite his friend, in a time just prior to the first-season television episode "Where No Man Has Gone Before." This episode first introduced Gary Mitchell, Lee Kelso and Dr. Elizabeth Dehner, and the reader may wish to use it as a referent.

Prologue

LEONARD McCOY WAS lost in the twenty-first century.

Not that he minded especially. He was so absorbed in what was going on around him he didn't care if he ever got back. He'd gotten himself stuck between the pages of a book that was creating controversies on several worlds, a book he'd initially approached with a great deal of skepticism, a book he now found he couldn't put down.

"Fascinating!" he muttered to himself, flipping pages on his office screen, amusing himself between consultations. He realized who he sounded like. "Well, I mean it's *interesting*. Oh, hell, nobody can hear me anyway— it *is* fascinating! Damnedest thing I've ever read!"

Jim would love this! McCoy thought, settling in for a good long read and hoping no one would page him. *I can't wait to recommend it to him.*

Book One

STRANGERS
from the
SKY

Garamet Jen-Saunor

Author's Foreword

There is no underestimating the sometimes serendipitous impact of coincidence upon the course of
history.

To say that the United Federation of Planets owes its
existence to the malfunction of a Vulcan scoutcraft in
the Terran year 2045 may seem exaggeration, particularly in view of Earthmen's response to that event.
Nevertheless, Earth at least might have condemned
itself to total isolationism in a vast and lonely universe,
were it not for the chain of events initiated by the arrival
of the strangers from the sky.

Every Federation schoolchild knows that Earthmen's first encounter with alien life was the result of the
voyage of the *UNSS Icarus* to Alpha Centauri in 2048.
The establishment of peaceful relations between the
two safely similar humanoid worlds made it easy for
Terrans to overcome any residual fears they might
retain about "little green men."

The rest of the history of that era reads like a utopian
dream. The cooperation between Earth and Centauri,
together with the genius that was Zefram Cochrane,
produced the breakthrough in warp drive technology in
2055. Subsequent contacts with Vulcan, Tellar, and

Epsilon Indii, homeworld of the Andorians, made the establishment of the United Federation of Planets in the year 2087 a logical progression.

The first encounter with Vulcans, according to official sources, came about when the Earth ship *UNSS Amity* rescued a disabled Vulcan craft adrift inside the solar system in 2065. Despite vast philosophical and cultural differences and the simple strangeness of this nonhuman race, the encounter with the Centaurians nearly two decades before made it possible for Earthmen to free themselves of prejudice and fear. Diplomatic relations with Vulcan were established in 2068 with the arrival of the first Vulcan delegation on Earth, and the alliance between the two worlds has been virtually untroubled since.

It is all readily available to us in history tapes and the *Amity*'s ship's log, yet another self-congratulatory example of how human altruism reached across the barriers of difference to offer the hand of friendship.

Except that it didn't happen that way at all.

ONE

Tatya raised herself on one elbow and gaped through the sleeping-room port at the night sky, her china-blue eyes wide. She hadn't imagined it.

"Yoshi? Yoshi, wake up. Look!"

He was sleeping on his stomach as usual, stirred and groaned, tried to burrow deeper under the thermal quilt, but Tatya shook him again. He pushed himself up on his elbows and vaulted out of the waterbed in a single graceful movement, padded across the floor to stand before the wide port in all his lean, golden nakedness.

"It's a meteor," he muttered, one hand holding his long black hair out of his eyes. "All day in the outback mending fences and you wake me for a stray meteor. Tatya, for gods' sake—"

"It's not a meteor," Tatya said emphatically. Lord knew they saw enough of those out here where the sky was two-thirds of their world. She stood at the port beside Yoshi, naked too—no one but fish to gawk at them this far out—as broad as he was narrow, as pale as he was golden, her heavy blond hair in two plaits down her back. She pointed to where the strange light moved down the arc of the sky. "It's not bright enough,

9

and it's moving too slowly. Steadily, not tumbling. Like it's on a set course. It's a ship, Yoshi."

"AeroNav would have signaled us if there'd been an accident." Yoshi yawned, dived back into the warm nest they'd made among the bedclothes. "It's a meteor. Or space junk. Somebody's antiquated satellite come hurtling down on our heads. It'll be all over the screen tomorrow. 'FAILURE OF SALVAGE OP; VITAL DATA LOST OVER SOUTH PACIFIC.'"

He considered putting the pillow over his head, as if that would protect him from things falling out of the sky.

"One of these days something'll hit us square on, you'll see. 'KELP FARM STATION OBLITERATED, TWO DEAD.' Wasn't enough we tried to destroy the ecology down here. Now we're cluttering up the whole solar system."

"Cynic!" Tatya clucked, crawling back into the bed beside him.

The strange orangish glow across the royal-blue bowl of mid-ocean starscape was gone now. Maybe it was only a meteor or space junk, but it had been awfully close; AeroNav should have warned them. Tatya imagined she could have heard its hiss and plop as it hit the water.

Silly, she knew, but perched on a tiny platform kilometers from nowhere, surrounded by acres of undulating kelp and in the company of only one other person, one got to thinking sometimes. Only those with unshakable psych profiles were assigned to the outlying agronomy posts; the screening was almost as rigid as that for deep space. Tatya and Yoshi were optimally matched and well adjusted to the isolation. Still . . .

"Yoshi?"

There was a feeble movement among the bedclothes.

"Just suppose—what if it was an alien spaceship? Seventy-five years ago Asimov stated there were tens of thousands of Class M worlds that might support

10

intelligent life. And the ship we sent to Alpha Centauri—"

"—won't be back for another nine years, if at all," Yoshi mumbled sleepily. "Any truly intelligent species would take one look at us and keep right on going. Million years on this planet, still haven't gotten the knack of not killing each other. Three World Wars, Colonel Green . . ."

"But that's all over," Tatya insisted. "We're a United Earth now. And someday we'll break the light barrier and our chances of encountering other species will increase a hundred, maybe a thousand times!" She jounced the bed in her excitement. "It has to happen. Maybe within our lifetime."

"Time-warp speed is still only theoretical," Yoshi the cynic stated, and suddenly he was snoring softly, unaware that his prophecy was about to be fulfilled. Something had already come hurtling down on their heads, and it was about to hit them square on.

Tatya was the first to spot the wreckage the next morning.

She and Yoshi were in the hydrofoil, performing their weekly tour of the perimeter to make sure the barriers had held (little worse than having to pick masses of jellyfish tentacles or decapitated squid out of the kelp braids after storm damage) and that no vessel had run afoul of their planted acreage despite the warning buoys. It wouldn't be the first time they'd had to rescue some private sea- or air-going pleasure craft caught in the weir, batteries dead, food and water depleted. But what Tatya saw was something other.

"Cut power!" she yelled over the thrum of the foil's motor.

They'd requested a replacement damper months ago, but it had gotten buried in bureaucracy. The kelp and algae and soybean farms, basis of all synthetic food production on this planet, which at long last had

11

learned to feed all its peoples, were supposed to get top priority on equipment requisitions, but that was the official story.

When Yoshi didn't hear her, Tatya reached past him and flipped the main drive toggle herself, answering his startled look by merely pointing off to starboard.

"There!"

As the hydrofoil settled into the water at cruising speed so as not to disturb whatever floated there, the shape of the wreck was unmistakable despite the extensive damage. This was an extra-atmospheric vehicle, a spacecraft. There were many such vessels used for exploration and mining operations throughout the sol system, including a regular ferry making the run between Earth, its moonbases, and the recently established Martian Colonies. But this vessel was none of theirs.

"It's not an Earth ship," Tatya said with that absolute bedrock certainty that always made Yoshi tease her.

"Since when are you an expert?" he started in on her now, his mouth twitching with amusement as he pulled athwart the blackened hull and cut the foil's motor to a standstill.

A fragment of what could have been lettering still visible on the seared and pitted hull, in no alphabet he would recognize, might have shaken him just a little if he'd bothered to look at it.

"Does it look like anything you've ever seen?" Tatya demanded, touching it tentatively, as if it might have been alive.

"Looks like it might have had somebody in it at one time," Yoshi said, avoiding her question. "May as well see."

He stood up in the bobbing foil and threw a line out to the wreckage, securing them together. Standing astride the two, his long skinny legs wobbling as he struggled to keep his balance, he tugged at what looked like a hatch, warped away from its housing by the impact, offering them access to the craft's insides and, very possibly, answers to all their questions.

"Well, does it?" Tatya insisted.

"Probably some top-secret new design we mere civilians aren't privy to," Yoshi said vaguely, intent on what he was doing.

He'd fetched a grappling hook out of the hold and was using the foil's auxiliary power to lever the hatch open with a raw, screeching noise. When he got it to where he could move it manually, he did so, peering into the darkness within, where all he could see at first in contrast to the brilliance of sunlit seascape around them were the lights of the monitors and what he took to be corpses. No one could have survived the outer hull temperature of the incendiary they'd watched across the sky last night. Yoshi suddenly pulled back, jerking his hands away as if the hull were still hot.

"Gods, Tatya, I think there's someone still alive in there!"

"Alive? But how?"

"I don't know! I don't see how, but—"

"Let me see!"

She pushed him out of the way to get a closer look. Tatya was a paramedic—at least one member of every station team was required to be—and if there was a chance to save a life, no matter whose—

First Mate Melody Sawyer of the *CSS Delphinus* handed Captain Nyere a cup of ersatz coffee from the dispenser and sipped at her own, trying not to be too conspicuous in her loitering. She had to know if what she'd seen in the sky toward the end of last night's watch had anything to do with the orders coming through on Nyere's screen right now.

Jason Nyere tasted the coffee and made the obligatory gagging sound (ironic that the hold was stocked with cases of the genuine article—hermetically sealed, time coded, inaccessible short of detonation—all

13

bound for agronomy station personnel, while he and his crew were consigned this stuff, concocted from the very kelp harvested on the stations, molecularly processed into something that tasted like a cross between parched sorghum and Nile Delta water at low tide on washday but sure as hell wasn't coffee), tore his slate-gray eyes away from the static-filled screen, and nailed his first officer with them.

"Sawyer, when this comes through it'll be Priority One," he rumbled at her, hoping she'd have the good grace to leave before he had to order her out.

"Coffee's that bad, huh?" Sawyer drawled, stretching her long, tennis player's legs in their belled uniform trousers, not taking the hint.

"'Coffee,' my Aunt Tillie!" Nyere grumbled. "Time was, I am told, when the navy got the best rations, not the worst."

"Time was, Captain suh, when the navy was a purely military entity," said Sawyer—whose several-times-great-granddaddy had seen military service in a place called Shiloh in a time when there were only nations or fragments of same, not a united humanity putting its world back together in the wake of juggernauts the like of Khan Noonian Singh and Colonel Green—"not the misbegotten agglomerate of research/surveillance/diplomatic courier/occasional deterrent/general maintenance/errand boy/chief-cook-and-bottle-washer/organized grab-ass entity that it is today. Suh!"

Nyere chuckled softly. Sawyer had these reactionary fits often; she was an incredible hardliner when it suited her. Personally, he preferred the enlightened demilitarization of today's Combined Services to what had gone before.

"You'd do things differently, I take it?" he inquired, though he'd heard this speech before.

"Damn straight! Jack of all trades is master of none,"

14

Melody snapped back. There was something incongruous about such macho opinions coming from this erstwhile southern belle with her freckles and her soft drawl, neither of which took the edge off the opinions or the willfulness behind them. Sawyer had been transferred four times in her early career before Jason Nyere decided her abrasiveness was exactly what he needed to keep him from going soft. "This ship being a prime example of the problem, suh. We are designated neither as submarine nor exclusively surface vessel, neither battleship nor merchantman, yet we are somehow expected to act as all four simultaneously. Suggest that in a real crisis we'd get tangled in our own lines and sink under our own weight. Suggest the absence of identifiable parameters is enough to reduce the entire crew to a state of permanent paranoid schizophrenia. Suh!"

"Speak for yourself, Sawyer," Nyere said. "Some of us would rather—"

The communications screen crackled and bleeped (MESSAGE COMING THROUGH), and Nyere remembered where this conversation had begun.

"Melody, I'm not kidding. Priority One. Take a hike."

"Captain, suh, respectfully suggest you try and make me!" she shot back. She was a hardliner only when it suited her; the rest of the time she was insubordinate to the point of—

Nyere sighed. The two of them had served on the same ships for over a decade. He'd saved her life once, she his twice, and he'd been godfather to the younger of her two kids. The tough-as-nails act had no effect on him. He waited for her to soften.

"Let me stay this once, Jason, please?"

"All right, damn you. But keep out of range of the screen. It's my neck."

"Tough neck!" Sawyer remarked, sidling over to where she could see without being seen.

15

The message was out of the Norfolk Island Command Center, from AeroNav Control itself.

Tatya, her hands full with the torch and the hydrofoil's emergency medical kit, had misjudged the distance and lowered herself none too gently into the damaged craft. It began to yaw violently and Yoshi lost his footing, tumbling backward into the foil. By the time he'd righted himself, nursing barked shins and an assortment of bruises, he could see that the spacecraft had settled considerably lower in the water.

"Tatya?" he called into the darkness below. "You're taking on a lot of water. How's the situation where you are?"

The sound of sloshing was her only answer.

"Get me the spare light down here!" she barked after some time. "Whoever said these things were waterproof . . ."

He lowered the second torch down to her, wondering if he should join her to hurry things or if that would only make the craft sink faster.

"Don't move around more than you have to!" he shouted down to her. There was no answer. "Listen, if it starts going under, I'm pulling you out. Never mind about anyone else. You hear me?"

He got no answer to that either, hadn't expected one. Tatya was intent on saving lives, could only concentrate on one thing at a time. Yoshi shifted his bare feet in his impatience. Tatya's unseen movements continued to rock the craft. It slowly settled deeper in the water, balanced precariously on the flexible cables of the barrier weir, listing inexorably away from the hydrofoil, pulling the securing hawser taut.

"Tatiana . . ." Yoshi called sweetly after he thought the silence had gone on too long. He never called her that when she was within swinging distance. "Can't you hurry? Or at least give me some idea—"

16

"There were four altogether. The two aft are dead. Incinerated," she reported flatly. "No surprise. What I can't figure out is why the other two aren't."

The two aft, she didn't bother mentioning, floated sluggishly in an ever-rising pool of seawater at the skewed lower end of the cabin. If Yoshi knew how bad it was, he'd order her out immediately, never mind the two survivors at the forward end, still strapped in their seats, unconscious and pinned under wreckage, but alive. Tatya inched her way through the rising water, gripping machinery and chairbacks against the slippery slant of the deck until she reached the other two.

"What pretty uniforms!" Yoshi heard her exclaim. "Everything here is so attractive—functional, but beautiful at the same time. The furnishings, the machinery. It's all so—so wonderful!"

Yoshi felt his scalp prickle. That didn't sound at all like old practical Tatya.

"How's the air down there? You're not making much sense."

"I'm fine. Rig the bosun's chair and don't bother me!" *That* sounded like Tatya. Yoshi went to work.

"Odd!" he heard her say, half to herself. "I can't find a pulse on either of them!" She raised her voice to make sure he heard her. "I'm going to start sending them up!"

"'Them' who?" Yoshi shouted as he scrambled to rig the rescue harness with its snap-away stretcher. He didn't expect an answer to that either. For some reason he couldn't explain he'd been scanning the horizon since Tatya had gone below, anticipating company. Certainly they hadn't been the only ones who'd seen it go down. "At least tell me what I'm rigging for!"

"The first one's male, approximately six feet, one-sixty to one-seventy pounds," Tatya recited, all professional. Yoshi could hear her sloshing around; the water level was rising, then. "Unconscious due to blow on the head, possible concussion. Some second- and third-degree burns and—damn! None of my readings on internal organs makes any sense, and it's too dark down here. We'll have to risk moving him. You got the full stretcher rigged?"

Yoshi snapped it to the aft hoist and tugged the lines.

"All set!"

"Okay, lower away. I'm checking the second one now."

"Male, young what?" Yoshi couldn't resist as he lowered the stretcher vertically through the hatch. "Sounds awfully big for a little green man. No tentacles, extra arms? You sure he isn't an android? How many heads does he have?"

"Yoshi, *dammit!*" She sounded more disappointed than angry.

"Just trying to lighten things up a little. You need some help lifting him?"

That earned him some of Tatya's favorite Ukrainian barnyardisms; in practical application she was stronger than he was. After a moment he felt her tug the line and started the foil's auxiliary to begin hoisting her patient out, guiding the line with his hands so the stretcher wouldn't bump the hatch.

"Male, young *what*, Tatya?" he had to ask one more time.

He caught a glimpse of her pale, concerned face in the cabin below as the stretcher emerged slowly into the sunlight.

"I'm not sure. You have any relatives on Mars?"

". . . located and if at all possible retrieved. Standard radiation and microorganism precautionaries to be implemented. Survivors, if any, to be quarantined aboard your vessel under Regulation 17-C until we contact you. Under no circumstances are you to break radio silence. Do you copy, *Delphinus*?"

"We copy, Control," Captain Nyere said to the

screen. "Commodore, what exactly is it that we're looking for?"

"Not your concern, Captain. Just follow your orders."

"And when—if—we find it?"

"If Regulation 17-C applies, you will stand by until you receive further orders. If not—General Order 2013, Captain. Methodology at your discretion."

The screen burst into static without so much as a signoff. Jason Nyere realized he was sweating.

"Jesus!" he whispered. "This is the kind of thing you have nightmares about. I never thought it would come down to me. I can't do that!"

"Can't do what?" Sawyer demanded, moving between him and the vacant screen; Nyere had forgotten she was there. "General Order 2013 is not in any reg book I ever read."

"It wouldn't be. The 2000 series is accessible to command officers only," Nyere said softly, vaguely. He kept dabbing the perspiration from his brow and his mustache, but it didn't help. He stared at his sodden handkerchief as if he'd never seen it before. "It's *Flag Officers' Handbook*, crisis activated only. It's none of your—I told you not to listen in!"

A number of smart-ass retorts sprang to Sawyer's lips; she clamped her rather horsey teeth down on them and didn't speak. She'd seen Jason stare down the muzzle of a loaded neutron cannon without breaking a sweat. She'd never seen him look this frightened. Unobtrusively she moved behind him and began massaging his shoulders. If any of the crew stumbled in now, there'd be hell to pay for insinuations. Let them dare. If one old friend couldn't comfort another in times of stress—

"Jason, what is 2013?"

"Two-oh-one-three—and I shouldn't be telling you this," he said tiredly, slumped in his chair, unresponsive to her ministrations, "is a contingency plan for possible alien invasion."

Melody's hands stopped. She laughed.

"You mean they're sending us out to look for a flying saucer? I don't believe it!"

Jason nodded dismally.

"Believe it. Ever since the first UFO sightings, there's been a contingency plan of one kind or another on the books to contain, assess, and, if necessary, destroy any incursion from beyond our solar system. Even when it was passed off as the hallucinations of a few crackpots, there was that much credence given to it. Now that we're capable of moving out of the system ourselves, now that we've been sending messages for over a century, it seems all the more likely that someone or something is going to answer us."

He paused. He was saying these things, his life and his command were being dictated to by them, but he couldn't bring himself to believe them, nor what he was going to have to do if they were fact.

"Whatever it was that went down out there last night, Melody, it wasn't one of ours."

Sawyer paced the confines of *Delphinus*'s fairly roomy captain's cabin, contemplating the calm and sparkling Pacific, somewhere in which a supposedly alien spacecraft had gone down the night before. Chances were it had simply plummeted like a stone into a pond and that was the end of it. General Order 2013 would be preempted by something as basic as gravity and the depths of the ocean floor.

"Why 'destroy'?" Melody asked at last. "I can see if they were hostile. An invasion force. But they'd hardly come in one ship at a time, would they? And the order wouldn't have turned you into the face of Armageddon in the time I've been sitting here. It's something else, isn't it?"

Nyere smiled wanly, unable to shake his awful dread.

"You're right. It's nothing so simple as any of that. What it is is our having a long, considered look at the alien or aliens and reporting our findings to Command. Command then decides if old Earth is ready—for the first time and for an absolute certainty—to know that such aliens exist."

"And if Command decides not?"

"Then it falls upon us to make certain that they—and any witnesses to their arrival"—he shook his head, unbelieving—"cease to exist."

"Relatives on Mars?" Yoshi said. "Tatya—"

Whatever comeback Yoshi might have had was throttled in mid-breath as the first survivor hove into view in the brilliant sunlight. The fact was that despite burns and abrasions and just plain dirt he did look Japanese, at least at first hurried glance as Yoshi swung the hoist and lowered the stretcher below decks to move him off of it and onto one of the bunks. Under closer scrutiny, though . . .

Yoshi felt his hands go numb and deliberately shut off the part of his brain that tended to extrapolate from what he saw to the extremities of what in all cosmic senses it could mean.

What if Tatya was right?

She was tugging on the line with a kind of urgency, anxious to get her second patient up, and Yoshi shrugged off his reverie and forced his hands to work, but even as he went through the motions, maneuvered the lines, kept an eye on the water level (another foot and it would reach the lower edge of the hatch, already the stray wave lapped inside—hurry, Tatya, hurry!), he still found time to stare over his shoulder at his newly acquired passenger.

It all happened rather quickly after that. Tatya's movements, to judge from the craft's renewed rocking, became little short of frantic. Yoshi heard her shout something as he hand-over-handed the stretcher up for the second time, and had to ask her to repeat.

"I said she seems to have smashed her face to hell,"

21

Tatya yelled. "I wanted to warn you. Knowing how you usually react to blood."

"Don't sweat it!" Yoshi yelled back, annoyed. It wasn't his fault he was squeamish, and she didn't have to be so superior about it.

He had no time to test his tolerance. Without warning the foundering craft tilted precipitously off the barrier, snapping the hawser, which caught Yoshi on the ankle. He howled in pain as his leg buckled, refused to work right for some seconds. The craft lurched and spun and water poured into the open hatch. Yoshi shoved the laden stretcher unceremoniously onto the deck, unsnapping it from the harness, which he flung desperately down into the filling darkness.

"Tatya, now! Grab the line and hold on!"

The auxiliary chugged and wheezed as it pulled Tatya upstream against the current. Yoshi flung her, gasping, drenched, and cursing onto the deck, left her to recover on her own while he veered the bucking hydrofoil as far away from the sucking maelstrom of the sinking craft as he could.

In an instant it was over. The sea was calm, and except for a slight fraying of the barrier cables, the spacecraft might never have been.

"You all right?" Yoshi asked over his shoulder, pointing the foil toward home.

"Waterlogged," Tatya admitted, hugging him squishily, water and kelp strands streaming out of her hair. "You?"

"Hawser damn near busted my ankle." He showed her the ugly red swelling that would be three shades of purple by nightfall. "Bruised my backside. Damaged my pride. I'll live. Better have a look at your patients."

Something in the way he said it had Tatya below in a flash. Yoshi said nothing more, pretended not to look as she examined them for the first time in full light.

"Yoshi, come here a minute," he heard her say, her

22

voice on the last calm edge of panic and beginning to fray. "Turn off the damn engine and come here!"

He did. She held out her hands to him in the sunlight. Considering the extent of the survivors' injuries she'd expected blood, but this—

"Tell me I'm not crazy," she pleaded. "Tell me I'm really seeing this."

"You're not crazy, Tatya. I see it too. I saw it when you sent the first one up."

"Bozhe moi!" Tatya breathed. "It's *green!*"

~~~

"Boy, do I remember that feeling!" McCoy sat warming himself at the fire in Jim Kirk's apartment. "First time I saw surgery on a Vulcan—I couldn't have been more than a first-year med student, never been offworld, didn't know a Vulcan to speak to—I'm telling you, I couldn't make a fist for the rest of the day! It was so *strange!* You expect blood to be red, dammit, no matter what the textbooks tell you."

It was evening. Kirk had put in a full day at the Admiralty. Spock was out on *Enterprise* for the next several weeks, taking his cadets through maneuvers. McCoy as usual managed to make himself to home wherever he was. He'd been telling Kirk about *Strangers from the Sky,* hoping to pique the amateur historian's curiosity.

"We've all had our moments of strangeness with other species, Bones," Jim Kirk said quietly, gazing into the fire. For some reason the topic made him uneasy. "And God knows there's been enough written on the subject, from abstracts in *Xenopsych Today* to those interspecies biology texts we used to pass around when we were kids. From the sound of it, this book of yours seems to fall somewhere in between."

McCoy cocked an eyebrow at him.

"That's a helluvan assumption from someone who hasn't read it."

23

"Nor do I intend to," Kirk replied pleasantly enough. "That particular era doesn't interest me. Never has. I don't know why, but—well. Freshen your drink?"

"Don't know what you're missing!" McCoy grumbled, keeping a weather eye on the level of the bourbon as Kirk poured.

"I remember the last book you recommended," Kirk said. Planetside the good doctor found far more leisure for reading—one of his tamer vices—than he did on double Sickbay shifts in space. "Gave me nightmares for weeks. You know the one I mean—*The Last Reflection?*"

"*The Final Reflection,*" McCoy corrected him. "Dammit, Jim, you're getting soft! Tell me that wasn't one of the most electrifying docudramas you ever read. Tell me you didn't enjoy it."

"It was and I did," Kirk acknowledged. "I just—didn't like the thoughts it left me with afterward."

"Such as?"

"Such as how there really are no Good Guys and Bad Guys. Just a lot of people falling over each other trying to do what they think is right. And about how fragile history is."

He had caught his breath then, the way he always did when he was about to spin off on one of his poetical monologues. McCoy settled back and let him fly, along for the ride. Damned if the man couldn't talk you to the gates of hell if you let him.

"I got to thinking about how one individual can sometimes change the course of history," Kirk was saying. "How if Krenn had been the kind of stereotype Klingon we'd come to expect, if Tagore had been a lesser human, we might have destroyed each other long ago. You read books like that and you realize how fragile the whole structure is. The old theory that if Hitler hadn't been born, Earth's Second World War

24

wouldn't have happened. Or that without Khan Singh there'd have been no Third—"

"—and if the archduke hadn't been assassinated at Sarajevo, there'd have been no First and no reason for the other two," McCoy cut in. "Bull! Jim, you don't really believe all that hokum? War was the human condition until we outgrew it, Hitler or no. That one-man-as-catalyst theory is a lot of horse hockey!"

Kirk shrugged. "I don't know that for sure. Sometimes it seems so much hinges on little things. One small incident, one misspoken word, one tiny misinterpreted gesture and the whole structure collapses. When I think of how much power we have, and how little common sense, I get the shakes."

"Which is exactly why you'll love this book, Jim," McCoy promised. "It deals with an incident none of us knew about until now. Our first *real* contact with alien life, the one the textbooks never told us about, and how we almost botched it so completely we might never have tried it again. Might have curled up in our little isolationist nest and pulled the covers over our heads and let history and the Federation pass us by."

"I don't buy that, Bones," Jim Kirk said, moving about the room winding those of his antique clocks that needed winding, a nightly ritual. "Sounds like a pretty big fish story to me."

"Not if you consider the era we're talking about," McCoy argued. "Earth was less than fifty years away from Khan's war, had just begun to consider itself a united world, and it had its growing pains. People still living who'd lost family and friends in that war and could never be reconciled, some cities still in ruins, a lot of grievances and old vendettas still festering. Depending on how you looked at it, it was either the best or the worst time for a bunch of aliens to come dropping in out of the sky."

"By the time *Amity* found that Vulcan ship adrift off

Neptune all that was over," Kirk said, resetting a particularly recalcitrant grandfather clock, half listening. "We'd already been to Alpha Centauri—"

"You haven't been listening to a damn word I've said, have you?" McCoy said disgustedly. "This happened a full twenty years before that."

Kirk restarted the grandfather's pendulum, closed the glass fronting, and frowned.

"What?"

"This Vulcan ship fell to Earth while the Centauri mission was still three years from its destination. We're talking sublight, remember? The crew heading for Centauri had no idea they'd find an advanced civilization, had no idea *what* they'd find. This was the Dark Ages of interstellar travel, and here's an interesting point: mankind had been sending and listening for radio messages from other worlds since the 1970s. We were actively seeking contact, but only on our terms. We had to be the aggressors. It was okay for us to go outside our system and find 'them'—whoever 'they' were—*out there*, but God forbid 'they' presume to set foot on our soil without knocking first. Worse, not only did they look funny and talk funny, but they had all these spooky habits like reading minds and suppressing their emotions and living practically forever from our standpoint, and being stronger and smarter and having warp drive . . ."

Kirk sat slowly, fiddled with the fireplace poker, watched the flames.

"Zefram Cochrane is credited with the breakthrough in warp drive," he said adamantly, as if it were set in stone somewhere.

"As far as *human* technology was concerned," McCoy corrected him. "The Vulcans already had it."

"That's impossible."

"Is it? They were out in space centuries before we were. You've heard Spock's lecture on ethnocentricity, on how just because *we* haven't discovered something doesn't mean it doesn't exist? How many superior species have we discovered since? That's the whole crux of the problem, Jim, the whole thrust of the book. It was the *timing* that was wrong. The *Amity* story makes good copy. Brave Earthmen rescuing injured aliens from their damaged ship and all that. But you of all people should know that human history is seldom that neat. By the time of the *Amity* incident we were receptive to alien contact. Twenty years earlier Vulcans or anybody else were just as likely to be burned as witches or blasted out of the cornfield with a 12-gauge as they would've been in any prior century. Neither Vulcan nor Earth wants to admit to that, but there it is. That's why it's been hushed up until now."

"Earth and Vulcan, joined in some—conspiracy—to keep this secret all these years?" Kirk mused, shook his head, rejected it. "Sorry, Bones, you've lost me there."

"The Vulcan Archives were sealed until the death of the last survivor," McCoy explained patiently. "Nothing conspiratorial about it. By reason of her credentials, Dr. Jen-Saunor was the first person—and the only human, by the way—to have access to them. On the human side, on the other hand, all contemporary Earth accounts were mysteriously 'misplaced.' Government files chewed up by computers, witnesses gone to ground, the usual nonsense."

"That much I can accept," Kirk said. "But not the sealing of the Vulcan Archives. It seems— uncharacteristic. Isn't the truth supposed to be accessible to all?"

"Not when it causes embarrassment to both sides," McCoy reiterated. "With the exception of the few who tried to help, most humans came out of this looking like hysterics or spoiled children. And the Vulcans could hardly be pleased with having to be less than completely truthful about certain pertinent details of the event."

"Convenient for the author, though," Kirk remarked dryly. "She's the only one with access to the files, no one on Earth knows enough to refute her. No wonder the book's so controversial. I'll refrain from calling it an outright scam, but—let's say it's an 'artful fabrication.' Fiction passing itself off as history. Like those *Ancient Astronaut* books a few centuries back."

"Now wait a minute—" McCoy growled.

"Another thing—" Kirk interrupted. "This novelistic style of hers. Reproducing dialogue as if she were actually in the room when it happened—"

"What's wrong with making history accessible?" McCoy wanted to know. "Anyone from a ten-year old to a Starfleet admiral can read this and understand it. And the dialogue, by the bye, was taken from the journals of one of the Vulcan survivors. As I'm certain you know from personal experience, once a Vulcan says something, he never forgets it."

"Sort of like studying Hannibal's campaigns from the perspective of the elephants," Kirk suggested. McCoy was not amused.

"You don't like your preconceived notions challenged, do you, you old dinosaur?" he badgered Kirk. "Don't like your safe little textbook version of history threatened. You're getting conservative in your old age, Admiral. Very bad business!"

"You want some coffee?" Kirk asked innocently, stifling a yawn.

"Not the kind you serve!" McCoy grumbled. "Closest it ever came to a coffee bean was in a dictionary. Right under 'bilge water.'"

"Well, don't mind if I do." Kirk meandered out to the kitchen, punched a single preset button on the synthesizer.

"Curious," McCoy heard him say.

"What is?" the doctor asked, contemplating the harbor lights.

"Assuming I believed any of it," Kirk said, returning from the kitchen sipping something that at least was hot, "and I'm not saying I do—here you have two Vulcans stranded on Earth twenty years too soon. Their ship is beyond repair, and they're totally at the mercy of humans and their primitive technology. How'd they get back home?"

"I'm not saying they did," McCoy replied.

"You're not going to tell me they spent the rest of their lives on Earth!"

"No, I'm not going to tell you that, either. I'm not going to tell you a damn thing."

"I can just see them putting in a request for a sublight ship," Kirk mused. "Or having to bob their ears and assimilate. I can't imagine a worse fate for a first-generation Vulcan. Or doesn't your highly acclaimed historian tell you?"

McCoy didn't answer.

"Time I was moving on," he said pointedly. "Got a six A.M. consult and a morning full of office hours staring me in the face."

Kirk tried to block his way to the door, only half kidding.

"Come on, Bones, tell me. What happened to the Vulcans?"

McCoy slipped his disk copy of *Strangers from the Sky* out of a pocket and held it out to Kirk, tantalizing. "Why don't you read it and find out?"

Kirk looked at the garish little plastic disk and almost took it. Something about that era of first contacts had always made him uneasy, perhaps the very thing McCoy had been on about all night: the innate Murphy's Law capacity of humans to botch whatever they put their hands to. He thought about an isolationist Earth, alone against a universe rife with unknowns. No

Federation, no Starfleet. No half-Vulcan first officer, who was also his friend . . .

Kirk handed the disk back to McCoy. "Thanks, no, Bones. Maybe some other time."

"Your loss!" McCoy growled, stalking past him to the door. "I'm going home to find out what does happen!"

TWO

"Destruction before detection."

It was the axiom etched on every scoutcraft commander's soul. Nevertheless, no commander could depart for what until recently had amounted to a several decades' journey without the formality of having the words reiterated by the commanding prefect. It might be illogical to hear repeated that which one knew as first principle of one's profession, yet it was required.

"Destruction before detection."

It was the definitive distillation of the precepts of *T'Kahr* Savar, first to hold the office of prefect for offworld exploration upon its creation some 170.15 years ago. It could also, of course, be inferred from the philosophy of IDIC as found in the writings of Surak long before such exploration was feasible.

"It is not given to us," Prefect Savar had written in his declaration of intent before assuming office those many years ago, "to influence or affect in any way the normal course of events upon any world we may observe in our journeys. The sociopolitical implications of any such intervention are too grave."

31

Subsequent study of those near worlds with advanced civilizations confirmed the wisdom of Savar's precept. It was found, for example, that the blue-skinned and antennaed inhabitants of one such world had grounded their cosmology in a complex polytheism that rendered their solar system the whole of the universe. To confront them with living proof of the existence of an alien species—pointed-eared, green-blooded, different in all respects—was to throw them into possibly irreconcilable theological turmoil.

In another instance, the suidaen inhabitants of the 61 Cygnus system, despite their own recent history of space exploration, were a conspicuously xenophobic species, prone to violence when their beliefs, however erroneous, were challenged. To communicate with such a species would only provoke the violence Surak had sought to eradicate among his people.

And while the inhabitants of the Sol system were highly advanced, heterogeneous, open to the new and strange, and had in fact been actively seeking communication with other intelligent life for over seventy of their years, they had only recently found peace among themselves after a series of global wars. Any threat to that tenuous peace from without was anathema.

"It is our purpose to study these worlds, with a view toward a time when first contact is deemed practicable, without giving any evidence that we ourselves exist," Savar had concluded in his declaration. "For that reason, any craft disabled within an inhabited system must self-destruct before its presence is discovered. Destruction before detection."

Destruction before detection. In the ensuing years it had never yet come to that, yet every scoutcraft was equipped with a self-destruct mechanism, and every commander was prepared at all times to activate it.

Destruction before detection. It was the first application of the Vulcan Prime Directive.

Commander T'Lera, offspring of the same Prefect Savar who had composed those words, stood before the current prefect, awaiting her final departure orders.

"The commander's choice of crew complement is of course at her own discretion—" Prefect T'Saaf began, contemplating the roster before her.

"—nevertheless the prefect is justified in questioning at least two of my choices," T'Lera finished for her, her voice perhaps a shade drier than the occasion warranted. "I am open to discussion."

T'Saaf moved her eyes away from the roster to the imperturbable face before her. It was said that T'Lera had qualified for the prefecture before her and refused it, preferring instead the reaches of space where she had spent most of her life. T'Saaf studied that face, handsome even in middle years, the eyes never quite fixed on any planet-bound thing but always elsewhere and afar, and could well believe it. So to her had fallen that which her abilities merited, but only because this one had refused it. T'Saaf would indeed welcome a discussion of the liberties T'Lera sometimes chose to take.

"The choice of *T'Kahr* Savar as your historiographer —" the prefect began.

"—was at his own behest, Prefect," T'Lera said. For once her eyes came close to focusing on the near-at-hand. "My father is old. He has not many years left to him. If he wishes to spend them in service, it is my judgment he is within his right."

"He *has* served," Prefect T'Saaf pointed out. "In the reaches of space, and in this office, for many years and admirably. No further service is required of him."

She got no answer to this. T'Lera's true reasons, and Savar's, were other than those stated.

"Does his healer deem him fit for such a journey?" T'Saaf demanded.

33

"He has made the journey thrice before the breaking of the light barrier," T'Lera reminded her, not precisely answering the question. "Six decades of his life have been spent in the void between the stars. It is logical to assume that this mode is more congenial to him than the confines of any planet."

"Nevertheless, if he is unable adequately to perform his duties . . ."

T'Saaf did not finish. The suggestion that her predecessor might be in less than optimum health or strength might be cruel, but its logic was unarguable. A scoutship's personnel space was at a premium, its food supply limited. Every crewmember would be employed to the fullest, and no one, not even a former prefect, had the right to voyage as a mere spectator.

"None can know the future," T'Lera replied, though she did not offer it as an excuse. "Savar is well aware of his responsibility to the rest of the crew. He will accept the consequences."

In another the tone might be pleading; in T'Lera it was only reasonable.

"If my father desires to make the journey one final time—"

"'One final time,'" Prefect T'Saaf repeated. "And if he does not return?"

"That, too, at his own behest," T'Lera replied. She unstiffened her rigid posture for the briefest moment, came as close as she could to making a personal request. "He has not long, and there is nothing that holds him to this world. One who has lived in space is entitled to die in space."

T'Saaf gave no answer, but locked her eyes with T'Lera's, forcing the latter to focus down, to remain with the planet-bound, the temporal, the personal.

"I accept the responsibility," T'Lera said, undaunted, her far-searching eyes all the more penetrating for their narrowed focus. "For my father's sake."

34

"Kaiidth!" T'Saaf acknowledged, and T'Lera had her will, at least in this.

Yoshi and Tatya brought the hydrofoil back to the agrostation without speaking. There didn't seem to be any words for this particular situation.

Yoshi steered the foil one-handed around the perimeter and down one of the access lanes that radiated like wheel spokes from the hub of the station, his eyes never leaving the horizon. The hand that gripped the wheel was white-knuckled; the other lay clenched in his lap.

Tatya stayed below with her patients, sitting on her heels on the deck between the bunk where the male lay and the stretcher that held the female. Now that she knew, or thought she knew, what they were, the idea of touching either of them made her quail.

You're going to have to touch them sooner or later, she told herself. You're a paramedic; it's your job. When you get them back to the station, what then?

She'd plunged her bloodstained hands into seawater up to the elbows, trailing them over the side until Yoshi started the foil again and it lifted out of the water. Her skin still tingled with the shock of it; she couldn't seem to get her hands clean. Now she forced herself to take a wad of sterile gauze from the medikit, dampen it with cool water from the galley, and swab the blood off the female patient's face, making sure none of it got on her hands. When they got back to the station, she'd have a proper scrub and put on her gloves and—

She finished what she was doing and tossed the gauze in the disposal, trying not to look too long at the strange female's face, which disturbed her deeply. The alien's nose was shattered, several of her teeth were loosened and the gums bleeding, at least one cheekbone was broken, the surrounding tissue bruised and beginning to swell. She must have impacted against the helm console during splashdown to do that much

35

damage. It wasn't anything Tatya hadn't seen before. What disturbed her was not the extent of the injuries, but the alien's response to them.

The alien, Tatya thought. Well, all right, what else am I supposed to call her? She's the alien, until someone tells me otherwise.

The alien, unlike her male counterpart, was at least semiconscious most of the time, and the broken facial bones, along with second- and third-degree burns similar to those the male had sustained, must have been excruciating. But except that the broken nose forced her to breathe through her ravaged and swollen mouth, she made no sound. Only her eyes moved. And those eyes . . .

The swelling had reduced them to slits, but they remained open as long as she was conscious—the color of jet, as sharp as lasers and, to Tatya, positively chilling. They fixed themselves on some distant point beyond Tatya's shoulder, and they made her insides quiver. If they ever looked right at her . . .

Tatya shivered, turned her attention to the male, whose eyes, mercifully, were closed. Fingertips tingling, Tatya forced herself to reach over and gently slap his face several times, bringing him up to a less profound level. When he'd stabilized, she sat back on her heels and studied him.

She had to admit he was beautiful. Even with burns covering a third of his face (further burns on his hands and visible through the charred fabric of his uniform), he was more beautiful, God help her, than Yoshi—his face all planes and angles beneath golden skin, his eyelashes thick and black and centimeters long, his dark hair silky to her tentative touch. She could almost forget that the blood beneath that golden skin was green, so mesmerized was she suddenly by the exotic upsweep of those alien eyebrows, and those ears.

Those ears. She'd thought at first they were the result of some form of cosmetic mutilation, like the custom of piercing on Earth, but on closer examination she could find no surgical scars, and the pinnal curve was simply too natural. They were supposed to be that way.

Tatya sat back on her heels and tried to imagine a whole race of beings like him. Perhaps a whole planetful, a solar system, a galaxy. She wondered what they would think of humans, red-blooded, stunted-eared, bizarre.

With a sudden thrill up her spine she realized that the female, still gasping for air through swollen lips, was looking directly at her. Tatya would have jumped up and fled (fled where, though, in a hydrofoil in the middle of the Pacific?) anywhere to escape those eyes, if just then the foil hadn't nosed against the dock, its motor dying to silence as Yoshi called down unnecessarily:

"We're here!"

"By virtue of his service, *T'Kahr* Savar could have requested and been granted a place on your expedition without your intervention," Prefect T'Saaf said to Commander T'Lera with particular emphasis. Let the proud one know that the exception was made because of who and what her father was, not she. "But the choice of Sorahl as your navigator is insupportable."

"On what grounds, Prefect?" T'Lera's voice once again held that dry, almost ironic tone. "Because he is without rank, or because he is my son?"

"There are six others of full rank as qualified as he," T'Saaf replied, and to address both issues: "Nepotism is not only illogical, it may in this instance prove dangerous!"

The charge of nepotism was grave, freighted as it was with implications of favoritism and a lack of judgment, equally serious violations of both a commander's code of ethics and a Vulcan's honor. T'Lera did not permit it to perturb her; she knew T'Saaf's methodology and had been prepared for this.

"If the Prefect will refer to the addendum to my preflight report." She struggled mightily to control her voice, which had slipped beyond the bounds of dryness into outright irony, if not sarcasm. "She will note that of the six of rank whose skillscans equal or surpass Sorahl's, four are already assigned to other ships, one is on leave of absence, and the sixth is Selik, who is already aboard my vessel as astrophysicist and cartographer. It was in fact he who recommended Sorahl, as the most promising of the senior cadets, to accompany us."

Prefect T'Saaf did not condescend to look at the addendum; she knew it would read as T'Lera said it did.

"As to the matter of rank . . ." T'Lera continued. Salt in the wound, a human might have called it; the Vulcan had no equivalent metaphor. "I respectfully remind the prefect that this is a technicality. The commencement ceremony for senior cadets transpires six days after our optimum departure date. Am I to delay my ship's departure by what may prove a dangerous margin? Or am I to deprive my crew of the best available navigator because he lacks the formality of rank designation on his uniform?"

She would not burden T'Saaf with the tale of how she herself had accompanied her father on his second voyage to the Sol III system when she was a child. T'Saaf would point out, and rightfully so, that regulations had been less stringent then and that as prefect Savar had been free to take certain liberties no longer permitted. That T'Lera had departed Vulcan a half-formed child of eleven years, to return two full decades later—in the days before warp speed the journey took that long—as a mature adult and unique among her kind for having spent those years in the void, was self-evident. Never again could a planet entirely contain her, and that was both her gift and her burden.

Did she presume to visit the same fate on her son?

But Sorahl was older, in his nineteenth year, and with the breaking of the light barrier a scoutcraft could now reach Earth within ten days, not ten years. The entire journey, including mapping and research, would be completed in a matter of months. It was not the same.

But these were deeply personal things, and none of the desk-bound, planet-bound, convention-bound T'Saaf's concern. The unarguable fact was that Sorahl was qualified and available, and his commander wished him to go. That his commander also wished to show her son what her father had first shown her—that there was that to be found in the misnamed void between the stars which knew no words in its exquisiteness, that there was that on other worlds which was as beautiful and diverse as Surak had envisioned it, juxtaposed with strangeness and squalor and a striving for perfection that no matter how imperfect was fascinating to observe—would not be spoken of in this official context.

But T'Lera would have her will in this as well.

"And if it is necessary for you to act upon the Prime Directive?" Prefect T'Saaf demanded. It was a last resort; she knew the answer.

Destruction before detection. It seemed to T'Lera that she had ingested it with her mother's milk.

"It is not given to me to violate that which Surak has taught and which Savar my father has labored all his days to promulgate," T'Lera said evenly. "The commander accepts the responsibility for the lives of all her crew, whether blood relative or no. I accept, and I will act accordingly."

Within moments Commander T'Lera was crossing the quadrangle of the Prefecture, on her way to the Academic Hall to bring the news to her navigator in person. There was no lightness in her step, no sense of triumph. Having argued for her father's fitness and her son's qualification, she had added to the already heavy burden of every scoutship commander. She, above all others, must not fail in her mission.

"We've got to be out of our minds!" Tatya muttered frantically as they brought the male inside and lifted him onto the waterbed in the sleeping room. "He's got a concussion, possibly a serious one, and my instruments can't detect intracranial pressure. He ought to be flown out by MedEvac or he could die on me. The other one's lost a lot of blood and she's going to need reconstructive surgery. What are we going to do? I can't—"

"Tatiana!" Yoshi was winded, more out of fear than exertion, and his nerves were shot. "It's too late to think about that now! We're committed. Pull yourself together!"

"All right," she whimpered meekly, all out of character. "I'll try!"

What was the matter with her? All her life she'd dreamed of space flight, of discovering life on other planets. Only a couple of mediocre scores on a simulator test had disqualified her from the AeroNav program and she'd opted for agronomy instead. Last night it had seemed so exciting. Why was it so terrifying now?

"Let's get the other one," Yoshi was saying, tugging on her arm. *"Hurry!"*

This time they both scanned the horizon for visitors.

Yoshi went below first, getting his first real look at the female alien. Her shattered face didn't bother him as much as he'd expected, but her eyes had the same effect on him as they'd had on Tatya.

"We won't hurt you," he blurted before he could stop himself. "We're trying to help."

He realized what he was doing and struck his forehead with the heel of his hand.

"Stupid! What's wrong with me? She can't possibly under—"

Tatya saw the alien's swollen lips form a single word.

"Under—understood," she breathed, and Yoshi felt the hair on the back of his neck stand on end.

"Our mission is to observe," then-Prefect Savar had written. "We will exert every effort to elude their observation telescopes and scanners, and avoid activating the defensive weaponry which every advanced world will perforce have pointed skyward against invasion.

"Approaching no nearer than their own artificial satellites, we will study the topography of their world, and learn their dwelling places and their natural phenomena. We will monitor the carrier wave messages with which they communicate with each other and those which they hurl into space in search of otherworlders. By analyzing all of their forms of visual communication, we will learn their arts and cultures, for these will tell us how they perceive themselves in relation to their world.

"Above all we will master their languages, for how else are we to communicate with them when the time comes?"

"Understood," T'Lera said in the official standard language of Earth, gleaned by previous scoutcraft crews from the audiovisual programs they had monitored over the years, computer-analyzed for grammatical structure, and stored in universal translators, a language she had learned from her father's lips as a child and spoken fluently with him and others in the Offworld Service ever since, though never before with one of its native speakers. "Understood."

She had spoken only to allay the fear she heard in the male Terran's voice, the anxiety she read on both of the concerned faces floating before her blurred and darkening vision. Had she not been in shock from her

41

injuries and the hours of exposure in the shattered craft, had she been less uncertain of Sorahl's condition and therefore better able to formulate a logical course of action, she might have taken into consideration the fact that a human's curiosity is as all-consuming as a Vulcan's, and kept her silence.

"You speak our language!" Yoshi whispered, incredulous. "But how?"

T'Lera's fading consciousness did not permit her to explain.

"I'd have thought," Melody Sawyer said, doing a visual all-points from the conning tower as *Delphinus* cruised at a leisurely three knots, searching, "they'd have everything that could float or fly out here looking. If it's what you say it could be. A worldwide alert, like in those old 2-D movies about men from Mars. You remember the one—"

She and Nyere were alone on the bridge for the moment, Jason working the scanners for the regular tech, who had gone below for a late breakfast, and Sawyer could afford to be loose-lipped.

"—the one we took the kids to at the Antique Films Festival? Where they built that whole military installation near some mountain in Wyoming just to welcome those little bald-headed, goggle-eyed critters coming down in this big old glittery flying whatsis . . ."

Her voice trailed off. Jason wasn't listening to her, wasn't looking at the scanners he'd so meticulously calibrated, sat squinting grimly at the far horizon hoping against hope that they wouldn't find what he knew was out there, though he was honor-bound, duty-bound, to try his damnedest to find it, and if he didn't, AeroNav would simply send out someone else who would.

"So how come, Jason?" Melody broke into his thoughts, grating. "How come it's just us out here?"

"Because the fewer people know about it, the fewer

have to be reeducated later," Nyere said, watching with perverse satisfaction as Sawyer's eyes went wide.

"You mean we'll have to be 'wiped'?" she demanded, hands on her hips. "The hell you say!"

Ah, the power of euphemism! Jason Nyere thought. "Reeducated," "wiped," whatever one chose to call it, it amounted to several mandatory hypnosis sessions to excise classified information from the memories of those who no longer needed it, and it was contained in every AeroNav reg book, a holdover from the reactionary days Sawyer pined for. Odd that she should be the one to object to it.

"Take it to a higher court," Nyere rumbled.

Sawyer sensed it was best to drop it for the moment.

"What'd you tell the crew?" she wanted to know.

"Told them it was routine salvage op. Derelict satellite with the databank intact."

"Think they bought that?"

"No. But as long as we're on radio silence they can speculate to their hearts' content." The captain glanced toward the stairwell to see if the tech was on her way back. "And that goes double for you. We don't want to risk alarming anyone else who might already have found what we're looking for."

He nodded unnecessarily in the direction of the agrostation some fifty kilometers off their port bow. The kelp farmers were the only other inhabitants of this stretch of ocean; *Delphinus* had been en route to them with supplies when the Priority One call had come in.

Sawyer whistled quietly. She was quite fond of Yoshi and Tatya; she and Jason and members of their ten-person crew had spent some wonderful long mid-ocean evenings in the company of the two young agronomists. But if civilians were going to get mixed up in this kind of thing, especially civilians with their own communications station and contacts on the mainland—

"As soon as we're in range, put a tracer on Agro III's

comm band," Nyere said as if reading her mind. "Close-monitor it yourself. Let's see what's new in their little corner of the world."

"Yes suh, Captain suh!" Sawyer said with a bit too much alacrity.

The scanner tech's footsteps on the metal stair treads curtailed further conversation.

"Sol system entry 24.01 minutes, Commander," Helm T'Preth had reported, her voice barely louder than the impulse engines whose control was at her fingertips.

(These were Vulcan minutes, based upon the beating of the Vulcan heart and the logic of units of ten, hence one hundred Vulcan heartbeats equaled one Vulcan minute. In human terms, based on standard time measurement, a Vulcan's heart beat 240 times per minute, therefore a Vulcan minute equaled twenty-five standard seconds, and twenty-four Vulcan minutes equalled ten standard ones. But the need for such conversion calculations did not yet exist. At present T'Preth's announcement signified only that their craft would cross the orbit of Sol IX, outermost planet and the one humans called Pluto, in the equivalent of ten Earth minutes.)

"Acknowledged," Commander T'Lera said from the conn, her voice almost as soft as T'Preth's, though it never lost its cutting edge. "All: duty stations, twenty minutes—mark."

Those already at station acknowledged with their silence. There was no extraneous talk aboard this or any Vulcan vessel. While every Vulcan appreciates the value of silence, perhaps nothing reinforces that appreciation better than the proximity of six other beings of varying temperaments within the confines of a scout-craft on a long space voyage.

In the early years before warp drive, those who kept watch in two-year shifts on this decade-long journey, while their fellows lay aft in cryogenic suspension, often reduced their conversation to nothing more than the relaying of essential data. Even now the ancient Savar, perhaps conditioned by those times, had not spoken for days.

The only one not at his station was the navigator. At his mother's command and well before the requisite time, Sorahl left off the private study he had been engaged in at one of the library screens and took his place at the navcon, though a trace of puzzlement on his face indicated a lingering preoccupation with what he had been studying. His mother and his commander took note, but said nothing.

Instead she devoted these waiting, interim moments to contemplating the faces of her crew, convinced from long observation that intense concentration upon that which one did best evoked a certain ethereal beauty in any face. As always, her crew did not disappoint her.

Truly her crew was a marvel to behold: a single unit of seven minds, seven distinct personalities and a multiplicity of gifts intermeshed and working together toward a single goal. They were seven and they were one, unity and diversity, the Vulcan ideal. T'Lera beheld them, and marveled.

Foremost was Selik, astrocartographer—tireless, methodical, his universe contained in his work as his work contained a universe. Veteran of several similar voyages, he was at present absorbed in plotting the course of a rogue comet that had altered the gravimetry of this sector since last he'd journeyed this way. The hunch of his narrow shoulders, the particular slant of his silvered head, evinced the degree of his absorption.

Beside him at her communications console and equally intent upon her work was the pale-eyed T'Syra, genetic rarity, Selik's consort, T'Lera's contemporary and cherished companion on all her voyages save the earliest. T'Syra's responsibility was the monitoring and recording of every radio wave that emanated from

45

Earth even at this distance, and her listening posture would vary little in the hours ahead.

The comet's trail created a great deal of static, disrupting the frequencies T'Syra had been monitoring. Before Selik could inform her of the cause of the disturbance, T'Syra acknowledged with a gesture. Communication between these two required no words.

It had been Prefect Savar's thought from the beginning that consort should accompany consort on long space voyages, not for human reasons of shared physical intimacy—such was impossible with any degree of privacy under conditions of scoutcraft travel, and the Vulcan required it with far less frequency than humans—but because two minds locked together since childhood could all the more readily intermesh with the minds of others within command structure. Hence Selik and T'Syra were paired, as were the somber helmsman T'Preth and the robust musician/ sociologist Stell, who, sight unseen from the living quarters, offered the contemplative strains of his *ka'athyra* for the diversion of his crewmates.

Ironic, T'Lera thought, that both the initiator of the consort principle and his offspring should themselves always journey alone. What had estranged Savar from her who was her mother was not her concern, and as for her own divorcement from Sotir, it was something she no longer permitted to enter her thoughts. And Sorahl was too young to concern himself with his duties toward his betrothed for some time.

Sorahl. His mild expression, his mother knew, masked a fiercely contained excitement as, his studies forgotten, he sought the first blue glimmer of Earth on the forward screen.

His hair wants cutting, T'Lera thought, seeing it curl over his collar. But were these a commander's thoughts or a mother's?

"Time, Helm?" T'Lera thought, not because she

needed to know, but to distract herself from her distraction.

"Five minutes—mark, Commander," T'Preth replied.

"Acknowledged."

Running on impulse engines, their craft would not reach Earth for hours yet. Officially T'Lera should have been midway into her requisite five-hour sleep cycle, but she had never yet missed this crossing and would not do so now. She could have left the center chair at any time since they'd stopped down from warp speed just outside the system, could have given the conn to Stell who was rotation crew for this ten-day stint, or to any crewmember for that matter. All of their roles were interchangeable; any of the seven could run the duty stations in an emergency, and each had specialized gifts as well.

T'Syra was a registered healer and xenobiologist. Both Stell and Sorahl held engineering degrees and could literally dismantle and rebuild the entire vessel. T'Preth was linguist, artist, and artisan, though the Vulcan made no distinction between the latter categories. Selik was third-ranked navigator in the entire Offworld Service and a member of the High Council; should this be the vessel that made first contact with humans, he would act as spokesman. And T'Lera, their commander, who would give no order she herself would not obey, was to some degree all of these things.

This too had been part of Savar's thinking from the first. If scoutcraft crews were to be the first other worlds saw of the Vulcan, they must also be the best.

"Crossover effected, Commander," T'Preth announced softly.

"Acknowledged," T'Lera said again, and, though as commander she need not say it, added: "My gratitude."

There was no other acknowledgment. A human crew

47

might have cheered. A Vulcan crew went on about its work.

At last T'Lera rose from her chair and entered the privacy-screened living quarters. Here in one of the sleeping niches—whether meditating or only asleep, only those who knew him well could be certain; the old one seldom closed his eyes for any reason now—lay the ancient Savar, point of origin of all aboard this vessel, of all who journeyed from Vulcan to the stars. His eyes, obsidian and glittering, gazed unblinking into that same nameless realm he had bequeathed his daughter.

"My father?" that daughter said now, kneeling beside his sleeping niche; the musician Stell had set aside his *ka'athyra* and gone to take the conn, leaving the two to their privacy. "We have made the crossover. I wanted you to know."

The ancient one raised himself slowly to a sitting position.

"My gratitude, Commander," he said, his voice rusty with many days' silence, insisting upon the formality as he had when their roles had been reversed. "It will be good to see Earth once more."

First Mate Sawyer ran the hand-held chemanalyzer over the suspect portion of the barrier weir surrounding the westernmost kelp fields of the Agro III station.

"Cables're tangled," she muttered as if to herself. "And they're frayed—here, and here. As if something heavy got itself caught, then pulled or slid off. Moy, keep this baby steady, can't you?"

Young eager Ensign Moy, falling all over himself on his first real sea voyage, struggled mightily with the small skiff in what was proving to be a choppy sea.

"Sorry, sir," he said by reflex; it seemed he was always apologizing for something. "MeteorCom says we're in for heavy weather."

His baby face shone with expectation as he tried to

48

read the analyzer over Sawyer's shoulder. "Whatcha got, sir? Anything interesting?"

"Could be, Moy," Sawyer muttered, preoccupied. "Could be real interesting."

It had been pure fluke that she'd been the first to notice something. Nyere had ordered the day watch to cruise the perimeter of Agro III before going inside, and Sawyer just happened to be taking a turn on the forward deck after hours bending over her instruments when the damaged cables hove into view. She'd persuaded the captain to let her lower the skiff and have a closer look.

"Those white patches are not paint," she said emphatically. "Not that I know what they are. Best we rub off a sample and take it back upstairs for a full analysis."

"You think it was a satellite like the captain said, sir?" Moy's words tumbled out in his excitement. "Or you think there's more to it? He's been real snappish since he got the word. I hear it was Priority One. You don't suppose—"

"Button it, Moy. Let's get back before my breakfast comes up. I'm not used to being this close to the water."

"Aye, sir," Moy said glumly, steering the skiff back to where *Delphinus* lay brooding behind them.

"It is not paint, Captain suh," Melody reported conclusively, the report printout in her hand. "It's a rhodinium-silica-based coating compound."

"So?" Nyere was studiously unimpressed. "You've heard Yoshi gripe about pleasure craft plowing up his acreage. Another slap-happy Sunday driver, that's all."

"I don't think so. Analyzer says its closest analogue is the kind of temperature-resistant sealant they spray on spacecraft."

Her particular choice of words was intended to catch Nyere's attention. It did so.

49

"What do you mean 'closest analogue'?"

"According to the analyzer, it contains trace elements not native to this solar system. They can be synthesized under lab conditions, but—"

"Then maybe it's something new the Space Service has come up with," Nyere said, grasping at straws. "I wouldn't call your findings conclusive, Sawyer. Not on this much evidence."

A long moment of silence hung between them. Nyere's heel dragging had begun to grate on Sawyer about as much as her impatience did on him.

"Jason, something fell out of the sky last night and got snarled up in that cable. It's my guess it's sitting on the bottom waiting for us right now." Nyere said nothing. "What I want to know is what the hell, in light of your orders, you intend to do about that, *suh?*"

"That will do, Sawyer!" He glared until she backed down. "Recommendations?"

"One, we go for a dive just where that cable's in such a mess and start scooping the bottom for little green men."

"Negative," Nyere said. "Weather's getting heavier, and we're losing the light. It can wait until morning."

"We *can* work under infrared, Captain," Melody stated the obvious.

"Not this close to the Mayabi Fault we don't," Nyere countered. "I'm not going to go plowing around down there in the dark with sand in our faces and end up falling down a crevasse. Tomorrow, when the wind's died and the sun's up. Tomorrow and not before."

Melody nodded, not satisfied. His argument might have made sense, except that he'd taken such risks before. How long did he think he could keep stalling?

"What else, Melody?" Jason asked, reading the expression on her face, not liking it.

"Recommend we go pay our farmer friends a visit."

Their eyes locked. She was calling his bluff and they both knew it.

"You've been listening on their comm band?"

"I have."

"And?"

"No outgoing calls all day," Sawyer reported. "No reports of anything unusual, no distress calls. Also no chat with the neighbors, no ringing up Mom on the mainland. Nothing."

"Maybe they're out doing their job. Or were until the swells started up."

"Except for one thing, Captain." Melody dropped it like a bombshell. "They've had the incoming on all day. As if they're just sitting there listening. Waiting for something to happen."

"You're fishing, Melody," Nyere said, though he didn't believe it himself. "It's a lax time of year. Maybe there's a good movie on."

"Jason, for Pete's sake—"

"Look, maybe they're making love in the middle of the day and they need it on for background music!" Nyere exploded. "Go find something else to do besides peeking through keyholes, will you? We'll be there at 1400 tomorrow anyway. It'll keep."

"If you say so, Captain *suh*," Melody said watchfully. "So long as you realize it ain't gonna go away by itself."

The door to the penthouse scanned Jim Kirk and shushed open, letting him in without a word. That was good. He'd listened to enough words, spoken enough words in a single afternoon to last a lifetime.

Damn staff meetings! he thought. Damn the life of the chairbound paper pusher who brought it on himself! What was I thinking of? The one thing I always hated most about a field command was the paperwork afterward. Locking horns with a Trelane or a Rojan could get you killed, but it was the reports after the fact that busted your—

Jim Kirk sighed. Now Spock had his *Enterprise* and all he had left was the paperwork.

He'd started fiddling with the closures on his uniform tunic while he was still in the turbolift. Now he threw its stiff red newness (almost the color of drying humanoid blood, he thought, as if noticing it for the first time. Whose brilliant idea was that?) over a chair, admiral's bars clanking disconsolately. He dumped his carrycase on top of it—pompous, silly thing with his name and rank holoscribed in one corner, hermetically sealed against all environmental conditions, equipped with a security lock that would implode and destroy the contents if it was tampered with.

Your tax dollars at work, Kirk thought. All it contained at the moment was a couple of medium-security tapes supplementary to this afternoon's meetings, which he would return unread in the morning, and The Book.

The book. He'd made a great to-do about having it made up in bound form, though it had cost him a bundle and sent the Troyian bookseller into a spasm over the inconvenience. "Surely the admiral has a speed-read degree!" the Troyian had clucked, fluttering his aquamarine fingers disconsolately over the order form for such an anachronism as a book with paper pages. "Why, a tome of this size can be scanned in an evening with comm-enhance. We even carry a 'read while you sleep' version. Such a waste of valuable time—turning pages, reading words instead of scanning paragraphs . . ."

"One of the reasons God gave man eyes and fingers, Purdi," Jim Kirk had said softly, but as if to suggest that the subject was closed. Troyians talked too much.

"Coffee-table book!" Purdi sniffed. "At least that's what they used to call them. That's why you want the antique version—part of your collection!"

Kirk had left him with his misconception.

"Over a Billion Copies in Scan!" raved holo-ads and vidvertising every time Kirk switched on Prolificom for a weather report.

Not only was everyone buying *Strangers,* everyone actually seemed to be reading it. Kirk caught Heihachiro Nogura scanning it on his office screen the morning after three civilian friends had tried to press their copies on him at a party. Even his students, whose tastes usually ran to *Astromance* and *Warmongoria,* were debating its merits in the corridors between classes. When they asked the admiral his views on its merit, Kirk waived comment on the basis that he was still weighing it in the context of his—ahem—personal experience in diplomatic matters.

The final straw was when he thought he'd managed to escape it for a day by attending to some business up at TerraMain Spacedock, about as far offplanet as one could go without leaving orbit. He'd stopped by the commissary for a cup of coffee and the latest gossip when he caught sight of Nyota Uhura and—

"Admiral, you remember Cleante alFaisal."

Silly question. Remember her? He'd once been madly in love with her, for nearly five minutes. *Enterprise* had been on a rescue mission, retrieving the two survivors, human and Vulcan, of a bit of Romulan nastiness at the edge of the quadrant. There'd been a moment's peace and respite beside a lotus pool, and this sad, beautiful creature with Byzantine eyes . . .

"Hello, Jim."

"Cleante."

He kissed her hand now as he had then. Uhura's eyes danced as she watched the two of them.

"Join us," she invited Jim Kirk, and he did.

"What brings you to these parts?" he asked Cleante pleasantly.

"Coincidence," she replied. Her voice was as lyrical as he'd remembered. "T'Shael had an appointment with Dr. M'Benga in Old Frisco and I tagged along to do some window-shopping. I ran into Nyota and she invited me up for lunch. I'd never been to Spacedock before."

53

"I see." Kirk nodded. T'Shael was the Vulcan survivor, genetically prone to some blood disorder that required periodic monitoring; Vulcan healers were hard to come by on Earth, and M'Benga was still the best of the humans. "Well, don't let me interrupt your conversation—"

"Cleante was just telling me the most fascinating thing," Uhura said brightly. "She's discovered a long-lost relative."

"Really? Something to do with your archaeology work?"

Cleante shook her head, her masses of dark hair an aura about her face.

"Surprisingly enough," she said, "he turned up as a rather mysterious character in a history book. Have you read *Strangers from the Sky* yet?"

Inwardly Kirk groaned, defeated. "No, not *yet.*"

"Well, I'm sure you're familiar with the premise. Here you have the entire military-intelligence community of Earth with its knickers in a knot trying to figure out what to do with two misplaced Vulcans, when this—character—by the name of Mahmoud Gamal al-Parneb Nezaj, if you can believe all that . . ."

That very afternoon, Jim Kirk beamed down from TerraMain and stopped by Purdi's Book Emporium, waving a white flag.

He'd had his copy of *Strangers* sent to the Admiralty on purpose, to pique the curiosity of the younger generation onstaff, most of whom wouldn't know what a book was if they fell over it. He'd sat at his desk holding the thing, still in the plain brown wrapper Purdi had so discreetly provided, delighting in the feel of it, the heft of it in his hands. There was something vaguely obscene about owning a copy of *War and Peace* or *Bleak House* complete and entire on a little plastic disk that could be read to you by a computer.

Aides and junior officers passed in and out of his

office all day, eyeing this audacious anachronism sitting plunk in the middle of Jim Kirk's desk, utterly mystified. Kirk did not bother to enlighten them, locked the book in a drawer while he locked himself into an endlessness of staff meetings, then smuggled it out of the Admiralty as if it might have been Klingon aphrodisiacs, instead of what it was.

Alone at last in the penthouse, he still didn't take it out of the carrycase. The longer he waited, the greater the pleasure when at last he took it out, settled himself by the fire with his feet up, and began turning pages, losing himself in another time, another place. He kept himself in suspense, poured himself a drink, and woke his computer.

"Computer?"

"Yes, Jim?" it answered sleepily; it had had the apartment to itself all day.

Kirk stopped himself from snapping at it for familiarity; he had requested a personality-specific model for home use.

"Read me tomorrow's sked, please. One item at a time."

"Of course, Admiral," it said more formally. "Beginning 0800: Quadrant Three commandants' tie-in briefing."

More talk, Kirk thought, complicated by time lags across an entire quadrant.

"Confirmed. Next?"

"Approximately 0930: workout with *kendo* instructor."

Kirk groaned; his arm was still sore from last week's session.

"Is that a confirm, Admiral?"

"What? Yes, continue."

"Ten hundred to 1200: Visiting Firemen."

"Say again?"

"Only notation you gave me, Admiral," the computer responded primly. "I took the liberty of tracing the

55

etymology through Linguistics and can report that the term originated on Earth in the then–United States of America *circa*—"

"Never mind!" Kirk snapped. Had Spock been tinkering with this thing behind his back? Some sort of Vulcan practical joke?

Of course, Vulcans did not engage in the employment of jokes, practical or otherwise, Kirk reminded himself. He could almost hear Spock saying it. There didn't seem to be a profound statement on any subject that Spock hadn't already uttered. Or was it just his manner that lent whatever he said an aura of profundity?

"Jim?" the computer intruded gently into his woolgathering. "Was it something I said?"

"What? Yes—no! I remember now. Visiting firemen. Means the command staff from Starbase 16 is in town and I have to give them the Cooks' tour."

"Cooks' tour? Shall I check Linguistics for that also?"

"On your own time!" Kirk said testily. It *was* ragging him, Spock's influence or no. "Continue schedule."

"Very well; 1200 to 1400: lunch with Admiral Nogura, his office."

Ulcer territory, Kirk thought. Heihachiro only schedules lunch with me when he wants something done yesterday.

"Next?"

"Fourteen hundred to 1600: tactics seminar, Blue and Gold groups."

Boredom, Kirk thought. How to keep myself awake so I don't put the cadets to sleep.

"Confirm."

"Sixteen hundred: *Kobayashi Maru*, Green group—"

"—and debriefing at 1700? Assuming they haven't incinerated themselves?"

"Would you care to do this for me?" the computer demanded, touchy about interruptions.

"No, continue." Kirk knocked back half his drink without tasting it, rubbed his eyes. "Sorry if I disrupted your train of thought."

"Not possible," the computer responded, literal-minded. "Seventeen hundred: Kobayashi Maru debriefing, Green group. 1800: Cocktail reception for—"

"Stop!" Kirk had clearly had enough. There was a cumulative uniformity to his days that was terrifying in its implications. He turned his thoughts toward the one thing he really cared about. "Computer, present position and status of *Enterprise?*"

"One moment." Pretty kaleidoscopic patterns played across the small screen. Kirk swirled the ice cubes in the bottom of his glass, waited. The rest of him might be parked behind a desk, but his heart was always with his ship. "Ready."

"Go ahead."

"Position and status *USS Enterprise,* NCC-1701: Stardate 8083.6. Crew complement comprising engineering officer and thirty-seven trainees: bridge crew comprising seven cadets, Captain Spock in command. Presently engaged in training patrol two parsecs off Llingri Star Cluster, to continue approximately three solar days. Employing Regulation 14-B standard maneuvers with accepted Vulcan variant. As of last report, all is well."

"I see," Kirk mused. Accepted Vulcan variant, indeed. That meant Spock was working their little human tails off under Vulcan regimen. Good for him! "Estimated return date?"

"Captain Spock had logged return date of 8097.4. Precisely."

Precisely. He would do it, too. Bring her into spacedock trim and unscathed and down to the minute by his calculations—ion storms, intervening interplane-

57

tary conflicts, and Scotty's lamentations about his engines notwithstanding. Good old Spock. *Enterprise* couldn't be in better hands.

Dammit.

Kirk ran himself through the sonic shower in record time, and slipped into an old sweatsuit. He padded into the kitchen and punched up a salad—McCoy had been on him about his weight again—then settled back by the fire, and lovingly turned the crisp new pages of his anachronistic book.

THREE

In the dying light of a stormy afternoon, Yoshi sat in the other room of the agrostation staring at the comm screen, neither hearing nor seeing it.

They had always called this the "other room." There was the sleeping room and there was this room—living room, kitchen, den, workroom, office, storage area, library, gym, entertainment center. The comm screen dominating one wall was combination computer, holovision, ship-to-shore, mail service—their only contact, except for *Delphinus's* monthly supply runs, with the rest of the world.

What Yoshi really wanted to do was to cut himself—themselves—off entirely from that world, pretend nothing had happened, retreat, hide out, wish it all away. But he kept the screen on, kept staring at its melange of images though most of them made no sense in his present state of high agitation. He seemed to think he ought to be watching for something specific, but whether or not he would recognize it when he saw it . . .

Did he actually expect MediaComm to announce that an alien spacecraft was being hunted in the South Pacific?

59

He'd thought of tapping into the AeroNav band. He was a good enough hacker to make it work, but figured their equipment was sophisticated enough to detect a tap and abandoned the idea. Instead he sat flipping from one news channel to another, mesmerized.

". . . following his attempted assassination by pseudo-religious factions calling themselves the Alliance for the Twelfth of November . . ."

Flip.

". . . threatening their mutual nonaggression pact with a renewal of hostilities unless . . ." Flip.

". . . when a riot, believed to have been instigated by spectators for the Southern Hemisphere team, resulted in twenty-three deaths . . ."

Good old Earth, Yoshi thought. Half a century since the last world war and we still can't keep from cutting each other up for anything from the rights of the persecuted to a disputed soccer score. Any aliens in their right minds would have taken a quick look around and kept right on going. Those poor souls we fished out of the water this morning must have been lost but good.

Flip.

". . . trading was active, the price of mixed SeaSources shares plummeting in the wake of reports that fungus infestations first noted in the mid-Pacific region continue to spread unchecked . . ."

Uh-oh, Yoshi thought, coming back from wherever he'd been with a bump. This one piece of local news was the only thing that could make him sit up and pay attention.

Word of a new and particularly resistant strain of kelpwilt had been rampant up north for months. None of the usual treatments worked, and the disease had been spreading inexorably in Agro III's direction. Stations to their north and east had already reported losses of up to a quarter of their acreage.

Yoshi shook his head, incredulous. Until this morning his most pressing task had been scooting up and down the access lanes in the hydrofoil examining random samples of the weed for possible infestation. Now he could sit content in the middle of his acreage and happily let it rot out from under them, as long as no one came near him and demanded he hand over the aliens.

He asked himself the same question Tatya had asked herself. What was he afraid of?

Nothing terrible would happen to him and Tatya. At most they might need some outside "help" to forget what they'd discovered. Their lives would resume their normal course, and it would be as if they had never discovered the aliens, or as if there had been no aliens at all. Wasn't that what he wanted?

But if he let them do what they wanted, what would AeroNav and the intelligence networks and the PentaKrem and the powers-that-were do to the aliens? And why did he care?

Yoshi told himself he wouldn't care, if it weren't for Tatya. He had a violent allergy to controversy; it was one of the reasons he'd sought the seemingly lonely life of the agrostations. Was he so caught up in Tatya's romanticism about other planets that he was suddenly willing to risk his life to prevent what could only be the misunderstanding, the hysteria, the detention and interrogation and possible exploitation—or worse—of two total strangers who just happened to look vaguely human, who just incidentally spoke a human language, and about whom he knew absolutely nothing else?

What if they had incredible super powers which, once awakened, could crush two isolated humans like bugs on a wall? What if they were criminals escaping from their own world, bent on murder and mayhem? What if they were the vanguard of an invasion force, whose mission was to infiltrate, win over poor unsuspecting humans, and conquer Earth?

And what if they were just two innocent star travelers

who had lost their way and almost died and were now totally dependent upon the kindness of strangers? Well, what if?

There were very few things Yoshi would risk his life for; he'd be the first to admit it. Unlike his adventurous partner, he'd never aspired to anything more grandiose than what he had here. The twenty-first century with its crowds, its noise, its technology, its potential for getting a person too deep into things too big and too complicated, intimidated him. All he'd ever wanted was to spend the rest of a long and uneventful life contemplating the sea, counting the stars, worrying about nothing more threatening than kelpwilt, and staying out of harm's way.

He might have turned the aliens in himself as soon as they'd gotten back to the station—to at least get them medical help, he'd reasoned—if it hadn't required more assertiveness than he possessed. And if he hadn't been certain Tatya would break every bone in his body.

And if the female alien hadn't spoken to him, in his own language.

Yoshi sighed, and flipped the channel.

". . . reportedly a defective recon satellite believed to have splashed down somewhere to the west-northwest of Easter Island . . ."

Yoshi stood up abruptly, capsizing his beanbag chair and making his sore ankle throb violently. He dialed the volume up.

". . . AeroNav vessel dispatched in an attempt to recover any portion of the satellite which may have survived. In other news . . ."

"Well, there it is," Yoshi said aloud.

"I'll bet it's the Whale," Tatya said from the doorway of the sleeping room. Yoshi hadn't realized she was there; they seemed not to have seen each other for hours. "She's due tomorrow anyway."

They had always called *Delphinus* the Whale, as a

play on her name, because of the size and shape of the ship itself, and as an affectionate joke at the expense of her captain, though never to his face. Jason Nyere was sensitive about his size. Suddenly the joke wasn't funny anymore. Nothing was.

"How are they?" Yoshi nodded toward the room behind Tatya; no need to specify who "they" were.

"Stabilized, I think." Tatya looked drawn, exhausted. "The male seems to be coming around a little. I don't dare medicate either of them, not even painkillers. As nearly as I can tell their entire physiology is different from ours. Organs in the wrong places, vital signs all screwy. I can't get accurate readings on anything, not even a blood pressure . . ."

Her voice trailed off. Yoshi had never seen her too exhausted to talk.

"Yoshi, what are we going to do?"

Yoshi shrugged. He didn't want to *do* anything. He wanted to fall into the Mayabi Fault and disappear.

"Pass them off as a couple of my relatives?" he suggested, groping for humor.

Tatya was not amused.

"I'd like to see you try telling that to Jason," she said grimly.

"I don't hear any brilliant ideas from your corner of the room," Yoshi snapped back.

Alone out here, they were accustomed to arguing as loudly and as often as they chose, but the presence of their unwanted guests had changed all that. Argue they did, but softly, counting on the rising wind stirring up whitecaps and howling around the corners of the station to keep them from being overheard should one of the aliens waken.

It did not occur to them that pointed ears had evolved on other worlds for a reason, that the wind had already wakened one of their guests, and that one such pair of ears was absorbing every word.

* * *

63

"They seem so primitive," Sorahl had said to his mother the first time she observed the frown with which he studied his private viewer and inquired as to what might be puzzling him. "I mean no disrespect, but I cannot help wondering why you and my grandfather find them so fascinating."

They had been two days from the Sol system, the scoutcraft traversing the Oort Cloud where so many of the comets visible from Earth originated. T'Lera and Sorahl were in the living quarters, she at the beginning of her offshift, he nearing the end of his. Shortly he would take over from Selik, who, with seemingly effortless proficiency, navigated with one hand while recording new comets with the other.

"'Primitive'?" T'Lera had inquired, making no effort to disguise her dryness of voice; of all beings, surely her son was most accustomed to it. "Specify."

Sorahl's gesture encompassed a number of record tapes strewn about his workspace, particularly those gleaned from Earth's holovision broadcasts by previous expeditions.

"Their forms of entertainment," he began, with the wariness of youth expecting to be criticized for its naiveté. "Their obsession with violence, with maudlin emotions, with humor at the expense of others. If these are the things they value . . ."

"Is this what your study indicates, my son?" T'Lera allowed herself to address him informally when they were alone and off duty. Were her father in attendance she would have refrained; where Savar had commanded, formal mode had been all.

"Mother, I am aware that I lack the experience of those who have made this their life work, but my observations indicate that this is a species perpetually on the verge of self-destruction."

"So many of its great thinkers would concur," T'Lera said dryly. "But what you have observed is not the sum

64

total of what they choose as diversion for their leisure, much less what they consider of value."

Sorahl lowered his eyes. His observation had been naive, and presumptuous. Before he could ask his mother's forgiveness she interrupted him.

"And what would you suggest, my son? That we abandon our efforts to learn of them?"

Sorahl's eyes came up to meet hers, barely masking the fire behind them in time.

"Not at all, Mother. Rather that we take the first step to which all our research has been leading. That we make first contact."

T'Lera hid her bemusement at his eagerness behind a careful sternness.

"Forgive my inability to follow your logic, Sorahl-*kam,* but if this is as you suggest a violent, unready, or—to use your word—primitive species, of what benefit would revealing our presence be to them? Would they not resort to precisely the violence you suggest in order to protect themselves from that for which they are unready?"

"I do not think so," Sorahl said quickly.

Curious, his mother dropped her pretense of sternness.

"Please explain."

"A recent paper by the political scientist Sotir . . ." Sorahl began carefully, watching his mother's face. Between them they always referred to his father and her former consort as an impersonal entity. There was a certain irony in this, Sorahl thought, in that much of his childhood had been spent under his father's care while T'Lera was off on yet another space voyage, but to refer to another's divorce, even within the family, was a serious breach of the proprieties. ". . . promulgates the theory that benevolent intervention in the evolution of a less advanced culture may actually spare another species the aggressions and loss of life which we as a species endured before finding the Way. In short—"

"Logic suggests that there are as many theories as there are theorists," T'Lera said abruptly. "And Sotir has never been offworld."

This fact among others, she did not need to say, had been one of the reasons for their estrangement.

"Does this necessarily mean his theory is without validity?" Sorahl asked with a familiar stubbornness his mother always found curiously satisfying. It was not Sotir's stubbornness, which could be both pedantic and strident, but her own and Savar's, a stubbornness that was nonaggressive, invisible until challenged, but then immovable.

"Any theory logically arrived at possesses its own validity," T'Lera admitted, masking her pride in her willful offspring. "Nevertheless, one is not free to test it on unsuspecting outworlders."

"Then why are we here?" Sorahl demanded with the impatience of youth, which even a Vulcan could fall prey to. "Why study these Earthmen for most of my grandfather's life and all of yours yet refrain from the logical next step?"

"It is not yet time," T'Lera said, in a tone that indicated the topic was not open for debate.

"In whose opinion?" Sorahl dared to ask, where one who knew his mother not quite as well might hesitate. "Yours, or Prefect Savar's?"

Destruction before detection. It was not Sorahl's question that gave his mother pause but the manner in which it had been asked. She had had cause herself to question whether after a lifetime under the aegis of that principle she could separate her own motivation from her father's.

"Savar and I are as one in our 'opinion,'" T'Lera said quietly, believing it. Her far-seeking eyes had gone hard. "But you, it would seem, prefer *T'Kahr* Sotir's 'interventionist' theory?"

Sorahl's jaw tightened imperceptibly beneath the full brunt of his mother's irony.

"I believe," he began, as if he had rehearsed it, expecting challenge, "that if Earthmen, or any intelligent species, were offered incontrovertible proof that it is possible to abandon violence and live by logic, millions might be spared the need to destroy each other. They could not help but see the advantage of our way."

"Despite their 'primitivism,'" T'Lera added.

"Mother, I am not suggesting that we are superior to them." Sorahl's voice had risen despite his best efforts and he lowered it forcibly. "Merely that we are different. That is consistent with IDIC."

"Precisely," T'Lera said, as if he had led himself to her side of the argument, which in fact he had. "And IDIC leads to Savar's Prime Directive, not to Sotir's interventionism. We are too different to judge what is 'best' for another species. And it is not yet time."

She stood abruptly, intent upon a sonic shower and sleep.

"Sotir may theorize at his leisure," she concluded. "It is I, as commander of this vessel, who must confront the reality. And you, as a member of this crew, who must obey. Before we enter Sol III orbit, Navigator, you will complete a thorough study of all record tapes designated 'Colonialism.' I will expect a full report."

Sorahl's voice, borrowing generously from the irony that was his birthright, reached his mother over the sound of the shower.

"Understood, *Commander,*" he said.

Which of them had been correct? Sorahl wondered now in the strange and utterly alien place where he found himself upon awakening. Or, rather, *more* correct, since logic dictated that no single individual could possess the whole of any truth. And what did it matter, now that circumstance had given them both into the Earthmen's hands?

He could hear them arguing in the room beyond.

". . . hide them here for how long? Even if they somehow magically recover all by themselves—"

"I don't know, Yoshi, I just don't know! But you said it yourself: we're committed. I feel responsible for them. And I won't have them hurt . . ."

Savar's precepts had never made provision for the situation his grandson found himself in, but like any Vulcan beyond seven years Sorahl was well trained in survival. Immediately upon awakening, he had assessed his circumstances and his surroundings, and attempted to rise from the waterbed. His unpracticed movements on this alien device, however, set it to undulating violently. The motion threatened to awaken T'Lera, who lay beside him, comatose as he had been, but in no immediate danger. Sorahl ceased his movements and considered what to do next.

He had been intrigued by the notion of a liquid-filled sleeping mat as soon as he determined its nature, added the sensation to the multiplicity of alien sights, sounds, and smells that assailed him. There was also the lighter gravity, with its accompanying strange sensations. Every waking moment increased the young Vulcan's knowledge about Earthmen and their world considerably.

This tiny room, safe haven from the strange and tumultuous seascape he glimpsed through the window port, spoke more eloquently of this world and its people than decades of long-range study. The homey furnishings and simple decor, jars filled with seashells and water-worn rocks, dog-eared paper books in several languages and on a variety of topics, bits of driftwood and Tatya's Ukrainian artifacts (Sorahl did not yet know them to be either Tatya's or Ukrainian, but would learn such things in time), the ordinary clutter of personal effects kept in the privacy of a sleeping room where one did not expect strangers to venture . . .

Sorahl did not move, touched nothing, would not presume to violate the privacy of those to whom he owed his life. Nevertheless their artifacts surrounded him, and he could not help contemplating them. Given an opportunity to examine his room at the Academy, what would Earthmen surmise about him and his kind?

He did not intend to eavesdrop on their argument, either, but how could he avoid it? Their voices assaulted his sensitive ears; their discordant emotions were more strident still. Yet their struggle to come to terms with what had been thrust upon them struck the young Vulcan profoundly. At last he began to understand his grandfather's obsession, his mother's fascination, with the species. He remembered that he had called them primitive, and was ashamed.

His shame was short-lived. There were things he must do. Gingerly he made another attempt to get out of the waterbed. This time he was successful.

Standing, he realized he was weak from hunger and shock (how long since the crisis that had brought them here, how long had their craft floated unnoticed in this alien sea?), but his youth and Vulcan stamina would work in his favor, and the human female in slapping him to lighten his coma had unwittingly given him the means to cure his own concussion. She had also dressed his burns, cutting away the charred tunic lest the fabric become embedded in the wounds. Barechested, Sorahl shivered. It was cold on this human planet; Selik's instruments had recorded remarkable extremes in temperature pole-to-pole.

Selik, my best teacher, Sorahl thought with a sudden flash of memory, seeing the stark face over his shoulder, instructing him. Circumstance has taken your life and spared me mine. Whatever I do henceforward must honor the memory of those whose lives were lost.

Again he shivered. The burns, residual shock, lack of sustenance, the lingering traces of concussion, exacted their toll. Sorahl wondered if it would be a breach of propriety to take the brightly patterned afghan thrown carelessly over a chair and wrap it around his shoulders.

Instead he put aside his own needs and went to his mother. Carefully he touched his fingers to the reach centers of her ravaged face. He was no healer, but if he could start her on the healing trance and stand by until she needed him to bring her out—

Mother, he thought to her knowing it was the one word that would tell her the most, bring her back through memories of the crisis, the abortive self-destruct sequence, the plummet to Earth, let her know that he was here and whole and required her presence. If she thought him dead, her mission would be complete; she would have no reason to preserve her own life.

Mother, he thought, searching for her through eddies of trauma and recent memory . . .

"Malfunction Retro One, Commander," Helm T'Preth had reported in her usual imperturbable tone. No matter that an irreparable malfunction of their retro-rockets could mean death for all of them this far from home.

"Compensate," T'Lera ordered with equal calm. "Are you in need of assistance?"

The others were already on alert: Stell leaning over Sorahl at the navcon to provide a third pair of hands should two prove insufficient, Selik and T'Syra coordinating readouts as they scanned for some external factor responsible for the malfunction. The ancient Savar had moved without sound to the airlock; it would be he who led the self-destruct if it came to that.

"Negative, Commander," T'Preth replied, nimble

fingers flying across her console. "Compensation adequate at present."

"Affirm," T'Lera said as the others returned to station as if the alert had been just another drill. "All stations, causative scan."

Silently all complied.

They had circled Earth for forty-seven of its days, pursuing their research and watching a thousand sunsets, undetected by the most sophisticated of Earth's scanning systems. Under Selik's tutelage, Sorahl had devised a remarkably flexible and intricate navigational pattern that brought them in under satellite tracking stations and maneuvered them around ground-based observatories, bringing them closer to the planet surface than any scoutcraft had dared venture before. Their impulse engines, recharging on solar while they were on dayside, allotted them fifty days of such observation, and then they must return home.

"Compensation insufficient, Commander," Helm T'Preth reported some moments later. "Retro Three now indicating variable instability."

Silently each resumed alert status.

"Causative, Science?" T'Lera addressed Selik crisply, pivoting her chair in his direction.

"Unknown, Commander," Selik replied at once. "No external damage. Calibrating for internal malfunction now."

T'Lera swung her chair forward again.

"Bring us up, Helm," she said sharply. "Twenty thousand perigee. Navigator, oblique angle. We must not be seen."

"Affirm, Commander," T'Preth and Sorahl said in the same breath, but T'Lera was already out of her chair and under the engineering con with Stell.

"Scanning Two and Four as well," Stell reported, and T'Lera merely nodded. She was listening to something else, sensing something.

71

"Status, Helm?"

"Retro One shutdown, Commander," T'Preth barely whispered even as it happened. "Three on blue line. Temporary hold at fourteen perigee. Downspiral estimated nineteen seconds—mark."

And the rest was nightmare.

Mother! Sorahl thought to her, drawing her away from such thoughts lest the healing trance prove impossible. *Mother!*

I am here, Sorahl-kam, T'Lera replied at last, and engaged the healing trance as he took his hand away.

Outside the wind was howling now, whitecaps churning, thunderheads roiling on the horizon. It was typhoon season, and someone was getting a lot of rain.

Several kilometers distant, along the bottomless rift known as the Mayabi Fault, the ocean floor slipped slightly, and a spacecraft of no known Earth design slid grating across the bottom. Under the silent silver stare of a thousand sea creatures it teetered and vanished over the edge of the crevasse in a churning of sand and was gone.

In the sleeping room of the agrostation, a young and shivering Vulcan wrapped a human-made afghan about his naked shoulders, keeping watch over his mother and looking out over the heaving sea.

And in the other room, two humans continued to argue.

". . . don't even know what they eat. Suppose they need some kind of special environment? We may be endangering them by keeping them here, doing nothing—"

"You just don't want the responsibility!" Tatya nearly shouted. "Shrug it off like you always do, dump it on someone else. You *know* what the bureaucrats will do to a find like this. Turn them into zoo specimens, destroy them. Over my dead body!"

72

"I beg your pardon—"

His voice was very soft, accustomed to speaking to more acute ears, but it brought them both to an instantaneous, electrified silence. Yoshi felt the hair on his neck start to prickle again.

"I mean no intrusion. It is obvious that we have caused considerable—disruption in your lives. We ask forgiveness."

Tatya moved toward him like a sleepwalker, reached out a hand, and almost touched him, exotic apparition like a genie from a lamp, except for the burn plasters on his chest and arms, then stopped herself.

"You're awake," she said unnecessarily, the para-medic in her taking charge, holding at bay the wonder, the incredulity. "H-how do you feel?"

"I am—well. Some physiological damage, but functional. As T'Lera will be, in time. Your concern for our physical well-being is no longer necessary."

He looked from one stunned face to the other. Was it possible they did not understand him? Or was it the incongruity of his speaking their language?

"But you had a concussion," Tatya blurted. "At least, I thought—"

"It is no longer a factor," Sorahl said. Studies indicated humans had no telepathy, no self-healing. There was no purpose in broaching such subjects now. It would serve only to confuse and frighten them. And in his hurry he had neglected the most basic of amenities. "Forgive me. I am called Sorahl. The other" —he gestured toward the sleeping room—"is T'Lera. My mother, and commander of our vessel."

It was Yoshi's turn to move forward. Instinctively he held out his hand in a typical human gesture. Sorahl, recalling the record tapes, extended his own hand and, the reluctance of the touch-telepath held firmly in check by the student of IDIC, made actual the first human-alien handshake.

"So-rall," Yoshi said carefully, sensing the reluctance, releasing the warm, dry hand; truth to tell, the moment terrified him. "And—Talera?"

Sorahl assented. Inaccurate, but it would suffice. Yoshi seemed pleased.

"My name's Yoshi. Yoshiomi Nakamura, actually. But Yoshi's fine. And this is—"

"Tatya," she said firmly, waving Yoshi aside. Tatiana Georgevna Bilash was someone she'd left behind on the mainland, along with three younger sisters and an inordinate number of bossy female relatives. She went to shake Sorahl's hand as well, was surprised to see him hesitate, seemed to shrink back slightly. "I'm sorry! Did I do something wrong?"

"No." Sorahl extended his hand a second time, touching hers briefly. How explain that among his kind a betrothed male did not . . . "It is simply not our way."

"I guess we have a lot to learn about each other," Yoshi said quickly, covering their varying degrees of embarrassment.

"Indeed," Sorahl said, and fell silent.

"You must be starved!" Tatya said suddenly, remembering the practicalities. "You just sit right here and I'll get you something to eat."

Halfway to the kitchen area, she stopped.

"I'm sorry, I—that is, we don't know—"

"We are vegetarian by philosophical choice," Sorahl explained carefully, remembering his amazement that other intelligent species could eat meat. "We will eat neither animal flesh nor the products of animals. Anything else is acceptable."

"I see," Tatya said slowly, temporarily nonplussed. It was an awesome responsibility, serving the first meal to an alien guest. What was appropriate?

"There's some tofu in the fridge," Yoshi supplied helpfully. He was consumed with curiosity, wished Tatya would stop fussing and give him a chance to ask a few of his thousand questions. "Dried fruit, brown rice. Look around." He turned toward Sorahl. "We're due for supplies shortly. Tomorrow, in fact." He shook his head. Tomorrow. Oh, gods, tomorrow! "The joke is, of course, that we're sitting on one of the staple foods of the planet, only it's not as if you can step out onto the porch and clip a few leaves for salad. What we grow is industrial-grade kelp. It has to be reprocessed."

"I quite understand," Sorahl said patiently. Food production had been Stell's area of expertise, and he had instructed his young pupil well. Yet another ghostly face, this one strong and benevolent, swam before the young Vulcan's vision.

"Tofu, then," Tatya was muttering to herself, clattering around in the kitchen area.

"You said, 'we,'" Yoshi said intently, taking the chair beside Sorahl's, marveling at the sight of an alien occupying his beanbag chair. He must not stare. If it weren't for those ears . . . "Who exactly are you? And how did you get here?"

"We are the Vulcan," Sorahl began, and proceeded to explain.

~~~

The Vulcan captain of a human crew continued the age-old tradition of his kind, asking nothing of those he commanded that he would not do himself.

The young cadet stood stiffly at attention as Captain Spock signed the end-of-shift status report. Spock allowed him a moment more of this posture, as good for the soul as it was for the spine, before favoring him with a mild glance.

"Stand at ease, Lieutenant. Is there anything else?"

The young human relaxed his stocky frame, though his spirit was still beset with the trials of serving under a Vulcan commander. Spock saw this in his eyes and addressed it.

"No sir, only—"

"Only what?"

"It's end of shift, sir. Owing to the drills this morning

you've been on the bridge since alpha shift. I was wondering if you planned to give over to anyone else for gamma, sir."

"As I read the duty roster," Spock said without having to look at it, "all who have requested gamma shift are currently at their posts. To have someone relieve me would necessitate awakening or otherwise intruding upon the offshift time of someone on alpha or beta. I see no logic in this."

"Only the logic that a commander shouldn't have to take a triple shift, sir," the young lieutenant suggested softly; he was met with a raised eyebrow. "Begging the captain's pardon, but it seems to me even Vulcans must get tired sometimes."

A quiet bemusement tugged at the corners of Spock's mouth.

"Mr. Mathee, are you offering to relieve me?"

"I would, sir," the young human said sincerely. "If I didn't think you'd think it was presumptuous."

"Thoughtfulness is never presumptuous, Lieutenant," Spock said, compounding the young man's confusion. "Nevertheless, I might point out that you would have to pull a double shift were I to take you up on your offer."

"Due respect, sir," the human said, finding ground at last to anchor on. "Logic suggests that if you can handle a triple, I can handle a double. Sir."

Spock nodded, pleased, and rose from the center seat.

"Very well, Mr. Mathee. The ship is yours for the next 7.94 hours. I shall be in my quarters."

Though far from sleep, the Vulcan thought as the turbolift brought him down the levels. There is something I must do.

He entered the dark cabin, deactivating the body scanner to keep the lights from coming on. His night

76

vision and the precise placement of every item in the room carried his body around petty concrete obstacles like furniture to where his mind had begun its journey while he was still in the lift.

In the briefest of moments he had discarded the Starfleet uniform (did it arrange itself so precisely in its place in the cabinet or were his hands so deft they conducted the busyness of mere *things* in such a way that they only seemed to move by themselves?) for the black meditation robe with its *Kohlinahr* glyphs, as easily as he exchanged the day's cares, concerns and calculations for the level of tranquility he desired.

As he knelt in the *loshiraq,* the "open posture," his hands formed in the double *ta'al* of Focus, his mind had already passed the purifying ritual, his heart rate slowed almost to human languor, his breathing almost to nil. His mind floated down, down, down, searching.

What he searched for was the answer to a most illogical question: how was it possible to remember that which had not taken place?

There is no true forgetting. Locked within the convolutions of every sentient mind is the exact recollection of every event that has transpired in the presence of that mind. Yet few humans would desire such total recall, and the human animal is notorious for its ability to forget, its memory lapses willed or unwilled. Not so the Vulcan.

The Vulcan memory is actively eidetic, unforgetting. Within the reaches of certain levels of meditation any past moment can be recollected in its entirety. It was this Spock sought to do.

His was not the realm of daydream, of preoccupation with things past. Yet something from that past had of late intruded upon his consciousness. Ever since he had read *Strangers from the Sky.* Tracing it back, he found no background, no event to surround it. Yet the memory remained, an indication to the logical mind that such memory was faulty. Ever intolerant of flaw in his own logic, Spock sought to correct the error.

All he remembered was a voice, female in timbre and, to judge from its inflection and coloration, probably human. It spoke a single phrase:

"You cannot do it alone."

There was nothing to which to attach that phrase, yet it persisted, floating in his subconscious, tantalizing. Spock must find the answer.

Down he reached, searching.

Indeed? the mind voice demanded in its language which owned no words. *And what precisely is the meaning of this?*

The fire crackled primevally—warm, comforting, mesmerizing. It had been a long day. Jim Kirk fought to keep the words from dancing off the page.

One more chapter, he thought, yawning, adjusting the comfort level of the chair, rubbing his bleary eyes. Bones was right. This book is fascinating; I can't put it down! One more chapter and I'll . . .

He nodded, drowsing. The book tumbled from his insensate fingers, over the arm of the chair onto the floor, its impact softened by the thick carpeting so that it made no sound. It landed spine upward, several fragile pages creasing under its weight.

Jim Kirk slept and, perchance, he dreamed.

"Commander," he began, *feeling his throat tighten around each word. A single wrong one would end everything. "What can I say to persuade you?"*

T'Lera studied him, the intensity of her eyes damped down so as not to intimidate him. How vulnerable these humans were! Was it logical, was it ethical, to leave them isolated in a galaxy fraught with unknowns? For the briefest moment she might have relented for this reason alone. But that decision was not for her to make.

"Do not think to persuade me with words, Mr. Kirk,"

78

she said slowly. "But if you offer a perspective which outweighs mine . . ."

A log snapped in the fireplace. Kirk jolted awake.

Huh? he thought, sitting upright and groping for the book, finding it on the floor, annoyed with himself for damaging it.

That was a strange one! he thought. When I was a kid I used to act out whatever I'd watched on vid the night before, tearing through the cornstalks, taking all the parts at once, Good Guys vs. Bad Guys back when I still believed there were such things, running myself ragged until Sam and his friends jumped me from behind the hayrick, laughing at me for a gullible, wool-gathering fool and we'd end up pushing each other into the creek.

And I'd dream about those silly 3-D melodramas, too, reliving them all night until I'd get tangled in the bedclothes or fall out of bed, and Mom would threaten to deactivate my viewer if I didn't calm down.

And God knows I've had nightmares aplenty about the real horrors in my life, Kirk thought with a shudder, now completely, coldly awake. The *Farragut* incident, Kodos the Executioner . . .

But this is the first time I've found myself playing a character in a history book.

He banked the fire, dumped his unfinished salad in the disposal, smoothed the pages of *Strangers from the Sky* before setting it on his nightstand, vibed his teeth clean, and went to bed.

And dreamed.

He staggered out of the room, slumped to the floor in the anteroom, numb and in shock from what he'd just witnessed. He'd thought he could stomach anything, but this—the horror!

Behind him, through the walls, a tumult of voices all

shouting at once poured into the room where it had happened, the noise of it drawing them like vultures, furniture slamming against walls as bodies shoved past each other in their haste to see. Reporters, security guards, diplomats, and their aides and hangers-on, pushed and jostled into a mindless mob, enacting the very Babel T'Lera had foreseen, a Babel of his, Jim Kirk's, creation.

Kirk clutched his head, clamped his hands over his ears in a futile attempt to block out the roaring chaos. He had done this thing, he! A world was unraveling under him and billions yet unborn, and it was all his fault!

"What is it? What happened?" voices demanded in all the languages of Earth. "Where are they? Where's Kirk? That stuff on the walls—Good Lord, it's everywhere! What is it?"

"It's blood, you idiots!" a woman's voice shrieked above the others.

Kirk's scalp prickled; his skin crawled in horror. Tatya, no! he wanted to cry. Tatya, don't! Don't look, don't see what I've done to your hopes, your dreams! It's my fault, mine! I tried, but it wasn't good enough! I'm sorry, Tatya, so sorry!

"Their blood is different from ours!" she was shrieking, hysterical. "It's their blood, don't you understand? You've killed them; we've all killed them. It's on all of our hands, all of us!"

Kirk clutched his head and moaned. No, my fault! Mine alone!

Behind him he heard the tattoo of bootheels, the blond woman's voice: "I told you! You cannot do it alone . . ."

". . . Alone!"

The bosun's whistle brought Spock back to the here and now abruptly enough to let him hear that he had spoken the word aloud and in Standard.

80

Fascinating! he thought, affixing this datum to the rest of the mystery he pondered even as he rose from his meditative posture to attend to the matter at hand.

"Scott to Captain . . . Scott to Captain . . ." resounded with unnecessary loudness in the utter darkness of his cabin. Interesting how Scotty never addressed him by name on the intership. For both of them there was only one true captain of *Enterprise.* Spock pressed the intercom toggle.

"Spock here."

"I dinna wake ye, did I?" Scott's voice was edged with its usual breathless anxiety. "I *am* sorry, but ye asked to be informed—"

"I was not sleeping, Mr. Scott. And, as I requested, you are personally reminding me of the Red Alert drill scheduled for 0601, so as not to breach security by letting the cadets know."

"Aye. And I wouldna have bothered ye this early, only there's a glitch in the readout on the intermix feed chamber, and before ye go taking her into evasives I'd like to take down to sublight for a wee bit and see can I get the bugs out."

"A reasonable request, Mr. Scott. How much of a 'wee bit' will you require?"

"No more than half an hour, Mr. Spock."

"Very well. Reschedule drill for 0631, and inform me when your exterminating operation is complete."

"When my—*what?*" It took Scott a moment to get the joke. "Oh, aye, I'll do that. Scott out."

Alone, Spock pondered.

Alone. Why had he spoken the word aloud? From the meditative depth he had engaged, the need to speak aloud signified a matter of grave seriousness. And why, out of all the languages he knew, had he spoken it in Standard?

There existed in Modern Vulcan alone some seven different words to describe varying states of solitude, excluding telepathic words unspoken, from "alone-not-alone" to "alone by circumstance" through "alone by need," each of which incorporated some seven further concepts from Ancient Vulcan including "alone by temperament" through "alone by outcastness," which in turn incorporated the "nonperson" modes. An etymological study of the concept through a single one of his languages . . .

But there was such a thing as being too thorough, and in the wrong direction. Spock cleared his thoughts and began again.

Solitude possesses many dimensions, the High Master T'sai had thought to him. Consider.

She had been preparing him for first *Kohl*, where solitude and the listening to one's own soul were All. In the end, it had been Spock who instructed her. Perhaps few knew firsthand as many variations on aloneness as he. Now, alone by his own choosing, he considered.

He began from the beginning as was logical, with the solitariness of the halfbreed child, alone by social outcastness, alone in the universe as the first of his kind. From such a beginning had he studied the alien solitudes he had encountered in his travels. From the loneliness of machine bereft of purpose and man bereft of memory to the loneliness of woman exiled in a world of ice, none knew as Spock did the degrees and dimensions of what it was like to be alone.

It was the one whose greatest fear it was to be alone that Spock considered last, for he knew this one so well. All he'd asked for was a tall ship and a star to steer her by, and the company of kindred souls in the adventure that was his life. Having surrendered both ship and adventure, Jim Kirk was nothing if not alone.

"Jim!"

This, too, Spock spoke aloud. Whatever it was that beset his meditations had its origins with Jim Kirk. But what was it? And who was the female whose voice insisted "You cannot do it alone"? What strange siren-metaphor out of Earth's mythology threatened his captain and his friend, and what could be done?

Were he human and by nature impulsive, Spock might almost have attempted to contact Earth. From this distance—

He considered. It would require nearly a full solar day. Illogical. If there were real danger, there was nothing he could do. Except . . .

Spock reached within, took up the silver thread that linked his mind with Jim's. Those whose minds had touched and been touched were given this.

Spock searched, found no immediate external danger to the human he so valued. He might have probed deeper to the unconscious levels, but to do so without permission was a grave breach of Vulcan privacy. Were he needed, he would know. Jim Kirk's voice had called to him from across a galaxy once before, drawing him from the reaches of *Kohlinahr*, and he had answered. He would do so again.

But not now. Within moments Mr. Scott would report that his readjustments were complete. The drill would proceed apace; duty would occupy the Vulcan's conscious mind for the present, perhaps sufficiently to block the insistence of disembodied female voices.

Further, *Enterprise*'s diurnal rhythms had been tied in with the Admiralty upon departure. It was morning where Jim Kirk was as it was "morning" aboard *Enterprise*. The admiral would still be sleeping.

("Sleeps like a baby," McCoy had observed once, having kept the vigil over a recuperating Kirk yet another time.

"A sign of a clear conscience," Spock had suggested dryly, having kept the same vigil, though not for medical reasons.

"Or no conscience at all," Kirk had shot back, yawning, embarrassed at all the attention, grinning at both of them.)

The bosun's whistle sounded yet again. Mr. Scott was nothing if not punctual. Spock roused himself into full command mode, grateful that whatever troubled his captain was at least held at bay by sleep.

"No, don't go! Please, no!"

Jim Kirk shouted himself awake. He was sitting bolt-upright in bed, clutching at something that was no longer there, some fragment of the nightmare that had jolted him from sleep. It was gone. A sudden attack of vertigo made him lie back against the pillow.

When his head cleared he glanced at the time: 0631. He didn't have to get up for another half hour, but any attempt to go back to sleep would be a joke. He sat up gingerly, wondering why the light was so strange. A mournfulness of foghorns from the bay below gave him his answer.

The penthouse was well above the fog line; Kirk could have stepped out onto the balcony and let a dazzling morning sun warm his face as he contemplated a world lost in cottony opaqueness below him. He did exactly that for a few minutes until the undulating whiteness brought a return of the vertigo and a touch of nausea.

So much for breakfast, he thought wryly as the glass wall to the balcony slid shut behind him. McCoy and his damned diets! To hell with green leaves!

Green. Oh, God, green! Green blood, Vulcan blood —everywhere. The nightmare came back to him in flashes. He could hear himself talking to T'Lera, to Tatya, saw himself as part of the horror that had caused the Vulcans' deaths, heard a voice—goading him or only warning him?—that he "could not do it alone." What in God's name did it mean?

Kirk sat on the side of the bed for a moment, thinking, mentally backing away from the impressionistic chaos of his nightmares and trying to find a different perspective.

Why was he rewriting history in his dreams, a history he knew had turned out reasonably successfully, but which he persisted in dreaming as a disaster, with himself as the causative factor? And who was the woman with the blond hair and the voice of doom?

She was always present in the recurring death dream, first as a disembodied voice, later as a shadowy female figure. Elusive, always just out of reach, poised on the edge of memory, she was nothing more than a flash of pale hair, a tattoo of bootheels, a single phrase repeated over and over in a voice Kirk was certain he ought to recognize. He never saw her face. Whenever he turned to reach out for her, she was gone.

He picked up *Strangers*, intending to search for her, but hesitated. Maybe he didn't want to know. He started flipping pages.

If you'd gotten this on disk, you old dinosaur, he chided himself, using McCoy's phrase, running one broad finger down the index on the odd chance that the word "blond" would pop out at him, you'd be able to code in that one word and the computer would present you with a list of every character in the book by hair color. Now, without a name or anything else to go on, you'll have to skim through the entire thing hoping to find her . . ..

He slammed the book shut. Or hoping *not* to find her, he thought, because if he came to know her as intimately as he knew the others, he might never sleep undisturbed again. His nights would be daubed with Vulcan blood and echoing with her voice for the rest of his life.

Kirk shoved the book in the drawer of the nightstand as if it might bite him, considered locking it in like a poisonous snake except that he was beginning to look foolish even to himself. He felt as if he was regressing into a wild-eyed boy hiding in the cornstalks. He

85

realized he was sweating, out of breath as if he'd been running. In the dream he had been. The blood, the shouting, his fault—

I have to know, he thought.

He pulled the book out of the drawer and began to read again.

FOUR

"Are you sure you've eaten enough? Are you sure it's all right?"

"It is—quite sufficient. Thank you, Tatiana."

She tried not to wince whenever he used her full name. At least he didn't know enough to add the patronymic; that would have driven her crazy.

He had made a meal of the bean curd and the steaming rice, cutting the dates and dried apricots she'd scrounged up into smaller morsels and adding them to the mixture, remarking on each item as he ate.

"We, too, cultivate a number of glycine species. The *dactylifera* and *prunus armeniaca* are also familiar," he reported solemnly. It was to pale-eyed T'Syra, geographer and botanist, that he owed his knowledge of Earth's flora. Hers was yet another spirit to whom he would do homage. "But this species *oryza sativa—* rice?"—Yoshi nodded, dumbstruck at the extent of the young Vulcan's knowledge—"is unknown to us."

"Maybe because it has to be grown in water," Yoshi suggested. "If, as you say, your planet is mostly desert . . ."

The human was hungry for details, plied the Vulcan with endless questions. He had dredged up the few astronomy books he owned and Sorahl had shown him the precise location of his world, using his navigator's skills to sketch enlarged-scale starmaps from the perspective of both worlds.

Tatya simply watched, speechless. She could not take her eyes off the young alien, memorized his every gesture, watched the movement of his long muscles beneath the thin sweater Yoshi had lent him, poured him endless cups of tea, which he drank hot and strong and without any sweetener.

"Species *theraceae,*" he observed between sips. In a human it might have been showing off. "Specifically *camellia sinensis,* I believe. We cultivate similar varieties on Vulcan, though we prefer the use of herbs."

"We drink herb tea also," Tatya said excitedly. "I just didn't have any on hand. When the Whale gets here I'll order whatever you—"

She stopped herself, horrified. What was she thinking of? She saw fleeting panic on Yoshi's face, saw that Sorahl was watchful, waiting, but did not ask her what she meant.

"You must be tired," she said quickly. "You really should rest."

"I cannot," the young Vulcan demurred. "I must keep the watch for T'Lera."

He did not elaborate, and they did not dare ask. There were so many other questions to ask first.

"It's amazing," Yoshi said, holding his long hair out of his eyes, watching the rain sheeting against the port, the grumbling flare of distant lightning. Tatya, exhausted, dozed in the beanbag chair, but the two males were beyond sleep. "Your ships have been out there, watching us, for how long?"

"Savar my grandfather was witness to your last two world wars," Sorahl said, watching Yoshi's eyes widen.

"But you're talking over a hundred— You said he was with you on this voyage. How old—"

"At his death he was 221.4, as measured in your years," Sorahl said softly. This memory, too, was part of him. "While he did not expect to survive the voyage, neither did he expect to meet death as he did."

"Your people live much longer than mine," Yoshi observed. It was yet another difference he must adjust to. But there was more here, some larger concept he was too fatigued, too wired up, to grasp. He sat beside Sorahl again, drawn to him. There was no longer any fear, and the strangeness diminished with each passing hour. In the dim light of a single lamp, all his human eyes could tolerate this long without sleep, they might have been brothers. Except for those ears, and a thousand nuances of cultural difference they'd only begun to explore. "And you say it was an accident that brought you here? You had orders to self-destruct rather than be seen? I don't understand."

"It was to avoid the situation which, because of our presence, now exists," Sorahl said. He too experienced the kinship, beyond the logic of biology or accident of birth, belonging more to the realm of IDIC, to a diversity so all-encompassing as to become similitude. "We did not wish to frighten, to create controversy. It would seem we have done both. How soon do you estimate your authorities will come for us?"

Yoshi flinched. A human might have bargained, threatened, pleaded for his mother if not for himself. There was none of that here. Another difference between them.

"Don't worry about it. We'll think of something," he said vaguely, not half believing it. At least if they kept talking he could put it out of his mind for a few more hours, and maybe by some miracle he would come up with something. "Tell me how it happened. The accident. It's important."

Sorahl understood. The human still required reas-

89

surance that these aliens, these century-long watchers, meant them no harm.

"Our scoutcraft are equipped with four retro-thrusters," he explained. "They are designed to work in tandem, so that as many as one on either side can malfunction without radically impairing ship's function. However, if two on the same side malfunction, and the odds against this are approximately 4,323.6 to one . . ."

"Retro Three on blue line," Helm T'Preth had reported, sealing their doom with a whisper. "Downspiral estimated in nineteen seconds—mark."

The downspiral alone need not have necessitated self-destruct; these small scoutcraft were incredibly maneuverable and could coast unscathed through atmosphere to touch down on land or water. Given a more favorable position they might have come to Earth in some obscure spot, repaired their retros, and departed unseen. But they were in the most cluttered of the satellite lanes and would soon be visible to any of half a dozen tracking stations. It was precisely this set of circumstances that Savar's Prime Directive had provided for, and every member of the crew was aware of it.

Sorahl, beside T'Preth at the helm as she made her announcement, would remember her utter calm all his days.

"Acknowledged," T'Lera said simply, sitting back in her chair. "Stop engines."

T'Preth did so. All was silence. A dozen hands ceased their tasks and folded themselves into waiting configurations. A dozen eyes sought those of their commander, and the message in all was the same. T'Lera's eyes sought Savar's.

"We are prepared."

It should have been simplicity itself. T'Lera had merely to activate the self-destruct timer and signal to

Savar to open the airlock. The sudden outtake of oxygen would implode their lungs instantly, even as the scoutcraft itself imploded, literally turning itself inside out with a minimum of visible "flash," reducing itself to fragments so small that should any survive the atmosphere, they would reach Earth as unidentifiable bits of charred metal.

It should have taken less than the nineteen seconds T'Preth had bequeathed them, except that for reasons as inexplicable as the failure of two tandem retros (and, with the loss of the craft, forever indeterminable), the self-destruct mechanism also failed, locking in midcountdown and refusing to respond to override.

"Kaiidth!" T'Lera said, as if it were nothing, though for her and one other it would mean the greatest sacrifice a scoutcraft's crew could make. *"T'Kahr* Savar, implement manual."

"Affirm, Commander," Savar said immediately. If his voice quavered, age was the cause and not emotion. He slid the pressure bolt on the airlock; the slightest outward pressure would unseal it. "At your command."

Ten eyes now looked to T'Lera; Savar alone had turned his eyes inward. As the physically weakest link in the chain, as the motive force behind the Prime Directive, it was doubly logical that he be the first to commit himself to the void beyond the airlock. Of the others, one must remain to assist the commander in destroying her vessel. They waited for T'Lera to choose.

"Status, Helm?"

"Orbit decaying, Commander. Downspiral commencing."

Screens had gone dark and could not be brought back up; whoever operated the craft from here on must fly blind, on instruments only, and half of them were frozen by the aborted countdown. T'Lera allowed herself the space of a breath, and chose.

There was a certain logic by which she might have selected T'Syra to remain, for they were lifelong companions and could read each other's thoughts. But by what right separate the pale-eyed one from her bond to Selik, even for a moment? No. Far-searching eyes sought pale eyes, and the choice was made in silence. T'Syra joined Selik and Savar at the airlock.

Stell also moved, not needing T'Lera's command. His usefulness had ended with the retro shutdown, and if T'Lera required T'Preth to remain, he would do what he must without her.

But with a glance T'Lera released T'Preth to join her consort. Sorahl, seeing that the choice had fallen to him, tried to interject. He would willingly give his life that any one of these might have a few moments more.

"Commander—"

"Kroykah!" T'Lera hissed without looking at him. "Terminal implement—now!"

She had flung herself into T'Preth's chair as the downspiral became more pronounced, locking her seat restraint and Sorahl's with a single motion. Sorahl hesitated for a heartbeat before reaching down two oxygen packs and handing one to his mother.

Neither looked back. Sound told them everything. With a violent sucking rush three hurtled into the void: the frail Savar, steeled by his conviction, the noble Selik, embracing the universe with outstretched arms, while beside him—

T'Lera felt the link with T'Syra snap with a pain that was physical. Her son heard her gasp and dared not witness, stayed riveted to his instruments, honoring her privacy.

For himself, he desired to make some brief farewell to the two who still remained, but to divert them from their task or himself from his was not only illogical but dangerous. His duty consisted of one thing only, to find a place in one of Earth's vast oceans where two

Vulcans and a scoutcraft could disappear without a trace.

"Hold!" T'Lera cried, her voice muffled by the oxygen mask.

She need not have spoken. The powerful Stell, his hands literally frozen to the airlock mechanism (it was very cold in space) knew intimately every conceivable sound a craft could make. He too had sensed the dying impulse flux in Retro Three, the one nearest the airlock. If it fired under these circumstances the craft would flare up like a comet—immaterial to its inhabitants, committed to death at any rate, but making it far too visible from the planet below. By main strength—a mere accident that he was the strongest of the seven—Stell wrenched the pressure bolt shut, but too late.

T'Preth screamed; Stell was permitted a single hoarse cry. The pain of becoming a living torch was more than even a Vulcan could shield against in time. The impulse flux, feeding on the outrushing oxygen, had hurled a roaring tongue of flame through the closing airlock, immolating them both. Their charred, still-smoking bodies fell backward into the craft like so much dead wood.

T'Lera closed her eyes and thought a mourning chant. There was nothing else she could have done.

Sorahl, who was yet young and lacking in the full mastery of the Vulcan, whose own life was measured in minutes, gripped the controls to keep his hands from shaking.

Retelling the tale, Sorahl saw that they were shaking still. Summoning all of his control, he made them stop.

"The reentry heat must have been ferocious," Yoshi said after a time. "We saw what was left of your ship."

"We are more acclimated to extremes of heat," Sorahl said quietly. His burns spoke for themselves. "And the oxygen packs spared our lungs."

93

"And you managed a controlled splashdown through all of that?" Yoshi asked, wondering if he would have had the courage. "Fantastic!"

"It was thought your Pacific Ocean would provide the optimum place of concealment," Sorahl explained. "Owing to its vastness and sparsity of population. We could not know that the locus of our splashdown would coincide so precisely with the boundaries of your station."

"Kismet," Tatya said drowsily, shaking off sleep and pulling herself out of the beanbag chair. She had been silent so long the others might have forgotten about her.

"I beg your pardon?" Sorahl gave her his full attention, although he seemed to do that with whoever was speaking.

"Karma. The power of fate," she explained lamely, wondering what kind of rumpled mess she must look to this stranger. She didn't usually bother about her looks, but suddenly it was important. "Different words for the same concept. It means there's a purpose to your being here. Some kind of pattern. Everything you've told us, all those instrument failures and bizarre coincidences, mean there's some special reason you were brought here, to us."

"Tatya, for crying out loud—"

"Perhaps so," Sorahl said not unkindly, though he might have argued the issue. "Though I for one do not subscribe to such fatalism."

"His grandfather and the rest of the crew died for that 'special reason'!" Yoshi snapped. "You're talking nonsense! If it was just to spare us the truth," he said to Sorahl, "you could have trusted us. Most people on Earth believe we're not alone out here."

"Yet confronted with such truth, your response is at best ambivalent," Sorahl observed, remembering his own insistence upon contact. His mother had been correct. Theory was one thing, practical application

94

quite another. "Even now you are uncertain what action to take."

"See?" Tatya said off Yoshi's chagrin.

"What will you do now?" Yoshi asked, disturbed that his uncertainty was that obvious. "We've seen you, talked to you. You've shared a meal with us. We can't exactly pretend you don't exist."

"That will be for my commander to decide," Sorahl said quietly, looking down at his hands.

As if on cue, there was a noise from the sleeping room—a hoarse, strained gasping that to Tatya's practiced ears sounded like someone suffering from lobar pneumonia and struggling for breath. She moved toward the sleeping room, but Sorahl was ahead of her.

He had to wake his commander from the healing trance. "Permit me," he said, not quite touching Tatya's arm. Tatya nodded, but followed him anyway, curious.

In the pink light of a rain-washed false dawn, T'Lera writhed on the alien waterbed, her head thrown back, fists clenched, gasping. Sorahl moved over her like a shadow and struck her, hard.

Tatya tried to throw herself between them, but Yoshi caught her by the shoulders and held on. Sorahl struck his mother again, and again. Tatya struggled as if it were she who was being attacked.

"He'll kill her!" she shrieked, trying to get free.

"He knows what he's doing!" Yoshi hissed in her ear with a conviction he only half felt. "Stay out of it!"

Sorahl struck again. Tatya turned away, clutching at Yoshi, who had his eyes closed. Had they been wrong? Had all Sorahl's talk of his logical, peaceful people been nothing but lies? Was this his way of wresting control from his commander, saving his own skin?

Then it was over. Neither human actually saw T'Lera bolt upright and seize her son's arm with a strength equal to his own, but both heard the authority with which she spoke.

"Sufficient," she said curtly, and proceeded to assess her surroundings and her hosts with those far-searching eyes as if nothing untoward had happened.

Yoshi just stood, as dumbstruck by the mother as he had been by the son. Tatya, as if to get out of the glare of those eyes, drew closer.

"May I?" she asked, reaching one hand out toward T'Lera's face, stopping just short of touching with mother as she had with son.

"You are a healer?" T'Lera inquired, understanding her intent.

"A what? I'm a paramedic. Is that the same?"

"Then you may examine me," T'Lera said with absolute equanimity.

Tatya limited herself to hands-on; she wouldn't have believed any of her instrument readings anyway. But her hands betrayed her as well, because except for the deformity of the nose, which would have to be re-broken and reset—

"You're completely healed!" the human said.

"Indeed," the Vulcan said, looking at her son for the first time. "My gratitude, Navigator."

"Kaiidth!" Sorahl said instinctively, forgetting where he was.

"We will speak the language of those in whose presence we are!" his mother/commander said sharply. Despite Sorahl's insistence that his people had eliminated emotion, this certainly looked like anger. "Do you forget so easily?"

A human might have made excuses. Sorahl simply lowered his eyes and clasped his hands meekly behind his back.

"I ask forgiveness, Commander."

"It is not I of whom you should ask forgiveness," T'Lera said, neither accepting nor rejecting his apology. "I must know what has transpired during my incapacity."

She was not exactly dismissing the humans, but she had effectively eliminated them from her consideration.

"Excuse us!" Yoshi muttered, pulling Tatya out of the room with him. T'Lera seemed not to hear.

The sun was coming up. Yawning hopelessly, Tatya set the coffeemaker and went to freshen up. Yoshi opened the port to let a soft breeze in, stood listening to the lap of waves, the burble of brewing coffee, seeing nothing.

Suddenly it was there. Hours ahead of schedule, looming on their horizon against a glare of brilliant sunlight. The Whale.

～～

"I'll go," Yoshi said when Tatya returned, rebraiding her damp hair. "See if you can persuade our friends to keep quiet and away from the windows."

Tatya watched him narrowly. If he was still unsure of his motivation, she was that much less sure.

"I'll tell them to leave everything dockside," he said off her look. "Or I'll go pick it up. I'll say you're not feeling well."

"Yoshi . . ."

"Look, what else do you want me to do? As soon as the rain stopped I was going to take the foil out alone, let them think we'd tried to run for it. Maybe it's better if we stay put, try to bluff it out. If they'd shown up this afternoon like they were supposed to . . ."

It was hopeless and they both knew it.

"We're still civilians," Yoshi said, suddenly determined. "We have rights. They don't get past the threshold without a warrant."

"Doesn't surprise me that your dreams are inhabited by strange women, Jim," McCoy said when Kirk told him about the nightmares. "Personally, I wouldn't worry unless they *stopped* appearing."

They were backstage behind the *Kobayashi Maru*

simulator, Kirk programming variations on the basic scenario for the latest batch of cadets.

"I'm not joking, Bones. This thing has me worried. You've finished the book, haven't you? Is there such a person as this mystery blonde?"

McCoy pondered on it.

"Not to my knowledge. Not that you give a man much to go on. Blond hair and boots, you said? Sounds like the beginning of a pleasant kind of fantasy, but as far as I know the only woman specifically described as having blond hair was Tatya Bilash. Maybe it's Tatya you're dreaming about," he suggested hopefully.

"The voice is different," Kirk maintained, his eyes on the simulator screen. "It's familiar somehow. I feel as if I should know who she is, but every time I'm on the verge of remembering a name, a face, she slips away."

"Maybe she's from another source entirely," McCoy suggested. "From one of your real-life memories or fantasies. Dreams are tricky stuff, Jim. You could be subconsciously mixing an old memory with what you've been reading and end up with a third thing that's neither one nor the other. I wouldn't worry about it."

"Maybe you wouldn't," Kirk said testily, punching in a series of codes with unnecessary vigor. "But I would. The woman is only part of the mystery. Why are these dreams so vivid, so consistent—and so consistently wrong? Why am I embellishing what I read in that book to the point where I feel as if I've *been* there?"

McCoy shrugged.

"You're just caught up in the hoopla like everyone else," he suggested, anxious to dismiss it, wondering why it had Kirk so agitated. "It's everywhere. You can't turn on the vid without some talk-show host or discussion group picking it apart. Walk into a party and half the people there are describing it to the other half."

"I deliberately avoided all that," Kirk pointed out,

pondering the final flourishes on the day's test. There were two Tellarite cadets in Green Group; he particularly wanted to test their response to pressure. "I wanted to read it for myself. No preconceived notions."

"Even so . . ." McCoy began, but didn't know what to say next.

He was back here with Kirk to monitor the cadets' interactions and responses to stress during the test for his Medical Officers' Report. While the *Kobayashi Maru* was always taped and he could review it at his leisure, McCoy wanted to watch the scenario as it happened. There was an immediacy that the camera always missed. Suddenly he found himself monitoring a response to stress from an entirely different quarter.

"Why are you making such a mountain out of this?" he asked his oldest, dearest friend.

"Because there's more to it than cocktail-party chatter," Kirk said grimly. "More than what's between the pages of that book. I can't put my finger on it, but there's something damned peculiar—"

"You always give 'em three Klingons," McCoy muttered, knowing the codes by heart, trying to distract Kirk from what sounded like an obsession in bloom.

"What?" Kirk asked vaguely, watching the monitor, half listening.

"I said: you always give 'em three Klingon vessels in the attack phase. Don't you think they compare notes with the groups that went before? You're getting predictable. Why not give 'em two Klingons for a change, or four, or one?"

"Because if you knew *anything* about Klingons, doctor, for all the years you've logged in space," Kirk said acidly, punching buttons with a zealot's fervor, "you'd know that *they* are predictable in their obsession with combinations of three. Hence a bracket of *K'tinga*-class battlecruisers has been and always will be composed of three. And *who's* getting predictable?"

"You are," McCoy said reasonably. "Or maybe I meant to say cranky. Short-fused, irascible, burr-under-your-saddle nasty . . ."

Kirk turned on him.

"You have a point, doctor?"

"Yes, I do. Low side of fifty's a little early for a midlife crisis according to today's demographics, Jim. You want me to prescribe something for the hot flashes? Or some*one* maybe?"

"Don't *you* make a mountain out of it, Bones," Kirk warned, returning to his console. "I get this way when I can't sleep at night."

"I can prescribe something for that, too," McCoy offered. "Or someone."

Kirk broke into laughter and punched McCoy on the arm.

"Damn you anyway!" He watched the cadets from Green Group file in and take their places on the mock bridge and almost pitied them. "And your *Strangers from the Sky*. Tonight that book stays in the drawer."

The book stayed in its drawer for the next three nights. Jim Kirk continued to dream.

"And I'll tell you something else," he told McCoy, pacing the confines of the doctor's offices in the Med-Arts complex. "I have whole conversations with them now. All of them—the Vulcans, Tatya, Yoshi, Jason Nyere. And Sawyer. Last night I got into a real knock-down-drag-out with Sawyer. Shouted so loud I triggered the computer alarm. Had some time convincing it I wasn't under attack or having a coronary. I can tell you what they looked like, what they sound like, what they ate for breakfast . . ."

"Jim," McCoy began, knowing it was useless. "You're projecting. Letting your imagination run wild. Listen, if you'd—"

"No, you listen!" Kirk stopped pacing, leaned across

McCoy's desk at him. "Bones, I'm making perfect sense, aren't I? You've read the book from cover to cover; you know who these people are. You know how the incident turned out. I'm telling you I do too, and I haven't touched the book since the last time we talked. How can I possibly know all these things?"

"Jim—"

"Did you know Sawyer was a crack tennis player?" Kirk went on, oblivious. "She was second-seeded at the Goddard Moonbase Semifinals in 2028."

"The book does mention she played tennis. I think." McCoy frowned. "I don't believe it goes into that much detail, however."

Kirk threw up his hands.

"There you are! Bones, I not only know that much about Sawyer, but I've seen her play! In fact, I've played against her! Last night's sequence—I don't even call them dreams anymore; they're like episodes in a serial—"

"Or chapters in a book you're writing in your own head," McCoy interjected, unheard.

"We were playing singles. I'd gone looking for her on the courts. Something I had to tell her about the Vulcans, something vital. She challenged me and we began to play. And by God, Bones, seventeen years off her form she was still good. Beat me in straight sets and she wasn't even breathing hard!"

"How old were you?" McCoy asked out of nowhere.

Kirk was momentarily startled.

"What?"

"In the dream. How old were you? Were you the age you are now, older, younger?"

"If this is leading to another crack about my being out of shape . . ." Kirk stopped, realized something for the first time. "I was younger. Much younger. Maybe not much more than thirty. That's why it bothered me so much, losing to Sawyer. Here she was with a good fifteen years on me, without the advantage of modern aerobic conditioning, and she beat me. That's why later, when she coerced T'Lera into playing . . ."

Kirk stopped. McCoy's blue eyes had that out-of-focus look that meant he wasn't listening to him but to the voices in his own head.

"Bones? That's not in the book, is it? About Sawyer playing tennis with T'Lera?"

McCoy didn't answer him.

"Do you think the age thing means anything?"

McCoy blinked, came back into focus.

"I don't know, Jim. It might. Mind if I ask you something?"

Kirk shrugged.

"Shoot."

"When did you have your last psychoscan?"

"Couple of months ago. Why? You know the drill. Regulation 73-C, Subsection A: 'All Starfleet personnel will submit to routine psychological profile scan no less than once per solar year. Those of officer rank, or whom medical personnel deem under more than usual stress—' "

" '—will be subjected to scan as frequently as necessary upon recommendation of senior medical officer,' " McCoy finished for him. "Jim, I'm recommending."

Kirk gave him one of those stopped-in-his-tracks looks.

"You're kidding."

"No, I'm not." McCoy returned the look with his best don't-argue-if-you-know-what's-good-for-you look. "I'll keep it unofficial, unless you get balky on me."

"You just want me out of your hair," Kirk said, trying to minimize it, shrug it off. "Or at least out of your office. I have been monopolizing your time, haven't I? I'm sorry, Bones, I'll—"

"Jim, don't try to charm me. I'm serious. You go voluntarily or I'll write you up, but either way you'll go. Now which is it going to be?"

Kirk looked genuinely hurt.

"I think I'm entitled to know why."

"Why," McCoy began, cranking up, "is because for the past four nights, from what you tell me, you've been playing a major role in a historical melodrama instead of doing what most normal humans do after a hard day at the office, which is engage in the entertainment of their choice and then go to sleep. Now, that kind of activity's bound to wear on a man. Affect his performance, maybe even his command ability—"

"Bones, I'm not exactly out on the edge lately," Kirk protested. "People's lives aren't hanging on my ability to command anymore."

"Maybe that's the problem, Jim," McCoy said. The response was a thunderous silence. "And since there's nothing physically wrong with you except for hyper-adrenal activity every time you get on the topic—"

"What makes you so sure of that?" Kirk wanted to know.

McCoy opened his left hand, where he'd palmed the smallest mediscanner Kirk had ever seen. It was silent, too, modified so that it made none of the whirring, humming readout noises of the standard models. McCoy had had it hidden in his clasped hands beneath the desktop, taking readings all the while Kirk ranted and raved.

"Why, you sneaky, son-of-a—" Kirk spluttered, torn between rage and laughter. "If that doesn't constitute a breach of privacy!"

"Not if you come into your doctor's office seeking a medical consultation," McCoy said mildly. "Look, Jim, there's nothing I can do for you without a scan. I don't know if this is boredom, depression, anxiety, an overdose of ground assignments, change of life, or some new virus that's going around. I do know, from my vast experience with certain personality types, that it's evolving into a full-blown obsession. It's driving you crazy, and before I allow it to drive me crazy I'm taking evasive action. You will report to Psych for that profile with all due expediency. Now, do you want that in writing, Admiral, or can we try to be adult about it?"

Kirk held up his hands in surrender.

"I'll try to fit it into my schedule." McCoy gave him a venomous look. "All right, all right. First thing tomorrow."

"Fine!" McCoy growled, pocketing the mediscanner and making paperwork motions. "Now get the hell out of here, will you? Some of us have work to do!"

And the next time I recommend a book to you I'm going to have my head examined, he thought to Kirk's retreating back.

Nowhere is it written that Vulcans do not dream. Nevertheless the misconception persists.

Logic suggests that the more highly evolved the intellect, the greater the potential, the greater the need, for the seeming formless randomness of dream. It has been proven that those centers of the brain which in some species produce telepathic impulses are closely interconnected with the places where dreams are born. It has been suggested that disembodied intellects—Thasians, Organians, Medusans—spend their entire lives in a realm of ever-flowing dream.

Among the Vulcan Masters, there are mind techniques that make logical use of dreams, channeling them to the solving of specific intellectual problems, suppressing them entirely to transform the time of sleep into the vast empty blankness where logic is All. It is said that the High Masters scarcely sleep at all.

For the average Vulcan, the realm of dreams may perhaps provide release for those emotions kept in check while waking. This is a matter for Vulcan privacy, and not for the curiosity of outworlders. Those who have observed the Vulcan in sleep may doubt that dreams transpire beneath the stillness of that repose. What the Vulcan dreams, what use he makes of such dreams are his concern, but that the Vulcan dreams is fact.

Sometimes it is necessary to dream.

Abandoning his nightly meditations at last for sleep, Spock dreamed.

"You cannot do it alone," the female insisted. "You cannot do it . . . You cannot do it . . . You cannot . . . You cannot alone . . . You alone . . . alone . . . alone . . ."

"Mother?" Spock asked the darkness, sensing rather than seeing her.

She was standing beside him, her hand on his arm in a gesture he tolerated from no other.

"Mother, if I fail . . . your people and my father's will never meet—"

"And you will never be," Amanda finished for him. "Is that what motivates you, my son?"

Spock shook his head.

"Personal concerns are of little consequence in a situation of this magnitude. It is the thought of Earth without the benefit of Federation—"

"And the benefit of Vulcan wisdom?" Amanda asked. "Poor little Earth! How ever will we manage?"

Spock stood on his dignity even in dream.

"Mother, it is a fact that without Vulcan intervention the entire food supply of Earth would have been endangered by the year—"

"And as even your father will admit, it is a fact that without the mitigating influence of humans, there was a 67.6 percent probability that Vulcans would have logicked themselves to death within a millennium," Amanda countered. "Assuming they survived the Tellarite Insurgency in a Federation that did not contain humans. And where was Vulcan, I'd like to know, during the Romulan Wars? Which of your worlds do you argue for, Spock? And why not both?"

Spock had no answer.

"Neither Vulcan nor Earth could have achieved what they have without the other. Neither could do it alone. Nor can you. You cannot do it alone . . ."

It was not Amanda who stood beside him in darkness, but T'Lera who stood before him in the light. Vulcan and commander, dweller in the void of space for more years than Spock had lived, she awaited his argument with the equanimity of her station and her years.

"Commander," Spock began, wondering for the first time in his life which of his worlds he spoke for. "What can I say to persuade you?"

T'Lera now studied him, making no effort to mitigate her gaze. This one, whatever he was, would not fear her. She must know why.

"Who are you?" she asked, slowly approaching him. "Who are you . . .?"

"I'm taking the afternoon off," Kirk told his Coridani aide. He had a sudden desperate need to be alone. "Get Kinski to cover my 1400 briefing, hold all my calls, and you can have the water-ballet tickets for tonight. If you don't mind sitting next to Commodore Hrokk."

"Thanks, but I'll pass." The girl lowered her bifurcate eyebrows at him. Commodore Hrokk had two hands more than the average humanoid. "Where will you be, Admiral?"

"Anywhere but here," Kirk said shortly, putting the time lock on his desk, jingling the activator for the aircar he'd left in the flag officers' hangar. Before the results of this morning's psychoscan came back he would be long gone. "And don't have me paged unless the world's coming to an end. Clear?"

"I thought you and *Enterprise* solved that the last time, sir," his aide quipped. Kirk stopped in his tracks. "I only meant—it's a running gag around here, sir. V'ger and all that."

"Yes, I know," Kirk said. "'Admiral Quirk' is what they call me behind my back, isn't it?"

When Coridani blushed, they went from gray to mauve.

"It's not that we don't appreciate what you did, Admiral, only—"

"Only what, Ensign?"

"Only it's a little awesome working for a living legend, sir. Particularly one who's so—down to Earth? Is that the expression I want?"

"It'll do," Kirk said grimly.

Living legend! he thought, navigating the corridors in quick time before someone waylaid him with some new idiocy. They'll cast me in bronze if I don't keep moving. Living legend! That hurts almost as much as the one about being "down to Earth." As Spock would say: precisely!

Kirk let the aircar down on its pontoons and waited for it to stabilize. The sea was calm, but he'd come in rather fast and kicked up a local wake; he'd have to wait for it to dissipate. Meanwhile he opened the overhead iris to 360 degrees and had a look around. He'd never been to this part of the Pacific before, had no idea it was so built up.

The picture of it he had in his head was two centuries old.

That clump of submersibles riding at anchor on a massive free-floating dock he'd passed to the west he recognized as belonging to DownUndersea, an entire underwater city built out from the coral reefs off Brisbane almost to the Solomons. But this far out, well east of Norfolk Island and south of Pitcairn, he'd expected open sea.

Instead he'd landed in the middle of a number of little pontoon villages built entirely on the surface of a reasonably quiet South Pacific. No doubt they had some kind of shielding against major storms; all the same he'd hate to be bobbing around like a cork on that ocean in a typhoon, Kirk thought. But the inhabitants of these villages were seafolk—Maoris and Samoans and the hard-as-nails descendants of descendants of *HMS Bounty*'s Pitcairners; they could probably weather anything.

Kirk opened the hatch on the aircar and breathed deeply of the salt air. It was beautiful here. He would have to come back sometime when he could stay a few days, get to know the people and their world. There was still so much of his own planet he knew nothing about, and he could find much to like in this part of it.

But what he'd come looking for wasn't here.

McCoy popped the results of Jim Kirk's psychoscan out of his viewer and scowled. This was more serious than he'd thought.

"Get me Admiral Kirk's office," he barked into the comm.

Within seconds he was talking to the Coridani ensign, who was extremely sorry, doctor, but—

"What do you mean he's gone for the day?" McCoy blustered. "Where the hell is he?"

He rang up Kirk's apartment and left a message with the computer. He called the museum at Alexandria on the odd chance he might be poking around in the library. He called all of Kirk's usual haunts. No one had seen Jim Kirk in over a week.

Ever since he got hold of that damn book, McCoy fumed.

Ordinarily he'd let it go. Jim was a big boy and could take care of himself. But in view of what had turned up on his scan there was something ominous about his choosing to disappear right now.

McCoy had one last resort, and that was to use his clout to have Kirk found via the intracranial senceiver flag officers were required to have implanted whenever they were planetside. McCoy had always hated the device, balked at it as a major invasion of privacy, and he wouldn't use it unless he was sure the man was in real danger.

And he wasn't at all sure of that. Yet.

Taking the scan tape with him, McCoy headed for the Psych Division. There were some people he had to talk to.

Kirk aimed the aircar toward the nearest of the float villages, adjusted its engines for oversea, felt it kick in like an outboard and churn up a great frothing wake. He lowered the overhead dome, keeping only the windscreen in place, enjoying the wind in his hair and the spray on his face. As he neared the piers extending out from the village like the spokes of a wheel and the variety of sea- and air-going craft moored to them, he slowed to a leisurely bobbing pace, cutting his wake to almost nil.

A boy of about twelve, shirtless and barefoot, sat dangling his legs over the end of one of the piers. When he saw this exotic craft heading in his direction, he jumped to his feet and waved it toward him excitedly. Kirk killed the engine to an idling purr and came alongside.

"Whattaway!" the boy called the local greeting, just loudly enough to be heard above the aircar's jets.

"Hello yourself," Kirk replied.

"Mine's Koro Quintal," the boy stated, jerking a thumb toward his bare chest. "What's yours?"

Squinting up at him in the afternoon sun, Kirk marveled at the diversity his planet could produce. Everything about the boy declared the variety of his ancestry. His first name, the wiry build, jet-black hair and tawny skin, even his abiding by the custom of not raising his voice close to the sea, revealed his Maori roots. His last name and the startling blue eyes in that burnished face made him offspring of one of Fletcher

Christian's crewmates. An Aussie accent the like of which Kirk hadn't heard since Kyle made commander and shipped aboard *Reliant* completed the picture. Here was a thousand years of Earth history, looking down at him from a pier in the middle of an ocean named Pacific, hands on his hips, grinning.

"Mine's Jim Kirk."

"You're lost, my word," Koro observed, cocking his head like a bird.

"May be, son," Kirk acknowledged, waiting for the boy to make the next move, enjoying the exchange.

"Could be I'd help y'find it," Koro said, digging one diffident bare toe into a rift in the prefab surfacing of the pier. "Can I have a go-'round in that-'ere rum-looking rig of yours?"

"Sounds reasonable, Koro Quintal." Kirk smiled, offering him a hand down. "Hop in."

They'd made the circuit of the entire village twice and flown over it once for good measure, Koro's eager hands on the controls, before Jim Kirk explained what he was doing here.

"Lot of outlanders been poking around this-here since that book come out," Koro observed as they idled and bobbed, watching the gulls wheeling and coasting back to the haunts of man with the sunset. "Weren't none of them a bloody admiral, my word."

"Don't tell me you've read it," Kirk asked, bemused. He'd worn his civvies, hadn't meant to tell the boy who he was, but news about living legends reached even here.

"*Strangers from the Sky*? Aye, sure thing. Assignment for school. Only it's ancient, don't y'see? Hasn't been a kelp farm hereabouts in a hundred years."

"If only there were someone who knew about that time," Kirk mused. "A local historian maybe. Koro, who's the wisest person you know?"

"That'd be Galarrwuy," the boy said without hesitation. "He's curator of the museum over to Easter. An outlander like you, Admiral-Jim-Kirk."

Time to use that rank to advantage, Kirk decided.

"Would you introduce me to this Galarrwuy sometime?"

"Now's as good as any," the boy said, scrambling back into the pilot's seat. "Can I steer her again?"

Kirk hesitated. It was early evening here, three hours earlier than San Francisco, and it would take him as many hours to get back. If he wasn't at his desk by 0800 tomorrow, they'd send out an alert for him, and he wasn't about to call in and let them know where he was. He decided to chance it. At least Easter Island was a thousand miles in the right direction.

"She's yours." He nodded at Koro. "Only take her up and over please."

"Why?" Koro gunned the engine. "You apt to seasick?"

"No, but it's faster."

"Ar!" the boy marveled. "Caught on to me already!"

"The minute that book hit the stands they started coming out of the woodwork," Dr. Krista Sivertsen told McCoy. "All the seekers and the searchers, every wide-eyed neurotic and flawed personality on the planet turned up claiming they were present in a previous incarnation when the Vulcans arrived, that they helped them escape or helped them pass for human or whatever. Some even claimed they were direct descendants of Sorahl by way of a variety of human females. Whatever it may have done for history, that book is playing hob with psychiatry. When your admiral told me why you'd sent him for a scan, I thought, No, impossible. He's not the type at all. He's strong, assertive, a totally integrated personality. McCoy's doing a number on me. Then I read the results of the scan.

"Let me put it to you this way, Leonard. If I sent you

111

a patient whom you diagnosed as having a serious communicable disease, would you let me plea-bargain him out of quarantine to run around infecting others?"

"He's not going to hurt anyone!" McCoy protested. "I'll personally monitor him around the clock for as long as you have him in therapy. But you can't relieve a man like Jim Kirk of duty and expect him to sit home and watch the wallpaper."

"On the contrary," the leggy blond psychiatrist said. "I want him hospitalized. Under sedation and under restraint if necessary, until we get to the bottom of this."

McCoy had argued himself hoarse since he'd stormed into Krista's cozy, informal office in Psych Division. Krista's digs looked more like a high-class ski lodge than a shrink's office, right down to the needlepoint on the sofa cushions and the choice of hot cider or schnapps-spiked coffee Dr. Sivertsen offered her patients as part of her unique brand of therapy.

McCoy had known her for years, had in fact had her as a student back when he was teaching. Back when he was still—unhappily—married, and the sight of her crossing and uncrossing those long legs in the front of his lecture hall had been enough to remind him just how unhappy he really was. But nothing would be served by bringing up that particular part of the past.

"Krista, be reasonable—"

"Leonard, I am being reasonable." She too was conscious of their shared history, remembered how his dry humor and the laugh lines around those sky-blue eyes hadn't disguised the pain behind them. To this day it was all she could do to keep from calling him Dr. McCoy all the time. "You saw his readout, and you're skilled enough to know what it means. I'll run it for you again if you need convincing."

She punched up Jim Kirk's psychoscan.

"Here, and here," she said, pointing out the anomalies. "Radical dysfunction in deep-level mnemonic patterns, and localized distortion of short-term focal memory."

"I see it," McCoy acknowledged grudgingly.

Krista shut off the viewer.

"Left untreated," she said, toying with the fringe on one of the pillows she'd stitched herself but looking McCoy straight in the eye, "it can result in severe stress, increasing disorientation, instances of selective amnesia. It can indicate possible latent schizophrenia." She leaned toward McCoy, put one hand on his arm. "I couldn't be more reasonable than in suggesting that this man get immediate and concentrated help. In an enclosed environment."

McCoy let it all sink in. How could a thing like this happen?

"Leonard?" Krista Sivertsen dropped her professional voice, exchanged it for a personal, caring one. Her hand was still on McCoy's arm. "I know he's a close friend of yours. I want to help."

"I know you do, Krista." McCoy patted her hand absently, baffled. "I just don't understand it. What could cause something like this to happen to a man like Jim Kirk?"

"We're not really sure," Krista said, back in her professional mode. "It's only recently been identified as a separate phenomenon. In the old days it was clumped in with all the other schizophrenias and treated with varying degrees of success. The only place I've ever encountered it these days is in certain kinds of drug addicts."

She chose her next words carefully.

"Sometimes a man like Jim Kirk, a man of great personal dynamism, finds it hard to adjust to a ground assignment. Is there any chance he might be experimenting with some of the new synthetic soporiffs the renegade labs have been peddling under the counter?"

"Of course not!" McCoy said. "I know the kind of dependence those alterants create as well as you do! Jim Kirk's not that kind of man!"

"I'm sorry," Krista said sincerely. "But I wanted to eliminate that as a factor right off. There are so many variables to consider. I ran his medical history before I sent you the results of the scan. It's incredible how many times the man's mind has been tampered with in his deep-space years. It's quite possible that any one of those old traumas . . ."

McCoy thought about it. From Sargon's initially benevolent "borrowing" to Parmen's literal mental cruelty to Janice Lester's outright theft, Jim Kirk had had more people poking around in his mind than any other ordinary mortal in history.

"Even a Vulcan mind-meld can trigger erratics in certain unstable individuals," Krista Sivertsen was saying. She had never met Kirk until he'd turned up in her office that morning, but the story of this human and a certain Vulcan was legend. "Do you understand what I'm saying, Leonard?"

"Yes. Yes, I do. But I can't believe—Krista, let me ask you: is it possible a Vulcan mind-meld could *undo* something this severe?"

"Oh, no you don't!" She knew what it cost McCoy to ask this; the story of *this* human and a certain Vulcan was legend also. "If you'd thought that, you should have gone to a Vulcan healer first. You dropped this in my lap, and it's my responsibility. No band-aid therapy and no pointed-eared witch doctors allowed." She was trying to make him laugh, but McCoy was preoccupied, beyond humor. "Leonard, trust me. With today's techniques it'll be a matter of a week or two. He can take some vacation time, and I promise you we'll keep it off his record. But only if you do it my way."

"How—how soon?" McCoy asked vaguely.

"As soon as possible. Tonight. I can free up a bed within the hour. Where is Admiral Kirk now?"

"That's the problem," McCoy frowned. "I don't know."

"Estimated arrival time Sol III?" Spock asked his navigator.

"Seven solar days, Captain," Lieutenant Mathee reported. "Stardate 8097.4, as per your original log entry, sir."

"Very well," Spock replied evenly, giving no evidence of how heavily that time would pass with him. "Helm, maintain warp two. We are going home."

And none too soon, he thought.

Rapa Nui. Easter Island. The World's Navel. It had many names. Kirk had of course heard of it, recognized the rows of solemn gargantuan statues facing out to sea, knew something of their history.

He was not prepared to find that the entire island had been transformed into a museum, the Museum of the South Pacific, centered in the ultramodern glass-and-rhodinium structure rising beside Rano Raraku, the volcanic crater lake near the island's eastern tip. Nor was he prepared for the museum's curator.

Dr. Galarrwuy Nayingul was an Australian of the ancient races—dark-skinned, deep-eyed, shorter than Kirk but solid, immutable, as if rooted in the Earth his people had inhabited perhaps longer than any others still living, his thick white hair and beard framing a face that was ageless. On this tiny island 9,000 kilometers from his birthplace near Darrinbandi, he was farther from home than Jim Kirk.

"A pleasure, Admiral," he said warmly when Koro had introduced them, gripping Kirk's pale hand in both his dark ones as if he'd known him all his life. "What brings you to this part of our, you'll pardon the expression, mundane little world?"

Kirk shared in his laughter, which was rich and deep and resonant with a more ancient, cosmic laughter.

"Curiosity, Dr Nayingul."

"Galarrwuy, please. Or if that's too much of a mouthful, Galar will do."

"Galarrwuy," Kirk said carefully. "I came looking for something Koro tells me is rarer than the American bison. An early kelp station."

"Ah!" Galarrwuy said, leading Kirk and the suddenly diffident Koro down the aisles of the closed-for-the-evening museum, its display cases filled with Micronesian artifacts and Maori bird masks lighting automatically as they passed. "You too have read The Book."

"I don't mean to sound like a tourist," Kirk began. "I imagine you're swamped with them."

"Only those I choose to see. And you would be one of them," Galarrwuy said, opening the door to his private office, offering his guests the comfort of low couches and freshly fermented pineapple juice. "Though not overmuch for you, boyo," he scolded Koro avuncularly. "You're going home soon."

"Ah, Galar, serious!" the boy protested, looking from one to the other to see where best to plead his case. *"Morla el do!* Tomorrow's good enough! I've come for to have a listen. As part of my education," he added winningly.

"Seriously," Galarrwuy corrected him, unimpressed. "Doubtless your kin know you're harboring with me yet again, but it does get wearisome having them ring me up every time you take a tail wind. Sit you down and finish your juice, then home for dinner. You can use my spare boat."

"Ar!"

The boy settled into silence in one corner, hoping they'd forget he was there.

"You seek information about the old kelp stations," Galarrwuy told Kirk rather than asking him. "In order to relive the experience of the young couple Tatya and Yoshi, all innocently tending their seaweed crop when,

116

on a crystalline night two hundred years ago, the Strangers from the Sky, our cosmic siblings the Vulcans, fell into their laps, so to speak."

"It's curious you should use the term 'relive,'" Kirk said sincerely. "Because in a peculiar way I feel I *have* lived the experience before."

Galarrwuy's deep-set eyes grew intense.

"Truly? Are you a reincarnationist, James Kirk?"

"No. At least I don't think so. Didn't think so." Kirk held out his hands helplessly. "I'm not sure anymore."

Then he told Galarrwuy about his dreams.

There was an almost interminable silence.

"Koro," Galarrwuy said at last. "It is time for you to go."

"I'm troubling n'one here," the boy grumbled from his corner. He'd been listening, wide-eyed. "Please, Galar, let me stay?"

Galarrwuy waited, as if he knew what the boy would say next.

"You'll Dream-time with him, won't you? You said you would teach me, when I'm old enough. I'm old enough now. Why can't I stay?"

"Koro," Galarrwuy said at last—emphatically, unequivocally. "You will go. *Now.*"

Kirk felt the hair on the back of his neck prickle. He'd thought only Vulcans could do that with their voices.

Whatever authority Galarrwuy had called upon, Koro obeyed. Within moments the sound of an aeroboat punctuated the island's uncanny silence. When it had faded to nothingness, Galarrwuy rose from his couch and went to the window, facing west, contemplating the darkness beyond. Kirk had not spoken since he'd told about his dreams.

"He is young," Galarrwuy said of Koro, as if by way of apology. "And, as they say in the islands, *eeyulla.* Impressed with his own importance."

"He's a boy," Kirk offered, excusing him. He'd

grown awfully fond of the young sea urchin in a scant few hours.

"In my ancestors' reckoning he'd be three years a man," Galarrwuy said sternly, his back still to Kirk. "If he survived the desert ordeals. The young today are spoiled. Undisciplined."

"I believe that's endemic, Galarrwuy." Kirk smiled, thinking how Vulcan this human sounded. Here was one he could trust, whatever happened. "Didn't Socrates make the same complaint in his day?"

Galarrwuy chuckled, relinquished the view at the window.

"So he did." He grew suddenly, deadly serious. "Do you know of Dream-time, James Kirk?"

"I know it once comprised the whole of your people's oral history," Kirk ventured. "That there were songs that accurately predicted the future. Cave paintings that depicted airplanes a thousand years before they existed. I assumed there were rituals not accessible to outsiders."

"You are partly correct," Galarrwuy said, showing no surprise at the extent of Kirk's knowledge. He would expect such a man to know as much.

The room seemed darker than Kirk remembered, as if something were absorbing all the light and only Galarrwuy's eyes were clearly visible to him. Some of the artifacts displayed around the room seemed less than inanimate.

"By the end of the twentieth century," Galarrwuy began, sitting across from Kirk again, "my people were almost extinct. They had lost their ways to the ways of the newcomers and no longer knew who they were. Only a few managed to preserve the old ways, and in time learned to use them in compatibility with the new.

"Today my people flourish, and Dream-time is recognized as being as 'legitimate' as any of the other ways humans attempt to touch the face of Creation. Nevertheless, to the uninformed the Singing still carries an aura of mumbo-jumbo.''

Kirk felt as if he were being offered a lifeline in this storm of recent origin. Could it work? Could a Dreamtime that could foretell the future also explain the past? He would try anything to exorcise the voices in his head.

"Galarrwuy, I've been to many worlds," he said. "If I've learned nothing else, I have learned that one man's 'mumbo-jumbo' is another's science and a third's religion. I have since tried to keep an open mind."

Galarrwuy chuckled again, partaking of the cosmic laughter.

"There is also an old saying from your part of Earth. 'Don't keep your mind so open your brains fall out.' I have never been to any world other than this," he said, serious again. "At least, not in body. Yet my experience is much as yours, James Kirk. There is more to what troubles you than dream."

"Galarrwuy, you sound like a Vulcan." Kirk smiled, trying to lighten things.

"No, I do not. I sound like a human who has lived within the influence of Vulcans, as well as other admirable species. Do you see how interdependent we have become? Do you understand why, in whatever reality your experience took place, you must return to that reality, and be certain it conforms to history, and not to your dream?"

Kirk struggled to comprehend exactly what Galarrwuy was suggesting.

"You mean you don't think I'm crazy? That there is some alternate reality present in these dreams?"

"I believe that you believe that," Galarrwuy said intently. "And you have far more experience with alternate realities than I. The logs you kept aboard the *Enterprise* are available in the archives at Memory Alpha. I have read them. Now, you tell me: what is reality?"

Kirk shook his head, as if that would clear it of the confusion. He held out his hands in submission.

"I don't know anymore. Will you help me?"

"I will try. Yet what I am about to suggest may place you in greater danger than where you are now."

Why am I so hesitant? Kirk thought. He could feel the fear cold in his throat, hard in his stomach. Why is it so much easier to confront external terrors than the darker corners of the mind? If Spock were here, I would have no doubts. He struggled with his fear, wrestled it into submission until it was only confusion, only puzzlement, yet he could not make it go away. Not alone.

Spock was still a hundred parsecs away; by the time he returned it might be too late. Kirk must trust in a human guide to take him where a Vulcan had walked with him before. To leave the matter unresolved, as Galarrwuy suggested, invited the greater danger.

"I haven't gotten this far by ducking danger," Kirk said, hoping he sounded more certain than he felt.

"I had assumed as much," Galarrwuy said, watching him intently. "Then Sing with me."

The room grew suddenly dark, and filled with shadows.

FIVE

Sorahl and T'Lera awaited the inevitable in the metaphorical shadow of an Earth ship, a seaship, a thing
that had no counterpart on their oceanless world,
named for a creature no longer extant on its own.

"Delphinus," Sorahl said, reading it off the prow of
the looming presence—instrument of their fate which
no doubt contained weapons sufficient to destroy
whole cities, much less two unarmed outworlders,
though no weapons were visible—through the windowport of the agrostation. "Named for the smaller
cetaceans—dolphins? The great whales are extinct,
are they not?"

"By the beginning of this century, as measured in
their years," T'Lera replied, perhaps wondering at a
species that could permit such things to happen, nay,
could actively cause them to happen. She wondered
also at her son. He knew the answer to the question he
had asked. For what reason, after all the words that
had poured from him at the Earthmen's behest while
she lay helpless in healing trance, did he find it
necessary to speak still? "You told them all?"

Sorahl stopped looking at the great ship through the
windowport but did not precisely look at his mother.

"I answered what they asked," he said, neither apology nor excuse, merely explanation. "And they asked much. I knew not what else to do, Mother. To speak half truth seemed neither ethical nor wise; its later contradiction might prove the more damaging. Yet to remain silent would only augment their fears. I thought it logical to allay those fears until such time as my commander could decide the optimum action. Was I in error?"

It is not what I would have done, T'Lera thought, but spoke something other.

"You answered to your own logic," she said with none of her usual irony of tone. *"Kaiidth!* It is done. And I no longer command you in this."

Sorahl gave her a puzzled look.

"I do not understand."

"The command mode as activated by Prefect Savar within the confines of a space vessel cannot apply to planetary situations," T'Lera explained. That her father's oversight in not providing an on-planet command mode placed her in an untenable position would remain unspoken. The circumstances that had brought her to Earth were not dreamed of in Savar's logic. "There are too many variables, too many unknowns. For a commander to require unquestioning obedience in a situation unfamiliar to her is illogical. Therefore I am only your mother, Sorahl-*kam*, and you are long since an adult. I release you from your oath. You must answer to your own logic hereafter."

Sorahl met the laser-sharp eyes in that ruined face for the first time and saw in them all that T'Lera was, all that mattered.

Restored to health, his mother had immediately risen from the alien sickbed, observing first with her eyes and then with her measured steps the room, the kelp fields beyond, and then the room again. She had stopped at the mirror hung over Tatya's dressing table, coldly assessing the extent of damage the ordeal had wrought upon her person.

The human healer had dared not move her alien patient overmuch, Tatya had explained, for fear of exacerbating her injuries, though Sorahl was certain this was not her only fear. At any rate, the human had wrapped T'Lera in quilts without removing the burned and brine-stained tatters of her uniform. Her hair was matted from the salt water, her face disfigured—less so than when she'd been brought here, but her nose was frankly broken at the bridge, a practical flaw and aesthetic offense against the dignity of one who had never been less than fastidious about her person.

Yet no iota of the dignity, the mastery that was T'Lera had been forfeit to the ordeal. All that was T'Lera was contained within those far-seeing eyes, no matter what had been wrought upon the outer shell. And the mastery that was T'Lera required a fidelity not contained in oath.

"With all due respect, Commander," Sorahl said, mustering his own fledgling dignity. "In wisdom and experience you are my superior. Therefore my oath remains."

"I am honored." T'Lera lowered her laser eyes briefly. "Yet neither a Vulcan's wisdom nor her experience is applicable where Earthmen are concerned. What they will choose to understand of us, what final disposition they will make of us, are beyond the realm of my logic. In this I know no more than you, Sorahl-*kam*. Perhaps less."

"Nevertheless," Sorahl demurred, placing his life in her two capable hands, "I acquiesce to your command."

His trust was profoundly affecting. A human mother might have embraced him, might have wept to have such a son. T'Lera had not the luxury.

"Hear me," she said sternly. "It may be that my command includes your death."

"It has already done so," Sorahl reminded her, though the memory of those last moments in the scoutcraft grew less credible with time. "And I have acquiesced."

"So you have," T'Lera acknowledged. "Very well. I accept your fealty, Navigator, on two conditions: first, that such fealty not preclude the offering of correction should you find your commander in error."

"Agreed," Sorahl said at once. Conditioned from childhood, he had automatically assumed the position of respect—posture straight, hands clasped loosely behind one's back, eyes meeting one's superior's with neither pride nor subservience.

"Second," T'Lera went on with no acknowledgment of his swift obedience; she was in full command mode now, "that there be no further discussion of the merits of revealing our existence to Earthmen. The time for theory is past. We are here, however unwillingly, and we must accept whatever happens. In this I will brook no contradiction."

Sorahl's hesitation was so slight a human would not have noticed it. But T'Lera was nothing human.

"I—" her son began, but she refused whatever he might have said with a gesture.

"It is well that you hesitate," Sorahl's mother-commander said. "I know now what it is given to me to do."

Outside on the landing dock, a confrontation of quite another order was transpiring.

"How'd you hurt your ankle, son?" Jason Nyere wanted to know.

Yoshi had forgotten the huge purple bruise on his leg from the snapped hawser, cursed himself for not wearing jeans instead of his usual cutoffs. Or would Jason have noticed that as well? Standing in the skiff at low tide, the captain of the *Delphinus* was about at eye level with the agrostation's metal deck looking up at

Yoshi, his slate-gray eyes reflecting simple curiosity, nothing more. Why did Yoshi feel all his prepared speeches drying in his throat?

"Oh, um, took a spill in the foil yesterday," he stammered. "Some chop came in ahead of that rain, wasn't it? Banged myself up pretty good."

"Not like you to be so clumsy," Nyere observed, avuncular. "Didn't expect to find you in. Thought you'd be out on the lower forty checking for storm damage."

"Yeah, well, getting a late start is all," Yoshi excused himself, feigning embarrassment, finding a hook for one of his prepared stories. "Truth is, Tatya and I had a bit of a blowup last night. Cabin fever or something. Lots of yelling, some dishes broken. You know how these things are. Lovers' quarrels."

"Um-hmm."

Jason Nyere waited rock-steady in the bobbing small boat, hands in the pockets of his windbreaker, trying to get the younger man to meet his eyes. Yoshi looked everywhere else but, his long hair flying in his face as he studied the far horizon away from the big ship, or his bare toes against the deck. Jason couldn't remember ever seeing him in shoes.

"So, I mean, we neither of us got much sleep, Jace, is what I'm trying to say," the younger man babbled on. "We're in pretty much of a mess right now. Ordinarily I'd ask you in, but Tatya doesn't want to see anybody, and I don't dare cross her. You know the kind of temper she's got."

Um-hmm, Jason thought. Like I know the kind you don't. "Lovers' quarrel!" Why don't you tell me the truth, son? Make it easier on yourself.

Sawyer had been furious with him for electing to go over alone.

"'Regulation 17-C, Subparagraph 3: Disposition of Extra-Orbital Vehicles and/or Personnel Aboard Same,'" she recited at him from the reg book as he clumped about his cabin deciding which of his uniforms would appear least threatening to indigenous and/or alien life forms. A lifetime of standoffs had taught him that the best way to get shot at was to flash a lot of fruit salad. "'Anything entering Earth atmosphere from beyond standard orbital range (as defined in Subparagraph 2) will be presumed to be potentially irradiated or contaminated with microbes or other organisms deemed harmful to human life. Said object, or any fragment thereof, or any living being found thereon, will be handled with extreme precautions, including the use of radiation suits—'"

"Melody, get off my case!" Jason had rumbled, settling on a work tunic with the least amount of braid and the windbreaker with its small insignia to wear over it. The overall effect was Just Folks, almost. "If there's anything that virulent over there, we're already in range of it and Yoshi and Tatya are probably dead. Anything else has got to be contained inside the station, and I can't step foot one on that deck if Yoshi doesn't want me to."

"You ought to at least wear a rad suit," Melody protested.

"And do what?" Jason demanded. "Assuming I could maneuver the boat in the damn thing, I'd scare the bejesus out of anyone. They'd think I was the alien!"

He buckled his belt, laced his boots, ran a brush through his close-curled, near-gray hair. He caught Melody's reflection in the mirror, and her face looked drawn. It was the face of an old friend, not a fellow officer.

"I don't like the thought of you going over there alone," she said, and her voice had gone all soft and concerned to match her face. "Let me tag along, Jason, please?"

"Absolutely not! You'd blow off and have us in trouble in no time."

"Then take one of the crew, at least to steer the boat and cover your back."

"The fewer people get a look at whoever or whatever's over there, the easier it's going to be after the fact." He zipped up his windbreaker, adjusted his cap. Goddamn scrambled eggs! Well, maybe an alien wouldn't understand their significance, would think they were merely decorative. Assuming they saw things the same way humans did. Assuming they had eyes. Assuming—Jason Nyere shut off his conjectures at the source. "Mel, get out of my way now; I mean it."

"You'll at least go armed," she begged, a last resort.

Nyere started to object, reconsidered, went to his private weapons locker.

"That I will do," he acknowledged, choosing the smallest laser pistol and secreting it in his belt beneath the windbreaker. "No need to advertise."

"I am going over there expressly to assess the situation," Captain Nyere informed his first mate, deliberately within earshot of Ensign Moy, who stood ready to lower the skiff. "You are to take no action whatever at this end. In the unlikely event you see me fall dead on the dock over there, you are to back the ship out of here with all deliberate speed and report to HQ on the situation. That is all. Do you read me, Sawyer?"

The convention of the military salute had ceased to exist with the activation of the United Earth AeroNav Forces. Jason Nyere was old enough to have seen it employed; Melody Sawyer was not. Nevertheless, she saluted.

"Loud and clear—suh!"

"Good. Carry on." Nyere stepped into the skiff and Moy lowered away.

"What's he mean, sir?" Moy pestered Sawyer as Nyere's resolute back in the small boat receded from them down the access lane of the agrostation. "About

127

him lying dead over there? Thought we were after a satellite."

"Microbes!" Sawyer snapped. It was what Nyere had instructed her to say, but it damn near killed her. "Thing was on a scoop mission and might've picked up some bugs."

"But, sir—"

"Break out the binoculars and give me a report on whatever happens over there," Sawyer cut him off. "Call it in on the intercom. I'll be in Spectrography and I'm not to be disturbed."

"Wasn't expecting you until this afternoon," Yoshi said pointedly. Sometimes the best defense . . . "How come the change in schedule?"

"I think we both know the answer to that," Jason Nyere said quietly, and Yoshi felt the Earth shift out from under him. "Want to tell me what it is you found out there yesterday?"

Their eyes met at last. There was no bluffing Jason Nyere. Never had been.

"I can't do that, Jason."

"Yes you can. In fact, face it, son: you can't do anything else. It's out of your hands. Too big for you. Why don't you give over to someone who can handle it? Make it easier on yourself."

Yoshi held his hair out of his eyes with one hand, extended the other in a gesture of helplessness.

"Jason, I swear to you, if it were just you— But it isn't. It's the people who cut your orders, and the people over them. It's the video people and the weirdos swarming around anything that's new and different. I—I can't explain it, but I can't let that happen to them."

Nyere listened, truly listened, to what Yoshi was saying. "Them." More than one, and living, intelligent.

"How many of them are there?"

"Two," Yoshi said, though he hadn't meant to say anything. It was all going wrong. He stood staring at the waves lapping beneath the metal deck, literally at sea.

"Are they—like us?" Nyere didn't know what he meant by that. Like humans in what way? In appearance, in outlook, in what? He needed something to hold on to.

"Like us? Jace, they're so much better than us!" Yoshi's face lit suddenly with a kind of rapture. "Better, different—I can't begin to describe them. But I spent last night sharing ideas with someone born ten light-years from here and felt like I was talking to a brother . . ."

What he described was a pristine, beautiful encounter. What Jason Nyere heard could have been only that. Or it could have been the ramblings of someone drugged, hypnotized, coerced. Something of what he was thinking must have shown on Jason's face. Yoshi picked up on it immediately.

"You think I'm nuts, don't you, Jason? You think they're in there holding Tatya hostage until I do what they want."

Mentally Nyere reached for his laser pistol, allowed his mind to caress its outline, feel the grip of it in his hand. If he inhaled, he could feel its real, hard presence against his side, reassuring. Thirty-seven years in the service and he had never killed anyone, had never wanted to. But if he must—

"You can tell me different, Yoshi. No human could've survived that crash. If they're so much like us, how did they?"

"From what Sor—from what one of them told me, they're more adapted to heat than we are. And they have this ability to heal themselves; I don't understand it completely, but it's some kind of mental process . . ."

He stopped, remembering how the healing had frightened him even after he'd grown accustomed to Sorahl's presence over a number of hours. Trying to explain it to someone who had not seen the Vulcans, could not know the magnetism, the centeredness they projected—

Yoshi shrugged, defeated.

"I don't know how to convince you we're all right, Jason. You want Tatya to come out too, so you can see? But I can't let you in. Not without certain—assurances."

Standing by the port in the other room, Tatya watched and listened, saw Jason Nyere secure the boat and, with surprising agility for a man his size, swing himself up to where Yoshi had finally calmed down enough to sit on the dock. Assured by the relaxed curve of their backs that the two men would go on talking for some time, assured by the quiet murmur from the bedroom that her alien guests were similarly engaged, Tatya decided to take the law into her own hands.

She sat at the comm screen and punched in a call to her favorite aunt, who incidentally happened to work for a news cooperative in Kiev.

"Tante Mariya?" she interrupted the usual exchange of pleasantries, lapsing into rapid Ukrainian in case anyone was listening. "Listen, I have a story to tell you. A scoop. But you must promise me you'll sit on it until—unless—something happens to me or Yoshi. . . ."

"Assurances," Jason repeated, pleased that Yoshi seemed unthreatened by his presence. "And what might those be?"

Yoshi inhaled sharply, as if he'd been rehearsing this in his head for hours; he probably had.

"For starters I need to know what your orders are in regard to—what Tatya and I recovered yesterday."

Nyere chuckled softly. He'd never have thought the younger man capable of such temerity. These aliens

130

must be something remarkable indeed to evoke such protectiveness.

"You know I'm not supposed to tell you that."

"I know." Yoshi grinned for the first time. "But you will anyway. Because you're my friend. And because otherwise I'll stall you under Right of Salvage."

Nyere shook his head in amazement.

"You've got this all thought out, haven't you? Well, I'll tell you: you can count on the first only up to a point," he cautioned the younger man. "And the second doesn't apply to human—" He stopped himself, realized how foolish it sounded, didn't know how to make it right. "You know what I mean, Yoshi. Whoever they may be, they have as many rights as we do."

"That's exactly what I'm trying to say, Jason," Yoshi said emphatically. "I don't want to see these people hurt."

"Neither do I, son," Jason Nyere tried to convince him. "Neither do I."

Tatya had scarcely begun her breathless tale to her aunt when a shadow presence cast itself over her like a physical chill. She jumped, looked up from the screen to see T'Lera. The Vulcan had not touched her, yet Tatya felt as if the temperature in the room had dropped ten degrees. She murmured something to her aunt about putting her on hold, and the screen went to snow.

"W-what is it?" she asked the alien presence in a voice smaller than any she'd known she possessed.

"You have communicated our presence to others." It was not a question. T'Lera did not need to understand the language Tatya spoke to understand her purpose. "It would have been preferable had you not done so."

"It's insurance!" Tatya said fiercely, finding her voice. "Somebody has to make sure none of us disappears or 'forgets.'"

131

"Is that a likely outcome?" the Vulcan wanted to know.

"You see that ship out there?" Tatya demanded. "Did you suppose they came all this way just to exchange greetings?"

"If it is their purpose to remove what they consider a threat to your people . . ." T'Lera began.

"Over my dead body!" Tatya said, not for the first time. A sudden burst of interference from the comm screen made her pounce on it, but too late. It went suddenly dead. No question in her mind who was responsible for that.

She glared at *Delphinus.* "They've been listening in," she seethed. "And they've cut me off!"

Melody Sawyer had been so absorbed in taking infrared readings on the agrostation she'd forgotten all about monitoring communications.

"What're they doing now, Henry?" she called to Moy over the intercom. She'd closed the spectrography booth off from the rest of the bridge. She was alone except for Lieutenant Patel, the scanner tech; she could hear her boots on the metal decking as she made her morning rounds.

"Just sitting, sir," Moy reported from the starboard rail, where he was leaning on his elbows to keep the binoculars steady. "Just the captain and Yoshi sitting out there shooting the breeze. Doesn't seem to be any worry about radiation. Wonder why they don't go on inside?"

"Don't wonder, Moy, just report," Melody snapped. "See anyone else over there? Has Tatya turned up at all?"

"No sir—" Moy started to say, but Sawyer had begun to curse and cut him off.

She lunged out of the spectro booth and clear across the bridge to the dead comm screen, nearly knocking little Patel flying in her haste. She'd shut the screen

132

down herself when she hit the sack around 0200 last night; God knew how much activity she might have missed in those few hours.

"Sorry, Reeta," Sawyer called over her shoulder, homing on Agro III's band. "Didn't mean to mow you down."

"No harm, sir," Patel replied, but Melody never heard her. She was mesmerized by the conversation between Tatya Bilash and a handsome Slavic-looking woman in what sure as hell looked like the city room of a major news service.

"What the hell language is that?" Melody demanded of no one in particular. Reeta Patel, thinking the first was addressing her, puzzled over it.

"None I am familiar with, sir. Perhaps something Slavic?"

"Never mind!" Sawyer barked. "I know what she's up to. Hellfire, if I cut her off, her contact'll get paranoid. If I let her spill the whole thing—damnation, where's my head?"

She saw the sender's half of the screen go to hold, saw the unidentified newswoman relax at her desk, waiting, and seized her chance. She hit the intercept, grinning evilly as the entire screen blanked. Tatya would probably assume it was a malfunction.

But Tatya was not so easily fooled. She was on Melody's frequency within seconds.

"Get out of the way of the screen!" she'd ordered T'Lera without thinking, then realized to whom she was speaking. T'Lera was not one to whom one gave orders. "I'm sorry! Move away from the screen, please! I know what I'm doing."

Her logic of no use, T'Lera complied.

"Agro III to *Delphinus:* come in, please!" Tatya called tightly, fighting to keep the fury out of her voice. "Agro III calling *Del—*"

"*Delphinus* here." Melody Sawyer's voice went from

133

molasses to icicles. "Not smart, Bilash. Don't do that again."

Tatya opened her mouth, but Sawyer cut her off.

"Listen up," she said, leaning into the screen for emphasis. "Your contact hails back, you tell her everything's all right. You speak to her in Standard, and you make sure she goes away happy, or I'll by God take this fish under that weed and on top of you like the one that ate Jonah. Do you copy?"

She didn't expect acknowledgment, flicked off at once. Had she waited a second longer she'd have learned all the Ukrainian she'd ever need.

"You talk to your—guests," Jason Nyere told Yoshi, neither of them aware of the *Sturm und Drang* raging over the airwaves around them. "Tell them I'm under orders to observe them. That I have to have them checked out for contamination. If they're interstellar, they'll understand that. Tell them it's what I have to do."

Yoshi hunched his shoulders, nodded miserably.

"Jason, I'm scared!"

"I know you are." The older man squeezed his shoulder paternally. You think *you're* scared! he thought. Your part of this is a cakewalk compared to what I have to do!

Captain Nyere lowered himself into his ship's skiff and started its small purring motor. He looked up at the young agronomist one last time.

"Don't fight me, Yoshi. You think I'm soft, and you're right. The worst I'd do is requisition your supplies and starve you out. But my superiors might not be as patient as I am. Whoever replaces me is bound to be someone who prefers more—direct action."

"Captain's on his way back, Commander!" Ensign Moy called over the intercom to Sawyer, who'd holed up in Spectro again, leaving the bridge to a bewildered Lieutenant Patel.

"As you were, Moy," Sawyer barked, all calm, cool, and collected again. "And lose the binoculars, will you? I get four body readings on the infrared, Captain suh," she announced as soon as she heard Nyere's boots on the bridge behind her. "And two of 'em are real weird!"

Nyere glanced reluctantly at the monitor.

"I gave no order for infrared."

"I know you didn't," Melody snapped back. "But you got it anyway. What're you planning to do now?"

"Aside from slapping you in the brig for insubordination? Not a damn thing!"

Jason Nyere had begun to sweat again. He wiped the cold trickle from his temple and tried to tear his eyes from the infrared screen. They were different, Yoshi had said. Different but somehow similar. Better, different, indescribable. Within the hour, Jason Nyere would find out for himself.

"Turn that damn thing off, will you?" he growled at Melody, as transfixed as she by the alien body readings moving about on the monitor, but suddenly protective of their privacy. Monitoring the station's communications before they'd known what they were looking for was one thing, but now— "Pack the counters and the scanners and go powder your nose. We're going visiting."

Some instinct nagged at Sawyer to tell him about the comm leak to Kiev, but she ignored it. She was confident she'd scared Tatya but good, and Jason had enough on his mind.

"Yessuh, Captain suh!" She was on her feet at once.

"Oh, and Melody?" Jason called after her. "Leave the pearl-handled Colts at home, okay?"

Melody started to squawk.

"Don't protest, dammit!" Nyere said. "That's the price of admission. The hardware stays here or you do. Which is it?"

Muttering, Melody clattered down the stairs. Jason

135

intercepted her a second time, coming out onto the stairs so Patel wouldn't hear him.

"How's your offduty wardrobe?"

It was an odd question.

"Shirts and jeans mostly. Tennis stuff," Melody replied. "You know the kind of thing I wear. Would've packed my crinolines, but didn't think I'd be needing them this time out, Captain suh. Why?"

Something about the situation was beginning to tickle Jason Nyere, lighten the load that had been pressing him between the shoulder blades since this time yesterday. The thought of the thousand little ordinary details that would have to be gotten through in order to accept these aliens on any terms . . .

"Well, considering that they lost everything when their ship sank, and all they have left is the uniforms on their backs," he began, as if it were elementary that "they" could wear human clothes without extra heads or limbs getting in the way. "Yoshi says the male's about his height, but I gather the female's closer to your size than Tatya's."

His hands involuntarily formed melon shapes at chest level, and Melody burst out laughing. Tatya was on the generous side.

"Sexist swine!" Melody snorted, before the impact of what he was saying truly hit her. "One of them's a female?"

Jason nodded as if to say, How about that?

"Commander of their ship, as a matter of fact. Why, Melody, I thought you knew the facts of life. If there were no little green women, where do you suppose the little green men come from?"

"Petunias." Melody sat on the cold metal steps and looked up at him, shaking her head. "Was it Sagan who said they'd look like petunias?"

"He only meant they probably couldn't crossbreed with us," Jason said after he'd figured out what she was babbling about. "Come on, Sawyer, don't fold on me now. Throw some things together and meet me at the boat in fifteen minutes."

"Sure thing," she said vaguely as he passed her on the steps. Twenty-four hours ago she hadn't believed in little green men. Now she was being asked to make up a Goodwill box for them. "Petunias!" she said, again, incredulous. "The whole thing's impossible!"

~~~

He's impossible! Tran Van Ky thought, holding her breath as her commanding officer loomed over her comm console.

"There has been no response to my transmission as yet?" Spock asked his communications "officer."

Tran tried to keep her voice from quavering, wondered if this was yet another test.

"Negative, sir," she managed crisply.

She'd wondered two days ago at Captain Spock's sending a coded personal message to a private transceiver on Earth at his own expense rather than using ship's normal frequency like everyone else. Either this was an extremely personal message, or it was yet another challenge to Tran's abilities, like everything else on this voyage.

There had been one shift where the computer fed her several dozen incomings of all classifications simultaneously, without bothering to inform her it was only a drill. Tran had fielded every last one of them in the proper order without screwing up or losing her cool and the captain had noted her down for a commendation, one of only three he'd given to the entire class all year, but Tran swore she'd aged six years in as many weeks and wondered if it was worth it. Whatever else they might be, training cruises with Captain Spock were never dull.

"Interesting," he was saying now, hovering behind her comm station in a way that always made her distinctly nervous. "Opinion, Mr. Ky?"

"I'm not sure, sir," she said, treading eggshells. "The

turnaround time is less than a day at this distance, and even if there was no one at the receiving end, there should at least have been a computer answerback. Unless that transceiver is no longer operative. That's the only answer I can come up with, sir."

"So noted," Spock said, giving her no indication as to whether or not he found that answer satisfactory. "You will inform me immediately, on the odd chance that there is any response."

"Aye, sir," Tran said, relaxing at last.

How simple their lives are at this age, Spock mused, watching her, knowing her to be preoccupied with nothing more serious than the approval of her commanding officer. Some of us have never found life so simple, though perhaps we are the stronger for it. His thoughts returned to his most immediate concern.

Ensign Ky's evidence indicated that Jim Kirk's private transceiver was presently inoperative. Only Starfleet Command or the officer himself could deactivate a flag officer's transceiver. In view of what Spock knew, there were several reasons why either might have done so.

His logic had yielded this much: he and Jim Kirk were being subjected to a series of subconscious impressions, masquerading as dream, threatening insanity unless some action were taken. Had Kirk, compelled by his very nature, already acted, and what had been the outcome?

Enterprise was less than six days from Earth. Would it arrive too late to help?

When he returned to the realm of light, Kirk found himself sitting upright on a narrow ledge against a cliff face, squinting into an early morning sun. His hands rested loosely on his knees, which were drawn up almost to his chest, and his head was tilted back against the cliff. He blinked against the light, felt a dryness in his throat, wondered where he was. And where was Galarrwuy?

His host sat cross-legged beside him, leaning against the same harsh red rock, smiling pleasantly, fresh as a daisy with the morning and, after the night's Singing, extremely familiar. But when had he exchanged his crisp tailored khakis—the Down Under business suit for generations—for the ceremonial garb and body paint of the Dreaming?

Kirk sprang to his feet, grazing his head on the overhang. Where were they? There were formations of the same red rock on Easter, the statues of the Long Ears were hewn from them, but these paintings were other.

He touched them reverently, recognizing them now: Thunder-man and the Turtle, the Snake-goddess and the Mimi. Had he been so lost in the Singing that Galarrwuy had somehow transported him to his homeland? What was this place?

"Nourlangie Rock," Galarrwuy answered him. "From the north near Woolwonga. Not my birthplace, but one I managed to salvage from the rains and the buffalo. I have, so to speak, brought the mountain to Muhammad."

Kirk leaned against the rock and laughed. The rest of the room came into focus. They were in a part of the museum he had not seen last night; it contained an entire rock wall from Australia preserved in a controlled environment. He stepped down off the ledge onto a man-made floor and Galarrwuy followed.

"Are you well?" the Australian inquired.

"Yes. I think so." Kirk touched his own face, as if to convince himself that he was really here. He was no closer to an answer, but he felt refreshed, better than he had in weeks, and, somehow, hopeful.

"That is good." Galarrwuy nodded, contemplating his own person in its other worldly garments. "Permit me to return to our century. Then we will talk about yours."

He went off to change. Kirk wandered outside, roamed the grounds of the museum, stood on the lip of the crater lake listening to the gulls and the silence.

But the silence did not last. The sound of an oversea craft of considerable size approaching the harbor filled Jim Kirk with dread long before it hove into view, its Starfleet insignia giving it the right of way past the small craft plying these waters. They had found him. And pulling a scene in public would only make it worse.

McCoy was the first to hit the beach, flanked by a couple of security guards and followed by a tall, leggy blonde. It seemed not only Kirk's dreams were populated by blondes, and for a wild moment he thought she might be the "someone" Bones had in mind to take his mind off his troubles. His hopes were dashed when he saw the medical uniform, the traditional caduceus of the Physicians' Branch replaced by the insignia of Psych.

Uh-oh. He'd really blown it this time. Nearly twelve hours AWOL and unaccounted for, after who knew what had turned up on his psychoscan. They were going to throw the net over him for sure.

McCoy was breathless and steaming by the time he'd made it up the beach to the crater lake.

"Don't give me a hard time!" he began without preamble. "It was all I could do to keep them from sending an armed escort and an elephant gun. Now you come peaceably or I've got a right cross will see that you do. Oh, by the way: Krista Sivertsen, Jim Kirk. Last time you two were together there was a one-way mirror between you."

His eyes met hers briefly and at least he had a face to attach to the voice that had led him through the scan less than twenty-four hours before. He wished he could show more enthusiasm, but he had a hunch they'd be seeing a lot of each other from here on. The medikit clipped to her belt no doubt held the elephant gun, just in case.

"How much trouble am I in, Bones?"

"You'll find out soon enough. Let's go."

"May I at least say good-bye to Dr. Nayingul?"

"You may not," McCoy stated, taking his arm and leading him as if he expected he might break and try to run for it.

The last person he'd wanted to see him this way stood watching from the pier. Koro Quintal had come back with the morning, to return Galarrwuy's boat and, he'd hoped, hitch a ride with Jim Kirk and get him to talk about the Dreaming. Now he only stood in the small crowd of arriving tourists ogling the Starfleet craft, and watched.

"I have to go," Jim Kirk said simply, his hand on Koro's shoulder. "Give Dr. Nayingul my regards."

Koro merely nodded, for once acting the man Galarrwuy insisted he should be.

"Galar will know," he said. He did not ask if Kirk would return. "*Haare raa.* Go well, Jim Kirk."

"*E noho raa,*" Kirk replied wistfully, not knowing how he knew the Maori farewell. "Stay well, Koro Quintal."

The Starfleet craft kicked up a considerable wake as it rose above the surface and headed into the sun.

It was McCoy who met *Enterprise.*

No matter how often she went out or how brief her run, Jim Kirk was always there to see her home. Sometimes he would be waiting in the officers' lounge at TerraMain, watching her coast into her slip through the big clearsteel window, but more often he rode shotgun on the shuttle traditionally sent to escort the senior officers off. The crew could beam directly down to the Admiralty and home, but Spock and Scotty had to report to branch HQ in the spacedock itself for debriefing, and Kirk was always there to greet them.

That he was not this time only confirmed what Spock already knew. Something was wrong. When he stepped out of the shuttle to find McCoy rocking on his heels in the corridor outside the hangar, he began to surmise how wrong.

"Here now!" Scotty chimed in, lugging a duffel bag of "personals" he didn't trust to the transporter (or, more accurately, to the transporter crew below on the mainland, who'd get their hands on the bag long before he did; there was a distinct clanking of bottles in the bottom). "Somebody's missing! And what're you doing up here, McCoy?"

"That's a long story," McCoy replied. He had circles under his circles. "Spock, can I have a word with you? I don't know why I had to greet you with this kind of news," he said after Scotty had wisely gone on ahead and Spock had heard him out. "Didn't want you to get it secondhand, I guess. And I needed to get it off my chest. Not that I expected you could do anything."

"I appreciate your confiding in me, doctor," Spock said in a tone McCoy had always taken as ironic, until he'd learned better. "And I may be able to do more than you know. How long has he been in Dr. Sivertsen's care?"

"You make it sound so pleasant!" McCoy said wryly. "It'll be a week tomorrow. Spock, I'm worried about him."

"With good cause, doctor, from what you have told me. Is he permitted visitors?"

"I'll arrange it," McCoy promised, struggling with something. "Spock, I—thank you. It's been a terrible burden, carrying this by myself. I don't know why, but I feel better about this already."

A number of possible retorts about the illogic of such a feeling when in fact nothing had yet been done to

142

alter the situation sprang to Spock's lips, but he made use of none of them.

Let us hope, doctor, he thought as he stood outside the briefing room and watched McCoy amble away, that your feeling is neither premature nor inaccurate. For all our sakes.

"The first phase of the patient's therapy was initiated by having him read *Strangers from the Sky* in its entirety," Dr. Sivertsen reported to her colleagues during her department's weekly consult. "The patient consented to this only after presenting me with a voice tape of his version of events as taken from his recurring nightmares."

"And how does Admiral Kirk's version compare with the account in the book?" One of the department heads wanted to know.

Krista Sivertsen fought to keep herself from screaming. The rest of the department knew she was treating a high-ranking official, nothing more. She'd tried to keep Jim Kirk's identity confined to the fewest number of people. That number had just been increased by everyone in this room.

"Except where the outcomes diverge," she began, counting to ten before she trusted herself to speak. "Admiral—the patient's—nightmares coincide with the historical account to an uncanny degree. The patient remains convinced that in some other reality, if you will, he was a participant in events which transpired over two hundred years ago. He speaks of historical personages as if he has known them personally."

"And he remains fixated on this one period in history?" someone asked.

"His attention is focused on this one event, the Vulcans' landing on Earth, yes," Krista corrected the questioner.

"Simple delusion," the questioner suggested. "Projection. Identification with historical personages as avoidance of his own feelings of inadequacy."

"The old Napoleon Complex," someone else added, and a few of the others concurred.

"I don't think so!" Krista said sharply, willing to risk her peers' disapprobation in this instance. She had lived with Jim Kirk through three intensive therapy sessions a day for nearly a week. The more she learned about the man the more she found to respect, the more she became convinced of the metaphysical truth of what he was saying, regardless of historical fact. "I'd ask you to consider the kind of man we're talking about. He's lived through, acted upon, more history than probably anyone else in this century. He doesn't need to compensate for feelings of inadequacy."

"But that was the past," one of her colleagues reminded her. "He's a desk jockey now. Perhaps in compensation for the boredom, a sense of failure—"

"Is it possible he's suffering from delusions?" someone else suggested before Krista could reply. "Maybe he had read the book before, but in a denial phase he—"

"That hardly explains the abnorms on his scan, does it?" Krista demanded, silencing them.

"What was his response after he'd read the book?" the department head wanted to know.

"He acknowledges the undeniable objective truth of events as stated in the book," Krista said carefully. How could she make them understand? "But he retains a belief in the alternate truth of his nightmares. Those nightmares are also increasing in frequency and intensity, to the extent that I've had to abandon dream monitoring and, in some instances, had to sedate him."

"Sounds like he needs an exorcist!" someone quipped, gallows humor.

"Maybe he does!" Krista snapped; she saw no humor in this situation. "I've tried everything else. I don't know what this is. Schizophrenia? Multiple personalities? Reincarnation? Possession? Ghosties and beasties? As I see it, there's only one thing left to do." She took a deep breath, looked at them looking at her around the table. "I'm going to try hypnosis. I intend to regress him past those memories."

But the hypnotism session was an utter failure. It left both patient and therapist drained, exhausted, and no further along than when they'd started.

"I've turned you inside out, Jim Kirk," Krista said, bringing the lights up. "I know as much about you as you know about the people in your dreams. But something's blocking this thing and I can't get through."

"You should have left me with Galarrwuy," he said, only half joking, sitting up on the consulting couch and absently plumping the needlepoint pillows. "He and I might have found the answer. If you'd let me out of here, let me go back to the Dreaming . . ." Something occurred to him. "Has Galarrwuy tried to contact me?" he asked. "I hated to leave him so abruptly. Without explanation."

"No," Krista lied. No point in telling him Admiral Nogura had tried to contain the rumor of his sudden disappearance by having his home transceiver deactivated, to make it look as if he were away on some top-secret mission. In his present state of defeat, she wasn't sure how he'd take that. "There have been no messages for you since you got here."

"None at all?" Kirk was incredulous, and suddenly wary. "What day is it?"

Despite the timelessness of this place and the fact that he'd smashed his chrono during one particularly violent nightmare, he knew the answer before she told him. *Enterprise* should have gotten in this morning. Would McCoy tell Spock where he was or was he sworn

145

to some kind of secrecy? They were shutting him away, treating him like he had some kind of dangerous disease. He had to get in touch with Spock.

"I have to get out of here!" he said, on his feet, suddenly agitated. "Krista, listen, there are some things I have to take care of. An hour or two—"

"Out of the question!" she said sharply, not about to tell him that the failure of this morning's session meant he might not be getting out of here for a very long time. "We're at a critical point right now. You can't just—"

"You said yourself it was a failure," Kirk began, but the beep of the intercom interrupted him.

"Yes?" Krista put the receiver in her ear so Kirk couldn't hear. "How long has he been waiting? The session went overtime; you should have let me know. All right, I'll send him right out."

"Truce, Admiral," she said, putting the receiver back. "You have a visitor."

"Spock!"

He gripped the Vulcan's shoulders in sheer joy, stopped himself from outright hugging him. He'd learned that in this place a mirror was seldom only a mirror, and the visitors' room had an unnatural number of them. He doubted he had any dignity left after a week in this place, but he was mindful of preserving Spock's.

The Vulcan accepted the embrace, and with it the turmoil in the human's mind. Masking his own concern, he allowed his eyes to smile.

"Jim" was all he said.

Spock sat while Kirk paced, listened as Kirk talked, provided as always the balance for everything Kirk was—shadow to his sunlight, coolness for his fire, calm against his agitation. Centered and impeccable, in contrast to Kirk, who was pale and tousled from the morning's ordeal, Spock was simply there, focus for Kirk's fears, center of his immediate universe.

Jim Kirk talked, couldn't stop himself. The weeks of anxiety, the puzzlement and fear, poured out of him. Spock listened.

"I should have kept quiet about it," Kirk said at last, running out of steam. "Asked McCoy for some sleeping pills, tried to ride it out. But no, I had to drive him up a wall to where he recommended the psychoscan. And then, to borrow Galarrwuy's expression, took a tail wind and ended up halfway across the planet. That was the dumbest move of all."

He sat, ran a hand through his hair, tousling it further, let Spock see the depth of fear in his eyes.

"Spock, I don't remember what it means to sleep anymore. Krista's as much as admitted she can do nothing for me, but they won't let me go. What do you think they'll do to me?"

"Perhaps nothing," the Vulcan said at last, and calmly.

He had needed to listen as much as Kirk had needed to talk, in order to be certain. He had heard what he needed to know. He leaned toward Kirk now, his long fingers moving gently toward the familiar places, seeking the familiar paths.

"If I may . . ." he began.

"What is this 'if I may'?" Kirk demanded, feinting as if to avoid Spock's Touch, laughing at the relief that flooded his soul. "Since when have you needed permission?"

"Indeed," the Vulcan said, and Reached.

When he withdrew his hand, and with it his mind, Kirk grew very still.

"That's incredible!" he said.

"Is it?" Spock asked mildly. "What you and I have experienced has always stretched the bounds of ordinary credulity. This is no exception."

"You're right," Kirk acknowledged. "God, I hope you're right! It doesn't give me any answers, but at least I know I'm not crazy."

147

"That does it!"

Their harmony was shattered by Krista Sivertsen's sharp take-charge voice.

"You simply insist on taking risks, don't you?" she flared at Kirk, charging into the room, ignoring Spock entirely. "First the Dreaming, now this! One of my aides was observing from the booth." She nodded toward one of the suspect mirrors. "And she called me." She turned on Spock, furious. "I suppose you've already done your damage?"

"There has been no damage of my causing, Dr. Sivertsen," Spock replied coolly. "However, unless Admiral Kirk is released from this facility immediately to seek an alternate form of cure, certain irreparable damage may ensue."

"I know you have a great many talents, Captain Spock," Krista said icily. "But I had no idea an expertise in psychology was among them!"

"It is not," Spock said evenly. "None is needed in this instance. Admiral Kirk's difficulty is not psychological in origin. He is not insane."

("Never try to second-guess a Vulcan," her best friend Liz had once written to Krista, years ago when she'd taken her first deepspace assignment, transferred from the Aldebaran Colony to serve on a ship with a Vulcan first officer. "They'll outflank you before you can shake your argument out of the mid-brain.")

Krista still kept all of Liz's letter-disks, still remembered all of Liz's pearls of wisdom. They'd been roommates during their internship, looked enough alike to be mistaken for sisters. Krista had adored Liz, treasured her sharp-cornered advice. But an innate restlessness had driven Liz offworld, and she had died not long after she'd left Aldebaran for her first starship assignment.)

But this was neither the time nor the place to resurrect those memories. Krista Sivertsen took a deep breath and readied herself. She would not second-guess this particular Vulcan—Liz had learned about him and his kind too late to save herself—but she wouldn't let him outflank her either.

"The term 'insane' is considered somewhat archaic in modern psychology, Captain Spock," she began, buying time as she showed him into her office. Kirk had agreed to wait outside; whatever else could be said about a Vulcan mind-meld, it seemed to have a calming effect upon the human participant. "We feel it has a connotation of hopelessness which, under contemporary advances in the field—"

"Whatever euphemism those in your profession currently employ," Spock cut her off, "the fact remains: Admiral Kirk is not insane."

"Would you care to look at his psychoscan?" Krista demanded heatedly. She could not abide amateurs, regardless of their species. "Or perhaps you'd like to read the transcript of my report on his condition, or a tape of this morning's hypnosis?"

Spock said nothing; his face told her nothing. She had the facts at her disposal. Why did she feel as if she were up to her ankles in quicksand?

"I know you're a close friend of Jim Kirk's," she said, trying the reasonable approach. "And I respect that. But if you think you can persuade me on that basis—"

"It would never occur to me," Spock said mildly.

What was his game? Krista wondered, groping. Her field was human psychology; she was out of her depth with Vulcans and this one seemed to know it. She felt the metaphorical quicksand creeping up to her knees.

"If you think you can pull rank on me, you can forget that, too. You're on my turf here, and my orders are to keep Jim Kirk confined 'until he is completely and permanently cured,' unquote. And they're signed by the Old Man himself."

Spock seemed to weigh this.

"Was the order deactivating Admiral Kirk's transceiver also signed by Admiral Nogura?"

"It was."

"May I ask why?"

"As a security measure. I'm sure you're familiar with the procedure. And to spare Kirk any unnecessary disturbances during the course of treatment."

"Meaning messages from Dr. Nayingul or myself."

"If you want to look at it that way."

"I shall have to persuade Admiral Nogura to rethink his decision," Spock said with utter equanimity, and Krista had no doubt he was one of the two people on the planet who could. "However, that is inconsequential at present. Dr. Sivertsen, I have heard your arguments regarding Admiral Kirk's condition. Will you grant me the courtesy of hearing mine?"

"I have the facts on my side, Captain, and I won't be budged. No one suffering such severe delusional nightmares will be allowed to leave this facility as long as I'm a member of the staff."

Spock appeared to arrive at a decision.

"Very well, doctor. Then I suggest you commit me to your facility as well. I have experienced the same nightmares."

Krista Sivertsen watched the results of Spock's psychoscan come up on her screen. When she had adjusted the readout for Vulcan Norm, it showed the same mnemonic dysfunction as Kirk's.

"I thought you were bluffing," she said.

Spock resisted the obvious response. The psychiatrist was staring at the readout in disbelief.

"I've never seen anything like this. The odds against it must be astronomical." Spock resisted responding to this as well. "Maybe it's what you get for messing around in mere human minds with your Vulcan techniques." She turned off the screen, as if not seeing the readout before her would somehow make it less uncanny. "I don't understand how this is possible. I understand even less the point of this Pyrrhic victory of yours, but it looks as if you'll be keeping the admiral company. I'll see you get adjoining rooms."

"Then I trust you have a Vulcan healer on-staff?" Spock inquired mildly.

"This is Earth!" Krista Sivertsen said incredulously. "There are probably fewer than a dozen Vulcan healers on the entire planet, and to my knowledge none of them is a practicing psychiatrist. Tradition has it your people don't suffer psychological disorders, but the evidence I have on that scan says otherwise."

"Seven," Spock said quietly.

"Come again?"

"There are at present seven Vulcan healers in residence within the sol system, including Luna and the Martian Colonies, and none is a practicing psychiatrist," Spock said. "The nearest healer so qualified is T'Sri of Rigel XII, and assuming she were immediately available, she could not arrive on Earth in less than seventeen Standard days.

"Consequently, doctor, unless you or someone on your staff possesses a degree in xenopsychology, you cannot keep me here."

"Why, you cold-blooded, manipulative . . .!" Krista Sivertsen flared, losing her cool entirely. "What the hell do you want from me?"

Spock told her.

"Forty-eight hours, no more," she told McCoy when she'd sent for him. "They'll be in your custody. They're not to leave Kirk's apartment, and you're not to let them out of your sight. If you need a couple of security guards—"

"Of course not!" McCoy blustered, not quite sure of that himself, considering the hijinks these two had pulled on him in the past.

151

"Forty-eight hours," Krista repeated. "Sooner if you see any indications of crisis. If they can't work their miracle in that much time—"

"You'll have them back," McCoy promised, hoping against hope that whatever his two charges were up to would work.

Krista delivered them to him at the Admissions desk with a kind of relief.

"Liz was right," she said to McCoy. "She always said, 'Never try to second-guess a Vulcan.' I should have listened."

"Yes, Liz always was good with the homey little Earthisms, wasn't she?" McCoy said sadly; obviously he knew who Krista was talking about if the other two didn't. He eyed Spock skeptically. "Pity I never had the benefit of that particular one. Might have saved me a decade or two of aggravation. Poor Liz!"

"A mutual friend?" Kirk asked, making conversation as they walked across the MedArts quadrangle. Now that Krista was no longer his shrink, at least for the next forty-eight hours, he could devote his full appreciation to her as a person.

"Friend of Krista's," McCoy specified. "Briefly a student of mine. Brilliant girl, untimely death. Come to think of it, Jim, you knew her, too."

"Did I?"

Kirk searched his no-longer-to-be-trusted memory for another lady psychiatrist. He'd gone through a phase where he'd found professional women—Ruth, Carol, Janet, Areel—particularly attractive, but as far as he knew—

"She was assigned as *Enterprise*'s staff psychiatrist when she died, Admiral," Krista said, keeping her voice level, her tone free of accusation.

"Liz," Kirk mused. "Elizabeth. Not . . .?"

"Elizabeth Dehner." Krista's voice trembled slightly, though her face would have done a Vulcan proud.

152

Kirk was less fortunate. The mention of the name froze him barely inches from freedom.

McCoy noticed the impact immediately, wished he'd kept his mouth shut. Liz Dehner would always be irrevocably linked with Gary Mitchell in Kirk's mind. To remind Kirk of Gary now, when he was so vulnerable . . .

But Kirk wasn't thinking of Mitchell at all. What had him nonplussed was a memory of Elizabeth Dehner before the incident on Delta Vega, a moment of déjà-vu that all but announced itself by a lightbulb over his head. An instant before it had not existed in any reality he knew.

"Elizabeth Dehner," he said incredulously, "is the blonde in the dreams. Spock, the voice—"

The Vulcan also stood transfixed, seemed to shake off some private reverie. "Yes. Yes, indeed!"

"Spock!" Kirk said, groping for something. "The landing party on M-155 . . . the Planet That Wasn't There."

"Interesting," the Vulcan said slowly. "A possibility."

McCoy, standing between them, felt his hair stand on end as if he were about to be struck by lightning. He had no idea what had just happened, but if it had anything to do with what they had less than forty-eight hours to solve, he was hardly going to let it take place here. Krista was looking at both of his friends as if she were strongly tempted to change her mind.

"Jim," McCoy interceded, grabbing his arm. "Spock, save your thought. Our meter's running."

"Bones, you really could take the time off," Kirk said winningly, over the ticking of his multitude of antique clocks. "We'll be good."

"Not likely!" McCoy growled, rattling around in Kirk's minuscule kitchen. "Don't you ever buy any real food? Goddamn synthesized, reconstituted . . ." He emerged finally with a prefab sandwich and a glass of amber liquid in his hand. "At least your bourbon's real. Where's Spock?"

"Talking to Galarrwuy on the bedroom screen," Kirk said distractedly, wondering what part of his brain the two were dissecting in his absence. "Did you think he'd shimmied down a drainpipe? It's over fifty stories to the street."

"I wouldn't put it past him! Can we get on with this? The more I think of baby-sitting you renegades for two entire days—I should have taken Krista up on her offer of security guards. Posted one at the front door and another in here to relieve me. I can see where I'm gonna have to watch the pair of you in my sleep."

"Considering the usual stentorian clamor which accompanies that activity on your part," Spock remarked, emerging from the bedroom, "it is unlikely any of us will derive much rest from this experience."

"Don't start with me!" McCoy began, but Kirk cut him off.

"Bones, our meter's running. Spock, what've we got?"

Spock settled himself by the inactive fireplace between Kirk and McCoy.

"The facts are these, Jim: you and I have, simultaneously and in the absence of communication, experienced a series of dreams relating to a particular event in Earth's history previously unknown to us. This in itself is neither surprising nor especially alarming. Doubtless many individuals, upon reading *Strangers from the Sky*, were sufficiently intrigued by its premise to incorporate it into their dreams."

"Krista said it was bringing the weirdos out in droves," McCoy remarked, fiddling with his medical tricorder. He looked at Kirk. "Sorry!"

"However," Spock went on as if McCoy had not

spoken, "that which began as dream soon increased in frequency and intensity, becoming more immediate, more 'real,' if you will, than our waking lives. There was a sense that we were involved with these historical personages, knew them intimately, including details that were not present in the book. There was also a growing sense of ominousness, of something indefinable gone awry. And there is more."

He watched McCoy fuss with the tricorder, preparatory to recording everything that transpired in this room for the next two days—though he would, of course, only pick up fragments of what had happened through the mind-meld—as evidence for Krista Sivertsen's files. McCoy noticed the prolonged silence.

"Go on, go on, I'm listening!"

"Several of our dreams do not overlap, but remain separate to each of us," Spock continued. "As if we were interacting with different individuals at different times. These separate dreams are totally in keeping with our personalities. You, Jim, engage in a tennis match with Melody Sawyer, with all of its subsequent consequences, whereas I—"

He glanced again at McCoy or, more accurately, at the intrusive presence of the tricorder, and hesitated.

"What is it, Spock?" Kirk urged him gently. "If it's too personal—"

"I," Spock said slowly, "dreamed about my mother."

Briefly he told them the content of his dialogue with Amanda.

"Dreamed about your mother, did you?" McCoy asked, sensing Spock's embarrassment, trying to bluster his way around it. "So what? A little of the old human nature creeping in. Even you must let your guard down during a REM cycle. Or are you going to tell me Vulcans have an Oedipus myth?"

"Doctor—"

155

"Or maybe it's symbolic," Kirk suggested. "Your mother subconsciously represents your human half, the half you're pleading for with T'Lera."

Spock considered it.

"A possibility. And so we come to the crux of the matter." He took a deep breath, gathered himself. The ticking of the clocks seemed to grow louder. He had both men's undivided attention. "The recurrent, virtually identical dream."

"The blood on the walls." Kirk suppressed a shudder.

"The dream which runs counter to history," Spock said. "The dream whose outcome is violent death and an Earth withdrawn from interstellar contact out of xenophobic terror. The dream in which each of us tries and fails to offer T'Lera an alternative to what she believed she must do. The dream which each of us experiences in precisely identical detail, with two very significant exceptions.

"One: each of us is the solitary protagonist of his own dream. It is as if we are interchangeable, and the words we utter identical. Two: each of us is haunted by the voice of an unidentified female reiterating the single phrase 'You cannot do it alone,' yet you are able to glimpse her, however incompletely, whereas I am not."

"Doesn't surprise me," McCoy chimed in. "Jim can't resist noticing things like the color of a woman's hair, what she's wearing, even in dreams. You can."

"Doctor, in an instance where the identity of the speaker hinged upon such incidentals as gender and hair color, I submit my powers of perception—"

"Gentlemen," Kirk interjected softly.

"Finally," Spock concluded, "our psychoscans indicate identical mnemonic dysfunction, implying identical incipient psychoses." He waited for McCoy to comment on this, but the good doctor was busy polishing his halo. "The odds against such an occurrence in

156

two unrelated individuals from such diverse backgrounds who are also acquainted with each other," Spock went on, "are in the billions."

"That as accurate as you can be?" McCoy couldn't resist. "You are slipping!"

"In my conversation with Dr. Nayingul," Spock continued, ignoring McCoy, "he informed me that the sharing of similar dreams is common among those who participate in mutual Singings in Dream-time. However—"

"That's useful," Kirk interjected hopefully. "Is it possible that you and I, because of the frequency of mind-melds—"

Spock shook his head.

"I had considered that. But if the dream 'belonged' to only one of us, we should both experience it with the same person in the central role. If it were your dream, for example, I should dream of you conversing with T'Lera, not myself, and vice versa."

"I see," Kirk said thoughtfully. "Conclusions?"

"I believe Dr. Nayingul is correct," Spock said evenly. "There is more to this than dream. As illogical as it may seem, Jim, I believe as you do that we were both in fact participants in this event. And our unshakable belief in this alternate reality, despite what we know to be 'true,' has caused what appears to be mental dysfunction on our psychoscans."

"'Appears to be'?" McCoy repeated. "Spock, much as I respect present company, and much as I hate to find myself in agreement with a machine, in the history of modern psychology no scan has ever been found to be in error."

"For everything there is a first time, doctor," Spock said. "I remain convinced that neither of us is insane."

"That's what they all say!" McCoy snorted.

"Bones!" Kirk warned. "An unshakable belief in an alternate reality," he said thoughtfully, reiterating

Spock's words. "And you think that belief has a basis in fact?"

"A distinct possibility."

"Meaning we were somehow transported backward in time . . ." Kirk pondered it. "Lord knows we've done it often enough, voluntarily and at the behest of others. But why don't we remember it?"

"Or why did we not remember it until now," Spock corrected him. "Perhaps someone or something does not wish us to remember. Following your hypnosis, Dr. Sivertsen stated that you were 'blocking' something. So, apparently, am I. My dreams have resisted all attempts at meditative resolution. Yet something in Dr. Jen-Saunor's book has triggered what I can only conclude is not dream but memory."

Kirk nodded, absorbing it. It was what he'd felt in his gut all along, what had driven him to the South Pacific to find Galarrwuy, who had said essentially the same thing.

"Then it's simply a question of determining when it happened and why we didn't remember it."

"Oh, is that all?" McCoy blustered, feeling distinctly left out. "All you've got to do is comb through nearly two decades of shared history to see if anything's missing. Every mission, every log entry, every time one of you sneezed and the other forgot to say 'God bless you.' Nothing to it; couldn't be simpler!"

"That *is* why we are here, doctor," Spock pointed out. "And we have forty-eight hours. And, thanks to you and Dr. Sivertsen, we also have a point from which to begin."

"Elizabeth Dehner," Kirk said after a long moment.

"Precisely."

"Of course!" Kirk said. It made perfect sense to him, even if McCoy was goggling at him. "Which reminds me. Will you accept an apology that's about fifteen years overdue?"

"Perhaps," Spock said, bemused.

"Then I apologize. You were right."

McCoy was heard to sigh thunderously. "This is what I get for leaving my decoder ring at home!" He addressed his familiar gods or perhaps only the ceiling. He directed his ire at Kirk. "Either you let me in on this particular mystery of the Intergalactic Brotherhood of Space Cadets or—"

"Or what?" Kirk teased. His mood had lightened considerably with freedom and present company. "Spock, should we tell him?"

"It has to do, doctor, with 'the sometimes serendipitous impact of coincidence upon the course of history,'" Spock said as if he were quoting something.

McCoy didn't recognize it. Kirk did.

"Then you have read it?"

"Of course."

"I find it intriguing that the author keeps such a low profile," Kirk observed. "There's no biographical material available on her at all."

"Dr. Jen-Saunor holds Vulcan citizenship," Spock said; he would know such things. "This implies a degree of privacy more pronounced than most humans would aspire to."

"Isn't that somewhat rare for a human?" Kirk wondered. "At least, I'm assuming she's—"

"Goddammit!" McCoy had listened to enough.

"Sorry, Bones." Kirk gave him his sudden undivided attention. "Do you remember who introduced me to Elizabeth Dehner?"

"Do I remember? I did, the first day she was assigned. Why?"

"Because until today," Kirk said, pacing—it always helped him think better—"I'd totally forgotten how I first met her. I thought it wasn't until Mark Piper brought her onto the bridge with—no, wait, Bones; it's important. I'm now convinced Elizabeth Dehner is the mystery woman in the dreams, even though I don't know why.

"I said I owed Spock an apology that was about fifteen years overdue? All right, ancient history: Dr. Elizabeth Dehner signs aboard at Aldebaran; you introduce me to her the same day. Mark Piper relieves you while you lay over at Starbase 6 for some unfinished business or other—"

"Yes, yes, go on!" McCoy said, uncomfortable with the memory even after all this time; part of his unfinished business had included a bitter accusatory commpic from his daughter Joanna, who was taking his ex-wife's side of the never-ending argument on alternate weeks. "I have to admit there was a bleak moment at the bar when I almost talked myself out of it. I'd never committed to a five-year mission before. But, hell, I thought. Burned all my bridges, and you've been stuck with me ever since. For weal or for woe, as they used to say. God knows it's been six of one ever since.

"While I was gone," he finished, watching Kirk carefully, "you managed to get into that mess at the edge of the galaxy, and both Liz and Gary—"

"Gary . . ." Kirk said softly—the hurt, the sense of a life unfinished, still evident in the catch in his voice. The admiral cleared his throat, pulled himself together. "Gary, Lee Kelso, and I went on only one landing party together while you were gone, Bones. Along with this Vulcan officer I'd inherited from Chris Pike, who, frankly, intimidated the hell out of me."

"I know the type, Jim," McCoy said, eyeing the silent Spock, sensing something ominous in the wings and trying to lighten up. "One of those superior, know-it-all sorts who—"

"We'd beamed down to have a closer look at this odd little planetoid that kept disappearing and reappearing," Kirk went on as if McCoy hadn't spoken. "Nothing unusual about the mission, except we never did find out what made that planet behave the way it did. Nothing unusual about the report that followed, except that historically it marks the first time Spock was right and I was wrong and I had to pull rank on him to make it come out my way." He gave Spock a wistful look. "God knows I wish it had been the *last* time, but—"

"Jim," Spock interjected quietly, "there is no need to recall that particular memory now."

"Oh, yes there is," Kirk said adamantly, beginning. "Planet M-155. Gary dubbed it 'The Planet That Wasn't There.' For a while it became a rather cruel joke at—someone's expense . . ."

Captain James T. Kirk sat in his quarters signing reports on the day after his best friend died.

"And thus ends the report on 'The Planet That Wasn't There,' " he said tonelessly, scrawling his signature across the slate with his bandaged hand, trying to rouse some enthusiasm for this, for anything, in the wake of Gary's death. "Unless you have something to add, Mr. Spock."

"I regret I have not, Captain," the Vulcan replied solemnly. "Records of like phenomena are virtually nonexistent, and all efforts to extrapolate from available data have proved inconclusive."

"Then that's sufficient," Kirk said flatly. "Tell Yeoman Rand to append my log entry on the mission to your science report and let it go."

"As you wish, Captain," Spock said, though the inadequacy of his findings gnawed at him. And there was something else. If he were not an innate perfectionist, he might have relegated it to the realm of human error and let it pass, but . . . "Captain, I have noted the omission of Dr. Elizabeth Dehner's name from your log entry on M-155."

"The landing party on M-155"—Kirk had the report on Delta Vega before him now; it was all he could do to keep his hands steady, much less his voice—"was comprised of you, me, Gary, and—and Lee Kelso. They're all listed in the log."

Ironic, Spock thought. Bitterly ironic that the very same individuals had comprised the landing party on M-155 and the ill-fated participants in the events of Delta Vega. Three once living, three now dead. The inclusion or omission of that final name would not alter the course of the cosmos, and yet—

"Captain, Dr. Dehner was with us on M-155."

"Dr.—Dehner," Kirk said tightly, ominously, his eyes locked on the report on Delta Vega, though its words were a blur to him, senseless, "joined us at Aldebaran and I never laid eyes on her until five minutes before we hit the energy barrier at the edge of the galaxy!"

"Captain, I must differ with you—"

"Spock!" Kirk fixed him with his eyes for the first time, eyes that burned with the tears he would not shed, eyes that would have made a lesser being quail and turn away. Spock merely held them with his own. The tension left Kirk's body; he passed a hand over his eyes and sighed. "Mr. Spock, it may not occur to you that your merely human captain has been through sheer hell in the past few days, and the last thing I need is to have the names of those three people—flaunted at me—"

"Captain, I assure you that was not my intention. If you wish, I shall make the correction to your log entry myself. It is unfortunate that those who accompanied us to M-155 are the same three who died on Delta Vega. Nevertheless—"

"Spock!" Kirk's voice was pained, his face bewildered. "I'm telling you I know who was on that landing party. Elizabeth Dehner wasn't there! Why are you doing this to me?"

It was Spock's turn to be puzzled. He knew little

enough of the function of human memory. Was the captain so blinded by grief he could forget the details of recent events? Or had something happened to him while they were on M-155, that dusty, treacherous anomaly that defied all their attempts at research, endangered all the humans' lives with its thin atmosphere, its extra-atmospheric disturbances . . .

"Captain, if you will recall, you lost consciousness briefly on M-155. Perhaps—"

"Spock, that's enough!" Kirk scratched his name on the Delta Vega report, thrust it at him. "If I say Elizabeth Dehner wasn't there, she wasn't there."

The error could be confirmed by eyewitnesses—by Mr. Scott and Mr. Kyle, who'd been in the transporter room—or by the duty officer's landing party roster, which bore Lieutenant Commander Mitchell's signature. But to what purpose?

"As you wish, Captain," Spock said, letting it stand.

Kirk stood beside the seated Spock, concluded his narrative to the chiming of several of his antique clocks. "How many times do you suppose I barked first and asked questions later?" he asked, smiling.

"I have never calculated them," Spock said in all innocence.

"Liar!" Kirk grinned at him, sitting between him and McCoy to form the apex of a most extraordinary triangle. The expression on his face was that of a man visited with a sudden revelation. "Elizabeth Dehner was in the landing party that visited M-155, Spock. You were right and I was wrong. I know that now. But I didn't know it then, or for all the intervening years. Why?"

"Possibly because something happened on M-155 that caused you to forget," Spock suggested. "And that is the point from which we must begin."

He had been preparing himself while Kirk told his

story, sat now with his hands in one of their myriad contemplative configurations, glanced at McCoy, who was quiet for once, stewing over something.

"Gentlemen," Spock said as another of Kirk's clocks chimed, out of synch with the rest. "As Dr. McCoy is about to point out yet again, our meter is running."

McCoy blinked, emerged from his funk. "Whatever," he said, turning on his tricorder. "I'm easy!"

Spock took this as acquiescence, and they began.

"My mind to your mind."

However often the words were repeated, in whatever language spoken or unspoken, however often the Touch was performed, it never lost its sacredness.

Between Vulcan and Vulcan, telepath and telepath, it was one thing—the active seeking and conjoining of mind to mind.

For Spock, half-Vulcan, sojourner among telepath and nontelepath alike, conjoiner with Horta and Medusan and every manner of human, it was something other. And with this mind most of all—a human mind at first unskilled, wary, resistant, but long since nurtured in the recognition and acceptance of at least one other mind—the Touch was unique unto itself.

When had Spock first touched Kirk's mind with his own? Had it been as late as the Melkot, as the spurious gunfight that his captain had known, objectively, was unreal and yet had needed Spock's unflagging conviction to enforce? Reaching his mind, disciplined from infancy, into that untried territory, Spock had first encountered, of all things, a joke. A feeble one at that.

"I think therefore I am. I think!" was how Kirk greeted him, able to laugh from the edge of the precipice, wanting the meld as a weapon against the Melkot but fearing it at the same time. The poor taste of the joke might have caused another Vulcan mind to withdraw, to leave so frivolous a mind to its own devices—almost.

But it was that very humor-in-crisis that had fascinated Spock, made him hold on—for weal or for woe, as McCoy would say—for as long as they both should live.

A wisdom older than Surak decreed: nothing that is is unimportant. Two minds met as one would find the answer, no matter how seemingly insignificant.

It might be nothing greater than a ship's log entry.

Book Two

Book Two

Chapter One

"CAPTAIN'S LOG, STARDATE 1305.4 . . ."

Captain James T. Kirk kept one finger on the log recorder button while with his other hand he set his knight in a direct offensive against Gary Mitchell's king.

"Check!" he mouthed silently so the recorder wouldn't pick it up. Pleased with himself. What Mitchell mimed back was also best kept off the record. Kirk tried to keep any trace of smugness out of his voice as he resumed the log entry.

"We are continuing our mapping of Sector Epsilon Z-3, scanning and cataloging individual planets in previously charted solar systems and seeking out possible additional undiscovered star systems. . . ."

Out of the corner of his eye he could see Gary making tentative passes at the board, mentally trying moves and taking them back. Kirk's grin widened, turned into a yawn as he returned to the log entry.

"To date we have cataloged some seventeen planets and four planetoids in a total of thirteen star systems. Planets scanned have proved to be Class D or lower. Following standard procedure, we have not found it necessary to send a landing party to a single one of these barren rocks. Needless to say the crew, and I, will be grateful when this aspect of our mission is complete. Estimate another three weeks, at this rate, before that occurs."

Kirk yawned again, missed the furtive flick of Mitchell's hand toward his queen and an improbable kamikaze ploy.

"Final note: in view of the meticulous scientific nature of starmapping, I have placed Science Officer Spock in temporary command for the duration.

"Besides," he said strictly for Gary's ears, shutting off the recorder, "in view of Mr. Spock's seemingly unlimited capacity for detail"—Gary laughed with him—"it gives me more time to polish my game. Problem, Mr. Mitchell?"

"Not hardly, *Captain*." Mitchell couldn't give him the title without a touch of sarcasm. In a flash his bishop had leaped up two levels, capturing Kirk's queen and leaving him wide open. "Check."

Kirk's jaw dropped.

"You son-of-a . . . How'd you do that?"

"Piece of cake, kid." It was Mitchell's turn to grin, loll back in his chair with his hands clasped behind his head. "I only have to do one thing at a time."

Kirk scanned the board, saw no way out, decided to make one final log entry before he conceded defeat.

"Addition to bi-weekly log RE: personnel changes. Yeoman Rand, please note and append to respective personnel files: McCoy, Leonard H.: away on leave, Starbase 6 until further notice. Piper, Mark: returned from leave pending retirement approximately Stardate 1401. Additions to crew effective immediately: Bailey, David: navigational trainee, assigned Engineering pending possible bridge assignment, and Dehner, Elizabeth: psychiatrist, assigned Sickbay. Out."

"Met her yet?" Mitchell wanted to know, watching Kirk stare at the board and sweat.

"You have, I suppose?" Kirk shot back.

Mitchell feigned a shiver.

"Never did care much for cold climates."

"Meaning there's at least one female in the quadrant who can resist you," Kirk muttered, pondering a counteroffensive as suicidal as Gary's offensive.

"Why be greedy?" Mitchell asked. "I was thinking of doing the charitable thing. Giving the lady a chance to practice some of those healing instincts on one of those grim, serious types who can't score for himself."

"I can't imagine who you're talking about." Kirk extricated himself from check, but less flamboyantly than he'd hoped. He was only postponing the inevitable. "The last time you tried to fix me up—"

"Oh, I wasn't thinking of you, son," Mitchell said laconically, clinching the game. "Don't you think Spock would be more her type?"

Kirk didn't answer right away, wasn't at all sure it was dignified for a captain to make fun of his crew, even in the privacy of his own quarters.

"Kind of makes you wonder what happens when two immovable objects collide," Gary persisted, until even Kirk had to laugh.

"Probably 'The End of Everything,'" he intoned, imitating one of their Academy professors.

Their laughter was all out of proportion to the real humor of what either had said. Why was it so easy to make fun of Spock with Gary? And, more to the point, Kirk wondered, why was it necessary?

He'd been warned it was impossible to warm up to a Vulcan, but that hadn't bothered him. He didn't expect his officers to be his friends; the fact that some like Gary and Bones McCoy incidentally happened to be friends first and fellow officers second was an unlooked-for bonus. All Kirk expected—demanded—from his crew was efficiency, loyalty, and compliance to orders. Spock possessed all of these to the nth degree. Why did he still feel uncomfortable with him?

Was it the Vulcan's absolute humorlessness, demonstrated to him all too frequently in the earliest weeks of the voyage? Was it something as immature as jealousy, envy of the Vulcan's effortless brilliance, his ability to do six things at once without looking as if he were half trying, his absolute accuracy in the most minute detail? Was it the fact that it was impossible to know what he was thinking, what went on behind that impenetrable gaze, and in not knowing, one concluded that he was looking right through this all-too-human captain and finding him inadequate to the job?

Truth to tell, the captaincy still rested uneasily on Kirk's shoulders; he wondered if it would prove to be more of a burden, more of a straitjacket than he'd bargained for. Maybe that was why he let himself get so silly when Gary was around. To everyone else on board he was The Captain—if not infallible, then expected to give the impression of being so. To Gary he was just a friend; there was something about that too precious to lose.

Odd how the thing you spent your life pursuing could turn on you once you got it. Kirk had wanted command. Wanted it? His entire life had been spent in preparation for it. He'd eaten, slept, lusted after it. A ship of his own. And now . . .

"Bridge to Captain Kirk. Spock here."

"Kirk here," he managed, with a warning look at Gary. "What is it?"

"You asked to be notified should we encounter an uncharted body of planetoid size or larger," Spock reported solemnly. "I believe we have done so, sir."

"On my way." Kirk snapped the screen off. "Coming, Mr. Mitchell?"

"After you, *Captain.*"

Spock stepped down from the command chair with a bit too much alacrity, Kirk thought, as if he could barely wait to return to his science station.

"Report," Kirk said over his shoulder, settling into the center seat.

"We are on elliptical approach to the unrecorded planetoid, Captain," Spock said, his concentration on the hooded viewer of the library computer. "Passing over its companion star now, sir."

"Main screen," Kirk ordered, and squinted into its brightness as Lee Kelso punched it up from the helm. A too-bright sun dominated the screen, obscuring the starfield and everything else in its vicinity. "Mag point-five on that screen, Mr. Kelso. And give us some rad dampers."

"Aye, sir," Kelso replied.

Reduced by half, its radiance considerably lessened, the star became more comprehensible, but it was still impossible to see past it.

"The star on the screen," Spock reported, "was designated as Kapeshet by previous expeditions. It was not previously known to have any orbital bodies, however. Kapeshet is a variable star with an outsize corona, which may explain why the dependent plane-toid has thus far gone unnoticed."

"All right," Kirk said, rubbing his hands together to contain his excitement. He was aware of Gary, stepping down to relieve Farrell at navigation, eager to be in on the discovery of a new planet, no matter how ordinary. "Size and location of your discovery, Mr. Spock?"

There was a silence, prolonged enough to make Kirk wonder if Spock had heard him. He swung his chair around to find Spock standing at attention in that waiting posture of his, hands clasped behind his back, an immovable object.

"I asked you a question, Mr. Spock," Kirk said tightly.

"Yes, sir. It was the nature of the question which puzzled me. The planetoid is not 'my' discovery, sir. Ship's sensors were responsible for its initial detection, consequently—"

There was muffled laughter from somewhere nearby, a waiting silence around the bridge. Kirk swung his chair slowly in a 180-degree arc, assessing the situation. It was common enough for an established crew to give a new captain a certain amount of ragging in the early weeks, but they'd survived a crisis or two together and should be over all that by now. Besides, most of this crew had signed on when he did; only a few were remnants of Pike's administration.

How many of them were in Spock's camp? Kirk wondered, failing to understand this early that Spock had no camp, and never would.

All right! Kirk thought, swinging the chair back in Spock's direction.

"Very well, Mr. Spock," he said slowly, his tone calculated to remind everyone on the bridge, but particularly his science officer, exactly who was in charge here. "We've had our moment of levity. Our— comic relief, if you will. Now kindly answer my question. Size and location of the object under investigation?"

Spock's gaze did not falter under Kirk's glare; it was almost as if he had no idea why Kirk was annoyed. He did not refer to his viewer, but recited his data from memory.

"Planetoid designated M-155, per standard Murasaki Index annotation. Circumference: 16,583 miles. Mass: four times ten to the twenty-first power metric tons. Mean density: 3.702. Quantitatively about two-thirds the size of Earth. Present location: in elliptical orbit around Kapeshet at 131 Mark 4, sir."

Kirk made an effort not to be impressed.

"Very well. Schematic, Mr. Mitchell. Let's have a look at it."

Mitchell plotted a schematic several degrees ahead and put it on the screen. The ship was almost through Kapeshet's corona; the planetoid should become visible momentarily. The entire bridge crew watched the screen. The sight of the dullest chunk of rock would offer them some relief from the previous week's monotony.

"I don't see anything," Kirk said, voicing everyone's impatience. Everyone but Spock, who didn't seem capable of impatience. "Helm, are you sure we're on course?"

"Affirmative," Kelso replied; "131 Mark 4, sir."

"Navigation?"

"Course confirmed," Mitchell said laconically, checking his instruments with a tilt of his head. "Except there's nothing out there."

Kirk frowned. Mitchell could be enviably relaxed, but he was seldom careless.

"Are you sure?"

"No orbital body at 131 Mark 4, Captain," Mitchell said, for once giving Kirk the title without irony.

"Confirmed, sir." Kelso turned to look at Kirk. "No planetoid at that location."

Kirk sat forward in the chair.

"Scan the area. Full sweep fifteen degrees about. Maybe it's in a rapid orbit or a retrograde. Maybe it's not in a fixed orbit at all. A rogue or an asteroid."

"Unlikely, Captain," the Vulcan said behind him without waiting to be consulted. "Planetoid was monitored on its present course for one Standard hour before verification."

It was precise standard procedure for the mapping of newly discovered planets. If nothing else, Kirk had to concede, Spock was precise.

"All right," Kirk said with exaggerated patience. "Then kindly tell me where it is now."

"Unknown, sir."

Kirk rose deliberately from the center seat, walked slowly, stiffly to the rail before Spock's station.

"Uh-oh!" murmured Lee Kelso, who knew that walk. He nudged Gary Mitchell in the ribs. "Duck, Mitch! It's about to hit the fan."

"Mr. Spock," Kirk said, carefully enunciating each syllable. "What is today's date?"

"Stardate 1305.4, Captain," Spock answered immediately.

"You're certain it's not April Fool's Day?"

"I beg your pardon, sir? I am not familiar with the reference."

"No, Mr. Spock, I don't suppose you would be," Kirk said long-sufferingly. "But tell me, has anyone else on the bridge seen this elusive planet of yours?"

"No, sir," Spock said quietly, aware that he had somehow displeased this volatile new commanding officer, though he was at a loss to explain how this had happened. Nevertheless he must give an answer that would only increase his captain's displeasure. "Due to the interference from Kapeshet's corona, I was monitoring on a frequency few humanoids can see. Further, I assumed that as commanding officer you wished to be the first informed."

"I see," Kirk said slowly. That last sentence was the tip-off, as he saw it. He had as good a sense of humor as the next man, but . . . "Mr. Spock, we're all a little fatigued with this starmapping, and I can appreciate an attempt at lightening the mood, when it's done well. But even the best practical joke can be taken too far!"

Spock stood on his dignity. "Vulcans, Captain, do not engage in the employment of jokes. Practical or otherwise. There was a planetoid. My only error lies in my inability to explain why it is no longer there."

If Kirk had been a little less of a greenhorn, he might have apologized right then. But he was still a greenhorn —and he didn't like to be second-guessed.

"Very well, Mr. Spock," he said, keeping his temper tightly in check. "We will—indulge you—for the next twenty-four hours. We will, for that amount of time, circle this variable star of yours in search of anything that remotely resembles a planetoid. For your sake, I sincerely hope we find it!"

He had planned a dramatic exit, strode toward the lift to find his way obstructed by his ship's new psychiatrist. How much of the scene had she witnessed, and what sort of martinet did she think him? Elizabeth Dehner followed Kirk into the lift.

"That was pretty," she remarked, her credentials giving her partial immunity from charges of insubordination.

"Is that a professional opinion, doctor, or are you just minding my business?" Kirk asked.

"I was wondering if that was some new command trend or if you had a personal reason for being so hard on him," Dehner said incisively.

"Neither, as a matter of fact," Kirk said. "I can't abide incompetence, and I can't abide a smart-ass. I was no harder on Spock than I had to be."

The lift had stopped. Kirk had given it no instructions, and Dr. Dehner apparently intended to follow him wherever he was going. Kirk decided to take advantage of that.

"Rec Room 3," he instructed the lift. "Besides, doctor, he's a Vulcan. Officially they have no feelings."

Dehner had been watching the numbers on the lift panel, might have gone to the rec room with him if it weren't for that last remark. She turned on him, her silken blond hair flailing about her face in her anger.

"Every intelligent being has feelings, Captain. The greater the intelligence the more highly developed the feelings. Mr. Spock is just better at hiding his than you are. Why do you dislike him so much?"

"I don't dislike him," Kirk defended himself. The lift had opened at the rec room. He stepped out but Dehner didn't. "I don't especially like him either. All I ask is that he do his job."

"Maybe if you were a little clearer on what your job was, Captain," Elizabeth Dehner challenged him through the closing doors, "you might be less paranoid about the way Spock does his."

Mixed reviews, Kirk thought grimly, striding down the corridors as if he were in a great hurry. The Vulcan won't mess with me anytime soon, but the lady shrink thinks I'm a bully. Nobody ever said this job was easy.

He was just stepping out of the shower the next morning when Gary strolled in without knocking. He and Kirk had always had the run of each other's quarters; Kirk's recent change in rank wasn't about to alter that.

"Feeling better?" Mitchell asked with exaggerated solicitude, lolling in the doorway with his arms folded.

Kirk grunted by way of reply. He seemed to remember Gary had been on his side yesterday.

"You'd better tread softly on that bridge this morning, kid. Spock's found his missing planet."

Kirk began to dress, looked at Gary's reflection in the mirror.

"Is it for real, or are you part of the gag this time?"

Mitchell shrugged off Kirk's paranoia; they'd both pulled a few in their midshipman days.

"Scanners say it's real. Oh, and FYI, they first picked it up on an infrawhite wavelength. Something Vulcans can see but we can't. That's why no one else spotted it."

"I wasn't aware of that," Kirk said quietly, humbly. Gary always seemed to know little out-of-the-way facts that he didn't.

"Spock's taken some pretty impressive pictures this time," Mitchell went on. "Verified and confirmed by everyone on each watch to avoid any further— misunderstandings."

"Why wasn't I informed?" Kirk snapped, on the defensive again.

Mitchell detached himself from the doorway, made himself comfortable in Kirk's best chair, propped his feet on the bunk.

"I guess in view of yesterday's tantrum he didn't

want to risk waking you," he said casually. "His pictures range from 2300 last night to about five minutes ago, at half-hour intervals."

Kirk stood with his shirt in his hand, stunned. "He's been monitoring this thing *all night?*"

"From what I understand, Jim, he never left the bridge after you called him into question in front of half the crew. Hasn't eaten or slept since he came on this time yesterday. I hear tell Vulcans get points for stamina, but . . ."

He let his voice trail off, let his silence do the rest. No one could put the guilts on Jim Kirk the way Mitchell could. He watched Kirk pull on his shirt, glance in the mirror one last time, then spin the entire vanity back into the bulkhead as if he didn't much like the face he saw in that mirror.

"I was rather—abrupt with him, wasn't I?" the captain of the *Enterprise* said humbly.

Gary grinned up at him. "Two things you never question about a Vulcan, James, are his competence and his veracity. You managed to do both simultaneously. Always said you were talented."

"I'll have to apologize to Spock," Kirk said, steeling himself.

He motioned Mitchell to his feet.

"Let's go have a look at the cause of the controversy."

Spock straightened from his viewer, sensing Kirk's arrival by the watchful quality of the silence on the bridge.

"Captain," he reported at once, "the planet is no longer there."

The silence deepened, grew profound, became so entire that the machine noise from the dozen bleeping, whirring, chirping, humming consoles seemed to heighten in an attempt to fill the vacuum, deafening.

Kirk felt his blood pressure rising. Was there no end

to this nonsense? He envisioned his ship trapped in endless orbit around this glaring, unfriendly sun like some interstellar *Flying Dutchman,* eternally in pursuit of a figment, a rumor of a planet, while he and his science officer remained locked in mortal combat, his hands forever gripping the Vulcan's throat. . . .

He took a deep breath, waited for the red haze to clear from his vision, and saw that Elizabeth Dehner was also on the bridge, tucking her blond hair casually behind one ear, watching him.

Paranoid, am I, Doctor? he thought.

"Mr. Spock?" he asked in the calmest of tones. "What do you mean it's 'no longer there'?"

Spock made note of the change of tone, as well as of its probable cause.

"Captain, as illogical as it may sound, this planet apparently has the capability to appear and disappear at random intervals, which I have plotted in this series of holo-images. It was literally here a moment ago, and gone the next."

The holos were genuine, verified by all three watches, incontrovertible. But what did they mean?

Garth of Izar had given an electrifying guest lecture at the Academy once. Jim Kirk had been there, crammed into the back of the SRO auditorium with about a hundred other cadets.

"Consider the minuscule portion of space we have managed to explore in our time," Garth had addressed them, his slender hands gripping the edges of the podium, his magnificent voice rolling out over them without need of augmentation. "As well surmise the nature of an entire ocean from a single surf-washed stone. Gentles, assume that space will always be more unknown than known, and nothing you encounter in its reaches will surprise you."

As a cadet, Kirk had taken those words to heart; they had saved his life more than once and his face more often than that. As commanding officer, Kirk seemed to have forgotten them. Maybe there was some phenomenon, operative in this area of space and as yet unknown to human science, that could account for an entire planet's whimsical appearance and disappearance. Maybe he should have thought about that before he shot off his mouth yesterday.

"Explanation?" he asked Spock now.

"Insufficient data, Captain," Spock replied evenly, as if yesterday's humiliation had vanished along with the planet. "I shall need to study this phenomenon further."

"No," Kirk said softly. "Not you, Mr. Spock. Have someone else from your department relieve you. Boma's Astrophysics, isn't he? Or Jaeger. Have one of them come to the bridge. You're long overdue for some rest. And—an apology."

"Sir?"

"I had—insufficient data—for coming down on you so hard yesterday. I'm sorry."

Spock hesitated. He had never understood this human concept of apology—so casual, so commonplace, so different from the formalized Vulcan asking of forgiveness. Among equals, he had learned, apologies were frequently dismissed with some offhand response like "that's okay" or "forget it," neither of which was logical. To state that the offense being apologized for was "okay" implied that it did not require apology in the first place, and to suggest that the offender "forget" the offense was not only unlikely, but apt to encourage a repetition of that offense.

Further, one could hardly tell one's superior officer to "forget it." What other responses were possible?

"'The first is to understand,'" Sarek his father, diplomat to all species, would say, quoting Surak. "'Thence to accept the one, not as you would wish to be, but as the one would wish to be, for this is the essence of Diversity.'"

Estranged though he was from his father, Spock

181

could respect his wisdom. First to understand. Spock had attempted to understand humans all his life, had come to understand only his lack of understanding. How was he to accept an apology he did not understand?

"Take it in the spirit it was intended and don't analyze it to death!" Amanda, his ever-human mother, would say, quoting no one's wisdom but her own. "And don't be such an infernal perfectionist!"

There had never been estrangement from his mother; could not be, for Amanda would accept him whatever he became. Spock took her wisdom as it was intended.

"I accept your apology, Captain," he said at last. "But I request permission to remain on the bridge. The study of this phenomenon would be a rare opportunity."

Kirk's first instinct was to deny him, but on second thought he realized Spock needed the vindication as much as he.

"Very well, Mr. Spock," he said, settling himself into the command chair for the first time that day; he felt he'd earned it. "Between us maybe we'll solve this thing. Who knows, we might even name the planet after you."

That will not be necessary, Captain, Spock started to say, but again his mother's wisdom intervened and he restrained himself.

"Main screen," Kirk said.

"Aye, sir," Kelso replied.

Out of the corner of his eye, the captain of the *Enterprise* could see his ship's psychiatrist leaning over the comm con chatting with Uhura. When she glanced in his direction, she was smiling.

Planet M-155 popped back into being within the hour.

Considering the uproar it had caused, it was an

unprepossessing little planet, essentially a drab greenish-gray rock with a tenuous atmosphere, little free water, and scant primitive vegetation. There was no evidence of animal life and nothing of mineralogical value.

And no indication, from this distance, of what was making it disappear.

Enterprise hovered at 40,000 perigee, as far away as scanners could work effectively. Kirk was not about to get his ship in too close.

"No evidence of structures or dwellings of any kind," Spock reported. "No evidence of any civilization past or present, or of any advanced life form. Dubious such a thin atmosphere could support sentient life."

"Then what's playing tricks on us?" Kirk wondered aloud. "Could there be some power source from off-world? A transfer beam or displacement wave from another solar system? Even a ship powerful enough to pull a planet off course?"

"Nearest inhabited solar system is forty-six parsecs distant," Mitchell reported from his station. "No vessel of any description within a radius of ten degrees."

"And no disturbance of surrounding space, Captain," Spock interjected. "Whatever the phenomenon is, it is affecting only this planet."

Kirk digested this. "Could it be a natural phenomenon? A time warp or—or something?"

"Exploring that possibility at present, Captain," Spock replied.

Kirk crossed to the science station, leaned on the rail. "Are we in any danger?"

"Inconclusive," the Vulcan said. "However, at this distance, I do not believe so."

Kirk didn't like the smell of it. "Shell game!" he muttered evilly. "Cosmic three-card monte with us as the rubes."

Kelso looked at Mitchell who looked at Kelso. They'd lived through enough of Kirk's metaphors to know what was going on in the captain's head. A more cautious commander would record the planet as an unexplained phenomenon, set out warning buoys, and move on.

James Kirk had not become the youngest captain in Starfleet history by being cautious.

"Spock, what's the longest it's been 'present' since it first appeared?"

"Four-point-one-three hours, Captain."

"And the shortest?"

"One hour six minutes, sir. However, that is no guarantee—"

One hour and six minutes, Kirk thought. More than enough time to beam down, have a look around, and, with Mr. Scott on the button, zip back up again.

He glared at the greenish-gray blob on the screen; it seemed to be taunting him.

"Mr. Mitchell, organize a preliminary landing party and have them on standby," Kirk said. "We'll give this beast one more prestidigitation. The next time it pops back in, we're going down there."

Chapter Two

"I REITERATE, CAPTAIN: the fact that the planet remained 'with us' for one hour and six minutes at minimum once before does not guarantee that it will not remain for a far shorter period this time."

"Mr. Spock, if you'd like to excuse yourself from the landing party, feel free to do so," Kirk said shortly, itching to start.

"Negative, sir. Mathematically, the odds are in our favor. I merely point out—"

"Good," Kirk cut him off, stepping up on the transporter platform with Spock, Mitchell, and Kelso. "Then let's get going!"

"Still waiting for Dr. Dehner, sir," Mr. Scott reported from the transporter control.

Kirk threw up his hands in despair, stepped down from the platform. It was his fault for insisting she tag along.

"I'd like a Med staffer along," he'd told Mitchell, who presented him with a preliminary landing party roster consisting of himself, Spock and Lee Kelso, when M-155 popped off the screen again and they waited for it to reappear. "In case one of you falls and skins your knees."

"Dr. Dehner's next up on the med list," Mitchell grimaced. "Jim, she's a shrink, for crying out loud. I'll lay odds she can't remove a splinter."

"Spock assures me the flora are pre-xylemic," Kirk said, deadpan.

Mitchell gave him a blank look.

"No trees yet," Kirk explained, having trouble with the corners of his mouth. "No wood, no splinters."

"Hilarious," Mitchell remarked, adding Dehner's name to the roster. "One lady shrink, per captain's orders."

"Give her a chance to get dirt under her nails like us ordinary mortals," Kirk said. "Opportunity to study interpersonal relations outside of lab conditions, that kind of thing. Be nice to me, Gary, or I'll see that you personally get to take her in hand."

Now Dehner was holding up the landing party and the joke had gone flat.

"By the time she gets here we'll lose our window on that planet!" Kirk lamented for the benefit of one and all. "Scotty, page her. If she's not here in one minute we'll—"

"Reporting for duty, Captain," a cool voice reported from the doorway. "I had to double-check my equipment." Dehner joined them on the transporter pods.

"Energize," Kirk barked to Scotty, the only way he could think of to have the last word.

"Fan out," he instructed his party. "Spock to six o'clock, Lee to nine. Gary to three, and I'll take twelve. We'll rendezvous back here on my signal." His eyes went from Dehner to Gary and he was tempted, but only briefly. "Doctor, you'd better stay with me."

The others moved off to reconnoiter.

"Making sure I get dirt under my nails, Captain?"

the psychiatrist inquired archly. "Or do you think you're apt to be the first to skin your knees?"

"Belay that," Kirk said, wondering how she'd gotten wind of what he'd said to Gary on the bridge. Gossip, like everything else aboard a starship, traveled at warp speed. "We're here to get some work done, not to play personalities."

He was not about to tell her his stomach was in knots, watching the people under his command moving off into the unknown. He didn't think he'd ever get used to it.

"Oh, I see!" Dehner said, seeing through the tough-guy act but playing to it. "Snide comments are your exclusive bailiwick. Rank hath its privileges, and all that."

"Did you bring that tricorder down for show or do you plan to take some readings?"

They traveled in silence after that.

Scotty had set them down on the night side; there was too much radiation from Kapeshet's corona, Spock had warned, for them to remain long on the day side unprotected. As it was, the raging sun spat enough of its radiance out over the horizon to lighten the night sky abnormally, obscuring all but the brightest stars, creating weird skittish aurorae at the poles, and giving the landing party an adequate if fickle fairylight to walk by.

The atmosphere was thinner than was strictly comfortable for humans, and Kirk cursed himself for not ordering airpacks. Well, he'd set himself a time limit of fifteen minutes; they could hold out that long.

Underfoot the soil was sandy and an unnatural cobalt-blue in color, though it could have been some trick of the light. It was fine and dusty and clung to boots and uniforms, irritated eyes and skin. Kirk heard Dehner cough more than once, but unobtrusively. He was probably the last person she'd let know she was uncomfortable. His own eyes were stinging, and he had a sneaking feeling this stuff was gumming up the tricorders despite their shielding.

"Anything?" he asked Dehner when she came to a halt, shutting off her tricorder with a shake of her head.

"Between the dust and the ionization from that infernal sun," she answered, disguising another cough, "I couldn't tell you."

Kirk wouldn't have expected her to find anything under ideal conditions; it wasn't part of her training. But he nodded to let her know it didn't matter, cleared his throat, and pulled out his communicator, motioning to Dehner to keep absolutely still so the dust would settle. He homed on Kelso's frequency.

"Landing party, report."

He heard static and the sound of coughing.

"Kelso here, Ji—Captain." Old habits die hard. "I'm about a thousand meters from where we split up. Can't find anything unusual, except that there are pockets where there's no air. Makes you a little light-headed if you're not careful. That and the dust—" He broke off, coughing again.

"Take it easy, Lee," Kirk advised. "Try to keep the dust out of your equipment. And your lungs. Rendezvous back at starting point in five minutes. Kirk out."

Mitchell's report was much the same, with more vociferous complaints about the dust. Kirk gave him the same instructions he'd given Kelso.

"Can this stuff harm us?" he asked Dehner, wiping his eyes on his sleeve, which only made them burn more.

"No worse than an attack of hay fever," she said, allowing herself to cough in earnest this time. "But cumulatively—"

"Understood," Kirk said. They weren't going to learn anything this way, he realized. "Let's go."

Against his own advice about gumming up the machinery, he tried to contact Spock as they hurried back the way they'd come, stirring up dust as they went.

Spock answered the communicator signal reluctantly. Neither the thin atmosphere nor the dust affected him; there were portions of his planet where such conditions were a constant. And the absolute normalcy of his tricorder readings for this kind of planet puzzled him. There must be an answer to its disappearances, and he must find it.

"Spock here."

"Time we were getting out of here, Mr. Spock. Get back to the beamdown point at once."

Spock had positioned himself on a small rise above the worst of the dust; with his acute vision he could distinguish the distant figures of the others gathering like ants around their point of origin. He did not require their dubious security in numbers, would be perfectly content to remain where he was, alone on the planet if necessary, in order to pursue his research.

"Captain, request permission to remain and continue my tricorder readings. There are still several possible explanations for the phenomenon which I have not yet had opportunity to explore."

The captain seemed to be having some difficulty getting his breath. Spock heard sounds of acute upper-respiratory distress.

"Negative, Spock . . . dust getting to all of us . . . back here on the double."

"Captain, I am unaffected by the dust. Respectfully request—"

"Dammit"—cough— "Spock, don't"—choke; splutter; cough—"argue!"

"Very well, sir," the Vulcan said reluctantly, and started back to where the others awaited him.

"Och, what d'ye make o'that, Kyle?"

"I dunno, Mr. Scott. Never seen anything like it."

Scott signaled to Kirk on the surface.

"Captain, is your landing party all together down there?"

"All but Spock," Kirk reported through a surge of interference from the corona, tapping the dust out of his communicator. "He's on his way in. Why?"

"I was afraid of that!" Scott said. "I had a fix on the lot of you like you ordered, in case we had to beam you up quicklike, and all of a sudden one of you popped off my screen, just like that blooming planet!"

"Stand by!" Kirk ordered, switching frequencies just as Elizabeth Dehner shouted.

"Captain! Mr. Spock—he's gone!"

She'd been standing a little apart from the others, facing in the direction Spock had gone, had caught a glimpse of the spare, angular figure moving purposefully toward them, as she'd watched first Mitchell then Kelso appear out of the swirling grit moments before. Suddenly, she saw nothing.

It might have *been* nothing—a larger swirl of dust obscuring the Vulcan, a sudden depression in the landscape momentarily hiding him from view; he might even have fallen and skinned his knees, Kirk thought bitterly, choking on the thought as violently as on the dust—were it not for what Scotty had just told him.

Kirk's mind raced. They'd been down here scarcely twelve minutes by his chrono. The planet had not disappeared that soon for as long as they'd been monitoring it. Was it about to vanish now, and take them with it?

"Spock!" Kirk called into the communicator, knowing it was useless.

The entire expedition was useless. Worse than useless because it had endangered his crew. It was all his fault. He was running toward where Dehner had seen Spock vanish, shouting into the communicator at the same time.

"Scotty! Beam the others aboard now! I've got to find—"

But the communicator failed, jammed by the interference and the dust he'd kicked up in his impatience. Kirk flung it aside, whirled as if to take one from someone else when he heard Kelso yell "Mitch!" and watched in horror as Mitchell, too, simply popped out of being.

The shout had not died on Kelso's lips before he too disappeared. Kirk spun around in time to see Elizabeth Dehner's eyes go wide as she—

Helpless to get a fix on anything, Scott and Kyle stood at the transporter control and watched as the landing party vanished one by one. Then the planet itself popped out from under them. *Enterprise*, suddenly robbed of its orbit, lurched violently before gravitational control compensated and the automatics locked in. Helping Kyle to his feet, Scotty looked at his screen in dismay.

"Bridge!" he called at once. "Who's up there, then?"

"DeSalle here," came the reassuring voice from the helm. "Uhura at Navigation. Somebody's rocking the boat."

"Aye, Mr. DeSalle," Scott breathed. "Take us out a remove from that blasted sun. There's namore between us and it. The whole kit's disappeared again and taken the landing party with it!"

Kirk hit the sand too hard to break his fall, landing on his backside in an undignified sprawl. He could see nothing. The first thing he heard was a voice, speaking heavily accented Standard.

"Oh, dear! I *have* done it this time, haven't I?"

Chapter Three

"SHOOT ME IF I'm wrong, Ji—Captain," Lee Kelso's voice echoed up the steps to Kirk and Mitchell. "This is going to sound nuts, but I think we're in Egypt."

There was no response at first from the dark at the top of the stairs, only the sound of both men scuffling and straining against the great stone slab that abruptly cut off the stairway, effectively imprisoning the four of them.

"You need any help up there?" Kelso asked.

"No," Kirk panted, and the sounds of scuffling were replaced by footsteps, echoing, growing nearer. "It can't be moved. We've tried."

First Kirk, then Mitchell, emerged from the darkness, down the ancient crumbling stone steps to the huge, echoing chamber where Kelso and Elizabeth Dehner waited.

"You did say Egypt?" Kirk said, dusting his hands, looking around.

"Either that or the best reproduction I've ever seen," Kelso maintained.

"Egypt," Kirk said again, incredulous. "First disappearing planets, then disappearing Vulcans, now you want me to believe we've been yanked off a planet a thousand light-years away and ended up back on Earth. Well, why not?" He sat heavily on the stairs, forgetting the bruises he'd earned on arrival here—wherever 'here' was—and tried not to wince. He gave Kelso the floor. "Convince me."

"For starters, I guess we all agree we're not on M-155 anymore," Kelso began, waiting for someone to contradict him. "Spock did say no structures, no evidence of civilization."

"Spock . . ." Kirk said with a sick feeling. The Vulcan was missing, had not turned up with the others. His responsibility.

"Well, here we are inside a structure, all right," Kelso went on. "And it's got all the earmarks of dynastic architecture: heroic proportions, mortarless construction; it's at least three thousand years old—I can tell you that even without a tricorder—and probably underground because there are no windows and the only way out is up—"

"Why don't you call it a dungeon, Lee?" Gary Mitchell chimed in. He'd ensconced himself halfway up the stairs where the light from some sort of antique electric fixtures was strongest, and was dismantling one of the communicators. "Because that's what it is. That stone upstairs won't budge. That means we're stuck here."

"Thanks, Mitch." Kelso grimaced, deflated. "Nothing like looking on the bright side."

"That's Mr. Mitchell's job," Elizabeth Dehner spoke for the first time from her chosen spot against one wall, deliberately distanced from the others, keeping her own thoughts on dungeons at bay. "Playing the cynic makes him feel superior to the rest of us!"

"Always expect the worst, doc." Mitchell grinned down at her. "You'll never be disappointed."

"Egypt," Kirk said for the third time, jumping down

from his step and beginning to pace. There didn't seem to be anything else for him to do, and he couldn't just sit. "Earth. It seems impossible. Megalithic architecture is common on humanoid worlds throughout the galaxy, Lee. What makes you so sure?"

"I've been studying the walls," Kelso explained. It was true. From the moment the foursome had picked themselves up from the sand-strewn stone floor, Kelso had been groping around the perimeter of the huge empty room, poking his fingers into crevices, measuring, calculating, at times crawling on all fours and muttering to himself until Kirk had demanded to know what he thought he was doing. "They're sandstone, originally dressed to fit so snug they didn't need mortar, particularly in a desert climate, although they've shifted in places, probably because of earthquakes. That's why there's sand on the floor. There were major quakes in Egypt in the twentieth century and the twenty-first—when they built the dam at Aswan, and again when they opened the old Gibraltar Locks. Too much water pressure in places where there'd never been water before."

"I see," Kirk said, but Kelso was just getting warmed up.

"If you look closely—" He began moving from place to place, pointing, scuttling around like a slightly crazed spider, his voice bouncing back and forth against the emptiness so that he seemed to be everywhere. "The blocks alternate headers and stretchers—short ones with long ones—in a pattern the Egyptians called *talatat* or 'threes'—no one seems to remember why—which was the pattern for interior masonry from the Golden Age, around 1400 B.C. Except for the women's temples, which were done in headers or short blocks only, like the temple of Nefertiti, which was dismantled after the worship of Aten was discredited, literally chopped apart stone by stone . . ."

He trailed off, as if realizing for the first time that he had said more in five minutes than he usually said in a day. Quiet, diffident Lee Kelso, known among his peers as Old Reliable—the man who could find anything, fix anything (and, as those who knew him from the Academy could verify, "organize" anything that wasn't nailed down) had suddenly revealed himself as a closet Egyptologist.

"Why, Lee, you amaze me!" Jim Kirk said softly when he'd done.

"It's a hobby." Kelso shrugged. "I've always been interested in architecture."

"What about the treasures, Lee?" Gary tweaked him, shaking cobalt-blue sand out of the communicator. It sprinkled like fairy dust down the stairs to mingle with the reddish sand on the floor, a reminder that where they had been was not hallucination, but no guarantee that where they were was not. "Where's King Tut's gold? Where's the ancient papyrus with the secret code? Where's the hidden passageway to get us out of here?"

"There are some hieroglyphs over here," Elizabeth Dehner said helpfully, interested in what Kelso had been saying and anxious to shut Mitchell up at any cost. "At least that's what I think they are."

Kelso had already investigated them.

"They're not true pictographs. Coptic graffiti. Centuries younger, and inferior to the real thing."

"Excuse us!" Mitchell murmured.

"At least the lights are a little more contemporary," Kirk observed, studying the wall sconces near the high stone ceiling, listening to the echo of his own voice. "For a minute there you had me expecting torchlight processions. All right, let's say Egypt, for the sake of argument. That puts us in a lot less difficulty than we would be anywhere else. All we have to do is find a way out of here, locate Spock—"

"Just like that," Mitchell remarked dryly, refitting the casing on the communicator and testing it. "Nothing to it!"

"Have you got that thing working yet?" Kirk demanded impatiently. "If we can home on a Starfleet frequency—"

"Oh, it's working, all right," Mitchell assured him. "But I can't broadcast. There's no range. Something's jamming it."

Kirk turned to Dehner. "What about the tricorders?"

"Same problem, Captain," she replied. "I can read anyone inside the chamber, but I can't get beyond the walls."

"There's some kind of damping field all around us, Jim," Mitchell reported, snapping the communicator shut with finality. "Something out there wants us incommunicado. And if it's the same thing that was strong enough to bring us here, offhand I'd say we're in pretty deep—"

"Very astute, Mr. Mitchell," said a voice behind them, a voice that did not echo, but spoke in the same heavily accented Standard that Kirk thought he'd imagined before. "However, allow me to assure you that your fears are unfounded. I mean you no harm."

He had not come down the steps, had not entered to the sound of stone walls sliding open to Gary Mitchell's suggested hidden passageway, was simply there with them—curious apparition out of another age or reality, turbaned and white-robed, too thin for his height or too tall for his weight—wraithlike, insubstantial, grinning like the proverbial Cheshire cat, and carrying (Kirk saw)—

—a bone-china tea service on a teakwood tray.

"You're the one!" Kirk advanced on him, finger pointed accusingly. "The voice I heard. Are you responsible for bringing us here?"

"Quite responsible, Captain," the wraith acquiesced

with a small bow, setting the tea service down on the steps in lieu of furniture, spreading his long fingers in apology. "Guilty as charged, though I assure you that was not my original intention."

Kirk opened his mouth and nothing came out. Nonplussed, he looked up at Mitchell for suggestions. Mitchell shrugged.

"What was?" Kirk asked carefully.

"I was attempting," the stranger said, fussing with the tea things, "an experiment in the manipulation of time. It was not intended to involve anyone else. You and your crew simply got in the way."

Behind him, Kirk could hear Dehner's tricorder whirring busily. Cool and collected, she was taking readings on the stranger. Good! Kirk thought, clearing his throat.

"I am Captain James T. Kirk of the Federation starship *Enterprise*. We were on a peaceful mission—"

"Oh, I know all that, Captain," the stranger said, waving it away with one long hand and nearly upsetting the teapot. "Though at present I do not know how I know. I know all manner of useless things. It is when I try to employ my knowledge in some way that might benefit me in my plight that I succeed only in making matters worse. Do you take honey in your tea, Captain?"

Before Kirk could refuse, assert himself, even shout something incoherent, Dehner's voice came from behind him.

"He's human, Captain," Dehner whispered. "More or less."

"What's that supposed to mean?" Kirk demanded.

"She means, Captain," the stranger said, still holding the teacup (seeing that Kirk had no intention of taking it, he offered it to Dehner, who shut off her tricorder and accepted it with a shrug in Kirk's direction), "that while some of my readings are within human norms, many are not. She will tell you that my neurological

197

patterns are paranormal, for example, particularly what you would classify as esper ratings, and that she is unable to determine my age."

"Exactly," Dehner said coolly, as if his knowing all that didn't surprise her in the least. She leaned against the steps sipping her tea as if it were the most normal thing to do under the circumstances. Kirk wondered if it was. "How did you know? Have you been tested before, Mr.—"

"Parneb," the stranger said, pouring a second cup of tea. "Mahmoud Gamal al-Parneb Nezaj, if you please, though Parneb is the one name I shall carry with me through all my incarnations. Mr. Mitchell?"

"My mama told me never to take tea with strangers," Mitchell quipped pleasantly from his perch near the top of the staircase. His arms were folded, he leaned casually against the wall, but a certain tightness about the mouth let Kirk know that he was coiled and ready to spring if he gave the word.

"Ah, but we are no longer strangers!" Parneb protested, offering the tea and some biscuits to Lee Kelso, who had never been known to refuse anything edible. "I know who you are, and I will tell you as much about myself as I can remember. And in due course I shall do all in my power to get you home safely. But you must first promise me you will not do anything— precipitous."

"It's mint!" Kelso said past a mouthful of biscuit, referring to the tea, to which he'd added a generous dollop of honey. "It's very good."

"From my own garden," Parneb said with a trace of pride. "And the honey is from my own apiary. Two skills which will hold me in good stead down the ages."

"One of my crewmen is still missing," Kirk interrupted, shaking off a kind of *Through the Looking-Glass* malaise that seemed to have captured Kelso at least. All this pouring and sipping, nattering and chattering, were getting to him; he had a sudden desire to smash crockery. "He was with us on that planet—"

"Yes, I know, the Vulcan," Parneb said calmly. "Pity, I don't quite know how that happened; you were all supposed to arrive here. *Malesh,* a single Vulcan can't be that difficult to find."

"We are in Egypt, aren't we?" Kelso wanted to know.

"Most definitely, Mr. Kelso. And I quite enjoyed your lecture on the subject." Parneb poured himself a cup of tea at last, folding his ectomorphic personage onto the stone steps to sip at it delicately. "You and your associates have managed to surmise a great deal despite the restrictions I have placed on you by confining you to this—cellar; it was not intended to be a dungeon, Mr. Mitchell, truly. I must also accept responsibility for jamming your equipment, Captain. I was aware that your training and your talents would demand that you attempt to escape or to seek help from outside. But, like you, I also have a manner of Prime Directive. I cannot have you announcing your presence in a century that is not your own."

Slowly Kirk began to comprehend what Parneb was really saying. He had by his own admission transported them across parsecs of distance. Why not time as well?

"Parneb," Kirk said with the last ounce of patience he possessed. "What century is this?"

"Why, one of mine, of course," Parneb seemed surprised that Kirk didn't know. "But as to which of them—let me think . . ."

It was more than Kirk could stand.

"I want answers!" he gritted out through clenched teeth. "I don't know who or what you are—sorcerer, con man, or just plain lunatic—but if you don't release us, tell me what's happened to my first officer and my ship, and get us back where we belong, I'll—"

"You'll what, Captain?" Parneb went on placidly sipping his tea.

Kirk lunged for him, found himself grabbing what felt sickeningly like cobwebs, until it melted out from under him. Kirk lurched forward, hit the steps hands first, broke his fall, and rolled onto the floor. Beside him Parneb's teacup tumbled, splashed, and smashed to bits. Parneb was elsewhere.

"Please don't do that again, Captain." Kirk leaped to his feet to find the conjurer standing in the center of the room, smoothing his clothing fastidiously. "It wrinkles the *djellaba* and is undignified for both of us. I *told* you I would do what I could. But I need time. And your present behavior is hardly conducive to my letting you out of here at all."

Kirk seethed, mentally adding his skinned hands to the bruises he already owed this disappearing dervish.

"Patience, Captain, for just a bit longer," Parneb advised affably. He saw that Kelso was examining the walls again. "Mr. Kelso, I would be most interested in how you rate this structure comparative to others of the same period . . ."

He linked his arm in Kelso's and within moments the two were off on a tour around the room, nattering away as if they had all the time in the world. Kirk collected his wits and looked around him at the others—Dehner sitting with teacup in hand as if she didn't know what else to do, Mitchell poised on the staircase like a deceptively sleepy cat. Alice through the looking glass, Kirk mused, had had to keep running in order to stay in the same place. Exhausted, he climbed up to sit beside Mitchell.

"Gary, I'm stumped," he said. "I can't seem to get through to this character at all."

His manner was not consistent with any regulation command technique he knew, but he was wise enough to recognize his own myopia and seek a second opinion. He had relied on Mitchell's advice for so long. . . .

"Patience and diplomacy, kid." Mitchell's lips barely

moved, his eyes never left the white-clad figure of their host, as if he suspected him of overhearing their conversation even at this distance. "Humor him, like Lee's doing now."

"Lee," Kirk said testily, "is off on his own little cloud somewhere. If I hear one more discourse on architecture I'm going to—"

"Is he, Jim?" Mitchell wondered. "You know Lee as well as I do. He can be a maniac sometimes, sure, but he's never lost his perspective. Ever since this Parneb character popped up, he's been playing him like a violin. Lee was the one who found out we were in Egypt."

Kirk watched the two figures on the far side of the room, suddenly saw Kelso's seeming flakiness in a new light.

"The Good Cop/Bad Cop scenario." He smiled.

"All I know is, it's old," Kelso had explained it to them, preparatory to using it to extricate them from some jam or other. "Earth origin, variation on the Devil's Advocate scenario. One guy plays the Bad Cop—real mean, ready to beat the guy in the middle to a pulp. The other guy plays it sympathetic, like it's all he can do to hold the first guy off. That way the guy in the middle trusts the Good Cop to protect him from the Bad Cop, and he'll tell him anything."

"And you're the Bad Cop," Kirk said.

"Perfect bit of casting, no?" Mitchell grinned. "And you're the quarterback." He grew uncharacteristically serious. "Lee and I'll block for you, Jim, you know that. But it's still your play."

Kirk smiled his gratitude. A man was fortunate to find such a friend once in a lifetime; a commander who could claim such a man as his confidant was doubly blessed.

"Captain?" It was Elizabeth Dehner, who'd been observing Parneb too. "Much as I hate to find myself in agreement with Mr. Mitchell, the technique is psychologically sound."

"There you are!" Mitchell said dryly. "Now that you've got the UFPMA Seal of Approval—"

"Easy, Gary, easy!" Kirk felt like laughing for the first time. "Save your act for Parneb."

"Who said I was acting?" Mitchell wondered with a quizzical look at Dehner.

Before she could say a word Parneb was suddenly, silently among them again. There was no telling how much he'd overheard.

"It is time now," he announced with a wave of his hand. "If you will all come with me . . ." He chose to make a conventional exit this time, moving up the stairs as if there were not several tons of stone between them and freedom. Kirk, right behind him, was strangely unsurprised to find that there were not.

Mitchell uncoiled himself from the steps and let Kelso pass him.

"Come on, Alice in Wonderland," he called down to Dehner. "Tea party's over."

Dehner shouldered her tricorder and glared up at him.

"Someday, Mr. Mitchell, I'm going to look inside your head and find the cause of that calculated misogyny," she said coldly.

"I've got nothing against women," Mitchell objected, trying to take her arm. "They're some of my favorite people. When they act like women."

"Maybe you're just jealous of my trying to get between you and your captain," Dehner suggested, wrenching free of him, ignoring the insult—not the first of its kind she'd heard, certainly.

"My advice has saved Jim Kirk's life more than once," Mitchell said stonily. Playing the Bad Cop already? Elizabeth Dehner wondered, or did he really mean to sound so menacing? "If he needs your advice, he'll ask for it."

The staircase spiraled upward through several narrow turnings within windowless, featureless stone walls that Kelso assured them, to Parneb's obvious delight, were of much later construction, opening out suddenly into a suite of airy, almost-modern rooms. Kelso was ecstatic.

"Mud-brick construction, domed ceilings, rounded arches!" he raved. "It looks like a Hassan Fathy. Parneb?"

"Close, Mr. Kelso," Parneb beamed at him. "The architect will be a disciple of Fathy's at the end of the last century."

Mitchell, meanwhile, was not looking at the architecture but at the mass of medieval miscellany contained within it.

"He's got all the trappings, Jim!" Mitchell sounded amazed. "Look at all this stuff! Everything the do-it-yourself sorcerer needs. Astrology charts, home remedies for everything from bellyache to unrequited love, all neatly labeled in English and Latin and what I assume is Arabic. Shelves lined with skulls, most of them human, all the latest up-to-the-minute necessities for turning lead into gold, eye of newt and toe of frog, even a genuine crystal ball!"

Something in the shape of a largish melon sat alone on a small table in the center of the room, glowing softly.

"You may sneer, Mr. Mitchell," Parneb said lightly, "but those trappings will earn me a marginal living in a less enlightened era than this. And the 'crystal ball' actually works."

Kirk had gone at once to one of the high arched windows; the view from there confirmed his worst fears. Centuries of debris had built up around the walls of their underground room, forming a tel that from the outside gave the appearance of a natural hill. At the base of that hill, some three stories below them, a busy street out of any Middle Eastern metropolis teemed with pedestrian and vehicular traffic. But it was all wrong. The vehicles, the clothes people wore, were at least two centuries out of date.

Kirk moved away from the window. Among the runes and glyphs and zodiacal symbols everywhere about the room, his eye caught a perpetual calendar, conveniently set at October 2045. Perfect! Kirk thought.

"Okay, Parneb," he said, rubbing his hands together. "We're convinced. What do we do now?"

"You sit," Parneb advised, availing himself of a small prayer rug on the floor. "And indulge me by listening to a fable."

"That does it!" Mitchell exploded, immediately in character. "Jim, how much more of this are we going to take? I've had it up to here with this clown and his mystical mumbo-jumbo—"

He lunged at Parneb as Kirk had downstairs. Kelso, playing along, intercepted him.

"Easy, Mitch—"

Mitchell shoved him aside, grabbed for the crystal ball, and let out a genuine yelp of pain.

"It gave me a shock!" He shook his hands to stop their stinging. "The damn thing's wired or something."

"Actually, Mr. Mitchell"—Parneb had not batted an eyelash during the entire performance—"it is attuned to my wavelength. That makes it—sensitive—to being touched by anyone else. Next time, consider that one man's 'mumbo-jumbo' may be another's science and a third's religion."

"Parneb?" Elizabeth Dehner was once again taking surreptitious readings with her tricorder, humoring the conjurer in her own psychiatrist's fashion. "Does your 'fable' have to do with getting us back home?"

"It most assuredly does, dear lady." He sighed, looking at Mitchell askance. "However, some require a demonstration first. *Malesh,* I will indulge Mr. Mitchell's skepticism!"

From beneath his *djellaba* he produced a thin silver chain, pendant from which was a smaller piece of the same "crystal" as the large orb on the table, except that neither was crystal at all, but some murkily glowing opalescent stone that at times seemed to grow softer, change its shape, become gelatinous, pulsating, almost alive. And, at its center, it created images.

Parneb closed his eyes, clasped the smaller crystal in his two hands, concentrated. The milky center of the larger crystal grew clear, became a starscape in which floated an angry flaring sun and its single gray-green unprepossessing planet.

"Kapeshet!" Jim Kirk recognized it. "And M-155."

"Is that what you called it?" Parneb wondered, opening his eyes. "Oh, dear, how boring! Well, but it is a boring little planet, isn't it?

"I chose this boring little world for my experiment," he went on, "because it was so remote and—I *thought* —uninhabited. Also, admittedly, the name of its sun intrigued me, Kapeshet being a contemporary of mine in Ancient Thebes. But how was I to know my interstellar sleight-of-hand would attract your attention and bring you poking around down there? By the time I saw you all stirring up dust it was too late. If I had not retrieved you and brought you here, well . . ."

He let his voice trail off, frowned at the crystal for a moment before reverting to his normal benign expression. "At any moment now you will see your *Enterprise* placidly orbiting as if nothing has happened. Because, you see, as far as they are concerned, nothing has— yet."

205

"How does it work?" Kelso gawked at the crystal, awed by a device that worked without visible mechanism. "Where does it come from? How do you—"

"Pretty impressive holography." Gary Mitchell sneered, still in character.

"Mr. Mitchell, I assure you—"

"I don't see the *Enterprise*," Kirk said tightly. "What's happened to my ship?"

"Undoubtedly it is orbiting the far side," Parneb said too quickly, slipping the smaller crystal back inside his robe. The image in the larger crystal vanished abruptly. "*Malesh*, I must rest now. Later we will devote ourselves to finding your Vulcan." He resettled himself on his prayer rug, waited for Dehner to finish her tricorder readings. "Yes, my dear?"

"Do you realize that when you go into that—trance —or whatever it is with the crystal," she said, "your body readings all go paranormal? Your pulse was over two hundred just now, and your neurological patterns—"

"Yes, it is quite exhausting actually." Parneb sighed. "The price one must pay, I suppose. Which is why you are best advised to do as Mr. Mitchell has suggested, and humor me."

Mitchell managed to look surprised at being found out.

"Which is not to say you are not a consummate actor, Mr. Mitchell. You almost had me fooled. But you see my hearing is also paranormal . . . A fable, then," he began once he had everyone's attention. "The tale of a being, seemingly human, who for some inexplicable reason was born backward in time, a being whose tomorrows are yesterdays, whose destiny it is never to be entirely certain if what he remembers has already happened or is about to happen at some future time, with or without his participation."

"Merlin," Elizabeth Dehner said out of nowhere.

Her three contemporaries goggled at her. "There's one version of the Merlin legend—I think it's T. H. White in *The Once and Future King*—where Merlin's magic is explained by his having been born backward, so that he can foretell the future because it's actually his past."

"Except that Merlin was only a legend," Kirk pointed out, vaguely irritated. One of his officers an Egyptologist, another suddenly an expert on medieval legends; it was all rather unsettling.

"Interesting," Parneb mused. "Except that it was not entirely true of Merlin." He looked fixedly at Kirk. "Merlin was not legend, Captain. That one's dilemma will be an immortality similar to mine, though he will have the advantage at least of running with the clock. I will know him as Ahkarin, in quite another century. If I live that long. Are you beginning to fathom the magnitude of my problem?"

"You're asking us to believe that you were"—Kirk struggled with it—"born in the future, and that you will live out your life in the past? How is that possible?"

"How is it possible that you are here, in a time before you were born?" Parneb countered mildly.

"But where were you born, when? Who were your parents?"

"I do not know!" Parneb said plaintively. "I have no clear recollection of my origins, though I know I was born not far from here. The past and the future flow together and switch back on each other until I scarcely ever know where I am. I seem to have lived in your twenty-third century; the scant knowledge I have of that time seems to confirm it. And I age far slower than an ordinary mortal. I have already survived several centuries and am doomed to live for several thousand years more, at least until the twelfth century B.C. when I shall—"

"Parneb," Lee Kelso said. He was not addressing the sorcerer by name, but recalling something he knew from history. "Parneb of Thebes. Construction boss under Ramses III, master architect under five pharaohs. You're not—you can't be—"

"I'm afraid I am, Lee," Parneb said sadly, familiarly. "Or will be. That is why I was curious about what you thought of the chamber beneath us. I will design a temple, and supervise its construction on this site, in 1198 B.C. It is one of the first and last things I remember."

Lee Kelso lapsed at last into silence. It was all too much for him.

Jim Kirk was far less awed.

"Now that you've explained it," he said to Parneb, "it makes sense—for you. But what does it have to do with us, with that planet?"

"I had hoped, by means of a science I mastered—will master?—in another century to use the crystal to focus my innate psychic abilities and reverse the chronology of my life," Parneb said, as if it were simplicity itself. "All I have ever desired is to be an ordinary human being, to live out my life in the proper order and to die in the fullness of time. When I succeeded in moving that lonely little planet across time and space, I thought I had found the key. But the experiment proved a failure, and in addition it endangered you and your people, Captain. I am sorry!"

No one spoke for a long moment. Suddenly Parneb seemed no more nor less a madman than any of them might be, given his circumstances.

"I ask you to consider"—there was no trace of joy on his usually smiling face—"the plight of one who awakens each morning not knowing if he is older or younger, who dares not give himself in friendship or love lest he watch those he cherishes grow younger even as his children live to become his elders. Consider one who must stand helplessly by as humanity unlearns what it knows, grows ever more superstitious and disease-ridden and primitive. If he tries to intervene, to speak what he knows, he is stoned for a fool or persecuted for a sorcerer. I will live to see six thousand years of war beset this part of the world, Captain, and there is nothing I can do about it. Even you, who are here because of my dilemma, believe me only because to deny my reality makes you the madmen!"

"It's insane!" Elizabeth Dehner said quietly. All of her professional cool was gone; she was genuinely moved. "How sad!"

"What's the crystal made of?" Mitchell asked, cutting across the mood, refusing to pity Parneb, refusing to succumb to any kind of feeling. "Where did it come from?"

"A meteor," Parneb said dispiritedly, as if the whole subject wearied him more than he could say. "A chunk of rock of no composition I can analyze, retrieved from the desert, whence it drew me on a moonless night, and probably not mine to keep. I suspect it will in its time become an object of great value, even of worship. Perhaps the celebrated Philosophers' Stone? I do not know."

Having told his fable, he seemed to gather it back into himself, put it back in its box while he resumed his characteristic affability.

"Vulcans have a saying, do they not, that none can know the future? Obviously no Vulcan was ever trapped in my situation. *Malesh*, at least I have managed to encounter interesting people in my times.

"I do not know entirely how the crystal works, lady and gentlemen, only that it works. In that respect I am not a scientist, only a sorcerer after all, Captain. But not a con man, nor quite a lunatic, if you please."

"I'm sorry," Kirk said sincerely. "As my first officer might say, I have a tendency to be—precipitous."

"Which is why we must locate that first officer, in order that he might continue to perform that invaluable public service," Parneb quipped, unfolding himself like an oversize grasshopper and taking out the smaller crystal again. "I surmise that in pulling him off the planet before I caught the four of you, I simply caused him to materialize somewhere else on Earth. The crystal is not without its flaws. I trust, Captain, he has sense enough to assess his situation and not tamper with present history?"

"Of course!" Kirk said impatiently; he was surer of that with Spock than anyone else. "Assuming you didn't dump him at the North Pole or in mid-ocean, he's perfectly capable of surviving on his own."

"And as he is the only alien on this pre-interstellar planet," Parneb said, leaning into the larger crystal as they all were, anxious for it to clear, "this should be quite simple."

But it was not. The large crystal did not clear, but continued to swirl and glow and pulsate. Only Parneb saw something in its depths and what he saw, to judge from the expressions that came and went like lightning across his face, at first delighted, then profoundly distressed him.

"Ah, there we are! Your Vulcan is in fact in the middle of an ocean, Captain, but altogether quite high and dry. He—oh, dear!"

"What is it?" Kirk demanded, nerves stretched to the snapping point.

"This is not possible! It is too soon!" Parneb cried, releasing both crystals and clasping his brow in distress. "I find not one Vulcan, but two!"

Chapter Four

WHAT DID MELODY Sawyer expect to find when she followed Jason out of the sunlight into the main room of the agrostation? Little green men, talking petunias, creatures so uncanny she could justify blowing them out of the water to protect future generations from the very sight of them?

They are not human, she told herself over and over again. They are something completely other, and we can't have any idea what they want here. That makes them dangerous until proven otherwise.

"You all right?" Jason inquired as she swung the rad-detector up to him out of the skiff. "You look a little green."

"Save that for 'them,' why don't you?" Sawyer said wanly. "I'd feel better if I had my hardware is all."

"State you're in, I'm damn glad you don't!" Jason rumbled. "If you didn't shoot your foot off, you'd get me in the back. Sure you don't want to wait in the boat?"

"And let them kidnap you for a love slave?" Melody swung herself up onto the dock and grabbed the medical equipment. "Damn the torpedoes and all that."

211

"Right," Nyere said, and they went in.

They'd had to wait on the dock while Yoshi brought the clothing bundle in. Now the young man held the door and tried to slip out past them. Melody's hands instinctively went for the weapon she didn't have.

"Where d'you think you're going, Buster?" she nailed Yoshi with her voice.

"Out!" he sulked. "It's too crowded in there, and I don't want to watch, okay? I have to go check my crops. I'll be back." He jerked his head angrily in the direction of *Delphinus*. "Besides, how far could I get?"

"Let him go," Jason interceded before Melody could get hard-nosed about it. "See you're back before dark," he told Yoshi.

"Sure!" Yoshi let the door slam behind them. The hydrofoil's motor made a prodigious noise pulling away.

They are not human, Melody thought, her eyes adjusting to the dimmer light as she picked out Tatya hugging one wall, looking simultaneously defiant and scared. There were two other figures in the room. Melody looked.

They are not human. They are not like us. If they go to heaven when they die, it's their heaven, not mine. They are not human. Killing one or both of them to protect my world is not the same as killing one of my own. They are not human. . . .

Her first thought when she actually looked at them— the tall young male so striking he'd have reduced her teenage daughter to a helpless puddle, the slender, stark-faced female with the oddly crooked nose, looking almost fragile in one of her old flannel shirts—was that this was a joke. Something cooked up by Command to keep them on their toes, some top-secret drill concocted behind closed doors at the PentaKrem to see how AeroNav personnel would respond to a real alien invasion.

Sure, Melody thought. Some HQ genius went and hired a couple of actors or maybe intelligence people, stuck those funny-looking ears on them, trained them to speak in those clipped, accentless tones . . .

Only the female actually spoke; she and Jason Nyere exchanged formal understandings in a way that always made Jason shine. He considered himself a front-line diplomat ("If I screw up there won't be anything left for the hair-splitters to do but pick up after me," he always said), and at the moment he was being magnificent.

The male alien stood silently behind the female, who was obviously in charge, almost mirroring Melody's parade rest behind Nyere's strangely reassuring shoulder; he seemed to devour each speaker's words, his eyes moving intently from face to face as each spoke.

". . . quite understand your position, Captain," the female was saying. "We will comply with whatever you deem necessary."

Her eyes, Melody thought, were like those ancient religious paintings where the eyes seemed to follow you around the room. She spoke solely to Jason, her eyes meeting his, yet at the same time they followed Melody. And talk about burning holes in a person!

She knows exactly how to work people with those eyes, too! Melody thought when it was her turn to go into her act, running the rad-scanners over both aliens without trying to look like she was hunting lice. Because now she's not so much looking at me as looking past me, as if I don't exist! I don't *like* this one; I don't care how peaceful her intentions or how many of her crew she lost getting here. I don't trust her, and excuse me for living, I don't like her!

In fairness, she tried being friendly to the male.

"Don't worry," she said off his serious face when it was his turn to submit to the scanner. "This won't hurt a bit!"

"I was not under the misapprehension that it would," he replied solemnly.

And they claim they learned our language from video? Melody wondered. They sure go out of their way to remember the big words! There's something pompous about a kid his age using words that size. Still, he has a nice voice.

"How old are you?" Melody tried, making conversation.

"Nineteen-point-six-five-eight, as measured in our years," Sorahl replied politely. The question hardly seemed pertinent, though perhaps there were medical reasons. "By conversion to your years, that would be—"

"Never mind!" Melody tried a different tack. "Do you ever smile?"

"Never," Sorahl said sincerely.

"Jesus!"

Melody tried not to notice that Jason was laughing at her.

"I'll have to ask you both to accompany me to our vessel for the present, Commander," Jason Nyere said. "For one thing, it's safer for all parties concerned. For another, my superiors will probably want to have a—talk with you."

He had almost said "a look at you," because that was what it would amount to, a lot of brassheads goggling at the comm screen and asking fool questions. He would see to it that it got no sillier than that.

Yoshi was right. There was something strangely compelling about these people, something that demanded respect and, considering their vulnerability on this alien world, evoked a kind of protectiveness.

Thank God! Jason Nyere thought, who had been so reluctant to assume the responsibility in the beginning. Thank God this has fallen to me and not to some hotshot looking for a place in the history books. The brass must be made to see the immeasurable value of these people, and the race they represent.

"As long as you're aboard my ship, you will be under my protection," Nyere told T'Lera. As one commander to another he had immediately sensed in her something simpatico, and in listening to her story his sense of who and what she was grew stronger. If the rest of her people were anything like this . . . "However, what my superiors will deem necessary after that will ultimately be out of my hands."

"Understood, Captain," T'Lera acknowledged with a tilt of her head. Without so much as questioning what Nyere thought would be the final solution, she indicated that they would go with him.

Tatya was less easily persuaded. She'd been tensed against the far wall like a trapped animal, watching her foundlings put through what she considered a series of humiliations, and she had had enough. She threw herself in T'Lera's path and all but attacked Jason Nyere.

"You haven't asked *me!*" she accused him. "As long as they're under *my* roof they're under *my* protection, and I say they're not going anywhere!"

Within no span of real time, three forces of will contended silently to change Tatya's mind. So strong were those wills that the thoughts of all three converged in Sorahl's telepathic mind, and he heard them as if they were speaking aloud.

They've given their consent freely and without duress, Jason Nyere would have said. Don't complicate this, Tatya, don't—

Make a scene, I dare you! Melody Sawyer would have hissed. Just you dare, and I'll tell Jason about the woman in Kiev, no matter if it makes me look bad—

We do not belong on your world, T'Lera would have said. Therefore we have no rights. What the captain chooses to do with us—

But Sorahl found his voice before the others.

"Tatiana," he said softly, and she turned to him, tolerating that name from him as she never had from anyone else, not even Yoshi. "It is logical."

"But it's not *right!*" Tatya protested tearfully.

"Are the two frequently incompatible on your world?" Sorahl asked, honestly puzzled, and because she could not answer him, Tatya was puzzled too. Unsure, she could no longer fight.

"I'm going with you!" she declared. "I won't let either of you out of my sight!"

Like I'm not going to let you out of mine! Melody thought. She and Yoshi would have had to go with them anyway.

Five sat in a skiff intended for a maximum of three and overloaded with equipment, so low in the water before Jason started the motor that the larger swells slapped over the gunwale and Sorahl, Vulcan-curious, marveled at the spray on his face, touched it with sensitive fingertips, smelled it, tasted it. T'Lera, erect and seeming unmoved beside him, noted her son's reaction and rejoiced that, whatever was to come, he had lived to experience this much.

Melody and Tatya sat squashed sullenly together in the bow, facing aft, both keeping an eye on the Vulcans for their respective reasons, each keeping an eye on the other for the same reason. Jason sat aft and steered, his mood strangely serene considering the unknowns ahead. In the center, T'Lera, wearing a colorful Ukrainian *babushka*—Tatya's last-minute solution to an obvious problem of ears—and Sorahl in one of Yoshi's hooded sweatshirts, looked like nothing so much as a pair of refugees.

"A question, Captain, if I may." T'Lera half turned to address Nyere, aware that the one named Sawyer tensed every time she made an unexpected move. "Forgive my curiosity, but how will you explain us to your crew?"

216

"I'd like to hear the answer to that myself!" Sawyer called over T'Lera's head. The Vulcan's eyes were upon her again, intent. "Last thing he told them was we were hunting a satellite." She addressed T'Lera directly for the first time, felt herself blushing, infuriatingly, like a schoolgirl.

"Indeed?" Could she have rendered her voice more neutral, T'Lera would have done so. But she was T'Lera, and Sawyer could not but hear the irony.

"Yes, ma'am!" she shot back rudely. "So what's the answer, Captain suh?"

"Actually, Sawyer, I thought I'd let you handle it," Jason Nyere said just under the wind, aware of how voices carried, aware of Ensign Moy waiting wide-eyed and twitchy with amazement on the foredeck to bring them in. "Suppose you call an all-hands briefing while I see our guests secured. Inform the crew from me that we were actually out looking for survivors of a Mars-base craft but, owing to security reasons and the need to notify next of kin . . . you know the drill. That ought to satisfy everybody."

Except me! Melody steamed, aware that he was laughing at her again. She vented her anger by shoving Tatya over on the seat, aware once more of a pair of laser eyes watching her, making her feel somehow foolish.

Two Vulcans, in this time? That's impossible!" Jim Kirk breathed, resisting yet again the urge to grab Parneb by the throat. "If you've lived in the future as you claim, you know the Vulcans aren't due to arrive for another twenty years!"

"Of course I know!" the sorcerer said plaintively. "Nevertheless, they are here. I cannot explain it."

The large crystal sat opaque and pulsing in the center of its table, mesmerizing. Kirk narrowed his eyes at it.

"You saw them in the crystal?"

Parneb nodded miserably.

"Parneb, it's time you told us how this thing works."

The conjurer weighed something carefully before he spoke.

"I am afraid I cannot do that, Captain. Now, do not get angry; you know it accomplishes nothing. I can tell you only that the stone works with my natural psychic abilities, as it might with anyone with a high esper rating, but it is activated by a science taught in a century after yours and possibly not on this planet. As I have told you, I also have a Prime Directive."

Kirk sighed, sat. Disgruntled, defeated, he glared at the throbbing orb.

"It's all connected somehow," he mused. "Spock's disappearance, the other Vulcans' premature appearance. And the fact that *Enterprise* was not orbiting M-155 when you looked for it, was it?"

Parneb sat fingering the folds of his *djellaba*, eyed Kirk warily before he answered.

"It was not where I expected it, Captain. I did not tell you that then, nor did I continue to look overlong, for fear you might lose your temper and attack me again, possibly damaging the crystal. For if you had done that, you would never get back home."

Kirk paced for what seemed the hundredth time that day, and it had been a very long day; he was running on one-hundred-proof adrenaline by now. Parneb, doomed to travel the millennia, seemed to need no rest. The others, endowed with lesser amounts of stamina, were in various states of repose. Elizabeth Dehner lay curled on a couch with her eyes closed, though she might have been only drowsing. Lee Kelso, adaptable as a cat, sprawled snoring on a pile of Kaffir rugs in one corner. Gary Mitchell sat staring at Parneb's vidscreen, anachronism in a room filled with anachronisms, watching a news program with the volume at minimum.

"Is it possible"—Kirk turned to Parneb, rubbing his brow in perplexity—"that by bringing us here—"

"I managed to wrinkle the fabric of time so to speak, causing things to happen out of sequence?" Parneb finished for him. "Quite possible, Captain. Quite alarmingly possible, and I must take full blame for not considering that before I began."

"And any change in the continuum of time—" Kirk began.

"—can have untold ramifications in the future," Parneb said unhappily.

Kirk crouched beside him, reasonable, beyond anger. "You've got to help us put things right. Can you imagine what would happen if mankind came face-to-face with Vulcans before we even knew there were other humanoids out there, much less—"

Much less the kind of alien I still can't get along with on my ship a full two centuries later, Kirk thought without saying. We think we're so sophisticated, so beyond all that, but we all still have our residual prejudices, I as much as any man. Imagine the men of this century . . .

"No need to imagine, gents." Mitchell switched off the vid, laconic as usual, but with a touch of cynicism. "Just tune in to the news for ten minutes on any given day. Border squabbles, unsettled reparations still outstanding from Colonel Green's war, terrorist factions. All this on a supposedly United Earth. I wouldn't give two lonely Vulcans a snowball's chance."

"And if anything had gone wrong, if anything goes wrong—" Kirk stopped himself, realizing he had begun to slip back and forth in time as Parneb did. "If any harm comes to those two Vulcans, there might be no Federation. No Starfleet, no *Enterprise*—"

"And no Spock," Mitchell chimed in.

No! Kirk thought.

∿∿

No!
Admiral James T. Kirk thrashed about, flailing his arms, catching Spock on the jaw. Ordinarily so minor

an annoyance need not disrupt the meld, but Jim Kirk's mind was flailing too, searching in vain for what was in fact at hand, hurling Spock backward out of the meld—

To where McCoy steadied him, gripping his arm.

"Enough, Spock, enough! Bring him up and leave off. It's too much for him!"

Spock oriented himself, shrugged McCoy off; his concern was elsewhere. Seldom was Kirk's force of will powerful enough to break the meld, yet that was apparently what had happened. Jim Kirk curled near-fetal in the deepest recesses of his chair, lost somewhere between now and memory, reliving who knew what nightmare in his mind. Spock touched him.

"Jim?"

Kirk flinched, shuddered, groped unseeing.

"Spock? . . . Spock!"

The voice was a child's voice, lost and alone. Spock focused all his will on bringing Jim Kirk home.

"Jim, I am here. Be with me!"

"Spock?" Kirk's vision cleared, his face lighted. "Spock, you *are* here!"

"Yes, Jim."

Slowly Kirk uncurled himself, aware of McCoy's hovering.

"I'm all right!" he insisted, drawing on all his dignity, lurching to his feet and straightening his clothes. "Spock, did I hurt you?"

"Of course not."

Kirk nodded, uneasy with the concern in his companions' eyes. What the hell had happened?

"Take Five!" he suggested, trying to make light of it.

He was no sooner out of the room than McCoy was rummaging for a hypo.

"It's happening too fast, Spock. Let me give him something so he can rest awhile."

Spock gripped McCoy's wrist, intercepting the hypo. "Doctor, we have scarcely begun. And there is very little time."

"Dammit, Spock, it's dangerous to keep pushing him like this! Maybe you can keep up this relentless pace, but I won't let you overtax Jim!"

"Do you think it does not tax me as well, doctor?" Spock asked softly, reasonably.

Only then did McCoy trouble to notice how haggard he looked; this thing was draining him as well.

"Thought you Vulcans were supposed to be indestructible!" he growled.

"Would that we were," Spock said sincerely. "But we are not."

"All the more reason why you ought to take it easy!" McCoy argued. "If you fold on me, what the hell am I supposed to do? Go back to Krista and say, 'Sorry, I lost them both'? You'd better make damn certain you strike a balance here between what you're searching for and how much you're willing to expend for it."

"We know what we're searching for," Kirk said, coming back from the bathroom looking, not refreshed, but at least ready for the next round. "And essentially we've found it. But Galarrwuy said something about being certain our reality conforms to history and not to dream. We haven't begun to find out why there's such a divergence, and I for one won't rest easy until we drop the other shoe. Whether we were pulled back through history by design or merely blunder, we somehow altered its course. I can't rest until I know whether what we did was, to use your expression, for weal or for woe. Spock?"

"If you are asking my opinion," the Vulcan said mildly. "It concurs with yours."

Jim Kirk smiled. "I thought it might. Insatiable curiosity is a trait common to both our species. What I was asking for was your consent to continue the meld, now. Unless you agree with the good doctor that we should rest first . . ."

The Vulcan raised an eyebrow. His tone was dry. "Would you be content to rest in nonexistence?"

Kirk took his point. "Which is essentially where we've left you, isn't it, old friend? Well, can't have you missing in action too long. Lord knows what sort of mischief you might get into."

"Jim, there's enough on that tape right now to convince the shrinks," McCoy blustered. "Let it go at that. Quit trying to be a hero!"

"I'm not!" Kirk snapped irritably, protesting too much. Was it heroism or pig-headedness that drove him on? "I'm trying to find answers! The tape solves our immediate problem, but it doesn't answer to history. And we have an obligation to answer to history."

"Even if it pushes you over some kind of edge where I might not be able to—"

"Bones, that's what you're here for—to keep us from going over the edge. But you've got to trust us to know our own limits, too."

McCoy glowered, fiddled with the tricorder, outflanked as usual. "Goddammit—"

"Come on, Bones," Kirk wheedled. "Double or nothing. We have to know."

Taking the doctor's silence for assent, Jim Kirk readied himself for a return to the meld.

"'Once more unto the breach, dear friends . . .'" he said, unable to resist.

Muttering to himself, McCoy turned the tricorder back on.

~~~

"Spock's half human," Mitchell explained for Parneb's benefit. "If Earth and Vulcan never get together . . ."

The information brought the conjurer violently alive.

"I did not realize!" he cried, jumping to his feet, wringing his hands. "Oh, dear! Oh, impossible! I am admittedly a bungler, but I will not be a murderer as well!"

When Kirk grabbed him this time, he did not turn to

cobwebs and disappear, but instead went limp and began to whimper.

"I never intended . . . all my fault . . ." he babbled.

"Pull yourself together!" Kirk ordered him, gripping his shoulders and shaking him. "You've got to help us! You're our only connection with this century. You've got to help us get to the Vulcans before it's too late—hide them, get them off the planet if possible, if we have to build a ship with our bare hands . . ."

Elizabeth Dehner, awakened by the uproar, sat yawning on her couch, beginning to understand why this man was a born leader. Gary Mitchell hauled a sleepy Kelso to his feet.

"Polish your Scout knife, Lee. Jim's leading us into the deep woods again."

Spock, meanwhile, far from nonexistent for all Parneb's concern, was visiting family in Boston.

Chapter Five

PARNEB HAD BEEN correct in one thing: his was a skill founded not on science, but upon the shifting sands of sorcery. His only too-fallible psychic ability, running counterclock and imprecisely at the best of times, augmented by the not-quite-understood power of an amorphous uncut alien crystal, was prone to error.

And as every jeweler knows, the most perfect of crystals possesses its hidden flaws. One perfect plane of Parneb's stone had brought four human wayfarers to his bosom in the nick of time. The minuscule asymmetry of another had cast their Vulcan comrade ashore simultaneously, but half a world away.

Unlike his crewmates in their Egyptian crypt, Spock had the advantage of coming to himself beneath a clear night sky. There was no disputing the logic of the stars, which stated unequivocally that the world they overarched was Earth. The logic of where was clear at once. The logic of how and why was irreducible under present circumstances. The logic of when was a function of the latter two and, on the whole, the least credible even upon proof.

What was to any Vulcan's disadvantage, Spock acknowledged at once, emptying brackish water out of his boots and his now totally useless communicator, was to find oneself in the middle of a frost-rimmed New England salt marsh during the Northern Hemisphere's quixotic autumn.

Vulcans, as a rule, do not subscribe to something as immeasurable as serendipity, and Garamet Jen-Saunor would not coin her phrase about coincidence for another two centuries. Yet there was no logical explanation for whatever placed Spock within a night's walk—at least at a Vulcan's measured, untiring pace—of one of the few places on Earth he would recognize even in a prior century.

He had not examined this world extensively during his years as a cadet, preferring the self-contained intellectual cloister of the Sciences Division of Starfleet Academy. Not until he was science officer aboard Chris Pike's *Enterprise* had he taken rare advantage of some leave time to place himself "on loan" to the Massachusetts Institute of Technology for participation in a botany project requiring the services of a Class A-7 computer expert.

In addition, he had visited the Boston Museum. And Boston had a significance to his family history shared by no other of his species. One of his mother's ancestors had made his home here in his last years. Among the many threads of oral history woven into the colorful fabric of the child Spock's memory was the tale of Professor Jeremy Grayson.

"He was my great-great-great-grandfather," Amanda had told her son, cherishing that small, somber, eager face turned up toward hers like a flower to the sun, craving knowledge as if it were life itself. Amanda had had to explain the periods of human generations to a child of so long-lived a species, as well as the vagueness of human genealogy as compared to the complexity of the Vulcan. Spock had listened, rapt and silent as always when an elder spoke, but most especially with his mother. "Jeremy Grayson was in a sense our first ancestor, because he is as far back as we can trace the line. Records were lost on Earth during the wars, and people with the same last name need not have been related. He was a remarkable man, an unshakable pacifist. He survived Khan's war, was responsible for saving countless refugees, was imprisoned and tortured. When he was very old he lived quietly in an old frame house in Boston. People came to him from everywhere, seeking him out through some underground network—strays and vagabonds, poets and pacifists, philosophers and dreamers. They were rewarded with a hot meal, clean sheets, and no questions asked. . . ."

Professor Grayson's house had not been Spock's original destination. Had he been *when* he thought himself to be as well as *where,* the logical course would have been to report immediately to Starfleet and wait for them to provide transportation. A touch of the door chime of the first household encountered beyond the salt marsh in Earth's virtually crime-free twenty-third century would have earned him instant access, the use of the householder's private comm screen, and an automated aircar dispatched from Comm Central to whisk him to the Admiralty to report on his misadventure, no matter how improbable.

But Spock's awareness that all was not as it should be began a scant few meters beyond the salt marsh, and was reinforced by everything he observed before retreating from the major highway he had chosen as his original path to seek shelter from human eyes in the shadows of off road trees. The scarcity of dwellings, the uniform antiquity of the vehicles that passed him, the strains of two-century-old pop music Dopplering from them in their haste, the absence of the weather shields erected over most of this inhospitably cold, damp, rainy, humid, muggy corner of Earth during his century

226

confirmed the improbable. The discarded small-town newspaper with the day's date blown across his path as he skirted the hamlet where it was still run off on hundred-year-old presses was unnecessary.

Spock evaluated his situation, and acted in the only logical manner open to him. Foremost, he must conceal himself from a world that did not yet know of his existence; then he must consider what, if anything, to do next.

He secreted the communicator in one of his boots for possible later use, detached the Starfleet insignia from his gold uniform tunic and buried it in the soil beneath a drift of leaves, tore a strip from the hem of that tunic to bind around his brow and conceal his problematical ears. With a Vulcan's innate time sense and unerring sense of direction he triangulated off the stars, and set out for Boston by the least populated route.

He covered the distance in half the time a human might, though the chill in the air lessened his efficiency. A roadside phone of a kind he recognized from some museum or other provided free access, with a little judicious tampering, to an electronic directory that yielded an address not far from the places Spock had known in another time.

Boston proper was waking to a brisk October morning when a chilled-to-the-bone stranger trod a mossy brick walk between overgrown privet hedges and touched an antique brass knocker whose nameplate bore the simple legend: Grayson.

Spock possessed no physical description of his ancestor, expected perhaps a wizened, enfeebled old man, shrunk into the shell of his former self as humans tended to be in old age. The human who answered his knock was nothing like this. He was powerfully built, much as Sarek was, and in fact taller in a shambling, stoop-shouldered way. Spock found he must look up to meet the eyes beneath tangled thickets of eyebrows in that craggy face, and those eyes were the pellucid blue of Amanda's.

"Yes?" the human inquired not unkindly, in a voice that by reason of its resonance might have originated somewhere in the vicinity of his toes. His heavy eyebrows were raised whimsically. "What can I do you for?"

"Professor Grayson?" Spock began tentatively, wondering what those clear blue eyes made of the alien apparition on his doorstep. "I do not wish to intrude, but I have been told you offer assistance to those in need . . ."

"Of course, son, of course!" Grayson said at once, offering a stranger access to his hearth and home with a sweeping gesture. "You certainly look like you could use a square meal, and you're hardly dressed for the weather. Come in!"

Only Grayson's walk betrayed his age, or some misfortune suffered long before age; he leaned heavily on a stout oak cane and shuffled painfully, listing precariously to one side.

("His legs were crushed during his imprisonment and never healed properly," Amanda had said. "When he was released, there were several attempts at corrective surgery, but one leg remained shorter than the other, and as he grew older . . .")

Spock, following his slow progress at a respectful distance down a long hall opening into several cosy, book-filled rooms leading to the kitchen, noted the small velvet skullcap Grayson wore on the back of his thinning gray hair and wondered at its significance. As if sensing that curious gaze on the back of his head, Grayson stopped, shifted the cane to his other hand, and felt for the object of that curiosity, removing it and looking at it as if he'd never seen it before.

"Senile dementia!" he chided himself. "I forgot to take it off. Don't mind me, son; at my age the memory isn't what it was. My wife passed away a year ago; the unveiling was yesterday. Afraid I've been sitting up feeling sorry for myself ever since." He gestured Spock ahead of him into the warm, bright kitchen. "Come, sit down. I'll make coffee."

The clutter on the kitchen table suggested that considerable coffee had already been drunk there, no doubt by an old man alone and beset by memory. Spock recalled all that he knew of human mourning customs and wished he had not come here.

"I did not know," he said simply. "Professor, I apologize for the intrusion. No doubt you wish to be alone at this time . . ."

"Probably the worst thing for me." Grayson hooked his cane over the back of a chair and braced himself against the sink so he could clear away the dishes without having to move too much. As an afterthought he stuffed the *yarmulke* in his sweater pocket. "Lord knows, Dora and I had forty-two years together. Gratitude seems more appropriate to that than mourning. Doubtless there's a Yiddish proverb for it; Dora would know, but I'm only an honorary Jew for having married her." He fussed with the coffeepot, shook off his contemplative mood. "Well, son, what's your pleasure? Bacon and eggs or something simpler?"

Spock sat at the kitchen table, though he had not intended to eat.

"I do not require sustenance, Professor. My need is only for shelter for a time. I will provide for myself in all other—"

"Nonsense!" Grayson would hear none of it. "You've got 'trouble' written all over your face, and trouble can't afford to stand on ceremony. It is an interesting face, by the way. Love to know the ethnic mix that went into creating you!"

Indeed, Spock thought. Grayson seemed to take his silence for apprehension.

"Sorry, son. Sixty years in the refugee business, and

you think I'd know enough not to ask nosy questions. Breakfast, then. Are there any dietary restrictions I should know about? Allergies, that kind of thing? My last customer was a Hindu poet who drove me nuts with straining at gnats, literally, but you—"

"I am vegetarian," Spock stated simply, hoping it would not prove a difficulty.

"Ah!" Grayson nodded. "That's easy. Some orange juice, a little old-fashioned oatmeal. I'm not the greatest cook, but I do well with the simple things."

He puttered while Spock watched, fascinated by the literal mundanity of miracle. By no logic that he understood could he have expected to find himself in the presence of an ancestor several generations removed, and in such ordinary domestic circumstances.

"There are a few necessary questions," Grayson said, dishing up oatmeal generous with raisins and cinnamon and joining his guest at the table with a great deal of shuffling and scraping of chairs. "I don't need to know the specifics of why you've come here. If you got my name through any of my regular contacts, I can assume your difficulty falls into certain benign categories. But I do have to know this: you're not running because you've killed someone, are you?"

"No, sir, I am not."

"Didn't think so." Grayson nodded. "The other thing is, I'll need a name for you. Doesn't have to be your real name, but I can't keep calling you 'son,' can I?"

In fact, you can, Spock thought. More legitimately than you will ever know! He considered what name he might give.

"I am called Spock," he said at last. Truth might prove difficult, but it was logical.

"Do you have a first name, Mr. Spock, or can't you tell me that?" Grayson asked, then interrupted himself before Spock could answer. "Spock—unusual name.

230

There was a Spock in the last century—a pacifist long before it was fashionable, one of the forerunners of the United Earth movement, and considered a crackpot for his troubles. Dr. Benjamin Spock. You wouldn't be related to him?" He took Spock's silence as negation. "Didn't think so. Lord, your generation probably doesn't even know who he was. *Sic transit gloria mundi!*"

"*Sed magna est veritas, et praevalebit,*" Spock replied without thinking; it was Amanda who had taught him Latin. He regretted his words instantly; Grayson was staring at him, a spoonful of oatmeal poised halfway to his mouth.

"I didn't think anyone knew Latin anymore," he said, studying his guest anew. "You're quite an enigma, Mr. Spock." He put down the spoon and pounded the table suddenly, startling his guest. "But it's not going to work!"

"Sir?" Spock's apprehension was tangible this time. Was it possible Grayson had penetrated his crude disguise?

"This last-name business," Grayson was saying. " 'Mr. Spock. Professor Grayson.' No sir. You're to call me Jeremy, understand? And I think I'll call you Ben, in honor of my predecessor. Any problems with that?"

"You may call me whatever you wish, Professor," Spock said formally. "But with all due respect, I cannot readily address one of your years in so informal a manner. Where I come from, the father image holds much meaning, and is worthy of great respect."

Grayson shook his head, bemused, went back to his oatmeal.

"Wherever you come from, they sure know how to rear the next generation," he said warmly. "Whatever suits you, Ben. I want you to feel as much at home as you can. Now eat that while it's hot."

* * *

In a terrorist bunker somewhere between Europe and Asia, a grubby hand yanked a translation out of a jury-rigged decoder.

"Wake Easter and tell him I got something," the one named Aghan grunted, kicking his companion's boot sole to get her attention. "Tell him I translated the Kiev bug. It's about spacemen!"

"Tell him yourself!" she snarled. She had her weapons dismantled and the parts spread over the stained and sagging couch; he'd knocked the recharger out of her hand and she had to crawl under the furniture to retrieve it, pushing her stringy blond hair out of her face. *"Verfluchte* cockroach! Spacemen!"

"I'm telling you!" Aghan grinned manically. He was called Aghan because it meant "November" where he came from, because he'd been a part of the Twelve November Uprising and rumor had it he bathed only once a year in honor of the rebellion. "I been bugging Kiev and Posnan Newscenters for months. Everybody laughs at me. 'Nothing ever happens in those backwaters,' everybody says. Even Easter laughs. Now I got something to show him. It took me a day and a half to translate this, but I got something. Something we could sell to a lot of people. Spacemen landing in the ocean. That's what the fat girl was telling Mariya Yevchenkova before she got cut off."

"Then she's as crazy as you are!" the blonde snarled, sliding the pressure bolt on her automatic back and forth with an ominous click.

"I'll tell Easter myself," Aghan said importantly, wiping his nose on the sleeve of his fatigues as if that made him more presentable. He headed for the one room in the bunker with a door that closed. "If he can't use it, maybe Racher will. Racher always pays."

Aghan's computer tampering was child's play compared to what was going on in the sub-basement of a data storage complex in Alexandria.

232

"Lucky I knew about this place," Jim Kirk remarked, hovering over Lee Kelso's shoulder, watching Kelso ply the keyboard as if he had all the time in the world. "I've spent some wonderful hours in the museum down the road. Lee?"

"Working on it, Captain," Kelso reported, unperturbed.

Kirk rubbed his hands nervously, forced himself not to pace lest he come within range of the security cameras. He was calmness itself compared to Parneb who, having traded his turban and *djellaba* for clothing more suitable to night stalking, stood tearing at his sparse hair in his distress. Elizabeth Dehner needed no tricorder to know that his pulse was running amok.

"Come on, baby!" Kelso coaxed the computer. "You can override that, sure you can! Atta girl!"

Footsteps down the supposedly deserted corridors made all but Kelso jump, but it was only Mitchell, checking up on the security guards he'd put out of commission to get them in here.

"Sleeping like babies," he reported. "And I managed to temporarily kill the cameras from here to one of the underground exits. They're on a timer, though. More than ten minutes and they'll trigger an alarm at police HQ."

"Come on, Lee, hurry!" Kirk urged futilely; Kelso the hacker was not to be hurried.

Parneb watched in utter amazement. The ease with which these future sorcerers had breached the most advanced security system this century could produce both delighted and frightened him.

"Gentlemen, if you please! If we are caught—"

"Don't sweat it," Mitchell reassured him. "We're the ones who'd have to face the music. You can always disappear."

"Here we go, people!" Kelso announced, punching one final button with a flourish.

Three separate printers went into simultaneous chattering action around the room. As each one completed its contribution to the creation of four sets of false identities to cover four displaced time travelers, Kelso scurried from printer to printer retrieving his creations, gleeful as a child.

Parneb had told Kirk everything he knew about the agrostations, AeroNav, the way things worked in this century. Kirk had taken it from there.

"We've got to get to the Vulcans. We'll need all our training, all our skills, to pass ourselves off as doctors, lawyers, Indian chiefs—whatever it takes to get to where they're being held."

"What then, Captain?" Elizabeth Dehner had wanted to know, questioning the end if not the means.

"That depends on what we find when we get there," Kirk replied grimly, holding contact with those cool gray eyes, for emphasis. "Humans are humans; they can't have changed that radically from our time. We'll need you to read the situation, recommend the solution least traumatic to all parties concerned. I know it's vague . . ."

"Understood, Captain." Dehner nodded, glad to have some part in the escapade at last. No one would know how much the thought of that responsibility frightened her. "As Mr. Mitchell would say—piece of cake!"

Kirk smiled faintly, admiring her cool.

"It's best if we split up," he instructed his troops. "We'll literally be scattered around the globe in order to do what we have to do. I don't need to remind any of you of the Prime Directive, of how essential it is that we do nothing to change the course of history."

"That means hands off the girls, Mitch!" Kelso had quipped, and Mitchell had just looked pained. Kirk ignored them both.

"We'll keep in communication constantly and arrange a rendezvous once we're all in place. We will also monitor what's going on around us. Any indication that the common man is getting wind of this thing, and what his response is. Parneb, we'll need currency from several regions and in several denominations, credit cards, travel accommodations . . ."

"Malesh!" Parneb sighed. "I would not be Egyptian if I did not have certain—connections. I will do what I can."

He had vanished into the twilight, returning with the necessities and a car to take them to Alexandria. On the road, Kirk had outlined to Kelso exactly what he wanted in the way of IDs. Getting past the guards had been almost too easy, and Kelso had gone right to work.

"All set!" he announced now, collating and distributing his works of art as they came out of the printers. "Each of you will find a set of identity papers, letters of reference, degrees and/or credentials where applicable, an updated planet-wide passport, and sundry other items. Captain . . ."

He handed Jim Kirk the first set.

"Colonel James T. Kirk, Ground Forces Intelligence, Americas Base. Thought I'd let you keep your real name; you'll have enough else on your mind," Kelso explained. "Besides, it's a cover name, and the average intell-agent changes that every other Tuesday, so I've left your file open in case you need to change it. All you do"—he demonstrated—"is stick your ID into any computer of this type—even an automated bank teller'll do it—punch in this code, which I trust you'll commit to memory, and the new name. I've laid in three backup files so you can be up to three other people.

"Now," he went on, leaving Kirk to marvel at the authentic look of his forgeries. "Mitch, I had a little fun with yours. 'Comrade Engineer Jerzy Miklovcik . . .'"

"'Assigned Gdansk Shipyards, Strategies Div,'" Mitchell read. "Very impressive, Lee. I like these."

"And you'll find a standing-orders file in the machine that you can alter for anywhere on the globe, using the same procedure as the captain," Kelso pointed out a little smugly.

"These are all fictitious?" Kirk wanted to know, fingering his papers thoughtfully before secreting them in various jacket pockets.

"All except our lady psychiatrist," Kelso explained. "We agree the PentaKrem probably wants a shrink to give the Vulcans a going-over, and whoever they pick is going to have to be pretty thoroughly vetted. So I tried to find a real shrink who was security-cleared and at least temporarily out of reach. That's what took me so long. However . . ."

He handed Dehner her papers with a flourish.

"Dr. Sally Bellero, former Assistant Head of Psychiatry at University Hospital, Marsbase, presently on leave of absence in her home town of Tezqan, Peru. There really is such a person stationed on Marsbase, and as luck would have it she's written several papers on space psychology and the parameters of possible alien intelligence. I figure even if they question your credentials, the turnaround from Mars is over two weeks on conventional radio this century, so that buys you some time."

"What about friends, relatives, people in Tezqan who might recognize me?" Dehner wondered, pushing the rest out of her mind for the present, even the ticking away of two weeks before her cover got dangerous.

"Tezqan was leveled by an earthquake ten years ago and has been almost entirely repopulated," Kelso reported. "Your entire family was killed."

"All right." Dehner nodded. Until this moment she'd felt virtually useless. "I can work with that. Thank you, Lee."

"Sure." He grinned, blushing. Beneath the admiring gaze of his immediate fan club, he produced the final set of papers. "Lastly, for me—I couldn't resist this one: Technician Howard 'Studs' Carter, member STEM Local 583 Itinerant, out of Hollywood, California."

"What's STEM?" Kirk asked, bemused.

"Stuntmen's, Technicians', Electricians' and Mediatricians' Union, of course," Kelso said. "Exploits all of my known talents and some of my unknown ones and gives me, shall we say, lots of 'lee'-way?"

No one so much as groaned.

"Lee, you're a genius!" Kirk said.

"I know," Kelso said modestly, erasing the menu he'd created from scratch, reinstating the overrides so that no one from this century would be able to detect any tampering.

"All right," Kirk said, ready for action. "Gary, how much time left on the cameras?"

"Minute and a half, Jim," Mitchell said calmly. "We can make it, if we hustle."

They hustled.

"Spacemen," Easter said. "You got the tape?"

Aghan showed it to him with a leer. "Already decoded."

Easter thought about it. He was a slow thinker, an odd trait in a terrorist, but in a century where his kind was ostensibly obsolete, Easter was an odd kind of terrorist.

He had chosen his code name after a rebellion of the previous century, one of countless gravemarkers in a grudge war twelve hundred years in the solving. One peculiar outcome of the Eugenics Wars was to get England at last out of Ireland, barely in time for both to become mutually cooperative pieces in the jigsaw puzzle that was United Earth. The final generation of IRA guerrillas, bred to street fighting and not much else from the time they could stand, had suddenly found themselves out of a job.

Their grandchildren held college degrees and meaningful jobs and a broader perspective on matters politic, but there were always throwbacks, and Easter was one of them. Spiky-haired, underground-pale, living on chips and Guinness and overdoses of sweets, crooning "A Nation Once Again" in his exaggerated brogue without ever understanding that its words no longer had meaning—where he found no war, Easter created his own.

He and his kind lived in a past that had never existed, created an edge to live on, a need to be hunted through the fetid undergrounds where they functioned best; it lent some spurious visceral energy to their emptiness. Easter and his motley band—Red, the stringy-haired blonde whose heroes were Abu Nidal and the Red Brigades, Aghan the greasy November soldier, and others scattered globe-wide to foment and instigate, and their arch-enemy and sometime-ally Racher, whose name meant Venger, a hardcore survivalist who would have them all dead, but only after they'd helped him destroy his enemies, who were most of mankind— had killed and maimed and laid waste without ever being so much as captured. For one like Easter whose every waking moment was a death wish, this was its own kind of agony.

"What's t'use of it, then?" he asked at last, after he'd mulled over Aghan's news until Aghan had begun to doze. "Spacemen. So what? Was it an invasion, I could see. We'd sit back and let 'em do the killin' for us. But two, y'said? What's t'use of it, then?"

"You are thick!" Aghan despaired. "Hostages. Trade-offs for whatever we want, or else we waste 'em. Then more spacemen come to avenge them. There's your invasion. A jihad to end them all."

Easter thought that over for a long time, too.

"How we gonter find 'em?" he asked at last. "If t'ship was gonter take 'em away, they could take 'em anywheres."

Aghan waited for him to finish his thought. Irish were as thick as legend. When Easter had run out of his simple syllables, Aghan spoke a single word: "Media."

Easter looked at him blankly. "Come again?"

"Slip this"—Aghan fondled the tape of Comrade Mediaperson Mariya Yevchenkova's conversation with her niece—" to some 'investigative reporter' for a rival service. Say the bleeding-heart North-Ams. They do the legwork, we follow in their footsteps. They get headlines, we get the spacemen."

Easter thought about it some more, tilted his chair back until his feet were crossed on the tabletop and he was staring at the damp on the ceiling. Six feet of reinforced thermoconcrete and twenty feet of earth separated him from the sky. He hadn't seen the sun in over a year.

He thought, and his thoughts became lurid in their violence. He and his band against the armed forces of Earth, with Racher's people deployed as backup to take as many of them out as possible, perhaps even Racher himself—it was sure death, death in a blur of blood and glory, the thing Easter craved most.

He swung his feet hard onto the concrete floor. Sure death.

"Contact Racher," he told Aghan. "We'll do it."

"Broadcast on the high frequencies only," Kirk instructed his troops, handing Dehner's communicator back to her. "Earth equipment won't be able to pick up that high. Lee, you'll be relatively stationary while the rest of us are moving around, so the others will call in to you at four-hour intervals. As soon as you get set up, contact Parneb and let him know where you are. Use an ordinary telephone or computer link and assume you're being overheard."

"What about you, Captain?" Kelso had not secreted his communicator in his new Earth-style clothes, held it out to Kirk. "You'll be in the greatest danger."

"I'll get your location from Parneb and try to call in whenever I can," Kirk said lamely. His communicator lay somewhere in the blue dust of M-155, a victim of his temper. Any junior officer that careless would have been chewed out for his stupidity, but who was going to chew out the captain? He would pay his own price. "I'll manage."

"It doesn't make sense!" Kelso objected. "I'll be playing around with some of the most sophisticated computer equipment in this century. Want to bet I can't find a way to reach the high frequencies? Besides, like you said, I'll be safe in one spot. Captain—Jim, seriously. Take it."

"I said—" Kirk began tightly, but Mitchell headed him off at the pass.

"Take the damn communicator, James," he said pleasantly. "We don't have time for heroics."

Kirk acquiesced.

"Thank you, Lee," he said humbly, pocketing the communicator.

Parneb drove them to the airport.

"I shall not rest, my friends, until you have all returned safely," he said sadly, clasping each of their hands in turn, Dehner's last. "Captain, if there is anything more I can do—"

"We'll be in touch," Kirk promised, thinking: You've done more than enough already!

"Mother, consider," Sorahl observed after Captain Nyere had left them in their well-appointed guest quarters deep within the great ship, away from human eyes and human questions, late into a night when several of those humans, enervated by the day's events, were thinking of sleep. The Vulcans, gifted with greater stamina, however overtaxed, were at least restful. "There is a curious irony to our situation."

T'Lera, Vulcan and commander lost to both her planet and her command, student of life's ironies,

240

considered all that had befallen them and wondered to which of a multiplicity of ironies her son referred.

"Indeed?"

"We have landed our ship in a vast body of water, thence been transported over water to a human-built structure, anchored, I am told, not on Earth but on a coral reef." Sorahl spoke these things with a quiet wonderment at this world's diversity. "From there we have been transported in a small water-borne vessel to within a larger one."

T'Lera said nothing while he finished his thought.

"Mother, we have, quite literally, not yet set foot on Earth!"

Chapter Six

IN THE WINDOWSEAT of a third-floor bedroom of an old frame house in Boston, overlooking a small rain-swept garden where an oak tree and a gingko vied in sprinkling bronze and saffron leaves respectively upon a patch of soggy lawn, Spock considered a worst-case scenario.

Logically, no natural phenomenon with which he was familiar could have caused him to be here; therefore his transport through time and space had been wrought by some manner of intelligence. Without knowing the nature of that intelligence or the reason for its action, Spock's options were limited, his outlook unpromising.

Assuming his companions had not been similarly transported, they would have conducted a Phase One search for him on the surface of M-155, then returned to *Enterprise* before the planet disappeared again. Having no possible way of knowing where further to look for him, they would eventually abandon the search for Spock and move on. As, logically, they should.

If his companions *had* been similarly transported, it was as likely that they were on Earth as that they were not. If they were not, there was nothing to be gained by contemplating where they might be. An intelligence

242

capable of manipulating time and space, yet so capricious as to transport other intelligent beings into the void of space or onto a planet of molten gases was beyond any logic Spock understood. Logic dictated that cruelty, and what humans called evil, were the offspring of ignorance and fear. Superior intellect, having transcended ignorance and fear, could only breed superior morality, or so Spock believed. He had not lived long among humans.

If his companions *were* on Earth, it was improbable that, sequestered as he must remain, they would be able to find him. He must therefore, against all odds, attempt to locate them.

Jeremy Grayson proved instrumental in this.

"Delicate question," the professor said one evening after they'd cleared the supper dishes and set up the chessboard. "How precarious is your financial situation? A temporary problem of liquidity, or are you plain broke?"

"I beg your pardon?" Spock had been pleased to learn that his ancestor held a grand-master rating; it eliminated the need for handicapping.

"Considering the condition in which you turned úp on my doorstep, I'm assuming you have no money," Grayson said bluntly, toying with a rook. "If there's anything you need, don't be coy about it."

What could he possibly require beyond the largess the professor had already provided? Spock wondered. He had food and shelter, his pick of closets full of clothing left by previous boarders, a room of his own, access to Grayson's private library, which literally filled the house to bursting. Grayson never questioned his keeping his head covered at all times, never invaded his privacy or questioned his need to be alone more than in company. If he must remain here indefinitely, surely there were worse prisons.

But as to anything he might need . . .

"There is one thing, Professor. Before I came here, I

was involved in a—project of a sort, with some colleagues. For reasons which I cannot explain, we—lost contact with each other . . ." He did not know how to continue.

"And?" Grayson moved his queen, sat back in his chair. "Check, by the way. You mentioned you were a scientist. Dare I ask what the project was about?"

"I regret I cannot tell you that, Professor." Spock rescued his king with a tricky knight-led counteroffensive. "Check."

"No problem." Grayson found himself seriously threatened for the first time in the game. "Didn't think you could. But you lost contact with the others, and?"

"I have reason to believe they may be in some danger," Spock explained carefully. "And since they will have no way of knowing where I am, I must communicate with them without attracting undue attention from—certain quarters."

"That should be easy." Grayson fiddled with his queen, a mischievous gleam in his clear blue eyes. "We can run an ad in the Personals." He moved. "Check and mate, Ben. Game for another?"

Spock reset the board.

Somewhere between the recipes and advice to the lovelorn, between agricultural reports and columns on pet care, the following evening's "newspapers"—broadcast to the home screen by a global media service for those who'd rather read their news than hear it—carried this terse notice:

> Kirk, James T.:
> Awaiting your command.
> Spock c/o Grayson/Boston.

"It'll run indefinitely on both the local and the global wire services until I tell them to pull it," Grayson said, wondering who this Kirk might be to inspire such loyalty from the likes of Spock.

"Doubtless the cost may prove prohibitive . . ." Spock knew something of the human obsession with profit.

"Not a dime," Grayson assured him. "Put your mind to rest on that score, Ben. I'm still owed a few favors out there."

All that remained for Spock to do was a thing most Vulcans excelled in: he waited.

At no time did he venture beyond the confines of the professor's house or garden. He made himself useful, doing whatever manner of housekeeping and repairs had been long neglected by a damaged old man. Despite Grayson's insistence that he need do nothing more than indulge him in a nightly game of chess, Spock cleaned the house from attic to cellar, raked leaves, climbed the precariously slanted gambrel roof to patch its leaks, completed the task of cataloging his thousands of books which the professor had begun years ago but left unfinished following the death of his wife. In all his activities, Spock was silent, unobtrusive, and for the most part lost in thought.

Others came and went through the professor's life—a daughter who Spock knew would be his great-aunt —and any number of friends and associates of every stripe who called or visited, often filling the parlor with stories and debate long into the night. Though it would have gratified his curiosity to attend these gatherings, Spock refrained, remaining in his room whenever Grayson had so much as a single other visitor, his sharp ears enabling him to partake of the conversation vicariously. He dared not do otherwise; there was too much at stake.

As he performed his household chores, Spock formulated a plan. With the professor's permission, he would remain with Grayson for one Earth year. If his companions did not find him in that amount of time, he would seek a more permanent place of concealment. Earth had deserts where no human could live. Spock was a desert creature born and bred; he would survive.

He did not permit himself to dwell upon the arduousness, the solitude of such a way of life. He would do what he must. At worst his self-imposed exile would last for an additional nineteen years, until the first arrival of Vulcans within the Earth system. Would it constitute a violation of the Prime Directive to reveal himself to his own kind and explain what had transpired? Even if it were not, and he were permitted to return to Vulcan with those rescued by the Earth ship *Amity,* what dispostion would be made of him on a planet where he had not yet been born?

The convolutions of such logic might drive a human mad. Spock had not the luxury of madness. He would do what he must; he had no choice.

Alone in what passed for a fleabag hotel somewhere on the west coast of the Americas, Jim Kirk wrote until his hand cramped:

"Captain's Log: No Stardate. Stardates will not exist for another forty-two years. If what we are attempting to do fails, they won't exist at all—at least on Earth.

"My people are all in place, awaiting further orders. Those with communicators have kept in constant contact with me. Lee Kelso has left me a commphone extension where he can sometimes be reached; the system is not ideal but is the best that can be managed. Kelso insists he will find a way to hook our communicators into a computer frequency even with this century's primitive technology; I have known Lee Kelso for years and believe he can do almost anything, but I am dubious about this.

"Dr. Dehner reports she has settled in comfortably in her new identity as Dr. Bellero, and has even set up a clinic to treat private patients. Despite her initial concerns, her arrival in Tezqan has not aroused suspicion. In many respects this century is infinitely easier to work in than our own.

"Mitchell has fitted in well at Gdansk, gaining access in ways I don't want to know about to AeroNav files on shipping routes and code-classified activities. He spends his evenings in waterfront bars telling dirty jokes in Polish and asking merchanters what they think about flying saucers. He has reluctantly agreed to limit his social activities to this much; we don't any of us dare tempt fate in ways that might alter history.

"Gary informs me that the area where the Vulcans were found is under the jurisdiction of AeroNav Command out of Norfolk Island, and has narrowed the number of ships possibly involved in retrieving them to three. Once he learns which of the three is the correct ship—and I have no doubt Gary will accomplish this by whatever sub-rosa means—we will need Kelso's skills as a computer hacker more than ever.

"As for Spock—I dare not allow myself to think about Spock. Our mad friend Parneb seems to think he still exists somehow; I can only attribute this to wishful thinking on Parneb's part, since Spock's nonexistence would be his fault. Nevertheless, something in me refuses to admit the Vulcan is dead or, worse, cannot exist in this version of history. How I would value his logic to help us now!

"Assuming AeroNav procedures to be not unlike that of the United Earth Space Probe Agency that will be its offspring, and which in turn will be the forerunner of the Starfleet in which we serve, the people in charge will be concerned with keeping the Vulcans safe and as far removed from the general public as possible. The only question is: Where?"

"Antarctica?" Jason Nyere repeated. It wasn't as if he hadn't heard it. "Commodore—"

"You have a problem with that, Captain?" the stolid face on the comm screen inquired. It was a paper-pusher's face, a bland, impersonal, just-following-orders face, and it was frowning disapproval at him. Jason Nyere seldom gave Command trouble; it didn't expect it from him now.

"You bet I do, sir! I have a problem with this entire scenario. If you people would take into consideration—"

"That's too bad, Captain. Are you requesting we relieve you?"

Nyere felt the blood pounding in his temples with the effort to stay calm. "Absolutely not, sir. I'm simply requesting—"

"Very well. Then I suggest you get under way at once. You will proceed beneath the pack ice to the old Byrd Research Complex. Once you've got your—detainees—secured, you will be joined by several wingboats. They'll be bringing some people in, and your crew—except for you and your first—out."

So that was the way of it! Jason thought. Take away my crew so I can't budge my ship until whatever little top-secret charade has been acted out to everyone else's satisfaction. Nyere leaned into the screen, trying to read his superior's mind.

"What 'people,' Commodore?"

"Not at liberty to tell you that yet, Captain. You're due at Byrd by 0800 Thursday. You will not break radio silence until then."

"Sir!" Jason cut across his attempt to terminate. "Commodore, goddammit, either I'm told the next move or by God I don't play! I want to know how many 'people' and from where—military, civilian, intelligence, who? None of you has had the courtesy to so much as speak directly to the individuals I am detaining here—with their complete consent and cooperation, Commodore; I'll remind you of that—"

"I have your report here, Nyere. Don't get snappish with me!"

"And another thing, sir!" Jason's slow, even temper was fired now. "Has it occurred to anyone in charge that these are citizens of another world, and that their government might not take kindly to the manner in which they are being treated—"

"That will be all, Captain!" The commodore's voice was shaky, as if he'd been sitting up all night with an itchy trigger finger contemplating exactly that. "You will radio Norfolk from Byrd upon your arrival. Out!"

Jason looked an apology at T'Lera, who had been listening out of range of the screen as Nyere felt she had a right to do, regulations or Melody Sawyer's temper tantrums notwithstanding.

"I'm sorry!" he said quietly. "But you see what I'm up against."

"I quite understand, Captain." T'Lera considered how her superior—the deskbound, planetbound Prefect T'Saaf—would respond, for all her training in logic and diversity, to a like situation. "This place where you are to detain us . . ."

Now that the screen was off, Nyere could dab the sweat off his face.

"Byrd is a polar research center, built and then abandoned in the Nineties, in possibly the coldest, remotest place on God's green Earth. The people who pay my salary would have me put you, literally, on ice."

"Captain?"

Jason chuckled quietly. He'd visited the Vulcan commander daily in her quarters in the six days Command had kept them waiting for a reply, had seen to it that she had ready access to him at all times provided she let him know in advance so he could clear the corridors. He found her remarkably easy to talk to despite the constant need to clarify the idiom, had stressed this ease of communication most emphatically in trying to get Command to stop hiding behind its cloud of jingoistic paranoia and confront the reality of Vulcans.

Vulcans, Jason mused. Pity their name for themselves transliterated so closely to the name of one of Earth's less popular ancient gods—crippled iron forger, hurler of lightning bolts. Surely that sort of subliminal silliness wasn't what was affecting the people who made the decisions for this planet?

I'm a ship's captain, not a shrink, Jason Nyere reminded himself. I haven't the foggiest idea what goes on in those people's heads. But I read this lady with the fancy ears loud and clear. She charts a straight course, and she's yare. Nyere found himself chuckling again. If nothing else, these mood swings had him marked for an early grave.

"One thing I am going to see to," he assured T'Lera, "is that whoever gets off those wingboats does not bunk on my ship. Let them keep each other warm inside Byrd; the main structure's little more than a glorified quonset hut, and I wouldn't vouch for the plumbing. The more uncomfortable they feel, the sooner they'll give up and go home. Then it will be my privilege to show you and your son my ship's true hospitality, instead of keeping you under wraps like criminals. Who knows, maybe I can strong-arm Melody into giving you tennis lessons!"

T'Lera understood that this last was meant as irony. Sawyer's general disaffection, her barely concealed fury at being shut out while T'Lera was let in to hear the comm from Norfolk Command (though doubtless she'd tapped in from her quarters; in a calculated oversight, Nyere had not forbidden it), her inability to be within ten feet of either Vulcan without, in Jason's words, "starting something," were sore points with the captain. He'd expected this kind of small-mindedness from his superiors, but with Melody turned on him he felt like he was getting it from all sides.

"Captain to First," he spoke into the intercom, not waiting for her to acknowledge; he knew she was listening. "Sawyer, inform the crew we will be under way in one half hour."

"Destination?" Sawyer asked, pure as the driven snow.

"Don't believe it's necessary for me to repeat what you already know," Captain Nyere said tightly. Did he read bemusement, or at least appreciation, in those steady laser eyes beneath their perpetually quizzical brows?

"Laying in a course for Byrd now," Sawyer shot back.

"Acknowledged." Jason kept it succinct. "Is Yoshi back yet?"

"Affirmative, suh! Aboard this past hour."

"Very well. Inform him and Tatya they'll be taking a little vacation."

True to his word, Yoshi had returned at dusk on the first day of the Vulcans' voluntary exile. He brought further bad news.

"It's the wilt!" he cried, finding Tatya in Sorahl's quarters, deep in conversation. He showed them both the dispirited-looking clump of kelp he'd brought back. "Beats me how, but it's got us. Half the north quadrant's affected."

Sorahl examined the kelp thoughtfully, mindful of everything he had learned of Earth's flora from his departed teachers.

"It appears to be a fungal infection," he observed. "What preventive methods do ploy?"

"None," Yoshi lamented. "And there's no known cure, either. The stuff doesn't respond to anything we zap it with, and we don't even know what causes it. A mutation, some little surprise left over from the last century's pollutants—we haven't a clue."

"The only thing we can do is slash and burn," Tatya said remotely. Forty-eight hours ago she might have shared Yoshi's despair; now little things like losing their entire harvest seemed somehow unimportant. "Although once it's gotten to more than 10 percent of the crop even that doesn't usually work."

"Well, I'm sure as hell going to try!" Yoshi declared. "Jason's got to let me back out tomorrow. Has he said anything about what they're going to do with us?"

"He sent a report to AeroNav Command," Tatya told him. "He's waiting for them to reply."

"Hell'll freeze over!" Yoshi plunked himself on Sorahl's bunk beside the young Vulcan, who was still studying the kelp, turning it over and over in his sensitive hands. "You're looking at our entire year's crop down the drain, my friend. And the experts say, if this thing can't be stopped it could put a serious dent in food production."

"Indeed?"

Yoshi nodded. "Some of the hysterical types are even talking famine. Luna has its own hydroponics labs, but Mars is still terraforming; they import all of their food, and it's mostly processed—kelp, algae, soybeans. If they can't get enough, they'll have to requisition our reserves or come home. At least, that's the worst of it. Anyway, what am I bothering you with this for? You obviously have nothing else on your mind!"

"May I keep this?" Sorahl asked, indicating the weed.

Yoshi found the request surprising. "Sure. Why?"

"I should like to study it," the Vulcan explained. "Captain Nyere informs me the *Delphinus* has a number of research laboratories aboard which are not presently in use. If I might have access to certain materials . . ."

"I'll ask him!" Tatya volunteered at once, and there

was a kind of animation in her voice Yoshi hadn't heard since this misadventure began. He wondered what she and Sorahl had found to talk about in his absence, did not like the trend his thoughts were taking and dismissed them. He too had more important things on his mind.

Jason Nyere was only too happy to honor Sorahl's request for a computer terminal and some of the chem lab equipment. Unaware of the rigors of a Vulcan's upbringing, unable to conceive of the limitations imposed upon the body and the spirit by the confines of scoutcraft travel or the mental disciplines mastered to compensate for them, he'd been troubled at having to keep the younger Vulcan a virtual prisoner.

All guest cabins were equipped with vidscreens, of course, and Ensign Moy had been kept busy trotting to the ship's library to fetch requested books and tapes, leaving them outside the visitors' closed doors, but Nyere found this inadequate compensation for denying his charges the freedom of the air. That the young Vulcan had a project to occupy him eased the captain's conscience considerably.

For his part, Sorahl was grateful for the intellectual exercise, but well aware of a more pragmatic concern as well. The unchecked destruction of the kelp would mean personal hardship for Yoshi and Tatya, and inconvenience for all of Earth. Though Sorahl was no biologist by his people's standards, any Vulcan held the equivalent of several science degrees, and there had been a paper published on his world some months ago regarding the treatment of a similar plant disease among the hydroponic farms of Vulcan. If he could apply the same research principles to plant life grown in salt water, Sorahl believed he could find a cure, and a way of repaying his debt to those who had saved his life.

He labored long hours over his research, sometimes

overtaxing the human-built computer at his disposal, sometimes outdistancing it with his mental calculations. Whatever humans decided to do about him and his kind, surely none of them could find fault with what he did here.

One of them did.

"He's good on that computer, Jason," Melody Sawyer remarked. "So good he's got it panting to keep up with him most times. I don't like it!"

"Seems to me you don't like much of anything around here lately." Nyere was using the endless wait for Norfolk Command's reply to catch up on the paperwork he usually ignored until he couldn't find his desk. "What's your beef this time? Or do you simply object to their breathing the same air as you?"

"It just occurred to me"—Melody ignored his sarcasm; it hit too close to the truth—"that this little Merit Badge biology project could be a cover. I don't buy Her Nib's story about them being the only ones out there. For all we know, Junior could be signaling in an entire invasion force right down on our heads."

"Not likely with you bugging him round the clock."

"It's an open computer system, Captain suh. He's gonna buy time on it, I have a right to tap him."

"Tell me, Sawyer, have you bugged the heads, too? Or don't you want to know if they do that the same as us?" Jason didn't wait for her to reply. "Besides, I really don't think he's calling in any big guns at this late date. I understand his grandfather had the opportunity during World War II."

He hadn't told Melody the history of the Vulcan scoutcraft as T'Lera had told it to him as a gesture of openness, told it to her now in yet another attempt to convince her that these people meant no harm. His narrative had the opposite effect. Melody listened slack-jawed, her face gone so white her freckles looked like they'd been painted on.

"Pete's sake!" she said finally, and stormed out.

Jason Nyere returned to his paperwork, seriously considering a request to Norfolk, if they ever got back to him, to have Melody Sawyer transferred off his ship.

Lee Kelso waited for the shift change at Media-Magix, Inc., his current home, before locking himself into a security terminal and keying in the final sequence he'd kept in his head all afternoon. If Mitchell was on time, and if he'd done everything right . . .

Beneath a roar of static and discordant microwave melodies, a laconic, skeptical voice seeped through.

"Mitchell to Kelso, Mitchell to Kelso, do you read? Lee, old buddy, you told me this would work . . . personally I think you're nuts, but I'll play along . . . Mitchell to Kelso."

There was far too much static, and a whine that reminded him of a three-day hangover he'd earned during a hard night on Argelius, but Kelso was inordinately pleased with himself. He tinkered and fine-tuned, letting Mitchell babble on.

"Lee, if you're listening, respond, will you? This is beginning to get very old . . . Seriously, old buddy, you've got another minute or two before I give this up . . . Oh, Le-ee, this is Gary! Hey, sailor, you come here often?"

Kelso made a final adjustment and keyed the answer back.

"Hiya, Mitch. Kelso here. How are things in Glocka-morra and Gdansk and points north and east?" He heard Mitchell's laugh through the static. Old Reliable had struck again. "And they said it couldn't be done!"

"Yeah, well, you did it, all right." Mitchell tried not to sound surprised. "You're actually doing this from a two-hundred-year-old computer terminal?"

"Affirmative."

"The man is amazing!" Mitchell marveled. "Yeah, but listen, old buddy, there's just one thing: I don't want to complain, but from the sound of things you've got a little tinfoil in the radar here . . ."

"Stand by, Mitch, I'm not reading you . . ." Kelso replied, tongue-in-cheek, stripping the static out. "Say again?"

"Never mind!" Mitchell's laughter was clear as a bell this time. "Listen, I'm due to check in with Jim in a few minutes. Anything you want me to tell him?"

"Save you the trouble," Kelso said, tapping in another frequency code. "Let me see if I can rig a conference call." Within moments he had tied in not only Kirk but Elizabeth Dehner as well.

"How long can you keep the four-way open?" Kirk wanted to know, as amazed at Kelso as Mitchell had been.

"As long as I don't get caught," Kelso said.

"Good. We'll need it," Kirk said tersely. Kelso knew what he could do and didn't need to be stroked. "Gary, what have you got?"

"Think I've narrowed it to one ship, Jim. She's the *CSS Delphinus,* classified as an SCC-MultiUse, meaning 'Sub/Carry-Cruiser.' She can go over or under at up to twenty knots, level a city, set up as a floating laboratory, carries enough cargo to feed a family of four for a hundred years . . ."

"Sort of a water-borne *Enterprise,*" Kirk said wistfully, wondering if her captain was anything like a starship's. "I've studied those old multi-use vessels. Incredible machines!"

"Exactly," Mitchell said. "And according to my info, *Delphinus* was diverted from her regular route around the agrostations, ostensibly to pick up a satellite, and has been on radio silence for four days."

"Sounds like she's the one," Kirk said hopefully. "Lee, can you tap a ship at that distance?"

"Sure, if Mitch could just get me some call numbers . . ."

"Have 'em in my back pocket, son."

Kirk left them to themselves and opened his channel to Dehner. "How's it going, doctor?"

"Hanging in here, Captain. Catching up on my reading."

"How's that?"

"I've been reviewing all of the papers and monographs my alter ego has written. Might as well know what I'm talking about if anyone asks me. Besides, I can't say much for the nightlife around here."

"Hey, if you're looking for a little action, doc," Mitchell chimed in, "just you let me know. Nights sure do get cold here in scenic downtown Gdansk. Anything I can do for a change of scenery . . ."

"Leave her alone, Mitch," Kelso griped; he'd had to listen to the two of them bickering all night on their flight out of Alexandria before they changed planes in Central Europe. But Dehner could take care of herself.

"Doesn't your celebrated charm work in Polish, Mr. Mitchell? Or am I the only game in town?"

"Captain said don't get involved with the native women," Mitchell said. Kirk listened, let them have their heads; he was blind—they all were—but he could see their faces, watch their little gestures, decided they needed the interplay, however acrimonious, to take their minds off the waiting, the uncertainty. "I'm just doing my bit to make sure I don't end up as my own great-grandfather."

"Of all the egotistical, irresponsible—"

Kirk could see her tossing her silky hair in her anger, her gray eyes flashing. But enough. He cleared his throat.

"Ladies and gentlemen, as you were!" He let the silence linger long enough for them to pull themselves up to attention. "Now then. Mr. Mitchell, the minute you see that ship so much as blink . . ."

"Got you, Captain. Mitchell out."

"Mr. Kelso?"

"Sir?"

"Keep your ears on. If you can read *Delphinus,* or the Command Center at Norfolk or, better yet, both—"

"Will do, sir."

"Also, check in with Parneb at regular intervals. If anything goes wrong, if you're in any kind of trouble, bail out and get back to Egypt and stay put, understood?"

"Sure thing, Ji—Captain. Last time I talked to him he was still looking for Spock. And he said nothing else about history was changed that he can see. Who knows, maybe—" Kirk said nothing. Kelso had the good grace to take the hint. "Ears on, Captain. Kelso out."

"Doctor," Kirk said at last.

"I'm with you, Captain." She'd been listening to the affection between this man and his old crew, wondered if that was the secret to his command ability—the simple, deep caring for every individual under his command. If that were the case, it must put him through hell every time he lost one. Elizabeth Dehner realized how much she had underestimated this man.

"All I can tell you is, hang on a while longer," he was telling her. "When this thing starts to move, you and I are going to be the front line."

Kirk could see her nod, though he couldn't see her. "Understood, Captain."

Captain Nyere had given Yoshi permission to tend his acreage while they waited. The young agronomist was out at dawn daily, sometimes with a member of *Delphinus*'s crew along to help him cut the infected kelp adrift and set it ablaze, letting the tide carry it away from the healthy weed until it had burned itself out and, presumably, incinerated the kelpwilt with it.

It was a last-ditch effort, primitive and unsanitary, polluting the water with ashy sediment, the air with greasy, roiling smoke that could be seen from the deck of the big ship all along the northern perimeter of the agrostation. Yoshi returned at dusk, bone-weary and covered with soot.

"You *could* help!" he accused Tatya on the third such night, falling across the bunk they shared in utter exhaustion.

Tatya soothed him absently, trying not to show her revulsion at the filth on his clothes, the grimy, smoky smell of him. Sorahl, when he permitted her to get that close to him, smelled like new-mown grass, or leaves in autumn, or something she'd left behind on the mainland and had a sudden nostalgia for.

"Jason would never let us both out at the same time," she reasoned, though in truth she'd never bothered to ask him. "And I don't dare leave the Vulcans. I trust Jason, but not Command. Someone has to keep watch. And I've been helping Sorahl in the lab."

"Oh, I'll bet you have!"

Tatya was genuinely startled by his vehemence, if not a little guilty. She and Yoshi had never formalized their relationship, had never needed to. They'd simply stayed together. Neither had ever been jealous; there'd never been any reason. Before.

"What the hell is that supposed to mean?" Tatya yelled, her anger edged with guilt and consequently exaggerated. *"Bozhe moi,* you don't think—?"

But Yoshi lay like a dead man, one long arm flung across his eyes, instantly asleep. Tatya left him alone and went to be with Sorahl.

"He is angry?" the young Vulcan asked, his velvet-dark eyes meeting Tatya's blue ones so steadily she felt herself melting all over. "I do not understand."

"He's jealous!" Tatya said bluntly, taking the used slides from him and popping them into the sterilizer, hoping their hands would touch. "He thinks I'm in love with you."

The young Vulcan knew the word, knew theoretically what it meant in human terms, but did not understand its coexistence with jealousy.

"Are you?" he asked with such absolute naiveté that Tatya dropped several slides.

"Of course not!" she lied, retrieving them from the floor and tossing her heavy braids back over her shoulders. The fact that I fantasize about you constantly, she thought—waking, sleeping, alone or with you, even when I'm making love with Yoshi—has nothing to do with anything!

"That is good," Sorahl said, without being able to tell her any of the myriad Vulcan reasons why this was so. "I owe Yoshi my life. I should not wish him to be angry."

Yoshi soon had more than enough to make him angry.

"Who's going to look after my farm?" he demanded when Jason told him they'd be under way for Antarctica within the hour. He'd come straight in from the burning —dirtier than usual, his hands blistered, his mood precarious. What Jason was telling him made the past six days meaningless. "I couldn't leave this close to harvest at the best of times. Now, with the wilt—gods, Jace, I could come back and find the whole crop gone!"

"Can't be helped, son," Jason said. "I thought we agreed the disposition of the Vulcans was of primary importance? And I have my orders."

"Screw your orders!" Yoshi shouted, completely out of character. He never shouted, never found anything to make him that angry. He seemed to be angry all the time now, and it frightened him.

Worse, after his argument with Tatya, what he'd really wanted to say was "screw the Vulcans." He, of all people, who a scant few days ago was ready to do anything to protect them—what was happening to him? Yoshi found a place of calm.

"At least let me call my contractors," he asked. "They can get someone in to replace us, at least continue the burning."

"I can't break radio silence; you know that," Jason said gently. Tatya, Sawyer, and now Yoshi would be furious with him. It seemed only the Vulcans understood what he was trying to do. "We can't wait that long. I'm sorry!"

"You're sorry?" There were tears of rage in Yoshi's eyes. "My crops, my farm, my whole life—and you say you're *sorry?* Who knows how long they'll keep us down there, or what they'll do to us? Who knows what's going to happen to any of us, even you? Sorry doesn't do it anymore, Jason!"

"I've been contacted, Captain!" Elizabeth Dehner sounded almost excited. "Two faceless, sexless characters buzzed their way into my flat at four in the morning, with sealed orders from the United Earth Council 'requesting' I pack enough heavy clothing for a week to ten days and report to the wingboat basin in Lima. And to make sure I tell no one, they've bugged my phone and there's a spook in an unmarked car at the end of the street."

"You know what to do?" Kirk instinctively lowered his voice, as if they could be overheard even with communicators.

"I think so." Dehner's voice was as cool as ever, but did he only imagine a slight tremor at the ends of her words? "I'm to go along. Mingle freely with the other medical personnel, do exactly what's expected of me, and try to report in to you at four-hour intervals."

"I'll follow you," Kirk promised. "As soon as Mitchell lets me know where." As if on cue, his incoming beeped. "Good luck, doctor. Kirk out." He switched frequencies. "Gary?"

"*Delphinus* is moving out, Jim. Heading south-

southeast, making twelve to fifteen knots in the general direction of the Ross Ice Shelf, Antarctica. Last I heard from Kelso he was going to have a tap on them by his next call-in."

"How long since you've talked to him?" Kirk wanted to know.

"Little over four hours," Mitchell said. "He said he might have to do some moving around. Some people wondering why he was logging so much overtime."

It didn't sound good. Kelso was resourceful, but not invincible. Not for the first time, Kirk regretted the communicator in his hand.

"Gary," he said ruefully. "When you talk to him, tell him to be careful. Dehner and I have to be moving too. I want you to sit tight until I give the word. If you get in a jam, like I told Lee, get back to Parneb and wait for us. Don't do anything—reckless."

"Who, me? Listen, kid, I'm not the one who's heading for Antarctica. If you need me, just holler, and I'll saddle up the sled dogs."

Kirk laughed in spite of the almost perpetual knot in his stomach. "Are you ever serious?"

"Not if I can avoid it," Mitchell admitted. "But I am now. Take care of yourself, James. I'd never forgive myself if you didn't."

In a furnished "sleeptel" cubicle, the twenty-first century's solution to the problem of cheap residency hotels, overlooking the flat, cookie-cutter scenery of the vast industrial suburb that had once been a state called Ohio, Howard "Studs" Carter a.k.a. Lee Kelso, formerly of MediaMagix/Hollywood, unpacked his very own personal computer, purchased in Canton that afternoon with one of Parneb's credit cards.

There'd been too many questions, too much heat at MediaMagix, and Kelso had quietly skipped town, setting up shop closer to the acres of microwave receptors meandering across Middle America. With a few minor upgrading adjustments, the little beauty at his elbow could be persuaded to eavesdrop on the world.

Kelso tuned the screen to a news program while he tinkered, with the volume so low it reached him only subliminally, until one item in particular almost made him drop his teeth.

". . . responding to an anonymous tip that what was removed from the agrostation was actually the fusilage of a space vessel which may have originated outside the solar system, and which may or may not have contained alien survivors. Spokespersons for AeroNav deny this categorically, and the PentaKrem insists that any connection between the incident and the mission to Alpha Centauri . . ."

Omigod, omigod! Kelso thought, as close to panic as he could come. It would take some more tinkering to get this baby to contact Jim Kirk, but Parneb could be reached by conventional telephone link. Kelso was on the horn to Parneb as fast as his fingers could fly.

"The reports are worse here!" the Egyptian confirmed morosely. "They are going so far as to speculate that the aliens are being held at a secret government installation, that they have at least three heads and are reproducing by cloning even as we speak. Ah, Lee, I am afraid even your century's magicians cannot remedy my mistakes now!"

"Don't let it get you down," Kelso consoled him, though he was feeling less than optimistic himself. "The more hysterical the rumors, the easier they'll be to laugh at later."

"Unless someone is harmed by them!" Parneb lamented. "In my experience, Lee, hysteria does not sit at home and brood. It takes to the streets in search of a scapegoat."

"There are ways we can plug the leaks." Kelso was

thinking aloud, eyeing his little computer. "If we could find out who the hell started them in the first place . . ."

" 'Tis cold," Easter observed in his lugubrious way. "Antarctica."

"Ja, so?" the other inquired in his clipped, metallic tones. "You are afraid of a little cold?"

Gray was Racher's color—gray skin stretched taut across a gray skull face, gray close-cropped hair, gray gunmetal eyes that glinted and clicked in their sockets rather than blinking like normal eyes, gray metal-on-metal voice. Legend had it Racher was more bionic than flesh, that his throat had been shot out or burned out or even ripped out and replaced with a robotic voice box, that other body parts had met similar metal-and-plastic fates. Easter, watching those eyes roll and click at him on the commscreen, could well believe it.

"I ain't afraid o'nothin'!" Easter retorted, having thought it through thoroughly. It was a lie. Death he did not fear, at least not his definition of it—death immediate in a flash of heat and fire with nothing to follow or, at worst, a hell of further fire. But death by cold—slow, creeping, numbing, Dantesque—that was fear. "I done my share. T'reporters is eating it out of our hands. And I said yez could have any of me people."

"But not you?" Racher's metallic sneer transmitted across a hemisphere from his base somewhere in Africa. "Easter keeps his rear covered while we freeze ours? *Nicht so*. You come with, coward, or there is nothing!"

"Who yer calling a coward?" Easter spluttered, then stopped.

Slowly it penetrated his brain that Racher intended exactly what he'd had in mind, the real reason behind this caper that made the capturing of spacemen secondary—a desolation of polar ice as the perfect arena for their true purpose, the elimination of the other for supremacy over the global terrorist ratpack. Only one King Rat would emerge from such a show-down. The white-on-white nihilism sparked some rem-nant of Irish heroic poetry buried deep in the detritus of Easter's murderer's soul.

"Listen, yer lousy scut." He chose his words careful-ly, for all their seeming rage. "I'll beat yer there!"

"Ever wonder about the others out there, Ben?" Jeremy Grayson asked his many-times-great-grandson.

Spock finished drying the dinner dishes, meticulously folded the dishtowel. " 'Others,' Professor?"

"I've never known quite what to call them," Grayson said, setting out his pawns. " 'Aliens' sounds like a slur somehow, and 'extra-terrestrials' is so ethnocentric. The Others, then. The intelligent beings on all those other worlds out there."

Spock sat carefully opposite his ancestor. Their nightly conversations had covered a variety of philo-sophical and speculative topics, but never this one. Was this some manner of test?

"Do you believe unequivocally that they exist, Pro-fessor?"

Grayson found that amusing. "You mean do I really think humans are all there is? A perfect God would hardly be so easily content. Oh, I believe in them, Ben. I only wonder if they believe in us."

He palmed a pawn of each color for Spock to choose from; his eye quicker than any human hand, Spock chose the black.

"I am not certain I understand."

"It occurred to me"—Grayson opened with a stan-dard knight gambit—"that they've probably been out there watching us for years, and if they aren't weeping, they're probably killing themselves laughing."

Spock considered the actual history of "alien" observation of Earth as he contemplated an unusual bishop defense. "I must confess, Professor, that I have never considered the question in quite that way."

"Captain's Personal Log, Day Six; Location: Aero-Nav Wingboat hangar, Staten Island, Tierra del Fuego:

"I wait with the other intelligence personnel in what passes for the VIP lounge of this desolate great barn in this more desolate corner of the world. Our destination: a place that gives new meaning to the word 'desolation': Byrd Research Complex, on the inland edge of the Ross Ice Shelf, Antarctica.

"My intelligence credentials have passed all inspections thus far, making it possible for me to infiltrate the system with remarkable ease. Special Commendation, Lee Kelso, appended. My fellow intell-agents are predictably featureless; even those obviously traveling in pairs do not speak to each other. At the opposite end of the lounge, a select group of civilians seems to be enjoying themselves a lot more.

"Dr. Dehner or, should I say, Dr. Bellero, has gone on ahead with the first boatload of military and medical personnel. She, at least, left knowing what she had to do. I only wish my mission were as clear.

"I have the virtually impossible task of seeking out two Vulcans, stranded on an ambivalent Earth twenty years before their appointed time, and somehow persuading them to trust me to extricate them from their velvet-lined captivity, lest they fall prey to human fear or permit themselves to be 'lost' in a bureaucratic gulag from which there may be no return.

"The only Vulcan I knew to speak to invariably rubbed me the wrong way without trying, and I am forced now to admit that most of the fault was mine, my insistence on trying to make him over in a human image, which simply cannot, and should not, be done. If only I had been able to understand that, we might never have been caught in Parneb's machinery at all, and if Spock is lost, as Parneb believes he is, it is my responsibility, and mine alone. A Vulcan is not a human with pointed ears; he is a Vulcan, with all of the difference and similarity this implies. I have learned this too late. How much more difficult will it be for humans of this century to understand; how ironic that it falls to me to make them see it!

"As for what I am to do about the human witnesses to this event—the logistics of escape are child's play by comparison. As for my only other contact with Vulcans, the celebrated Vulcanian Expedition . . ."

Jim Kirk stopped jotting in his notepad, aware that at least one other intell-agent was pretending not to watch him behind dark glasses. This compulsion to record his thoughts was a blatant threat to his cover, and Jim Kirk cursed himself for a fool. When the boarding announcement came, he stopped in the lavatory, first incinerating his notes, then flushing the ashes. Taking his seat in the wingboat, he continued his log entry in his head.

The Vulcanian Expedition. Its very misname was evidence of a fiasco masquerading as a serious mission.

According to official statements, the convergence of four starships in orbit around the dry red planet was intended primarily as a show of unity to impress the empires. That it also served to remind the Vulcan Council of the scarcity of Vulcan nationals in Starfleet was purely coincidental.

The Articles of Federation clearly stated that every member planet was to provide a certain percentage of its population for service to the UFP. Vulcan had no objection to that, had in fact been one of the major proponents of the article, and her scientists and students provided far beyond the quota of volunteers for research and exploration, as well as such inglorious tasks as clearing brush and planting crops on colony planets. But certain other Federation members, Tellar in particular, found this inequitable. Vulcans should serve in Starfleet in equal numbers as well, they maintained. Why should humanoids take the brunt of combat missions while Vulcans raised flowers and gave seminars on safe outplanets? By what right did Vulcan waive a military draft, leaving Starfleet service only to those who wished it? Thus the Vulcanian Expedition.

The outcome was the commissioning of the starship *Intrepid,* built and manned entirely by Vulcans, the only starship in the Fleet never to fire its phasers against a living being. Rumor had it the phaser tubes were sealed, the torpedo bays empty, but any Vulcan would assert that this was illogical. The weapons' existence did not necessitate their use.

It was a logical response to a no-win challenge. Starfleet chose to view it as a compromise, a concession on the part of the Vulcans, and the four starships left orbit with a feeling of relief. Vulcan considered *Intrepid* neither compromise nor concession, but a statement of logical purpose—a shipful of scientists without a single combatant aboard. Vulcans would indeed participate in Starfleet, but only according to their own convictions.

Starfleet's concession was to send *Intrepid* solely on research missions, leaving potential combat situations to those who had manned them before. Tellar lodged an official protest, but this was not unexpected.

And a generation of young Starfleet officers could tell their grandchildren that they'd been to Vulcan, though it wasn't entirely true.

The *Republic* had been one of the starships sent to flex its muscles over Vulcan, and her navigator, one James T. Kirk, was one such participant in the expedition who never set foot on the planet. Unneeded at his post once they were in orbit, he'd been drafted as a glorified security guard, shepherding diplomats to and from transporter rooms, getting no closer to the world itself than Vulcan Space Central, the vast orbiting space station, over a thousand years old, with its red-draped walls and torrid temperatures. He'd managed to keep his nose clean—how not, on a world with no words for the concept of a barroom brawl?—and never once spoke directly to a Vulcan, had to be content with snatches of conversation overheard in corridors to give him some vague notion of who these beings were. What he had or had not learned would not help him now.

Jim Kirk watched as the wingboat lifted off from the frigid waters off Tierra del Fuego and soared over an expanse of gray whitecapped sea on its way to Antarctica.

If only Spock were here! he thought, not for the first time, but for a different reason. I don't know if I can do this alone!

Lee Kelso yawned, stretched, checked the time. Captain Kirk would still be in transit to Byrd; there was no way to contact him until he arrived and probably it was just as well. Better to save him a few hours' grief over these news leaks.

There was nothing else to do tonight except possibly key down and get some sleep. Kelso had barely turned off the lights in his cubicle and wished his trusty little computer pleasant dreams when the door buzzer sounded.

Kelso frowned, half sat up, remembered the cubicle's low ceiling just in time. He'd left a wake-up call at the front desk, but that wasn't for another four hours. Unless the buzzer was defective, or whoever it was had the wrong cubicle . . .

It buzzed again. Uh-oh, Kelso thought. This has to be trouble. He looked around the tiny cul-de-sac, as if there were any means of escape. Bracing himself for just about anything, he leaned against the entrance door and yawned.

"Yes?"

A baleful eye met his through the peephole. "Mr. Howard Carter?"

Definitely trouble, Kelso thought, scanning the room to make sure he'd left nothing incriminating lying around. "Who wants to know?"

A badge replaced the eye at the peephole. Comm-Police, here to question him on suspicion of tampering, using computer time without paying for it. "We'd like to talk to you."

Kelso laughed inwardly. If they had any idea what else he'd been up to . . .

Opening the door slowly, looking like nothing so much as a sleepy small boy standing there in his skivvies, Kelso was inclined to be philosophical. They'd have caught him eventually; it had only been a matter of time.

Chapter Seven

WITH JASON NYERE at her right hand and her son at her left, T'Lera of Vulcan faced a United Earth and attempted to answer its questions. Among the representatives of the military, intelligence, and several diplomatic and peace organizations, Jim Kirk listened, and marveled.

He did not know what preparation the Vulcan commander had made for this ordeal, only knew from her answers and her unflagging patience that she was prepared. He could not know that her transit here in the big ship that lay now with its conning tower thrust up through the pack ice like some fantastical city mushroomed overnight in the wilderness, had been spent kneeling in meditation on the unyielding metal deck of her guest cabin deep in the belly of the Whale, letting its vibrations subsume her body and enter her very soul.

Another Vulcan might have found the unrelenting noise of this human-built behemoth unbearable as it plowed its inexorable way first over, then under, a cold dark Earthsea where dwelt creatures so seeming-alien most humans would be utterly repulsed by them, carrying far from the reach of most humans two not so alien that those humans could not accept them, given the chance. But T'Lera had lived in motion most of her days, and however strident this pounding, thrumming machine noise compared to the lissome slipstreaming of ship through silent space, it was as much a part of her as her own heartbeat.

A human's heartbeat, loud and slow and strong; in close proximity these past days T'Lera's acute ears had heard such hearts pulsing urgently, all but engulfing the soft swift susurration of her own. Thus this ship, slow and loud and strong, traversed an ocean that had engulfed the silent swiftness of her craft. Thus this species—loud of voice, slow to reason, strong by virtue of its numbers—sought to exile the silent swiftness of her and her son in a living desolation of cold white Earth, where she had sought the peace of death in cold black space. Overlong contemplation of such ironies could threaten even a Vulcan's mastery. T'Lera had moved her thoughts elsewhere.

Father, she had thought, addressing Savar's *Katra* not in prayer but as a kind of focus. Father, my logic is uncertain where Earthmen are concerned. Were it for myself alone I would know what to do. But for my son . . .

A hundred years' observation of Earthmen indicated that they had evolved enough not to kill indiscriminately but only when they perceived themselves threatened. If they had considered T'Lera and her son a threat, the task of executing them would have fallen to Jason Nyere from the beginning. Had he hesitated, the one named Sawyer would have only too willingly fulfilled the duty he refused; it needed no telepathy to read this in her eyes. Not death, then, but some other fate, awaited outworlders on this world. What price would Earthmen exact for what they obviously considered an act of trespass?

Were aliens stranded on her world, T'Lera knew,

they would be provided unquestioningly with a ship to return to their own. Could humans be made to see the logic of this? Or did they still disbelieve that Vulcans presented no danger? If neither death nor freedom, what alternative was there?

Delphinus's destination provided its own answer: exile in a place no Vulcan could escape unaided, but exile of what duration? The young human female seemed convinced her leaders were capable of 'losing' two unwanted visitors. Would they be left alone in this wasteland of ice or, perhaps more humanely—the word was Earth origin, derived from Earthmen's name for themselves—would they be provided with some less inhospitable cage which was a cage nevertheless?

For herself T'Lera would accept this, but not for her son. Whatever she could bargain for Sorahl's safe return to their world, up to and including the limits of a Vulcan's honor, she would give.

Would they free Sorahl if she agreed to remain as surety, possibly for life? She whom no planet could contain would be no more an exile on Earth than anywhere else. She who as a growing child had remained awake for the first half of the twenty-year journey while the adults rotated in two-year cycles through cryogenic suspension, knew what it was like to be alone.

That she might never again share a Vulcan's thoughts with a kindred soul might have given her pause. Surely there were humans with whom she could hold such discourse—Jason Nyere had the potential to be such a one—but the powers who would decide for her life would make certain she never encountered them. Yet she who had lost her soul's companion in the death of T'Syra could endure this as well. And if a Vulcan's mourning belonged to the realm of solitude, what opportunity would she have to mourn those she had lost!

Let permanent exile be her fate, then. She might only request a desert less frigid than the one for which the ship was bound.

This for herself, but not for Sorahl. The time would come when he must return to Vulcan, for reasons no Earthman could comprehend. She must find a way to return her son to their world, by ten-year voyage in a sublight Earth vessel if need be, and alone, but this was what she must do.

The only alternative, that which she had attempted in the destruction of her ship, might no longer be available to her once she was Earth's hostage.

The noise of the great ship surrounding her had increased then, became a grinding, crushing ferocity as *Delphinus* pushed its way upward through the polar ice as Captain Nyere had told her it would do. The engines had stopped, the noise ceased. They had arrived. All was silence, and the swift susurration of a Vulcan heart.

Holding the inquiry into the Vulcan Problem in the big cold dining hall at Byrd had been deliberate, intended to impress the panelists with their own importance, if not the Vulcans. The high-domed room, entirely surrounded by armed Ground Forces sentries (two deep in places, not counting the snipers on the roofs of the auxiliary buildings), dwarfed its fewer than two dozen inhabitants, transformed their voices into echoes and their breath into vapor in the inadequate heat. Jim Kirk's feet were cold through boots and heavy socks; he wondered how the Vulcans could stand it.

The medical team had seen them first, submitting them to a battery of tests that took up the entire first day. They'd been poked and prodded physically and psychically until medical personnel had arrived at the satisfactory conclusion that they were what they claimed to be.

"They've put them through so much!" Dr. Bellero,

née Dehner, lamented to Kirk when they could snatch some surreptitious time together. Officially, when they passed in the halls or sat on the same inquiry panel, they did not know each other. "Most of it's legitimate, but some of it's downright silly, not to mention humiliating. I'm embarrassed for them, Captain, and for us!"

"Stay with it, doctor," was all Kirk could tell her. "And hold on to your files. You're our best hope for containment there. How'd they do on the psych tests?"

Dehner smiled her wistful, crooked smile at him.

"Flying colors, of course. I'm doing my best to spoon-feed the results to my 'superiors.' Can't make them look too brilliant or integrated. And I've glossed over the scary stuff—the self-healing and the telepathy. No sense making them seem too different."

"Good," Kirk said, half listening. His primary concern since he'd gotten here had been the search for a way out. Considering the heavy artillery, there didn't seem to be any. "What's the feeling among the rest of the medical people?"

"The internist walked away shaking his head," Dehner said wryly. "He's been holed up in his cabin ever since, probably on a bender. He doesn't like finding hearts where livers should be; I think it shook him rather badly. The neurologist was a lot more sympathetic. She was the one who suggested reconstructive surgery for T'Lera, if they could risk transfusions from Sorahl."

"What did T'Lera say to that?" Kirk wanted to know, expecting a typical Vulcan response.

"She was very appreciative, but she 'questioned whether the aesthetic merits outweighed the risk to the physician of losing a patient.' Unquote."

Kirk smiled. "Meaning she'd rather have a broken nose than a posthumous malpractice suit."

"Smart lady," Dehner said, and they went their separate ways.

* * *

275

Elizabeth Dehner managed to sit in on all of the inquiry panels even when she wasn't required, citing "professional curiosity." Whenever Kirk sought her out at the other end of the L-shaped table, she made eye contact and gave him a vague little shrug.

The arrangement of the tables had also been designed to impress, if not intimidate. The interrogators, anywhere from ten to fifteen of them at any given session, sat at two long tables arranged in a chevron, bracketing and slightly higher than the single table provided for the Vulcans and their human sponsors. Jason Nyere had appeared steadfastly at every session, but the two civilians who had rescued the Vulcans, after repeating their story for about the sixth time, were no longer there. The young woman Tatya had burst into tears at the previous session, and on the recommendation of Dr. Bellero, she and her male companion had been escorted back to the ship.

The questioning had continued throughout the second day, with the Vulcans the only ones showing no signs of stress or fatigue. Sorahl answered only those questions put directly to him. As commander, T'Lera answered everything else, no matter how aggressively phrased or how often repeated—calmly, rationally, and with an almost embarrassing honesty.

"So you're saying in essence that there will be no search parties, no one to come looking for you?" one of the military types—a three-star general who, from the embittered look of him, had spent his life in a futile search for a war to fight—demanded.

"That is correct," T'Lera replied evenly. "Once gone to ground, a craft is considered lost. There will be no attempt at search or rescue."

Jim Kirk winced. Did she have any idea how vulnerable that made her and her son?

"That's strictly on your say-so," the general said belligerently. He held an expensive gold pen in his hand despite the recorders, used it more as a bayonet than to take notes. He had it pointed at T'Lera now.

"I beg your pardon, General?"

"All we have is your word that your people won't launch a search or worse," the general said loudly. "I'd ask you to prove that."

T'Lera seemed momentarily taken aback, as if she'd forgotten that this species could lie, did lie, had in some contexts—the military among them—elevated the lie to an art form, and would thus assume that she was lying without concrete proof to the contrary.

"You *have* my word," she said slowly, precisely. On her world it would have been enough. "Could you raise my ship from the ocean floor, you would find it carried no weapons, nor did any of my crew. And surely your planetary defenses have detected no additional vessels within your system?"

The general had the good grace to look embarrassed at that. All the defense systems around Earth, Luna, and Mars had been on a full-scale alert since the crash, had detected nothing as big as a flea amid the clutter of satellites and space debris of Earth origin.

Score one for the Vulcans! Jim Kirk thought as the delegation's chairperson banged her gavel to settle the murmurs in the big room. It was bleak comfort, Kirk thought, chafing at the endlessness of the proceedings, and what he saw as no escape. None of this should be happening, and the further it spread, the more impossible his task became.

"Now, as I understand it"—the general had apparently recovered himself sufficiently to continue his line of questioning—"you've had ships out there observing us since 1943, you say?"

"The first mission to your world arrived 102.4 Earth years ago," T'Lera explained for the fifth time. "If that is how you number your years, the answer is yes."

"So you were orbiting up there spying on us all that

time," the general began, but T'Lera could not allow his misconception to go uncorrected.

"I resist the term 'spying,' General. Our purpose was nothing more than to observe a world which has been studying other worlds since the time of your scientist Galileo. If you consider this an invasion of your privacy, I must ask forgiveness for my people. But since your radio telescopes have been 'eavesdropping' on other star systems since—"

"That is not the point!" the general bellowed, and the murmurs broke out again. The chairperson hammered them into silence, but not before Jason Nyere, T'Lera's long-suffering right-hand man, began to chuckle.

"You find something amusing in all this, Captain?" the general demanded hotly, glaring the chairperson's gavel into silence in midair.

"Sorry, General. Must be battle fatigue," Nyere replied. "It just seems to me the lady's got a point. If we had the technology, we'd be doing the same thing— what the hell else did we send a ship to Alpha Centauri for?—and with a lot less grace about it than these people have shown."

"Suggest if you're that tired you put in for a few hours of R and R, Captain," the general advised humorlessly, ignoring everything else Nyere had said. The internecine war between AeroNav and Ground Forces had its roots in navy vs. marines and probably went back to the time of the Caesars; it would hardly be resolved here and now.

Worse, the pacifist contingent, relegated to the lower ends of the tables and not permitted to approach the Vulcans informally, had taken to Nyere from the beginning and applauded him now. Jim Kirk, in his intell-agent guise, wished he could do the same; he had great respect for the burly ship's captain, considered him a worthy antecedent and a potential ally, possibly the only one in the room.

The general, aware of Nyere's growing popularity, was hardly about to yield the floor to him and a bunch of peaceniks. He tapped the table with his gold pen until he had everyone's attention, then jabbed it toward T'Lera again.

"You mean to tell me your people sat out two of our world wars and did nothing?"

"Correct," T'Lera acknowledged. She had restrained the intensity of her far-searching eyes these two days, mindful of their effect on every human she'd encountered save Jason Nyere. Now she permitted those burning laser points some of their intensity and directed it at the general. "What would you have had us do, General?"

"Well, if you're as damned peaceful as you claim"— the general lost himself momentarily, feeling the heat of T'Lera's eyes but not yet knowing its source—"why didn't you intervene somehow? Stop the wars, prevent all those millions from being killed?"

The general's face had gone an alarming color and he was breathing hard. T'Lera chose her next words carefully, knowing they would condemn her and her kind in the eyes of many in this room.

"I regret I must point out, General, that our Prime Directive precluded the role of avenging angel. It was our duty, however unpleasant, to permit you to make your own mistakes."

There were murmurs from all sides at this. Some of the pacifists seemed to be wavering, a few of the intell-agents nodded knowingly, drawing from T'Lera's statement conclusions that no one who wasn't an intell-agent could fathom, and Jim Kirk found himself thinking uncomfortably of the Vulcanian Expedition.

". . . one of the most callous, inhumane attitudes I have ever . . ." the general was saying, and by the time the delegation's chairperson restored order he was totally out of breath. Jim Kirk seized the moment.

"The chair recognizes Colonel Kirk."

"Commander T'Lera," he began as heads turned; he had not spoken at all yet, and most of the factions had no idea who he was.

"Colonel Kirk," the Vulcan acknowledged.

This is it! Kirk thought. "Commander, if you were in charge of this situation, how would you resolve it?"

The question brought the entire oversized room to an uneasy standstill, silenced the ill-mannered mumbling from the diplomats' quarter, caused the military types to straighten in their seats and the intell-agents to lean forward in theirs, silenced the very echoes in the corners. Above and outside, the sentries could be heard changing shifts in the frigid air, boots scraping, automatics clicking.

"Colonel Kirk." T'Lera spoke undaunted into that silence. "I would not presume to dictate policy to those who know your people far better than I—"

Damned Vulcan hair-splitting obsession with protocol! Jim Kirk steamed, wishing she'd just answer the question.

"Let me put it to you another way, Commander." He had to clear his throat to hear himself. "If you and your son were free to leave this room, what would you do?"

The silence became a startled, angry murmur, through which the general's stage whisper to an aide carried like cannon.

"Who is that man? I want his credentials! Who the hell does he think he—"

Whatever answer T'Lera might have given was lost in the groundswell and in the tumult that followed.

The abrupt sound of wingboats, twice the number that had brought the delegation here, punctuated the icy stillness outside. Sentries could be heard running across the pack ice; two of them, flanking a Ground Forces lieutenant, burst into the room. The lieutenant whispered something urgently in Captain Nyere's ear, and he and the Vulcans were escorted abruptly out of the room.

The chairperson sought futilely for order. Kirk found himself pushing through the delegation, all of whom were on their feet trying to get past the sentries who were blocking all the exits.

Something's happened, Kirk thought. Something outside, up north, in the rest of the world. Something bad. Gary, Lee, my people—

"You did *what!*" Jason Nyere's voice shook with anger, and he had begun to sweat again.

Messages had been streaming across the comm screen for over an hour, messages from Norfolk Command, from Ground Forces Central and the PentaKrem. Someone had leaked a news story about alien invaders being held incommunicado somewhere in Antarctica, and it was all over the media. Every major information source carried some version of it, from the mildest hearsay to the most fantastical eyewitness account, and any number øf reporters and thrill seekers were chartering transportation to go and see for themselves. Unless they were stopped on the shores—and the legal ramifications of that were mind-boggling—they could be on the ice within hours, and those perceptive enough to guess at Byrd could be here within a day or two.

It was why Jason and the Vulcans had been so unceremoniously pulled out of the inquiry; it was why everyone still inside Byrd was running around like chickens wondering what to do next. It was why Melody Sawyer finally broke down and told Jason about Tatya's aunt in Kiev.

"You did what?" Jason repeated, looking down at Tatya, who had collapsed all in a heap on the carpet in his quarters, crying again. It seemed all she'd done for the past two days had been cry for one reason or another.

"I thought if people knew it would help," Tatya blubbered. She looked up at Jason tearfully. "When Melody cut in, I did what she told me. I told Tante Mariya not to break the story. She wouldn't have, without my telling her. Someone else must have overheard. I only wanted to help!"

"Oh, you helped, all right!" Sawyer spat at her from where she stood guard at the door, ready to cave in the skull of the first Ground Forces flunky who so much as set big toe across the threshold. This was a family problem, and she would see it stayed in the family. The whole family was here, too—she and Jason, Yoshi and Tatya, and—and the other two. Whatever happened, it would happen inside this room. "You fixed it so the brass have to make the media out as liars no matter what. And if they have to kill your friends here in order to kill the stories—"

"Goddammit to hell, Sawyer!" Jason roared, knocking his chair over and advancing on her; Melody had never seen him so angry. "You! You've been sitting on this for how long? Why the hell didn't you tell me?"

Melody pulled herself up so straight she was trembling.

"Assumed the situation was contained and no need to trouble you, suh!" she barked. "I heard her retract her story and assumed the aunt bought it, and—" She broke, came as close as she could to apologizing. "Hell, Jason, I thought—"

"That's always been your trouble, Sawyer!" Jason spluttered. "How many times do I have to tell you—don't *think!*"

T'Lera passed a look to her son, a look that said simply: Do you still question that it is not yet time? Sorahl hung his head, wished only to return to his makeshift laboratory and his research, away from this human turmoil that gave him cause to question everything he believed.

"It's done now," Jason Nyere said helplessly, his anger gone, replaced by a great weariness.

"What's going to happen to us?" Yoshi seemed perpetually bewildered, got up from where he'd had his arm around Tatya, left her to dry her own tears. "Jason?"

"Ground Forces will probably evacuate their people and whoever else is willing to be 'wiped' and returned home," the captain said. "I think we can be sure it's their intention not to be here if any reporters get through the security cordon. As for the rest of us . . ."

All nonmilitary personnel in the dining hall were escorted back to their quarters until such time as Ground Forces decided who was to go and who would be allowed to stay. Rumors about the media leaks grew more ominous with repetition. What had started out as a few individuals' concern over a stray flying saucer was beginning to sound like an Earth-wide panic. From the white-on-white perspective at Byrd, there was no telling what was truth anymore.

Jim Kirk had been among the first to return to his room voluntarily. Now he sat on his bunk and slapped his communicator shut with a grimace, hiding it in a secret compartment in his luggage. Broadcasting for too long was dangerous even on the high frequencies, and he hadn't been able to reach Mitchell or Kelso. Lee had warned him there might be too much interference this close to the Pole. Not only that, he couldn't even get through to Dehner, who was caught up in the chaos with the rest of the medical personnel. Deaf, blind, and on his own, Jim Kirk decided it was time to act.

He retrieved his communicator, slipped it into a pocket, and replaced the intell-agent ID in his wallet with one of Kelso's backups, which he'd had the presence of mind to activate before he left Tierra del Fuego.

Taking advantage of the confusion still reigning in the corridors among those who balked at leaving, Jim Kirk blended in with the pacifist contingent, blessing Lee Kelso for his ingenuity and offering a silent prayer of thanksgiving to John Gill for his lecture on the Dove Society.

"An anomaly," the noted historian had called it in his lectures on pre-Federation history at the Academy. "Possibly the first time in human history that the intelligence community stopped looking upon pacifists as the enemy and joined with them in preserving the unity of Earth. The society endured for over a century, until the Romulan Wars focused intelligence attention outward against a new enemy . . ."

Collector of esoterica even then, a certain eager young plebe had absorbed every shred of information he could find on the Dove Society, used its techniques and code words in a covert operation, with several fellow victims, in a brief abortive foray against a common enemy of peace in the person of an upper-classman named Finnegan. Their victory had been short-lived and Finnegan's vengeance swift and murderous, but Jim Kirk's memory for useful trivia endured.

To his surprise, the pacifists immediately accepted him as one of their own.

"I had a premonition," their leader confided when she'd secreted him in her cabin with the others, out of Ground Forces' earshot, "when you asked that rather pragmatic question of our unfortunate visitors this afternoon. Pity T'Lera never had a chance to answer it. I presume the 'Colonel' is cover?"

"Naturally." Jim Kirk grinned at her. She was a plump, grandmotherly type, but not impervious to his charm. "It lends me more credibility with the brass-heads. Do you think they'll send us home?"

"They've already told us as much." The pacifists' leader sighed. "We're to be airlifted out, then detained somewhere while they 'wipe' our memories, then dropped on our respective doorsteps as if we'd been away on a skiing weekend. We agreed to those terms from the beginning or they would never have allowed us in. But we'd hoped for a better outcome than this."

"Outcome?" one of her companions demanded. "This is no outcome at all! The military intended all along to 'disappear' these people. The news leak is just a ploy to keep us from speaking to the Vulcans directly!"

"We should have called Grayson in," another said. "They'd have listened to him."

They all began talking at once.

". . . hear he's been ill . . . lost his wife last year . . . wouldn't matter. You don't know Grayson. You're too young to remember, but—"

"We asked for Grayson from the beginning!" their leader finally silenced them in exasperation. "They refused to let us contact him. Obviously he carries too much clout."

"Excuse me," Jim Kirk said, sticking his neck out. "Who is this Grayson?"

They all looked at him, owl-eyed.

"You are rather young," their leader said, eyeing him suspiciously. "And I suppose it has been that long. Jeremy Grayson is professor emeritus of the University of Pacifist Studies at Vancouver, one of the founding members of the United Earth Movement, and a hero of the Third War. Less flamboyant than some of the others, certainly, and he's been in retirement for years, but I would have thought—"

"Of course!" Jim Kirk lied, thinking fast. "He was one of my heroes as a boy. I wasn't sure he was still alive. It seems a little awesome that he'd be the same one. . . ."

They seemed to accept that. Kirk promised himself if he ever got out of this, he'd learn to be a little less glib.

"If you could get in touch with Professor Grayson . . ." he suggested.

"Impossible!" somebody said. "We won't be allowed to communicate with the outside until after we've been 'wiped.' By then we won't remember why we came here, or even *that* we came here."

"But if someone else could?"

"Jeremy would be able to find a sane solution to this; I'm certain of it," the leader said sadly. "And he commands sufficient respect from world leaders to make it stick. But it's too late for that now."

"Maybe not," Jim Kirk said, and reached a decision.

Starfleet's Prime Directive, he reminded himself, precluded interference with any normal culture progressing at its own pace. There were no regulations on the books pertinent to time travel. Ergo the only directive that applied to time travel was the moral obligation not to do anything that would alter the future. He didn't know if his mere presence here had already irrevocably changed history, but now that he was here, he had to do what he could to bring about a peaceful resolution to this crisis.

He whipped his communicator out of his back pocket.

"I have a device here," he began as the assembled pacifists gathered around to get a closer look. "It's highly classified, and I can't tell you how it works, but it's quite possible I can get a message to your Professor Grayson with it. If you can trust me to remain here as your spokesperson . . ."

Before the media had broken the space-aliens story, and before Ground Forces and the PentaKrem sought some legal way to cordon off the entire continent of Antarctica, two small pleasure copters skimmed in low

286

over the floe ice and settled on their pontoons on the seaward edge of the Ross Ice Shelf some five hundred kilometers from Byrd. The individuals who emerged from them, ruffling the feathers of the penguin population with the crash and clank of several snowmobiles sliding down the unloading ramps, were anything but tourists.

"We split up," Racher decreed at once, leaping onto the ice in his arctic fatigues, his face gray against their blinding white, his metal voice whirring and clicking in the frigid air. "You that way, we this. A pincer, with them in the center, so!"

His mittened fist closed like a vise in demonstration.

His people, an even dozen of them—nameless, faceless, sexless, and armed to the teeth—stood in solid ranks behind him to face Easter's ragged crew, Red and Aghan and the only others he could gather on such short notice: Kaze the self-styled ninja and Noir, who was either Rastafarian, born-again Mau Mau, or Avenging Angel of Allah, depending upon the day of the week. The contrast was not lost on Easter, who was immediately on the defensive.

"Says you!" he snarled, coming as close to the armed Racher as he dared, glaring into those unblinking metal eyes. "Think yer God, do yer?"

Aghan rolled his eyes at Red, who ignored him. Their leader was hell-bent on prolonging their stay in the cold with this show of bully-boy arrogance; better to be snug inside the plush, well-heated snowmobiles, gift of an arms dealer experiencing some lean times since Colonel Green's demise and looking for fresh territory.

"Yer don't give me orders!" Easter growled, scuffing his feet against the ice when Racher did not deign to respond. "Hear me?"

"Together we are too visible," Racher stated flatly. "You wish to be captured? Perhaps you do not trust me? Or perhaps you are afraid?"

This earned him a string of curses which he dismissed with an indifferent shrug; even his shoulder joints had a metallic sound. He fondled his small laser rifle and glanced over his shoulder at his troops, who smirked in unison at their leader's cool.

"You are finished?" Racher asked when it looked like Easter had run out of spit. "We split up."

Easter cursed a final time, motioned his lot into their two snowmobiles, though not before Aghan decided to take some target practice at a flock of penguins.

He aimed his automatic and let off a full clip, laughing manically at the splatter of blood and guts and feathers and the prodigality of noise rolling flat out over the ice with nothing to rebound it.

"Lookit, Easter, look!" He danced in delight. "I got me a whole bunch of spacemen!"

Racher spat on the ice. *"Verrückter!"*

His troops in their snowmobiles soon vanished over the horizon, far from already gelid splash of innocent blood, across a landscape of white on white.

White lather foamed in pleasing soft billows against the sides of the shaving mug as Spock stirred it with the badger-hair brush. The brush had given him pause the first time Jeremy Grayson asked him to assist an old man with shaking hands in the ritual of shaving, but Spock considered finally that the badger might not have minded overmuch the honor of offering its small life in service to a fellow creature who had done as much good as Grayson.

"Hate to put you through this rigamarole, Ben," Grayson said as Spock, expertly now, stroked the lather onto his weathered face and began to ply the razor. "I'm probably the last man on Earth who cherishes an old-fashioned barbershop shave. Consider it a point of vanity. I like to look my best even if no one can see me. Does that make sense?"

288

"Of course, Professor," Spock replied. One of such age was permitted his own illogic. "And the 'rigama-role' does not inconvenience me."

Rather, it is something of an honor, Grandfather.

They were in the kitchen again—Jeremy Grayson seemed to live in the kitchen, except when he had visitors—and the vidscreen was just coming up for the early morning news, Grayson's way of "keeping a finger on the pulse of mayhem" as he put it.

"I've decided it may be safe for me to pass on soon," he remarked, watching the screen with the volume down as Spock trimmed his sideburns. "I do believe we've finally gotten over the need to kill each other on a global scale. I'll leave the minor skirmishes to the younger generation. Lord, I do get tired sometimes! Though I may stay around to learn if the *Icarus* mission finds anyone on Alpha Centauri."

Spock wiped the remaining lather off the professor's face in silence. Grayson was scowling at the vidscreen.

"Turn that up a bit, would you, Ben? Your ears are obviously better than mine. This looks like something that may need our attention."

Together they listened to several of the saner versions of the space-aliens story.

"Well, what do you think of that?" Grayson mused.

"Possibly a hoax?" Spock wondered aloud, his mind awhirl with permutations and calculations, none of which made much sense in the abstract. If the stories were true, if there were in fact aliens present on Earth, might their presence be connected with his untimely arrival?

"Maybe, maybe not," Grayson said, pulling himself to his feet and groping for his cane. "But if it's anything like the truth, I have a fair idea the next thing I may have to ask you to do is help me pack a suitcase."

As if by some prearranged signal, the commphone began to beep. Grayson looked at Spock, eyes twinkling beneath their tangled brows. He switched the vidscreen from news to the commphone. Within moments he was conversing with a former student, now head of the Peace Institute in Stockholm.

Shortly Spock would indeed be helping him pack a suitcase.

"Oh, Sally?"

For a sinking moment Kirk thought Elizabeth Dehner would fail to respond to her cover name, but it was only his tone of voice that made her hesitate—a particular tone in the male voice she was too accustomed to ignoring in her role as Elizabeth Dehner. But training got the better of reflex, and she turned to find Jim Kirk standing in the doorway of his cabin, smiling his charming-as-ever smile and crooking his finger at her. When she approached, he grabbed her, pulled her inside, and shut the door.

"Captain, what the hell . . . ?"

" 'Colonel,' if you must call me something. As you were, doctor." Kirk dropped the act immediately, became all business. "Don't jump to conclusions. Unlike Mitchell, I'm concerned with a different sort of—diversionary action."

Dehner seemed visibly relieved. "Sorry."

Kirk dismissed it. "We've got more important things to worry about.

"I want you to do whatever you can to remain here when the others leave," he instructed her. "Up to and including faking an affair with me as a reasonable excuse. We can't take the risk of their moving you somewhere where we can't find you."

Dehner relaxed, sat on Kirk's narrow bunk. "Okay. What do you want me to do?"

"How much do you know about this 'wiping' process?"

"Mandatory reading for any history-of-med course,"

Dehner replied. "Mostly the administering of large doses of meperidine and the neo-dopamines combined with selective hypnosis. Banned during the Mind Control Riots. It's crude by our standards, but effective."

"Could you do it if you had to?" Kirk wanted to know.

Dehner thought about it. "Theoretically, given the right drugs. But I'm not sure if I'd want to—morally, I mean."

Kirk sat beside her on the bunk. "If it meant the difference between this—mess we're in now—and getting history back on course, could you? Morally?"

"I think so," Dehner said after a long moment.

"Good!" Kirk patted her knee fraternally, was on his feet to check the door and the corridor beyond. Satisfied that no one could overhear them, he shut the door and stood with his back to it. "As nerve-racking as all this is, it's working in our favor. The government will make sure everyone who leaves retains no memory of what happened here. That leaves only the people aboard that ship. And you and I, doctor, are going to get aboard that ship."

He told her about his encounter with the pacifists and how he'd managed to contact their Professor Grayson via Stockholm. The pacifists' wingboat had lifted off less than an hour before.

"If Grayson turns up, he'll be one extra factor we'll have to consider," Kirk said grimly. "But I understand he's an old man, and not well. He might not show. We may get lucky. What about the other medical personnel?"

Dehner smiled her wry smile. "They couldn't wait to get out of here. I think they were looking forward to being 'wiped.' Being confronted with anything so different was frightening to them."

"'So different,'" Kirk repeated. "Wonder how they'd cope with some of the *really* different types we've encountered. We forget how parochial we were in these times."

In these times? Dehner thought, but said nothing. Kirk was already off on another tangent.

"You all have had to file reports."

"Right," Dehner confirmed. "They're stored in the computer system down the hall. It's an antique even by today's standards. Took us half a day to figure out how to store things instead of dumping them."

"That's useful," Kirk said, suddenly animated. "See if you can get back into the computer room. Sweet-talk the guards, do whatever you have to. Get into the system and dump whatever you can—your reports, the other medics', anything the other civilian personnel might have entered."

"Is that all?" Dehner asked dryly, already on her feet. "Where will you be?"

"Right here," Kirk promised. "At least until morning. Mitchell hasn't reported in for two days. He may just be moving around, or he could be in trouble."

Watching the Ivory Coast slip rapidly by to his left, Comrade Engineer Jerzy Miklovcik tried not to grin as the captain of the speedcruiser grunted and handed him back his departure orders.

"Beats me why they have to divert an entire ship to transport one engineer to the ends of the Earth," she growled. "What the hell you going to be doing in Antarctica anyway?"

"Building igloos," Gary Mitchell joked in his best Polish accent. "Ours not to question why—correct, Captain?"

She gave him a sour look and went below. Mitchell stood at the rail with the wind ruffling his close-cropped hair and hoped he'd be in time.

Jim Kirk had told him to stay put in Gdansk unless and until he ordered him to come to Byrd. Mitchell was acting against orders, acting on an internal order—an absolute psychic certainty that Jim Kirk would need him soon, if he didn't already. Mitchell had had such flashes of insight with uncanny regularity all his adult life; they rarely misled him. He hoped he was wrong this time, hoped he'd get to Kirk in time to earn a reprimand for disregarding orders over something as harebrained as a "feeling." But, better safe.

Besides, considering what Parneb had told him to look for in the Western Desert on his way here, Jim Kirk should be pleased to see him no matter what.

"Lee's gone to ground and I can't take the time to look for him," Mitchell had told the sorcerer, popping in on him unexpectedly, if it were possible to do that with a true psychic. "It doesn't feel right to me, but right now I've got to get to Jim. I figured if you wanted something useful to do . . ."

"I too have been searching for Mr. Kelso since his last transmission," Parneb announced in an injured tone. "As I continue to search for your Vulcan companion."

"Yeah, well, you keep at it," Mitchell advised, not expecting results on either search, but it kept Parneb out of further mischief. "See you around. I've got a ship to commandeer."

"Mr. Mitchell." Parneb pulled himself up to his full height in an attempt at hauteur; in such a comic-opera figure it was hopeless. "There will never be any love lost between us; I can appreciate that. But there is a larger consideration here, which is why I will tell you one thing: if you chance to be passing over the Western Desert in your travels, you might wish to observe from your window what appears to be an abandoned petrol refinery. It is in fact an installation left over from the Third War . . ."

* * *

Flying over the neatly disguised half-ruined silos in the special AeroNav plane reserved for transporting high-level personnel, and using the on-board computer to cross-reference certain files he'd left open in Gdansk, Gary Mitchell wondered if Parneb was a total bungler after all.

A sudden blizzard waylaid Easter's band less than a hundred kilometers from where they'd started, bringing both snowmobiles to a standstill. Worse, one of them had developed a fuel leak, the result of a stray shot from Aghan's penguin massacre.

"Must have ricocheted and hit the tank," Aghan offered, as if it were nothing.

Even if they siphoned some fuel from the second mobile there might not be enough, and there was no way all five of them, with their weapons, could travel in a single vehicle. Easter sat at the controls and cursed himself hoarse. Red, disgusted, kicked the hatch open and braved the flailing ice storm to huddle in with Noir and Kaze, while Aghan shrugged and went to sleep, oblivious to the rage of his leader and the wind outside.

Meanwhile, Racher's dozen, unstopped by either storm or stupidity, continued on their deadly way.

"You look unwell, Professor," Spock observed, pausing in his task. "Perhaps if I could accompany you . . ."

"Accompany me?" Grayson wheezed, breathless from the preparations and perhaps something more. "Lord, Ben, I almost wish you could go in my place!"

He sat on the bed beside his single battered suitcase as Spock packed it for him in his purposeful, methodical way.

"Quite seriously," Grayson said. "I'd take you if I could. Even send you alone. I don't know what it is about you—maybe it's nothing more than the way you look a person in the eye when he talks to you—but I believe I could trust you with my life. Or any number of lives, for that matter."

There was no logical response to such an accolade. Spock's hands continued their work, folding sweaters and shirts and extra handkerchiefs, while his eyes met his ancestor's blue-eyed gaze in their characteristic steady way.

"But there's a strong chance they'll turn *me* back at the borders," Grayson went on. His breathing was labored, as Spock had never heard it before. "I'm sorry, but I can't risk antagonizing them. They'll have to make their best use of one old man, that's all."

Spock had heard the report from Stockholm, and Grayson had added his knowledge to the journalese still pouring from the vidscreen on the topic. Extrapolating from these scant facts and his knowledge of the time and place and of Vulcan scoutcraft procedure, Spock had come to the disquieting conclusion that the aliens in question were in fact Vulcans.

Their untimely presence must be linked to his own, to the disappearance of his crewmates, to the distortion of present history. Ironic that it was to be his ancestor who attempted to set things right, while he could only stand helplessly by. But if Grayson failed . . .

"Professor, if I may ask"—Spock closed the suitcase, set it near the bedroom door preparatory to bringing it downstairs— "if these are indeed beings from another world, what can be done about them?"

"Oh, they're from another world, all right!" Grayson stated unequivocally, pulling himself off the bed suddenly and rummaging in a bureau drawer for something. "No human would have tolerated the nonsense they have without raising hell. If it rested with me—and that's a rather improbable 'if'—I'd see they got a ship to return to their world and hope to God they can forgive us our immaturity!" He found what he was searching for, a small odd-looking talisman on a tangled silver chain. Grayson proceeded to try untangling it. "Mind

295

you, if you think the powers-that-be are going to take the advice of one decrepit pacifist—here, give me a hand with this, can you?"

The tremor in his hands made him drop the talisman; Spock retrieved it from the floor and examined it curiously.

"Doubt if your generation would know what to make of that little object." Grayson's breath came in shorter gasps now, but his eyes remained untroubled, studying his mysterious lodger under his eyebrows, glinting mischievously.

Spock disentangled the talisman from its chain and studied it. It was a simple thing—a circle enclosing a modified inverted "Y" or perhaps a runic "K"— simple, but of great significance.

"I believe it was commonly called a peace symbol," Spock observed. "Of obscure but possibly ancient origin, first used extensively during the antiwar movements of the 1960s."

Grayson nodded, as if he'd expected Spock to know this much. "It became our symbol in the underground during the Third War—a way of knowing whom we could trust. Now that peace is the majority opinion, the symbol has fallen into disuse. Though if I fail in what I've been asked to do—well, this small thing has gotten me through many a dangerous situation; let's hope it can get me through one more."

He sat heavily on the bed, his breathing growing more and more labored. He seemed to be listening to some inner voice. Spock watched him with growing concern. Unaware that he was doing so, he had untangled the fine silver chain and extricated the talisman; he held it gently, reverently in his hands.

"You have extraordinary hands, Ben, has anyone ever told you that?" Grayson's voice sounded dreamy, far away. "I've watched them do things—strong, deft, accustomed to work, but gentle at the same time . . ."

Those same hands caught Jeremy Grayson and pre-

vented him from falling as he was suddenly taken by
some sort of seizure.

"You are ill," Spock said, steadying him, activating
the alarm on the commphone, which would alert the
nearest hospital. He lifted the old man effortlessly in
his arms and carried him downstairs to await the
ambulance.

"Ben . . ." Grayson gasped, clinging to Spock as if to
life itself. "Benjamin . . . favored son . . ."

He suffered a second seizure, which sent him into
cardiac arrest. Spock laid him out on the living-room
carpet and began CPR, breathing life into him to whom
he owed life.

Mahmoud Gamal al-Parneb Nezaj abandoned his
crystal-gazing with something like despair. Lee Kelso
was nowhere to be found, and whatever hope he'd had
of finding Spock was finally exhausted. Parneb made
himself a pot of mint tea and absently flicked on his
vidscreen. Voices trickled in and out of his consciousness as he waited for the tea to steep.

". . . in major capitals and small villages alike, de-
mands from groups of every political stripe calling for
the aliens to be brought forth and made available for
questioning, if they in fact exist. Meanwhile, planetary
defenses continue on the alert, and countless millions
scan the heavens nightly, waiting with dread for the
appearance of further strangers from the sky . . ."

". . . have gone so far as to suggest that the arrival of
aliens is in fact a reprisal for the launching of the *Icarus*
mission to Alpha Centauri. Spokesmen for the Back to
Earth Movement, at a prayer meeting hastily assembled in Salt Lake City, called for a halt to all further
space exploration, and one source was quoted as saying
there would be nothing morally wrong with abandoning
the *Icarus* in space if this would put an end to the alien
invasion . . ."

". . . eyewitnesses claim that such aliens have landed

before, and have been secretly interbreeding with human stock since the first UFO sightings nearly one hundred years ago . . ."

". . . seventeen people injured when an unidentified person or persons spread the rumor that alien invaders had taken over the airports . . ."

"Oh, dear!" Parneb sighed, stirred his tea, and changed the channel. In a moment of serendipitous coincidence, he found something he'd been searching for for days.

". . . Awaiting your command. Spock . . ."

"Virtually no one suffers from stroke anymore," Jeremy Grayson's daughter told Spock when she arrived at her father's house from the hospital to pick up some necessities. "But the injuries suffered during his imprisonment, and some of the drugs they used . . ."

"How is he?" Spock asked quietly.

"He's not regained consciousness," Grayson's daughter said.

"And the prognosis for his recovery?"

"It's too soon to tell. He's an old man, Mr. Spock, a very tired old man. But it would upset him to think that you were leaving because of this."

"I am needed elsewhere," was all Spock could say. Around his neck, beneath a high-collared shirt, he wore the small peace symbol on its silver chain; he could only hope that it would help him achieve what Jeremy Grayson could not.

"All right," Grayson's daughter said with much of her father's warmth and concern, traits that would someday be characteristic of a certain great-grandniece. "My father spoke very highly of you, Mr. Spock. There were a number of promising young people whom he 'adopted' over the years. I think you might have been among that select group."

"Indeed," Spock said, struggling with something that was very like emotion.

"If you ever need a place to stay . . ."

Spock merely nodded and took his leave of her. The small silver talisman dangled cold and hard against his alien flesh as he set off to do the impossible.

Jeremy Grayson's daughter locked the house behind her and returned to the hospital. Inside the big, empty house the commphone began to beep. It beeped continuously for the rest of the afternoon. Somewhere in Egypt, a sometime sorcerer sipped his mint tea and sighed.

Chapter Eight

JASON NYERE SAT listening to the proposal being made by the bright young peace representative and his psychiatrist friend, and seriously considered mutiny.

He'd been surprised, stepping out of the conning tower for some fresh air and a chance to rejoice in the silence following the departure of the last wingboat, to see these two emerge hand in hand from the main structure at Byrd, stroll across the snow, and casually request permission to come aboard.

"We've refused transport out," Jim Kirk explained once the reintroductions were out of the way. "We've signed all the necessary waivers, and we're here on our own recognizance."

Nyere listened, trying to read between the lines. There was more to this bright young man than met the eye. "I suppose my first question would have to be why? Why put yourselves at risk of getting caught up in this thing when you don't have to?"

"Maybe it's the reason we're here," Jim Kirk suggested, at his charming best. "To get caught up in what could be a critical moment in history. Dr. Bellero's studies on space psychology and the possibility of alien life are what brought her here in the first place."

"I can't tell you how gratifying it is, Captain, to find my speculations confirmed in the person of these Vulcans," Elizabeth Dehner said sincerely. "They confirm what most reputable scientists have maintained for years: that a civilization advanced enough for interstellar travel must be a peaceful one."

Not counting Klingons, Romulans, Orions, Jim Kirk thought, distracting himself.

"As for my people," he went on, hoping Nyere would take that to mean the Dove Society, "we are committed to a peaceful solution, as I believe you are, Captain. The way you've stood by the Vulcans during the questioning indicates to me that you want exactly what we want—a just solution, with nobody hurt. Dr. Bellero and I have a mission to perform here, Captain, and we need your help."

"My 'help' or my 'cooperation,' Mr. Kirk?" Jason asked dryly; he was familiar with this particular variety of hotshot. "Or is it 'Colonel'? Twenty-four hours ago you were passing yourself off as an intell-agent. I'm still not entirely clear on whom you're working for."

Jim Kirk grinned at him, disarming. "Do I look like an intell-agent?"

"No, your color's too good." Jason Nyere chuckled at the joke he was about to make. "You look as if you spend more time on the rocks than under them." He did a sudden about-face into seriousness. "I don't know what you are, Kirk, and I don't know if I can trust you. But I'll tell you something you can pass on to your 'people,' whoever they are—even if it means my neck. I have sat by and watched two innocent people—and they may not be 'human,' though I'm not sure anymore if that's a privilege or a disgrace, but they *are* people—poked, prodded, put through all manner of foolishness, and treated like they're carrying some sort of disease, all because they are 'different.' Historically speaking, I believe I know something about that."

"I'm certain you do, Captain," Elizabeth Dehner offered sympathetically.

"And if I had the means to bust out of here and let these people go—"

"Captain"—Jim Kirk gestured ingenuously at the vast ship surrounding them—"it seems to me you have the means."

Nyere narrowed his slate-gray eyes at him. "Don't think I haven't thought about it, Kirk. But there's a question of what Commander T'Lera wants—oh, and don't underestimate the lady; she has very strong opinions about what's to be done or not done in her name—and there's also the little matter of where we go from here."

"Suppose I told you that my people were prepared to take it from there?" Jim Kirk asked eagerly. Was it to be this easy? "Suppose I told you we had the means to conceal these people where no one could find them— not the media, not the PentaKrem, not anybody. Suppose . . ."

But Jason Nyere was shaking his head; it was not to be that easy. "No, Kirk. That's one of the tamer scenarios the Council's toying with even as we speak. I won't have these people sent into exile, no matter how pleasant."

"Will you stand by and let the Council exercise a more extreme option?" Kirk asked incisively.

"That's my business," Nyere snapped back, but he'd given Kirk the answer he was looking for.

"Suppose I said we had the means to send the Vulcans home?" he ventured, out on a limb.

Nyere chuckled. "Now you're creating fantasies. Don't I wish!" He shook his head sadly. "No, people, I'm sorry. There's nothing I can do until Command gets back to me with the Council's decision. After that . . ."

No one spoke for a long moment. Jim Kirk shrugged at Dehner and they got up to leave. But not before Jason Nyere asked them for a favor.

"You're both free to come and go as you please, of course. Talk to T'Lera and Sorahl. I don't mean convince them to try to escape with you; I doubt if you could. But let them know that all humans aren't like the ones they've had to deal with across that inquiry table."

"We'll do our best," Elizabeth Dehner promised.

"Captain . . ." Jim Kirk shook his hand, feeling optimistic that at least Nyere wouldn't prove an obstacle; he'd hate to see the man hurt.

Jason Nyere did not share Kirk's optimism. When his guests were gone, he glared at the silent comm screen—locked on two-way silence until the council reached its decision—and willed it to speak, at the same time as he dreaded what it might ultimately tell him. After all this struggle, he was faced with the same moral dilemma thrust upon him when the first retrieval order had come down from Command. If the trigger was to be pulled, he would be expected to pull it.

When he was sure that he was totally alone, Jason Nyere put his head down on his arms and wept.

Gary Mitchell's snowmobile made excellent time over the fresh powder laid down by the recent blizzard; he skimmed merrily along with the late afternoon sun, skirting the horizon as it did this time of year, directly in his face. It wasn't the best of travel conditions; even with his goggles and the mobile's photosensitive windshield he was virtually snowblind, and he could as easily fall into a crevasse in this unrelenting brightness as he could in total darkness. The captain of the AeroNav ship that had dropped him on the edge of the shelf had wanted to provide him with a snocat to get him safely over the crevasses, but the thing was armor-plated and heavily tracked and much too slow for Mitchell's purposes. He'd taken the mobile and headed directly into the sun, running on instinct.

It was instinct that made him veer off to avoid the two identical snow-covered hillocks directly in his path before he actually saw them. Skidding around them to leeward, Mitchell saw why they were identical and got out of his mobile to rap on Easter's windshield.

"You guys all right in there?" He framed his face with his mittened hands and pressed it against the glass to see better. "Want some help digging out?"

"We are fine, thank you, sir!" a cheery voice said from the backseat. Mitchell could barely distinguish a flash of white teeth in a dark face. The death-pale spiky-haired figure in the driver's seat seemed mute as well as sullen. "Excepting, if you had a spare fuel block . . ."

"Sure thing!" Mitchell was halfway back to his vehicle when the windshield on the strangers' mobile slid down and the sullen figure spoke.

"We don't need nothin' of yours," it said. "Bugger off!"

"Hey, no skin off mine, man!" Mitchell grinned. A crawling sensation at the back of his neck told him what he didn't need to turn and see: someone had stepped out of the second mobile and aimed an automatic at his spine.

Mitchell himself had brought no weapons, hadn't wanted to take the risk of being searched, had assumed a vessel like *Delphinus* carried sufficient armament to provide him with whatever he might need once he got there. He'd also had a hard think about the Prime Directive; if it forbade creating new lifelines in the past, what did it have to say about destroying existing ones, even if they belonged to the scum of the Earth?

He backed slowly toward his snowmobile with his hands raised and the grin frozen to his face, slid in, and gunned the motor with one hand while he slammed the hatch shut with the other, swinging away in a great arc that he prayed was out of firing range, and roared back the way he'd come. When he was sure the lay of the land hid him from view, he switched off the engine and sat there sweating, listening to the ticking silence.

What the hell had that been all about? They might only be poachers, predators still bagging seals regardless of the bans, but what were they doing this far in on the shelf? They could be prospectors or tourists or even, though he doubted it, natives out joyriding. Or—

Mitchell listened to his inner voice. It told him that even if these friendly souls were acting alone and running low on fuel, he'd better make damn sure he got to Byrd before they did.

He reset his controls for a route around the strangers and fed the snowmobile as much speed as she'd take without shaking apart, caution to the wind. If there were crevasses between him and Byrd, he figured he'd fly right over them.

Yoshi was alone at the crew's table in the mess hall when Sorahl brought him the computer printout.

The dinner crowd varied nightly. Yoshi, Tatya, and Sorahl invariably ate together; most times Jason joined them, less often T'Lera. Melody preferred leftovers in her cabin and her own company.

It was Tatya's turn to cook; she could be heard rattling around in the galley, the strains of Borodin's "Polovetsian Dances" weaving around the sounds of cookware. Tatya had chosen the music as well; perhaps the festive mood was in celebration of the inquisitors' departure, or only false hope.

Yoshi frowned at the printout in his hand, mystified. "What's this?"

"I believe it will prove efficacious in the cure of the kelpwilt," Sorahl said simply. "Once you are able to return to your station and actualize it, of course."

"It looks complicated," Yoshi said, avoiding the issue of his return to the agrostation and what he would have to sacrifice to get there. He deciphered what molecule chains he recognized, puzzling over the rest. "What's this thing over here?"

"A synthetic enzyme similar to one developed not

long ago on our world," Sorahl explained. "I was unable to find an analogue in any of Earth's texts, which may account for the unresponsiveness of the disease to present methods. However, I believe it can be implemented under Earth conditions."

"You mean you just made it up?" Yoshi was incredulous.

"I assure you the research is accurate," Sorahl said, mistaking his meaning. "To within 99.44 percent, as measured under laboratory conditions. Whether or not it will prove so under actual field conditions—"

"I didn't mean that," Yoshi said quietly, getting to his feet as if in homage. "I meant, all by yourself you've discovered something a dozen agronomy experts with a million credits' worth of grant money couldn't find under their noses in two years of research, and you pass it off as if it's all in a day's work. I meant—you'd do this for us, after all we've done to you. After all we may yet do to you."

"It is no more than any Vulcan would do, given the same circumstances," Sorahl said, puzzled that humans still could not understand this.

Yoshi shook his head, amazed and ashamed. Amazed at Sorahl's people, ashamed for his own.

"I also meant—thank you—my friend."

For the second time in history, human and Vulcan exchanged the handshake of friendship in spite of difference.

"Soup's on!" Tatya announced loudly, blundering in from the galley with her hands full, shattering the moment. Yoshi laughed for the first time since he could remember, and Sorahl raised both eyebrows in astonishment. Yoshi folded the printout very small and slipped it into a pocket of his jeans, and the three sat down to dinner.

"I'm told we have someone aboard who makes the best chicken Kiev in the Southern Hemisphere," was

Jim Kirk's entrance line. If it was calculated to have Tatya eating out of his hand, it succeeded.

"If I can twist Jason's arm into freeing up some of the real chickens he's got frozen in the hold, you're on, Mr. Kirk!" She giggled.

"Complaints, complaints!" the accused party rumbled as Jason too joined them. He had recovered from his earlier moment of despair; if his eyes were bloodshot it might only be fatigue. "I let you have the real coffee, didn't I? You've been eating a lot higher on the hog than my regular crew. Real eggs, fresh fruit and vegetables—"

"Only because of the Vulcans!" Tatya teased him, returning to the galley for more plates and replacing the Borodin with some Prokofiev; the composer's "Kije" also joined them for dinner. "You'd never be so nice if it was just us!"

The good-natured banter went on, with Yoshi joining in, and Sorahl at least managing to look less somber. Jim Kirk exchanged glances with Dr. Bellero when she came in. Whatever was going on in the world beyond, morale was high in here.

"Maybe too high," Elizabeth Dehner whispered, reading Kirk's thoughts. "It could be false euphoria. The calm before the storm. Overcompensation for recent events and future uncertainties. I'd be careful."

"So noted," Kirk whispered back. "How do you do that?"

"What, read your mind?" Dehner teased; if they were going to pretend to be lovers, she would give it her best shot, in public anyway. "You telegraph with your face, didn't you know that? I also have a high esper rating. Though not as high as Parneb's."

"I'll keep that in mind!" Kirk grimaced, aware that Sorahl could not help overhearing. He was searching for an opening gambit to talk to the young Vulcan when T'Lera was suddenly among them.

She made no entrance, in fact made no sound, but her presence was such as to reduce them to silence and draw their attention to her. An officer and a gentleman, Jason Nyere was on his feet at once; the other males, excepting Sorahl, followed suit. Accepting Earth's antique chivalry with her silence, T'Lera seated herself beside Jim Kirk.

"I am told you are sent to offer us freedom," she began without preamble, including Dr. Bellero in her careful, damped-down gaze, but primarily addressing Kirk. "I am also told you are not what you earlier purported to be, 'Colonel' Kirk. Is my information accurate?"

"Yes, ma'am," Jim Kirk responded almost humbly, daunted by her proximity for all her containment. "Right on both counts."

T'Lera disregarded his attempt at lightness. "If I may be so bold: what are you, Mr. Kirk?"

"A friend," Kirk said at once, without meaning to. He'd been running prepared speeches in his head for days. Where was his celebrated glibness when he needed it?

"Apparently our definitions of friendship are somewhat dissimilar," T'Lera suggested.

Jim Kirk heard Jason chuckle. The captain had broken out the ship's liquor supply; Kirk accepted a scotch on the rocks with silent gratitude.

"Perhaps it was a poor choice of words," he told T'Lera. "Or a less-than-precise choice." Damn! he thought. He'd learned nothing since his encounter with Spock on the bridge, was left falling over his tongue in an attempt to clarify himself. "Perhaps what I mean is that what I am is less important than what I am attempting to do."

"Forgive me, Mr. Kirk," T'Lera said dryly. "But the limits of my perspective render me unable to separate motivation from motivator."

A sharp, humorless laugh announced Melody Sawyer's arrival.

"Save your breath, Kirk! She can't accept your help; you're only human!" She plunked herself down next to Dehner, as far away from the Vulcans as she could be while still at the same table. "Thought it might be refreshing to eat with human beings again," she announced, helping herself from the serving platters.

The Vulcans had the good grace to say nothing. Yoshi and Tatya looked embarrassed, and Jason Nyere looked as if he was about to chew Sawyer's ears off.

"Does their presence threaten you, Commander?" Dehner asked ingenuously.

"It does not!" Melody snorted.

"Then why do you act out in such a hostile manner whenever they're in proximity?"

"Listen, honey." Melody pointed a fork at her. "You may be impressed with your own credentials, but I've got nearly twenty years on you and I don't impress. You can look in my file; you'll find I don't suffer from paranoid delusions or feelings of persecution—"

"Just bad manners!" Jason rumbled.

"I have the perspicacity to recognize a threat when I see one, suh!" Melody barked back.

"What exactly do you see as the threat?" Jim Kirk chimed in, finishing his drink and changing direction. Maybe he'd struck out with the Vulcans, but a fellow human's distrust of the alien was familiar territory. "I see us sharing a meal with two quiet, well-mannered fellow beings who have neither taken hostages, blown up our military installations, nor demanded that we 'take us to your leader.'" Nyere was chuckling again. "I don't understand—"

"What I 'perceive as the threat,'" Melody mimicked him, "is what all those people up north looking for flying saucers are afraid of. It may not have a name, or maybe it does. Maybe it's the simple deflation of ego accompanying the realization that we're not supreme in this corner of creation. Maybe it's the fear that everything we've fought through three world wars to preserve on this lowly little dustball will have to change now. Maybe it's the idea that these people have watched us, learned our language, and happen to look a little like us, but they aren't like us; in fact they take an inordinate self-inflating pride in *not* being like us. Maybe I sit here thinking 'would I let my daughter marry one of them?' I don't know what it is; all I know is I don't want it happening in my lifetime. And the response from the rest of the planet sure as hell indicates I'm not alone."

That said, she put her food on a tray and stalked off. Jason looked as if he might be tempted to go after her, if only to dump her overboard in her underwear. He shook his head, put his fork down, and excused himself to return to his solitary vigil at the comm screen.

No one but Kirk ate much after that, and he unobtrusively, convinced that whatever lay ahead he'd need the strength for it. Tatya began to clear away the dishes; Yoshi and Sorahl retreated to one end of the table to consult over something on a computer printout. Elizabeth Dehner poured herself a cup of coffee and watched it grow cold at her elbow. In the galley, the last melancholy strains of "Lt. Kije" wafted away and no one bothered to replace the disk. The false euphoria was gone.

Only T'Lera, her hands folded in a configuration not unlike one Spock might have chosen, Kirk noted with a pang, sat unmoved and unmoving in the midst of emotional outburst or the disintegration in its aftermath, centered and certain. If he could get to the core of that certainty, Jim Kirk thought, and somehow challenge it—

He sighed. Here under the ice day and night were indistinguishable, but topside the sun would be going down about now. Another day shot to hell. He'd told his people it would be easy once he got to the Vulcans; here he was sitting right beside one of them and he had no idea what to do next.

He felt rather than saw T'Lera's eyes on him.

My God, he thought. How often have I gotten that same look from Spock—assessing, weighing, and, I always assumed in my paranoia, finding me unworthy. But Spock's gaze, however incisive, was always tempered with—with something; I'm not sure what. Certainly nothing as emotional as compassion, but something softening, mitigating. There is nothing soft in T'Lera's gaze, nothing soft about T'Lera at all.

"You realize, Mr. Kirk, that Commander Sawyer is correct," T'Lera said.

"I'm not so sure," Kirk said, swallowing the last of his dinner and pushing the plate away. "There are at least as many humans who would welcome you, given the chance."

"Provided we did not move in down the block," T'Lera said dryly; she'd been getting a handle on the idiom after all, with Jason's help. Across the table, Elizabeth Dehner tried not to choke on her cold coffee. "Tell me my presence does not make you uneasy, Mr. Kirk, and I will remember that humans have one skill Vulcans have never mastered, and that is their ability to stretch a truth."

I've struck out twice in ten minutes, Kirk mused. What have I got to lose by going up a third time?

"Commander," he began. "What can I say to persuade you?"

"Persuade me of what, Mr. Kirk? That your people are at best ambivalent about mine? Of this I need no reassurance."

Kirk shook his head. "Of the fact that some of us want to help, and we may be empowered to get you off the planet, if only we can get you out of Antarctica." He heard Dehner inhale sharply; he had no basis for making that last statement, but he made it anyway. He

311

got as close to T'Lera as he dared. "I asked you a question yesterday at the inquiry, Commander; you never got a chance to answer it. What would you do if you were free to leave here?"

He saw Sorahl's head go up, saw that Yoshi was listening, too.

"Is this an intellectual exercise, Mr. Kirk, or some manner of test?" T'Lera wanted to know. "I had thought the tests concluded with the departure of the inquiry panel. As to intellectual exercises . . ."

"Commander T'Lera, sometime over the next few days"—Kirk felt his temper simmering, decided to use it—"your fate, and your son's"—he included Sorahl in the conversation—"is going to be decided for you, either by the United Earth Council or, God help you, by 'public opinion,' in the shape of whatever nosy reporters manage to sneak through the security cordon and find their way here. I'm offering you a chance out. I have no time for intellectual exercises!"

He subsided, wondering not for the first time if he'd blown it completely. T'Lera let the silence continue interminably, let it settle on them both, oppressive.

"Mr. Kirk," she said at last. "What I have attempted to do to prevent this you know. What I am permitted by my conscience and by my oath to do next is contingent upon what is best for your world and for mine. Isolated from both in this place, I cannot accurately know what that is. Yours may be a simple question, but it has no simple answer."

"All right," Kirk acquiesced. Jason had left the liquor cabinet unsecured, and he helped himself. "Let's say I'm simplifying matters for the sake of expediency. Let's say I'm as aware as you of the danger here—not only to you and your son, but to both our worlds. Perhaps more aware than you can know."

"Jim," Elizabeth Dehner said correctly, in character, "you're telegraphing again."

"Why, Sally." He grinned, also in character, returning to his seat with drink in hand. No, I wasn't going to tell her who we really are! he thought, hoping she was reading him loud and clear. If I'd wanted a watchdog or a lecture on the Prime Directive, I'd have brought—well, Spock, if I could have. "Don't you trust me?"

"As far as I can throw you!" Dehner said sweetly.

T'Lera, assuming this to be some human lovers' quarrel, as Dehner had intended her to, lowered her eyes in respect for human privacy even in this public forum. Her high beams off him for the moment, Kirk stopped sweating and thought hard.

"Commander, I'm told your people pride themselves on logic, on the ability to predicate future occurrences based upon present events. Am I correct?"

"It is not a matter of pride, Mr. Kirk. These are our gifts, and we make use of them."

"But you could, for example"—Kirk held his temper this time—"project a time when Earthmen, in the course of space exploration, would happen upon Vulcans or—others—out there. Assuming there are others out there."

T'Lera was watching him closely. "Perhaps."

"Then I put it to you that if your ship had not entered Earth's atmosphere and crashed, and created who knows what repercussions in terms of human fears and misunderstandings, there would come a time in Earth's technological evolution when we would reach out into space and encounter other technological life, whether Vulcan or not, if such life existed."

"Mr. Kirk," T'Lera answered. "Three of your years ago an Earth ship was launched toward the system you call Alpha Centauri. I suggest that your scientists would not have dispatched so dangerous, time-consuming, and costly a manned expedition without the expectation of finding intelligent life."

"What do you think, Commander?" Kirk asked incisively. "Is there intelligent life on Alpha Centauri?"

"I have never been to Alpha Centauri, Mr. Kirk,"

T'Lera replied, and Elizabeth Dehner excused herself to get another cup of coffee.

She's not going to violate her Prime Directive, Kirk thought. Not even to the degree of revealing her knowledge of other life forms, not even if it could save her life. He had to admire her for it, at the same time he felt like throttling her for bringing him so close to violating his own. Was there no other answer?

"Hypothetically, Commander," Jim Kirk began, feeling an extra gear kick in somewhere in the back of his brain as he found the persuasiveness he'd been searching for all evening. "Assuming your ship had not crashed, assuming the scoutcraft missions proceeded without incident, how long approximately—in your opinion—before Earthmen and Vulcans encountered each other?"

"Based upon your present level of technology and exploration correlative with ours," T'Lera answered after the briefest moment of calculation. "Approximately 19.285 of your years."

Practically down to the date and time! Jim Kirk marveled, wondering if the famed rescue mission by the *Amity* had been accident after all. He risked a glance at Dehner when she returned from the galley to see if she'd overheard. She had. And, Kirk realized, so had Sorahl.

"You know, it's always amazed me," Kirk mused, "the sacrifices in time space travelers are willing to make. The crew of the *Icarus* will take six years to get to Alpha Centauri and six to get back. I'm curious, Sorahl—how far is Vulcan from Earth?"

"Approximately 58,782,000,000,000 Earth miles, based upon our ship's trajectory, Mr. Kirk." The young Vulcan was too new at interaction with Earthmen to suspect the trap Kirk was laying for him.

Kirk whistled softly. Elizabeth Dehner wanted to hit him. "That's quite a distance. How long did it take your ship to go that far?"

The young Vulcan knew his mother's thoughts as he walked blindly into the trap. Perhaps, indeed, it was not yet time.

"Perhaps my commander could better answer that, Mr. Kirk," he said politely, knowing it would not serve.

"But you were the navigator," Kirk challenged him. "I'm asking you. That much distance—I'm no physicist but, my goodness, that comes out to about ten light-years, I think. You couldn't have been in space that long; you'd have had to be a child when you left Vulcan. How long, Sorahl?"

The young Vulcan hesitated, though not out of doubt as to what answer he would give, only in search of a way to give it without offense. "With all due respect, Mr. Kirk, I cannot answer that question."

"Nor will I, Mr. Kirk." T'Lera was on her feet and Sorahl followed suit. "If you will excuse us—"

They were gone as silently as T'Lera had come. Jim Kirk pounded the table in frustration.

"Am Morgen." Racher's lips did not move when he spoke. His voice was metal against metal in the cold of the unheated outbuildings at Byrd. "When there is sun."

"That's nearly twelve hours!" one of his followers complained; Racher had forbidden heat flares lest they attract attention should anyone chance to look out from *Delphinus*'s conning tower.

They'd hidden their snowmobiles behind the ancient glacial ridge some hundred yards distant, waited for dark to creep and crawl across the ice to the deserted complex. They had not questioned why it was deserted; waited now, their attention focused on the grim gray conning tower jutting above the ice, giving barely a hint of how much ship lay beneath.

"Ja," Racher replied, unperturbed. His bionic eyes were infrared-equipped; through the starboard port he

could discern a human figure—Jason's—alone in the dark of the bridge, and was tempted for the briefest moment. But he had built his reputation as a terrorist upon merciless dawn attack; he would not change that now.

"I want them to know who kills them. We breach from the conning tower." He motioned with the muzzle of his favorite automatic; the laser rifle was only to impress thugs like Easter. "And we go in. Search and destroy. Everyone."

Some of the white-clad figures murmured in the darkness. They'd been promised hostages, trade-offs, reparations for their various causes, not a night of subzero cold and a dawn of profitless slaughter.

"Everyone?" someone asked.

"Ja." Racher's eyes glinted metallically in the darkness. "Everyone!"

"You deliberately tried to corner them into revealing their warp-drive technology," Dehner said, amazed at Kirk's temerity. "What did you hope to accomplish?"

Kirk shrugged. "I thought T'Lera might see it as a way to bargain for their lives."

Dehner shook her head. "When will you learn?"

"About Vulcans? Probably never." He was thinking about the general and all the other experts, pounding at T'Lera with the wrong questions. "Those idiots! They could have had access to warp-drive technology a full decade earlier if they'd gotten over their paranoia and—"

"What makes you think T'Lera would have told them any more than she told you?" Dehner asked quietly.

Kirk didn't answer her. "I can't get through to her!" he said, amazed at himself. "I feel so—so helpless!"

He and Dehner were almost alone, still across the table from each other in the mess hall. Yoshi could be heard in the galley unloading the dishwasher; everyone else was gone, somewhere in the big empty ship. Yoshi had replaced the Prokofiev with some Bach; the "Air for the G-String" matched Kirk's somber mood.

"Does that surprise you?" Dehner asked mildly.

Kirk looked at her askance. "What—that I can't get through to T'Lera? Or that I feel helpless?"

"Either. That you as a captain without a ship, a leader with no one to lead, should feel helpless. Or that you still don't know how to talk to a Vulcan." Dehner leaned across the table at him, playing the lovers' tête-à-tête to the hilt; she could learn to like this. "Or that there's at least one female in the galaxy who's impervious to your charm?"

The conversation reminded Kirk too much of one he'd recently had with Gary.

"Don't play doctor with me, doctor!" he said tightly, knowing she was right on all counts. "Maybe you'd like to try this yourself?"

"Who, me?" Dehner stretched, cracked her knuckles, put her elbows back on the table. "I've got my evening cut out for me trying to find a way into the pharmaceuticals locker."

Kirk gave her a puzzled look. "How's that?"

"If you're serious about my having to 'wipe' people," Dehner explained, "I'll need the proper drugs for the job." Kirk nodded. "Meanwhile, why don't you go another round with Scarlett O'Hara cum John Wayne?" she suggested. "You two seem to understand each other."

"If we ever get out of here"—Kirk was on his feet; he'd intended to track Melody anyway; was Dehner reading his mind again?— "remind me I owe you a reprimand for insubordination."

Dehner just smiled at him.

Melody Sawyer stood rooted to the gym floor in her tennis whites, repeatedly whacking a tennis ball off the same spot on the handball wall as if it were a bull's-eye, or possibly the back of a Vulcan's head. She'd thought of working off her rage in a few fast sets with the robot, but she knew all its moves by now and was usually one step ahead of it. There'd never been anyone on board she couldn't beat one-handed.

Whack, whack, whack! She slammed the ball at racquetball speeds, not needing to chase it because it homed to her like a boomerang. Whack, whack, whack! If anything, she was building tension instead of relieving it.

Feeling positively murderous, she programmed the robot for high lobs and determined to sweat it out.

"Service!" she yelled, triggering the robot while she was still on the wrong side of the net. It spat out the first ball and she waited on it until she really had to chase it. About twenty lobs later she was beginning to loosen up when she saw that she was not alone. She gave the solid figure in jogging clothes a once-over without ever slowing up.

"Great form," Jim Kirk tried for openers. "Captain Nyere tells me you were on the pro circuit."

"And I bet you came all the way down here just to tell me that, didn't you, Mr. Kirk?" she asked, all molasses and sarcasm and never missing a beat.

"Actually, I thought I'd do some running," Kirk lied, picking up a spare racket and testing the grip. "I thought the gym would be empty this time of night."

The robot had run out of balls and Melody scrambled around the court retrieving them. Kirk's attempts to help only irritated her.

"Listen, Buster: you want to run, go run."

"Sure." Kirk grinned, casually lobbing the ball in his hand over the net and making it look easy.

"You play?" Melody challenged rather than asked.

"Well . . . I'm a little rusty," Kirk said diffidently.

Melody kicked the last of the stray balls off the court and threw Kirk one. "How rusty?"

* * *

Yoshi was stacking the last of the clean dishes in the pantry and had started on the silverware when Elizabeth Dehner brought her coffee cup out to the galley.

"I'll do this one," she told him when he tried to take the cup from her.

She put it in the sink and rinsed it, awkwardly, too accustomed to her era's disposable, recyclable containers, and saw that the young man was watching her out of the corner of his eye, she hoped not because of her domestic technique.

"What is it?" she asked when he continued to stare. Her voice was cool, clinical, but with the right note of accessibility.

Yoshi responded to it. "Can I talk to you for a minute, doctor?"

They sat in the deserted mess hall and he told her whatever she didn't already know about him and Tatya, the events of the last few days, the Vulcans, the kelpwilt, his fears for the future.

"Tonight Sorahl gave me this," the young man finished, showing Dehner the formula, sweeping his long hair out of his eyes in the characteristic gesture. "It's probably a miracle cure, and he just gives it to me. After I've done this jealousy trip on him and Tatya, after everything else. And he *gives* it to me. No 'shall we share the discovery,' no 'what about patent laws,' nothing. A gift. No strings, no applause, nothing. 'We who are about to die salute you,' or something. I'm so confused!"

"We all are, Yoshi," Dehner assured him vaguely. How could she possibly explain Sorahl's behavior without explaining how she knew? "That's really what this whole thing is about. When we don't understand something, it's natural to fear it."

"I thought I understood," Yoshi said sadly. "In the beginning, that first night when Sorahl told us about his people and his world—I could see it; I could feel it! It was this weird gut feeling that maybe I'd been born on

319

the wrong planet. I wanted to see the world he was describing—a world without war or violence, a world of peace and order and common sense where a person can live and work according to his gifts. I come from a tradition of discipline and respect for elders and spiritual awareness; I would have thrived on that. The more Sorahl talked about Vulcan, the more I felt homesick for a place I've never seen. Do you think I'm crazy?"

"No," Elizabeth Dehner said sincerely, thinking that if they could set history right again, Yoshi might yet live to see this world of his dreams.

If everything that brought Yoshi and me to this time and place hadn't happened, Dehner thought, suddenly visited with a bad case of *Weltschmerz*. She shook her head. No, she didn't think Yoshi was crazy, only depressed, and justifiably so.

"Yoshi," she asked in her best clinical manner, "how much would you be willing to do to get the Vulcans home safely? To make it possible for you to visit that world you envision?"

Yoshi's eyes widened in a kind of rapture, which sparked and died almost as quickly as it had come. He shook his head sadly.

"I lost that chance when I handed Sorahl and T'Lera over to Jason. And if you're asking me what I'd do now that it's too late—I'm no kind of hero."

"There are many kinds of hero, Yoshi," Dehner said, getting to her feet. "I need a walk. How well do you know the inside of this ship?"

Yoshi grinned shyly. "About as well as the people who run her. Would you like a guided tour?"

Dehner linked her arm in his. "Please."

"Forty-love!" Melody announced a little too smugly. "Always suspected you peaceniks were cream puffs. Sure you want to go a whole set?"

"Just play!" Kirk's grin was feral, masking his

breathlessness. He wished he hadn't been so ambitious at dinner. Not that it would have made much difference; the woman was a killer.

"Masochists, too!" Melody's serve was a rocket.

"Okay, where were we?" Kirk huffed, getting under the ball just in time and sending it wobbling back into a clear fault. With a kind of noblesse, Melody allowed it.

"You were asking why an intelligent person like me couldn't overcome my prejudices, just walk up to one of the Vulcans, and 'engage in dialogue,' is how I think you put it," she said, sending him running again. "Is that what happens when you sleep with a shrink? You start talking like one?"

"Maybe," Kirk gritted, feeling his racket scrape the flooring as he volleyed back, lost his balance, and slammed into the far wall. If she got this point, she wouldn't get it easily. "Well, why don't you?"

"Because"—Melody got the point, easily—"somebody has to keep a clear head until this thing settles out."

Kirk rubbed his shoulder and went to chase the ball. "I don't understand what that means."

Melody bounced on her toes and laughed humorlessly. "You know, Kirk, I'm beginning to believe you are a pacifist after all. No one else would be so naive. Haven't you figured out what happens next? Or do you really believe those people will be allowed to go home?"

He couldn't answer for several moments, needed all his wind to keep the ball in play. By the time he could draw breath the score was thirty-love.

"All right." He mustered the last of his charm. "Indulge my naiveté. What happens next?"

"The United Earth Council is going to decide that these people don't exist," Melody explained. "Then it's up to AeroNav to 'disappear' them, and Jason gets the tag." She whacked the ball. Kirk got under it and whacked it back, barely. "And if you think that big old softie is going to be able to train a weapon on these people and march them into exile"—whack—"or, worse by his standards, cleaner by mine, pull the trigger on them, you are grossly mistaken."

To his surprise, Kirk actually saw an opening and scored his first point in a game and a half. "You, then?"

"Damn straight!" Melody shot back. Whack!

"And that's why you're keeping your distance," Kirk countered. Whack! "The good soldier. Just doing her duty. Like the Gestapo, and Colonel Green's troops. Just obeying orders. As long as they aren't human—"

"They aren't!" Melody yelled. Whack! "Nothing you say is going to make them human! And don't give me that 'good soldier' crap, Kirk! You civilians always think it's black and white!"

"Oh, no!" Kirk assured her with what little wind he had left. If she only knew! "I know exactly how many shades of gray there are in any command decision, believe me."

That point made them thirty-even. Melody stopped play and came up to the net, ferocious.

"I don't know why I'm telling you this, Kirk. Maybe it's because I won't give your shrink friend the professional satisfaction, and there's no one else aboard this tub I can talk to. But aside from all that soapbox stuff I gave you at dinner—and don't get me wrong; I meant every word of it—there's one little thing I won't even tell Jason, and that is that whatever I end up doing over the next few days I'll do because of him, even if he hates me for it."

She was back in play without warning, and Kirk was recovered enough to chase whatever she belted at him.

"I love that man like a brother!" Melody Sawyer stated. Whack! "He took me on when I was nothing but a loudmouth maverick, insubordinate to the death, transferred off nearly every ship in the fleet and just this side of a dishonorable discharge, and he stayed

322

with me. Turned me into something resembling an officer, and maybe even a gentleman." Whack!

"I have worked beside him for fifteen years. I know him better than I know my own husband." Whack! "I've held his head when he was sick, and he's held my hand when I damn near died. He's not only my CO, he's my best friend, and I've watched him bleeding for these Vulcans from the outset."

With a final murderous flourish she punished the ball across the net and Kirk didn't bother to go after it. He conceded the game with a gesture and collapsed in a corner, nursing a stitch in his side. Melody wasn't even winded.

"Paint me the villain of the piece, Kirk; it doesn't matter." She was all but attacking him. "History won't get it straight anyway. I'll do whatever I can to spare Jason Nyere whatever agony I can, if it means I have to pull the trigger myself."

"I hear you!" Kirk wheezed, thinking of himself and Gary and the parameters of friendship. "But it doesn't have to go that way if—"

"That's a girl's set," Melody cut him off. "Or do you want to go three out of five like a man?"

He would have gone the full set if it killed him, partly to have another go at her philosophically, partly to salvage his pride, but Melody had found another target for her fury. "Goddamned if they aren't everywhere you turn!"

She slammed her racket against the net post, advancing on someone hidden in shadow just outside the gym. "Have those big ears of yours gotten all that? Come out here where we can see you!"

T'Lera emerged from shadow. "It was not my intention to eavesdrop; I was merely uncertain of the protocol of interrupting your competition. However, the experience was most illuminating." She crossed the gym floor precisely to the boundary of the tennis court and stopped. Jim Kirk did not recall scrambling to his feet, but there he was. While T'Lera's eyes included him in her awareness, her words were solely for Melody. "If I understand the terminology of the game correctly, I believe it is accurate for me to say: your form is excellent."

"Thanks!" Melody said grudgingly and by reflex. The Vulcan's compliment confused her, reduced her to an angry silence in her confusion.

"An interesting game, this tennis," T'Lera went on. "Pleasing to the observer as well as to the participant, in that it combines physical skill—speed, grace, agility, and strength—with intellectual acuity—the insight into the opponent's thinking, the striving to improve one's skills to the limits of one's ability."

"Sounds like you've done your homework!" Melody sneered. "Did you study up on all that in your cabin just so you could impress me?" She jerked her head in Kirk's direction. "You two in cahoots or what?"

"I beg your pardon?"

"I don't suppose they play games on your planet!" T'Lera's impervious cool was making Melody blush again. "All locked in their ivory towers being cerebral all the time."

"On the contrary," T'Lera was saying. "We are not so very different from you in that respect."

Jim Kirk, silent for once and watchful, was reminded of the only time he had chanced to observe a Vulcan in some solitary physical routine.

He knew the stories of Vulcan superiority in strength and agility, had always thought them exaggerated, until he came upon Spock, alone on a practice mat in a deserted corner of the rec room late into ship's night, engaged in something that was neither dance nor calisthenic, neither aerobic nor isometric exercise, yet somehow a harmonious blending of all of these with something purely Vulcan and, Kirk was to find out the hard way, virtually impossible for a human to master.

324

He had merely stood and stared, until Spock became aware of him.

The Vulcan came to a complete standstill, hands locked behind his back. "Captain?"

"Don't you ever sweat?" Kirk had joked lamely, embarrassed for them both.

"Not with such minimal exertion, Captain," Spock had replied stiffly, and Kirk had choked back a laugh. Minimal exertion? That last routine would have put a human's neck in a sling for a week. Maybe the stories were true.

"It's an interesting routine." Kirk was still trying to warm up to his first officer; this was some weeks prior to the M-155 incident. "Could you teach it to me?"

Spock had hesitated. "It is not often taught to humans."

"But there's no—taboo forbidding it, is there?" Kirk had persisted. It would be a long time before he would learn to hear the silent alarm behind Spock's reluctances. "I'm in pretty good shape; I'm sure I could handle it."

"Undoubtedly, Captain. However, I do not think you would find it—desirable."

"Why not?" Kirk had found himself growing annoyed. Every time he tried to understand this Vulcan he found doors slammed in his face. "I'd welcome the challenge. I may be only human—"

"Captain," Spock seemed to have difficulty finding the correct words. "The routine you observed was a basic warm-up. It is mastered by most Vulcan children before the age of infant school. If you will excuse me . . ."

Dehner's right—I never learn! Kirk thought, snapping himself back to the present and what he suddenly perceived as T'Lera's interest in quite a different pastime than tennis.

"That the term 'love' is used when referring to a null score," the Vulcan was saying. "Perhaps you could enlighten me as to its origin?"

Melody was being engaged in dialogue with the enemy in spite of herself. The effort made her diffident. She shrugged.

"I don't know. No one does. It's one of those obscure things that's lost in the antiquity of the game."

"Nevertheless," T'Lera pursued her thought relentlessly, "one might perceive an interesting irony in the use of the term in a sport not noted for its 'love' of anything, except perhaps aggressiveness. Might one consider the use of the term an instance of 'adding insult to injury'?"

Kirk stifled a laugh and Melody glowered at him. She'd gone back to hitting the ball off the back wall. "I never thought about it."

"One wonders if the game would retain its essence were the aggression factor eliminated," T'Lera mused.

She made to leave the gym then. Melody turned on her.

"Listen, you're such an expert, why don't we go a few games?"

Jim Kirk's head came up at the same time T'Lera's did, and he caught the gleam of something in those laser eyes, something it would take him years to learn meant "I accept the challenge."

"I would be honored," T'Lera replied, extinguishing that gleam aborning. "However, I suggest such a contest might prove inequitable."

"Why?" Melody was suddenly intrigued by the idea. "Because I'm a pro and you've never played? We'll treat it like a lesson, then. Just for the exercise, no points. You look like you're in good shape, and you can't be more than a few years up on me. I'll handicap if you like."

T'Lera continued to demur. "I doubt you could

handicap sufficiently for the differences between us. Forgive me, Commander, but I would prefer not."

"Afraid there's something you can't one-up a human at?" Melody held her racket like a weapon. "Mr. Kirk here says I should try interacting with you instead of 'objectifying' you. I'm not a diplomat like Jason; I believe actions speak louder than words. I've listened to all the heroic words about how you scuttled your craft and how you were willing to die rather than let us discover you. Just words. I want to see what you're really made of."

The challenged and accepting look had returned to T'Lera's eyes. Jim Kirk found himself intervening.

"Melody," he interjected. "I don't think you want to do this . . ."

"Shut up, cream puff! You're out of this!" Melody barked, still focused on T'Lera. "Well?"

"As you wish, Commander," T'Lera said, and Jim Kirk wanted to scream.

Chapter Nine

"CAPTAIN'S PERSONAL LOG:

"This has to be a joke, a single great cosmic joke, probably at my expense. Here I stand, on a tennis court buried deep within an Earth ship, awaiting what may literally turn out to be the match of the century, played out before an audience of one whose role is nothing more than unofficial referee.

"I consider myself fairly well read. I am familiar with the Faust legends, the tales of mortals dicing with the devil. I seem to remember an old 2-D film whose outcome had something to do with a knight playing chess with Death for possession of his soul. But the fate of the Federation hanging on the outcome of a tennis match? It is simply too much.

"Maybe history derailed cannot be set back on course, and my crew and I have been exerting ourselves for nothing. Maybe I, captain without a ship, leader with no one to lead, deserve to be caught between two of the most impervious females, two of the most immovable objects, in the galaxy.

"The urge to scream has passed. I am now possessed of an almost uncontrollable desire to laugh. Only the thought of all the bad things that may yet happen makes it possible for me to contain myself. At the very least, I may be able to prevent these two from killing each other."

Kirk and Melody stood around waiting for T'Lera to change into borrowed tennis clothes. Melody had insisted on it, and Kirk felt he deserved points for not strangling her on the spot. She stood glaring at him.

"What are you grinning about, cream puff?"

Kirk just shook his head; he didn't trust himself to speak.

"You don't have to hang around!" Melody growled, pacing the service line like a tigress, perhaps having second thoughts. "Why don't you go make yourself a cup of hot milk and—"

"Sawyer, if you think I'd miss this match for anything . . ."

"Kirk, let me ask you something." Melody stopped pacing and came over to him, confidential. "Do you really think she's as old as she says?"

Kirk shrugged, bemused. "Who knows? I understand from the medical findings that their lifespan is more than twice ours. You should have asked me. Getting cold feet?"

"In a pig's eye!"

Kirk smiled outright; *that* response had a familiar ring. "Melody, out of curiosity—what if you lose?"

Her laugh was more a bark, a forewarning of her bite. "I haven't lost since Goddard, and I played on a busted ankle that day! Besides, Kirk, she claims she's a hundred years old. Give me a break!"

Melody had blundered into the age factor all by herself.

"I suppose your space service has some pretty tough fitness requirements," she'd sounded T'Lera out in the locker room. She really was trying; Kirk's remark about good soldiers had stung her more than she cared

329

to admit. "You look to be in fair shape for your age, if I guess right."

"One-hundred-thirteen point-four-six," T'Lera supplied deliberately.

The information rocked Melody, as every new and different datum about these people did. She shook her head and went to wait on the court.

"Good night, Yoshi, and thank you!"

Elizabeth Dehner shut her cabin door, listened as Yoshi's sneaker soles faded down the corridor, took a deep breath, and counted to a hundred. Willing herself to remain calm, she rummaged in her luggage for a small hypersonic lock pick, the very one Lee Kelso had jury-rigged to get into the computers at Alexandria. Stepping back out into the corridor, Dehner returned the way she and Yoshi had come, heading for the pharmaceuticals locker three decks below where she'd made note of it during their walk.

Tatya flipped open the hatch on the conning tower, reached out, and scooped up a handful of snow. Cupping it in her two hands, she tiptoed down the metal steps, past Jason Nyere, snoring in the captain's chair beside the defiantly blank comm screen, and presented her offering to Sorahl. The young Vulcan took the uncanny melting stuff from her, marveled at a cold that burned the hands.

"My teacher Selik once calculated that a moderate storm of one minute's duration, over an area of one square mile, would contain a number of these hexahedral crystals equivalent to—"

"Shut up and stop breathing on it!" Tatya hissed, exasperated. "Look, it's melting already. Your hands must be incredibly warm."

"In its present state it is most untidy," Sorahl observed, watching the melt drip between his fingers

330

and onto the floor. "Is there someplace where I can dispose of it properly?"

"It's only water!" Tatya dismissed it, wiping her own hands on her trousers, suddenly disappointed with the venture. It wasn't that Sorahl's childlike wonderment wasn't what she'd expected; it was the sense that everything was melting—everything. "When my cousins and I were small, my Tante Mariya used to pour hot syrup over the new snow on a really cold day; it would freeze hard in seconds and we'd eat it like candy. It tasted like—oh, I don't know—like something you knew you had to enjoy for that moment because you could never have it again . . ."

She stopped babbling, turned away from him to hide her tears. What an idiot she was to offer him something as cold and ephemeral as a handful of snow! What she wanted to offer him was freedom. She wanted to grab his hand and run with him across the pack ice to the mainland, to roll in the powder until it was in their hair and their eyelashes and down inside their boots and parkas, though she imagined he'd hate that. She wanted to flee with him to the nearest settlement—no matter that it was a thousand kilometers away—to go to ground where no one could find them. She would travel with him for years until everyone had forgotten, until it was safe. They'd send for Yoshi, and the three of them could build a life together, somewhere, somehow.

She realized Sorahl felt nothing for her, perhaps believed his people knew nothing of emotion as he claimed. His response would always be polite interest, nothing more. Somehow it no longer mattered. What she felt for him was pure and cherishable in and of itself, and if only she could set him free . . .

"I wish I'd never met you!" she whispered through her tears.

"Truly?" The young Vulcan stood with the snowmelt still dripping from his fingers. "If I have given offense, or committed some error—"

331

"No!" Tatya whispered sadly, and she touched him then, put her hand against his cheek as she might have with a favored brother, or a child. "No, you're close to perfect! It's we who've got it wrong!"

The border towns were in chaos.

While it continued to deny the presence of extra-terrestrials anywhere on Earth, much less within the boundaries of Antarctica, the PentaKrem was being an awful nuisance about letting anyone travel inland without proper authorization. The backlog of media types and UFO groupies in the raggedy little settlements dotting the coastlines made the natives irritable, and they shut their doors in stolid silence, letting the rabble of outlanders cool their heels quite literally in the sub-subzero cold as they scrambled for hot meals, hotel rooms, and rarer-than-hen's-teeth travel permits.

Tensions mounted. Daylong blizzards, the occasional earthquake, and a mysterious delay in arrival of supply ships only added to the turmoil. Some of the groupies grumbled and went home, but the media reps held their ground, disregarding the fact that it wasn't theirs to hold. Drunken brawls were common, the jails filled up almost as fast as the hotels, and sanitation robots could not possibly keep up with the excess.

In the midst of chaos a solitary figure stood out by virtue of his refusal to succumb to it. Finding no order, Spock set about creating his own.

He waited all day and half the night in the anteroom of the PentaKrem's temporary headquarters in the tiny prefab town of Sunshine, where a squadron of aides processed media personnel through their offices in an attempt to convince them that there really was no story, so would they all kindly go back home? Looking distinctly out of place in the noisy, ill-mannered mob packed to the walls in the dank, windowless anteroom, the silent figure in the watchcap and heavy dark

332

overcoat simply awaited his turn. Near midnight, when even the most entrenched of the reporters had given up and gone to supper, Spock alone remained.

An exhausted secretary was locking the inner offices when she found him.

"Everyone's gone," she told him. "You'll have to come back tomorrow."

"You are here," Spock pointed out reasonably.

"Yeah, well, I'm going home. And even if I weren't, I'm not authorized to review travel applications."

"But the assistant director is. If I am not mistaken, he is still in his office."

The secretary eyed him warily. "Says who?"

"Between seven A.M. and twelve noon today," Spock said, "seven persons including yourself entered these offices. You are the sixth to leave. I believe the person remaining is qualified to issue travel permits."

"How do you know who—"

"I was here," Spock said simply. "I watched them."

"You've been here for over seventeen hours?"

"Seventeen hours and twenty-one minutes."

The girl nodded, amazed. "And I'll bet the next thing you're going to say is that you're not leaving until you speak to the assistant director."

"Correct."

"Okay!" She sighed, sat at the reception desk, reached for a stylus and a computer form. "Let me have your name, Mr.—"

"Spock."

"First name?"

He hesitated for only a moment. "Benjamin."

"And which media service do you represent, Mr. Spock?"

Spock shook his head slightly. "I am not a reporter. I have been sent by Professor Jeremy Grayson of the Peace Fellowship."

He showed her the readout of the message from

Stockholm. Her manner toward him became suddenly deferential.

"We were told to expect Professor Grayson himself."

"The professor was taken ill," Spock said, wondering if that fact had altered radically during his travels. "I have been sent in his place."

"I see," the secretary said. "Everything seems to be in order. I'll just need some identification, Mr. Spock."

It was the one thing he had hoped to avoid. If the single item that had gotten him across borders and oceans alike to bring him here should fail him now, he could go no further. Reaching inside his collar and slipping the fine silver chain over his head, Spock cradled the symbol of peace in his hand.

It hardly compared with navigating a starship through hyperspace, Gary Mitchell thought, checking his coordinates in his jouncing snowmobile, but it had its own excitement. With luck he would reach Byrd within the hour.

Yoshi sat cross-legged on his bunk in total darkness, contemplating the rest of his life.

"He'd thought sleep would come easily after his long soul-searching talk with the psychiatrist, but her words had only replaced his old fears with new ones. If his small life was so profoundly affected by the presence of Vulcans, no wonder the rest of the world was hysterical.

Suppose T'Lera was right, and Vulcans might have come to earth within his lifetime? Suppose Dr. Bellero was right, and there were things he could do to help?

The least he could do was to go find Tatya and apologize for his caveman behavior, Yoshi decided, groping for his jeans in the dark. He would find her—and Sorahl; he knew they'd be together, possibly for the last time; the council might decide as soon as tomorrow—and tell her, tell *them* he was sorry.

Something fell out of his jeans pocket and brushed against his foot. Yoshi flicked on the reading lamp and retrieved it.

"Stupid!" he chided himself aloud, unfolding the computer printout. Anyone else would have put it in a safe place before—

Before it fell into the hands of people who would try to make him forget who had given it to him, Yoshi thought. He'd told Dr. Bellero he was no kind of hero, but maybe he could preserve something of value. With sudden determination he found a pencil, bracketed Sorahl's newly created enzyme off from the rest of the formula, and gave it a name. Then he refolded the printout and hid it in the bottom of his duffel bag, and went for a walk in the belly of the Whale.

T'Lera took the first game, forty-love.

She had come onto the court barefoot, her feet too narrow for human tennis shoes, yet another reminder of her difference.

"Never mind!" Melody waved off any objection. "Some of the best of the Aussies play barefoot." Nevertheless, she kept staring at T'Lera's feet.

"Quite within the norm of human acceptability," T'Lera assured her, extending each foot in turn against the floor as if for inspection. "Unlike the ears."

"Hey, I didn't mean—"

"Perhaps if Earth is to be our final home, your surgeons might be called upon to remedy that defect, that we might be more pleasing to the eye of the beholder." The T'Leran irony was radiating full strength. From his place on the sidelines, Jim Kirk could taste it; it made his back teeth ache. He wondered how Melody could withstand the full intensity. "Unless of course you prick us and we bleed . . ."

Have they all read Shakespeare? Kirk wondered. And was there anything more than a difference in degree between Sawyer's attitude toward Vulcan intellect and his own?

"Your serve!" Melody barked from her side of the net.

The human's sneakers made a great thumping, squeaking Earthbound protest against the surface of the indoor court, where the Vulcan seemed to float against a gravity lighter than that of her world. Melody's savage two-handed volleys were met with effortless agility, answered with lofting nonaggressive returns that gave no hint to the human opponent as to where they would vector off and descend. Jim Kirk's call of "Game!" in T'Lera's favor was merely salt in the wound, insult to injury.

"A hundred and thirteen, huh?" Melody huffed, wiping her brow with the backs of her wrists.

"Point-four-six," T'Lera replied.

Jim Kirk found himself hoping she'd beat the pants off her.

Yoshi's footsteps on the metal stairs to the bridge roused Jason Nyere from uneasy sleep.

"Wha?" The captain pulled himself upright in his chair, instinctively going for the laser pistol he'd returned to the weapons locker eight days ago; his dreams had been that troubled.

"Easy, Jason," Yoshi told him. "Just me. Not used to wearing shoes. Decks get cold at night."

"Have to fix that," Nyere muttered, orienting himself, eyeing the void of the comm screen wistfully. "The Vulcans—"

"—are becoming acclimated to the cold, Captain," one of them assured him. More awake now, Jason noticed Sorahl and Tatya as well. "Please do not trouble yourself about that."

"—time is it?" Jason wondered, squinting at the chrono.

"Time for you to get some shut-eye." Yoshi tried to help the big man out of the chair. "You can keep the screen on in your quarters, can't you? Nothing's going to happen up here; they've probably sealed off the whole continent by now."

"Ought to be on the bridge when it comes," Nyere said halfheartedly, easing himself up. He was getting too old to sleep upright in a command chair. "Captain's duty to keep the watch . . ."

He staggered. Yoshi supported him on one side, Sorahl on the other.

"Want us to call Melody to the bridge?" Yoshi asked. He got no answer; Jason was asleep on his feet. Together Yoshi and Sorahl half carried him into the radio room where there was a daybed. Tatya removed Jason's boots and found a blanket.

"Poor old man!" Yoshi mused as the three of them tiptoed out.

Except for the stray monitor light, the bridge was in total darkness. Beyond its wraparound window lay a jumbled expanse of snow-covered pack ice, trampled and dirty around the buildings at Byrd, stretching as far as the rise of the glacial ridge that marked the beginnings of the mainland. Above the ice sprawled a breathlessness of stars.

"I guess we can't see Vulcan from here," Yoshi whispered as the threesome stood together on the tower. Whatever else he was made to forget, he must somehow condition himself to seek out the small red point of Epsilon Eridani for all his nights.

"Only from your Northern Hemisphere," Sorahl replied solemnly, "my friend."

Had he sensed what emotions brought Yoshi here or, being a Vulcan and without such emotions as jealousy, did he simply disregard them in others? No one spoke, no one dared look anywhere but at the stars. Yoshi wrapped one long arm around Tatya.

She rested her head on his shoulder, recognizing as if from long ago the familiar smell of him—of sea breeze and sandalwood and something uniquely Yoshi, Earth things, human things—and sighed, content.

Yoshi's other hand went instinctively to push his lank hair out of his eyes, but stopped. Instead he tossed his head back and reached out to clasp the Vulcan's shoulder, gesture of fraternity in spite of difference.

Sorahl accepted the gesture, and with it the un-shielded turmoil of a human mind. This would be the legacy of any Vulcan who dared call human friend. Perhaps it was not yet time. But he would devote whatever remained of his life to making it time.

A metal-cold figure with infrared eyes picked out the three figures standing as one at the window of the conning tower, targets so easy even he was tempted. His weapon shifted and rose in his hands as if of its own volition; he sighted off the central figure and pondered whether it would be better to take him first, then sweep side to side to pick off the other two, or to start at either side and sweep straight across. Either way it was a matter of seconds. All three would be his.

"Racher?" A voice behind him. "There's someone there. On the bridge."

Racher lowered his weapon reluctantly.

"Not yet." His breath made no vapor on the deadly cold air. "Not yet."

"Game!" Jim Kirk called a second time, raising his hands at Melody and shrugging as if to say, What did you expect?

"Three out of five!" Melody barked, though her sides were heaving and the sweat stung her eyes even under the sweatband.

T'Lera seemed to weigh the dangers, if not the gratuitous violence, of trampling so fragile a human ego for the third time. Yet there was no question of holding back. She had accepted the challenge; she would do what she must.

"I said three out of five, goddammit!" Melody yelled across her hesitation, swinging wooden arms to keep them limber, bouncing on an ankle that hadn't hurt like this since Goddard.

T'Lera gathered herself, her bare toes gripping the service line. "As you wish, Commander."

"It's all over for you come morning!" Melody taunted her across the net as they played. "I hope you realize that!"

"Indeed," was all T'Lera said.

"I—don't understand—you people," Melody huffed, playing for her pride if not her planet. "Do not— understand you—at all! You could have—grabbed Yoshi and Tatya—and held us off. You could—grab me and the cream puff here—right now—single-handed— you're that strong. Take over the ship—hold off the whole goddamn planet! What I don't—understand—is why you don't!"

Jim Kirk had not cut across her monologue to tally T'Lera's points; it was about to be over and all he had done was witness. T'Lera's final return was a butterfly, a dove, whose wings lightly brushed the high ceiling of the gymnasium before floating slow-motion down with a precision beyond any human's saving. Jim Kirk would wonder forever after if T'Lera had intended it to be so flamboyantly poetic. As for him, he was speechless.

"Must might always make right, Commander?" T'Lera wondered, becoming very still as the ball rolled unmolested across the floor. "Are there not sometimes greater considerations?"

"'Greater considerations'!" Melody snorted, at the net. There was no attempt to concede the match, no consideration of the traditional handshake. Shake hands with a Vulcan? Impossible! "Logic and lofty ideals! You're all so noble, aren't you? You know, I think you could almost change my mind if you'd just

339

once admit to being a little less than perfect. If you'd show a little weakness, a little selfishness—a little concern for your son if nothing else.

"I have a daughter and a son not more than a year or two either side of your son's age," Melody finished. She was still out of breath, though not from tennis. "If I were in your place, I'd be on my knees begging for them!"

It would require years under the tutelage of another Vulcan to teach Jim Kirk the constant tension in the Vulcan soul between the pull of diversity and the preservation of what it means to be a Vulcan. All he could think of now was that T'Lera had met her Vulcanian Expedition, and depending upon whether her response was seen as logic or compromise . . .

"Would such a display gratify you, Commander?" There was Vulcan logic and a thousand years of peace in her voice, Vulcan pride and forty thousand prior years of ferocity in her eyes. "Is it my humility you require, or my humiliation?"

Before Melody Sawyer could find words, before Jim Kirk could move, T'Lera of Vulcan, still somehow unridiculous in her borrowed tennis clothes, was on her knees at Melody's feet. What she might have said no one would ever know; the ship's loudspeaker shattered the silence before she could speak.

"Red Alert! Red Alert!" it boomed throughout the huge empty ship in Jason Nyere's command voice. "Red Alert! First officer to the bridge!"

Sawyer took a split second to throw down her racquet and grab a sweater. Jim Kirk was already running.

Sorahl had heard the snowmobile first.

Bundled in a heavy parka—gift of the departed pacifist contingent, who had provided clothing for him and his mother, neglecting only tennis whites—he'd opened the hatch to breathe the night air, marveling at

340

a cold so different from that of his world's desert nights. If he had been listening then, he might have sensed the shifting intensity of Racher's shadow troops, who, seeing him clearly silhouetted against the stars, could barely contain themselves. But Tatya had been on her way up to join him, and the sound of her footsteps distracted him until—

"What is it?" she asked, seeing his faraway look.

"I hear something. An engine, perhaps."

Tatya listened, shook her head in amazement. "Those ears! I don't hear anything!"

But they remained very still, and after a moment she heard it too. So did Racher.

"Shoot before my order," he whispered fiercely, to make certain everyone heard him, "and you are dead before the one you shoot at."

He still somehow expected Easter's band to turn up even this much past their rendezvous, wouldn't mind at all catching them in the crossfire except that he still wanted to wait for a dawn attack. The sound was of a single engine, not two. Was Easter fool enough to approach so near with this much noise? Racher was still puzzling over it when Gary Mitchell's snowmobile crested the glacial ridge like a motocross racer and roared straight for *Delphinus*.

"Don't shoot, don't shoot!" Racher risked a shout over the mobile's roar.

There were mutters of disaffection, and he could feel his people coiling dangerously tighter. But curiosity conquered tension as the unfamiliar vehicle fishtailed to a halt in front of the great gray conning tower and a figure stepped out. Gary Mitchell took off his goggles and hailed the twosome on the tower.

"Evening!" he called up pleasantly enough. His voice was easy on the cold air. "Looking for a fellow name of Jim Kirk. Any idea how I can reach him?"

Yoshi had heard the snowmobile too, and gone to fetch Jason Nyere.

341

"Who wants to know?" Jason had ordered everyone off the tower without a word. Weaponless, groggy with sleep, and missing his boots, he was in charge nevertheless.

"A friend," Mitchell replied easily, though something he thought he'd glimpsed in the dark as he shot over the ridge, in conjunction with his strange encounter on the way in, was beginning to coalesce in an uneasy equation in his head. "He'll know me when he sees me, Captain Nyere."

Thank God he recognized the voice from Kelso's wire taps, Mitchell thought. Something was out there in the dark behind him; he had no time for formalities.

The mention of his name in conjunction with Kirk's decided Nyere to trust this apparition out of the night, for the moment. Slowly he began lowering the gangplank to the stranger. Mitchell danced in the snow like a boxer.

"Captain, I appreciate your need for caution, but aside from the fact that I'm freezing out here, there's something I think you should know about hidden just over that rise there—"

No one knew who fired first, whether it was one of Racher's dozen made crazy with waiting, or Racher himself, to cover the incredible blunder of leaving the snowmobiles plainly visible against the snow. Racher did not make blunders. Someone began to fire; all hell broke loose.

Mitchell dived for cover between ship and snowmobile, wondered as he watched tracers kicking up spurts of ice in search of him whether the mobile's thin aluminum construction offered any protection at all, wondered if he dared chance a leap to the half-lowered gangplank or if that would only make it easier for them to pick him off.

He realized he was probably dead. Nyere would assume he'd been sent to decoy the ambush and leave him to get chewed up in the crossfire. Mitchell burrowed into the snow with his hands clasped over his head and tried to remember how to pray.

Jason Nyere had ducked down from the conning tower at the first burst, sealed it behind him, and lowered the louvers over the ports while he activated the Red Alert.

"Get below!" he bellowed, grabbing Sorahl's arm, shoving Yoshi and Tatya toward the stairs. "Find T'Lera and the doctor and seal yourselves off in the infirmary until you hear from me personally. Move!"

He was breaking out hand weapons and scanning the Byrd Complex with infrared when Melody and Kirk barreled in.

"Kirk, I want to talk to you!" Jason tossed an automatic at Sawyer, who caught it one-handed.

"What the hell, Captain?" She was about in the mood to blow somebody's head off.

"I don't know yet!" Jason huffed. "Mr. Kirk here's going to tell me. Whoever they are, they're holed up in the buildings with some heavy hardware." He briefed her as rounds from the terrorists' weapons rattled off *Delphinus*'s thick hide like so many dried peas, shoved a string of sonic grenades and a helmet at her. "Get up there and keep 'em busy. I'll have a head count for you in a minute. Don't lose yours!"

"Suh!" Melody bolted up the stairs to the gunnery slit halfway up the tower; visibility was for spit, but she'd have to be damn careless to get hit from there. "What about the guy under the mobile?"

"Cover him until we find out whose side he's on!" Jason shouted back. "Kirk—"

"Captain," Jim Kirk seized the moment, "I've had weapons training. I can help."

Nyere narrowed his eyes at him. "I'll just bet you can. The question is, whom?" Bursts from Melody's automatic punctuated their sentences; the stench of overheated lubricant permeated the bridge. "You want to explain to me how a guy in a snowmobile slips through the security cordon to get here, asks for you by name, and before I can lower the drawbridge I find myself fighting World War IV?"

"Gary . . ." Kirk said with a sick feeling. It had to be. No one else would be so reckless. "I don't know anything about who's shooting out there, Captain, but the man in the snowmobile is a friend. You can trust him as much as you can trust me. Just let me get him out of there and—"

"As much as I can trust you!" Nyere exploded; he was charging a laser rifle, stringing sonic grenades around his neck as they talked. "Where the hell are my boots? Trust him like I can trust a self-proclaimed pacifist who's suddenly a weapons expert? Trust him when he's tailed by who knows how many crazies attacking on God knows what premise an AeroNav vessel which, if I could get clear of this ice could—" He began to wheeze, breathless, needing breath for more than argument. "Kirk, I *don't* trust you, and if we live through this, the first thing I'm going to do is—"

"You've got to believe me, Captain, Mitchell has nothing to do with this attack!" Kirk cut across him. He had no idea how Elizabeth Dehner managed to be beside him in the thick of things, but he gripped her hand, tried to explain. "Gary—it has to be! I have to get him out of there—"

"Cap—Jim!" Dehner's voice was shrill, her pupils dilated with fear, a fear of more than terrorists. "The Prime Directive. You can't! If you kill anyone—"

"I have to!" Kirk shouted, then got control of himself. "Captain, you've got to—"

"Doctor, I ordered you to stay below!" Jason rumbled, leading her toward the stairs. He had overheard, not that he understood. Prime Directive? What the hell . . .?

Dehner gave Kirk one last backward glance. "Jim—"

"All right, doctor!" he said tightly. "As you were!"

The military parlance suited Kirk, Jason saw. He was going to take a chance. He shoved a limited-range laser rifle into Kirk's hands.

"Go give Sawyer some backup."

But halfway up the stairs with weapon in hand, Kirk realized Dehner was right. He couldn't. Not even for Gary. But he had to do something.

He plunged up the stairs and threw himself in beside Melody at the gunnery slit; Sawyer never took her eyes off her gunsight. She was single-handedly holding the line, keeping whoever they were inside the outbuildings with steady bursts of fire, but for how long? From his limited perspective, Kirk could see the buildings of the complex, their shattered windows spitting varieties of death, and the roof of the snowmobile, but no Gary.

"Thought a ship this size would be equipped with more than hand weapons," he remarked, realizing the one he held was of such antique design he probably wouldn't be much use with it if he could figure out how to fire it.

"Brilliant deduction, cream puff!" Melody spat between rounds. "We could take out a whole city, except the heavy artillery's under the ice, and we can't move this hulk under these conditions without a full crew. If it were up to me, we'd seal off and wait for them to run out of spitballs, but captain seems to think your friend's worth saving."

She stood up and used her backhand to lob a sonic grenade damn near inside the nearest building to keep the crazies busy while she reloaded. When the shock waves subsided, Kirk tried to get her attention.

"Is there a way out of here besides topside?"

"Auxiliary hatch 'round back of the radio room. Puts the tower between you and them." Melody slid a full clip home before it dawned on her what he was suggesting. "Are you crazy?"

345

"If I can get Gary in, you can seal off," Kirk said hurriedly. "If I can't, you're rid of both of us and you can seal off anyway. Give me your grenades."

"And have you slam-dunk one in on me before you go join the opposition! Like hell!"

"Melody," Kirk said patiently, the laser rifle easier in his hands than it ought to be. If he only had a hand-phaser. "Right now I could vaporize the top of your head and the conning tower simultaneously. Will one of you for God's sake trust me enough—"

"Captain suh!" Melody shouted past him, fired another round, waited for Nyere to respond. "I read ten to twelve of them, assorted light-to-medium armament. And the cream puff wants to go play in the snow!"

"Jesus!" Nyere breathed. He would have been up there with her, but he was still on the infrared trying to get a fix on each terrorist, and he was anticipating trouble from below. Sure enough, T'Lera was there.

"Captain Nyere."

Her voice seemed to strike him like a blow, and even he for once cringed from the fire in those eyes. She had disregarded Yoshi's instructions about repairing to the infirmary for safety, had for that matter disregarded Yoshi, deflecting him and all things human until she did what she must. She was in full command mode now, formidable. Sorahl followed her without word, as if to the gates of hell, Jason thought, if Vulcans had subscribed to such things.

"Dear God," Nyere breathed, seeing her. "You're the last thing I need!"

"Captain." T'Lera had been briefed by her son, held out her hands in a gesture of surrender. "If it is us they want . . ."

Jason groaned. "Don't you understand? This is my ship! I'm not in the habit of tossing lambs to the slaughter, and until I know who and what I'm combatting, you are in my way!" His hands too made a gesture of surrender. "For the love of God, T'Lera." He had never addressed her by name before. "Please!"

It cost her much, but T'Lera acquiesced. It was not given to her to dictate to another's command, even if lives were lost. She nodded once and was gone, Sorahl with her.

Now all Jason Nyere had to contend with, aside from a dozen terrorists, was this enigma named Kirk.

A ship's captain's greatest skill lay in split-second gut-instinct decisiveness, in any century. Kirk recognized the struggle Nyere fought with himself and for once kept his mouth shut. Nyere's hand was on the string of grenades around his own neck, when—

"Pete's sake!" Melody shrieked, hurling herself backward and halfway down the stairs as a wave of flame shot through the gunnery slit, dissipating in a greasy-stinking fireball that would have fried her in an instant if not for her tennis player's reflexes. "They've got a flamer!"

Twenty-first-century flame-throwers, Kirk remembered vaguely, having heard Sulu raving about them once, were napalm-fed, laser-powered, and had a range of over a hundred yards. Hardly kid stuff, even by his century's standards. He felt Nyere thrust the grenades into his hands.

"We can't hold up long under one of those," the captain breathed. "Leave the slit open and they'll cook us one by one. Close it and they'll fine-tune the thing and slice us open like a tin can. You've got three minutes to get your friend. I'll lower the gangplank in two. When you see the tower light go on, move."

Kirk gripped his arm briefly, warriors' gesture of gratitude too ancient to eradicate, and moved.

He hadn't bothered with outdoor clothing, wouldn't have wanted the encumbrance of it, gave no thought to the incredible cold until he had to pry his hands loose from the ladder rungs as he let himself down the far side of the tower and flung himself onto the ice. He half ran, half slid until he reached the little of the prow that stuck up through the ice, his last bit of cover. Another wave of flame shot out of Byrd toward the tower, illuming a scene out of somebody's hell before plunging it back into darkness. In that instant Kirk spotted Mitchell facedown in the snow and prayed he was only covering.

Something exploded, knocking Kirk sideways off his feet. Melody was throwing grenades again, covering him. This one sent the flame-thrower back into hiding and sent Kirk into motion. He leaped, rolled, scuttled forward on hands and knees, crawled on his belly like a reptile, ran the last few yards zigzag around a burst of automatic fire that Melody quelled with yet another grenade as Kirk dived behind the snowmobile and smack on top of Mitchell.

"Gary, it's me!" he screamed above the racket, shaking Mitchell to keep him from reflexively ripping his head off. Recognition brought wild laughter and a great deal of mutual back pounding.

"Are you all right?"

"Sure, kid!" came the answer, but Mitchell's voice was ragged, his lips trembling from more than cold.

Kirk saw the tower light strobe on and sweep across the battered facades of the outbuildings, sending the terrorists scattering back from the windows out of range. The gangplank started down. Kirk shoved Mitchell toward it.

"Go! I'll cover for you!"

He thought he remembered what to do with an old-style sonic grenade; he was about to find out. He allowed himself to watch Mitchell leap for the gangplank and scramble upward to the hatch, then slipped two grenades off the string, flipped the safeties and sent them rolling in opposite directions down the alley between the complex and the ship as far as he could throw. Let them figure out *that* strategy, he thought, head down to weather the synchronized blasts. The tower light swung over his head again. Mitchell was safe inside. Kirk ran for it.

In the twisted synapses of Racher's mind, it was all Easter's fault.

He and his dozen had had great fun at the expense of the monosyllabic Provo and his traveling circus with its cumbersome killing toys—rocket launchers and vaporizers and a neutron cannon so unwieldy it took two people to fire it—toys so powerful they could not be used in close-quarters hand-to-hand without destroying attacker along with victims. Cowards' toys, Racher had called them, wishing he had them now.

If all had gone as planned, Racher thought, spitting fire with his flame-thrower, they'd have had no need for such awkward hardware, would already be inside carving their way inch by bloody inch to victory. Now only the flame-thrower stood between them and total rout. The heavy toys were with Easter, wherever the bloody hell Easter was, and there was no way to breach the ship.

"Pointless!" one of Racher's lieutenants screamed in his ear. "We can't get inside! Call it off!"

"Never!" Racher shrieked back, spitting flame across the distance, feeling his own heat and power to the exclusion of all else. A lick of flame caught Mitchell's abandoned snowmobile, incinerating it in a thunderous fireball that rocked the pack ice and the great ship.

The conning tower shuddered under the impact. Melody had barely slammed the hatch shut behind Kirk when the blast sent her sprawling the full length of the stairs this time, right into Gary Mitchell's waiting arms.

"Some reception committee!" Mitchell grinned, his humor restored now that he was inside. "Can I play?"

"Civilians!" Melody spat, dismissing him, and Kirk, who stood wringing his hands (with fear, she thought), lurched over to where Jason was getting readouts on blast damage.

"You all right?" Jason grabbed Melody, concerned.

"Been better!" she remarked, feeling around her teeth with the tip of her tongue. "Think I bit my tongue. Look at us, will you, Jason—tennis togs and stocking feet! Some defense team! How bad?"

Nyere showed her the readout. "Exterior stress fractures and partial bulkhead rupture. We'll know the next time we try to go under."

Melody meanwhile was scanning the body readings on the infrared, memorizing where they were inside the buildings. She took Jason's as-yet-unfired laser rifle from him without resistance.

"Time we put a stop to this!" she declared, bolting the stairs to the tower with eight generations of Alabama marksmen behind her.

Laser rifles make very little sound. Melody picked off three of Racher's dozen before they knew what hit them. One was the lieutenant who had pleaded for retreat. He fell inches from his leader, who never turned to look. The others, recognizing futility at last, wheeled and ran for the snowmobiles.

Only Racher remained, his metal-and-plastic body, lizard-cold, yielding no heat reading on infrared. In full awareness of a cause lost, he did not relent. Revving the flamer to its highest setting, he leaped into the clear, charging the great ship alone, spitting flame, admixture of dragon and perverse Quixote, howling vengeance like some reborn Teutonic berserker.

Whatever else Racher was, he was part of the diversity of creation. His weapon, human-made, fueled not by vengeance but only napalm, proved the less invincible. Its semisolid fuel, rendered too solid in subzero air, jammed in the feeder tube and began to drip onto Racher's arctic fatigues, saturating them. Racher's destiny came in a howling column of flame, beacon in a frozen hell, transmogrifying whatever might have been human in him into a charred lifeless hulk toppling under its own weight, smoking feebly in the snow and stolid starlight.

"They are in retreat, suh!" Melody reported, scanning the fleeing snowmobiles from the helm. The ultimate irony of Racher's incendiary end was that no one saw it. "Request permission to have a look around, see if they left any wounded."

She knew the three she'd dispatched were dead—she never missed—but she had to somehow goad Jason out of the well of weariness in which he was in danger of drowning.

"All right, dammit," he breathed now. "Let me at least get my boots on. Kirk, how'd you and your friend like a breath of air?"

"So fill me in, James," Mitchell said out of the side of his mouth as Sawyer none too subtly led them out onto the ice at gunpoint. "What have I missed? What fun times have you and the lady psychiatrist been having in my absence?"

"You'll be briefed," Kirk mouthed back, eyeing Melody over his shoulder. "As soon as you tell me what the hell you're doing here against orders."

"Oh, we-el . . ."

Kirk understood completely why Jason wanted them out here for the body count; if he were in command, he'd have done the same—kept the unknown quantities out in the open and away from the Vulcans, seen if they reacted with anything like recognition to the bodies in the buildings, or if there was anything on the dead to connect them with the living. Then, too, if there were any live ones still lurking in the vicinity, Kirk and Mitchell would do for cover.

"No ID on the three inside," Melody reported. "But the weapons were Ground Forces–issue."

"Doesn't necessarily mean what you're thinking,

351

Sawyer," Jason grunted, watching a pale newborn sun flush the ice at his feet from blue to pink. A heaping yellow-gray storm front on the opposite horizon, promising blizzards, moved in on them with ominous speed. "Lot of terrorist splinter groups have access to GF hardware—"

"Sold to them by GF regulars looking to foment insurrection and keep themselves in business. It's an old trick, and one I wouldn't put past that tin-star general who was here."

"Sawyer, conspiracy theories are as old as—" Jason began, but Jim Kirk saw an opportunity and seized it.

"Excuse me, Captain, but maybe it's not so farfetched," he offered. "Who else would know that you're out here with the Vulcans, without your crew, and on radio silence? Would it be the first time Ground Forces acted ahead of the council's decision?"

Melody was nodding sagaciously, but Jason had had enough.

"Kirk, do me a favor?" His voice was pained. "Shut up!"

Kirk did, but not before planting the seed of doubt in Nyere's mind.

"Wait'll you see what else I found," Melody said, leading them across the ice to where Racher's smoldering remains left an ugly smear of ash against snow and ice melt. "I hear tell GF is doing android research. You tell me what you make of that, Captain suh."

Together the four of them examined the mass of burned flesh and plastic fused and melting into charred metal.

"Never mind this!" Nyere looked ill. He'd been crouched over the carcass, got to his feet now, listening. "Tell me what the hell you make of *that*!"

"Chopper, suh," Melody confirmed, picking the uneven eggbeater sound out of the silence and a sudden vicious wind coming in ahead of the storm front. "Question is, whose?"

"Back inside!" Jason ordered her against the wind. "Make sure the others are secured. Swing the tower light around if that chopper comes in; that storm's going to make it darker than midnight in a minute."

"Suh!" Sawyer was running.

The helicopter Jason heard was only the lead chopper in a convoy. Further out toward the coast, before the sun was up, the inhabitants of two snowbound snowmobiles had watched them go over.

"No markings," Noir observed, scooping snow off the roof of the second mobile while Kaze checked the runners. "Could be anybody."

"Too many of them," Red said, hunched inside her parka. "It's heating up. I'm for getting out."

She'd become the unofficial spokesperson for the traveling circus following Easter's unofficial abdication. Easter hadn't moved from the driver's seat of his snowmobile throughout the long arctic night, sat singing antiquated Sinn Fein marching songs until even Aghan had gotten disgusted and scrambled out.

"His brain's froze," was the November terrorist's cheery opinion. "Not that it wasn't always stuck between gears. His fuel's gone, leaked out overnight. He's off his head. I say we leave him."

"We could've blasted that guy that came through last night!" Red spat. "If that idiot hadn't stopped us. Took his mobile, made it to the rendezvous."

Aghan shrugged. "It's all over now, with or without us. Racher's probably dead. Crazy to go up against a ship that size alone."

"It was your idea, cockroach!" Red reminded him, stamping her feet on the ice. Several more choppers went by overhead. "Enough! It's running?" she yelled to Noir, who was back inside the mobile. Noir nodded. "Good! Unload the hardware. We'll give it to Easter to keep him warm."

The motley foursome unloaded the back of the

353

second mobile, toted rocket launchers and grenades and vaporizers and the neutron cannon into the back of Easter's vehicle. Their supplier could always get them more; they could travel lighter without them. Throughout this brilliant piece of deduction the sullen Provo didn't move, sat with his eyes glazed staring through the windshield, singing his anachronistic songs.

"Now we all fit!" Red announced as the foursome squeezed back into the second snowmobile. "We go home. Anyone asks, we tell them we're journalists looking for spacemen. Only there aren't any."

They were gone in a roar and a skidding of runners, back in the direction the choppers had come, heading for the coast and a way out.

Aghan's assessment was correct. Easter's brain was frozen, partly by paralyzing cold, partly by paralyzing failure. He should have captured last night's cruising tourist, blown his brains out, taken his vehicle. He should have beaten Racher to the rendezvous and ambushed him. He should have captured the spacemen single-handed, or died in a blaze of heat and light.

Instead he sat paralyzed, living out the death he feared most.

"'A nation once again . . .'" Easter crooned hopelessly, his eyes frozen on nothingness, his rancid breath the only heat source, fogging the windshield. The numbness crept up past his knees, deceptively warm. "'And Ireland long a-promised be, A nation once again . . .'"

"We've lost 'em," the lead chopper's pilot told her VIP passenger as they emerged from the cloud cover without their unwanted escort and roared in ahead of the storm, swooping down like an oversize grasshopper on the three figures transfixed on the ice.

From inside the ship, Melody nailed the chopper with the tower light. Jason, watching it loom on him, gripped his weapon and wondered if maybe Melody

354

and Kirk were right, and this whole thing had been orchestrated to eliminate the Vulcans and blame it on untraceable terrorists. He kept Kirk and Mitchell well out in front of him for cover; the laser rifle rose slowly in his hand.

The chopper pilot had a voice augmenter. "Hold your fire, Jason. I'm a friendly!"

Jason had to laugh, recognized Raven Takes-the-Bow, AeroNav Aux South's ace pilot.

"Raven!" he shouted, waving both arms to let Melody know it was okay. "What the hell are you doing here?"

"Can't stop to chat, Jace. Got a VIP to unload and a passel of reporters on my tail."

"Reporters?" Jason repeated. Raven was still hovering; could do it for hours, she was that good. "Come down here and quit blowing my hair around!"

The chopper lowered ponderously onto the ice and cut her motor to half. A solitary figure in a dark coat and watchcap stepped uncertainly over the pontoons to confront Jim Kirk, whose face lit up like the sun coming out from behind a cloud. Of all the improbable chimera this old Earth had to offer—

"Spock!"

Chapter Ten

"Spock!" Between the wind, the chopper's noise and sheer disbelief, Jim Kirk could barely draw breath to speak. "I can't tell you; I never expected to see you again! Certainly not here."

"Indeed, Captain. I might say the same of you."

"We have to talk!" Kirk shouted. "Captain Nyere, shouldn't we go inside? The storm—"

"Hold your water a minute, Kirk!" Nyere shouted back; he was leaning inside the chopper to talk to Raven. "Who is this guy? And what reporters?"

Raven shrugged. "He's from the Peace Fellowship. Reporters're from everywhere. Had to let 'em through. Freedom of Information Act, or some such. Best you take your guest aboard and maybe roll up the shutters for a few days. Law says we have to bring 'em in here, but no law says you have to bring 'em aboard."

"There's one more thing!" Jason shouted, and he told her about the terrorist raid, the three dead inside the buildings, the one in the snow. "Tell Command. Someone's going to have to come in and get them out of here."

"Not till this blows over." Raven nodded in the

direction of the storm front. The wind had gone from freight-train roar to banshee howl, and stinging sheets of sleet threatened the rotors. "Give the reporters something to work on. Have to go."

Jason had barely stepped over the pontoons before she lifted off, wheeling around the worst of the front and heading back with a cheery wave. Nyere led his charges inside.

First Mate Melody Sawyer was not on the bridge where she should have been.

Maybe it had to do with her killing three people, something she'd only had to do once before, and then because Jason's life depended on it; Jason alone knew how soft she was beneath the John Wayne exterior. Maybe it had to do with conspiracy theories and the arrival of yet another of Kirk's mysterious friends, on the heels of a terrorist attack and in a VIP helicopter no less. Maybe it had to do with her not sleeping well since she'd first set eyes on a Vulcan, and not sleeping at all within the past twenty-four hours. Maybe it had to do with nothing more than the descrambled message still beeping through on the comm screen:

Council's decision expected within the hour. Stand by.

Melody wasn't supposed to know Jason's Priority One access code. Obviously she'd known enough of it to descramble the message, which had flung her into action without bothering to acknowledge it. Jason acknowledged by reflex, thinking: What action?

"Oh, dear God!" he breathed, seeing the weapons locker open, the marksman's laser rifle replaced, his small hand pistol gone. "Kirk, you and your people stay here."

Jim Kirk had sized up the situation at the same time Nyere did. Maybe it was having most of his crew back that galvanized him, but this time Kirk wasn't taking no for an answer.

"Melody said she'd kill the Vulcans if she had to, to keep you clear!" He gripped the big man's shoulders, shook him hard. "You've got to let us help. If there were time, I'd tell you who and what we are—"

"There's no time!" Jason roared, flinging Kirk back to where Mitchell had to grab him.

Footsteps made them all turn. Elizabeth Dehner came up to the bridge, unaware of any new crisis.

"Melody said Jim was looking for me," she explained, saw Mitchell and Spock, stopped in her tracks. "I—"

"Where is Sawyer now?" Jason demanded, wild-eyed, voice shaking. Unthinking, he slipped a second laser pistol into his belt, then stopped, put it back inside the locker, slammed it shut. Dear God, was this what it came down to: friend against friend for the sake of strangers and a difference of opinion?

"She said she was going to the infirmary to give the others the All-Clear," Dehner said, totally bewildered.

"Captain," Jim Kirk began.

"No, Kirk," Jason said. "My ship. My responsibility."

It was the one argument that could stop Kirk, even momentarily. And in that moment Jason was past him. The four on the bridge heard Nyere double-time down the steps, heard a rush of air and clanking of bolts that meant he had sealed the bridge off from the rest of the ship. They were trapped.

Jim Kirk rushed down the steps, pounded on the sealed bulkhead, too late.

"Jason!" he yelled. "Jason, listen to me!

"Damn!" he whispered tightly, returning to the bridge, collapsing unawares in the captain's chair. "I tried to stay within bounds, tried to do it by the book, and I've failed! My fault!"

Mitchell had no time for self-recrimination. He and Spock were already stripping down for action, removing their heavy outdoor clothing, though Spock wisely retained the watchcap. Mitchell was soon at the gunnery slit, casing the joint. He whistled softly. "Oh, boy!"

Kirk was on his feet. "What is it?"

"Well, take your pick," Mitchell said. "A major blizzard packing about eighty-mile-an-hour winds, or three big old choppers grounded and stuffed to the gills with media types. Getting out of here isn't going to be easy."

"Out is not the way we want to go," Kirk said emphatically. "Spock, there has to be an override to trigger that hatch." He sat the Vulcan down in his seat at the console.

"Captain, I am still uninformed as to the reason for Captain Nyere's actions or our need for urgency."

"Later, Spock, later. If there is a later," Jim Kirk said. "Gentlemen, let's go to work."

Melody had been only too pleased to find the lady shrink floating the corridors against orders; sending her to the bridge had eliminated one major stumbling block. Jason's laser pistol, concealed in the pocket of her tennis sweater, would eliminate the rest.

"Over there!" she ordered T'Lera without preamble, locking the infirmary door behind her, bracing her back against it for cover, the laser pistol aimed right between those quizzical eyebrows. "Junior, you too. Yoshi, Tatya, stay where you are. Don't even breathe!"

Tatya gave a little involuntary cry. "Melody!"

"I—said—don't—breathe!" Melody rasped, not taking her eyes off the Vulcans. "Sit still! This time tomorrow you'll be on your way home and it will all be a bad dream! They'll be 'wiped,' their memories erased," she explained offhandedly to T'Lera, wondering why she bothered; she owed the Vulcan nothing. "We all will."

"Indeed?" The Vulcan had risen to her feet at once, unfaltering. Not an overly imposing figure, but one to whom attention was due nevertheless. "And this permits you to take our lives?"

"Better me than Jason," Melody said, her jaw set.

"I quite understand," T'Lera said. "But would it not be preferable that I accept the responsibility?"

Melody's gun hand faltered. "You'd do that? Take your own life, kill your own son?"

"I had thought to spare my son," T'Lera said, a color to her voice that none of them had heard before, except perhaps Sorahl, in a time before memory. "On the tennis court you suggested my weakness would move you. This is my weakness: I would plead for my son, for his life and his freedom in exchange for mine. Would you have granted me this?"

"I wouldn't have had the authority," Melody began, but it was Sorahl's voice T'Lera heard.

"My commander has instructed me to inform her should I detect a flaw in her logic." As he had aboard their scoutcraft, he sought to dissuade her from sacrificing another's life for his.

"Be silent!" T'Lera cautioned him, knowing what he was attempting. Her eyes never left Melody's "I see, Commander, that—"

"Mother," Sorahl said now as he had then.

"*Kroykah!*" T'Lera hissed now as she had then, violating her father's dictate and her own in regard to languages unknown to all who could hear her voice. If her son above all did not understand what she did and why—Her control was all but shattered; gathering the shards she had left, she focused all her will on Melody. "I see now I was in error. You cannot give my son freedom, only death. But it must be by my hands. I *will* ask for this. Then you may do with me what you will."

Melody shook her head. "You could really do that?" She looked at Sorahl, as if expecting common sense from him at least. "And you'd permit it?"

The young Vulcan had stood with head bowed beneath his mother's reprimand. Now his velvet-dark eyes met Melody's.

"It was our intention from the beginning," he said with some fledgling mastery that might someday have flourished to equal his mother's.

"Aboard your ship, in a crisis—I can see that!" Melody's hand was frankly shaking now; she two-handed the pistol, lowered it more toward T'Lera's heart, or where it was supposed to be. "But in cold blood? I don't—"

"Our blood is no colder than yours, Commander," T'Lera said, deliberately misunderstanding. "The weapon is not needed. Only give us a place where we may be alone."

"I do not understand you people at all!" Melody shouted, very near hysteria. Even two-handed she could not keep the pistol still. "I don't want your nobility, your pity, your goddamn condescending Vulcan 'understanding'—"

"Looks like you're stuck with them anyway, John Wayne," Jason rumbled from the side, stepping in beside T'Lera.

Melody cursed herself for a punchy sleep-deprived fool; she'd forgotten all about the waiting-room entrance. How much had he heard?

"Captain suh," she said, chin up, control regained, voice colder than the blizzard raging outside. "You are in my line of fire!"

"And *that*," Kirk concluded, watching Spock manipulating switches at the helm control while Mitchell and Dehner worked over the weapons locker with Kelso's lock pick, "is how we end up gathered here today.

Except for Kelso. Only God knows where Lee Kelso is."

"Only God and Mr. Kelso," Spock corrected him mildly, touching a final toggle and sitting back as the hatch below clanked and slid open like magic. "I should like to meet this Parneb. A discussion of temporal dynamics with such a being would be most illum—"

"Later," Kirk cut him off, grabbing a weapon from Mitchell. He thought fast. The fewer people who got a look at Spock— "Mr. Spock, you and Dr. Dehner will wait here. Don't let anybody else aboard. Mr. Mitchell, let's go!"

"Tatya, don't be an idiot!" Melody said.

"I know what I'm doing!" the young woman said with a quietude and dignity that surprised everyone. She had used the distraction of Jason's arrival to move across the room to where the Vulcans were, blocking their bodies with her own. "I can't let you take them away again! I can't live with never knowing what happened! If you can kill two innocent people, Melody Sawyer, the third can't be all that hard."

Exasperated, Melody almost lowered her weapon. "Yoshi, do something! Talk some sense into her, can't you?"

The young man stood alone on the far side of the room, separated from everything he believed in by the point of a laser. He'd told Dr. Bellero he was no kind of hero. Was it heroism to admit he couldn't stand by and watch these people destroyed?

"I never could talk her into anything; you know that." He swept his hair out of his eyes, moved to join the others casually. "Give it your best shot, Mel. No one'll blame you."

Did she only imagine she heard Jason laughing at her again? He was out of her range of vision, off to the side where she'd bullied him with the pistol, not realizing he

362

was that much closer to grabbing it from her if he'd wanted to.

"Well, John Wayne?" he rumbled. "Looks like you've got the whole shooting match. What're you going to do with it?"

Melody lowered the pistol, let it fall to the floor, flung herself at Jason and began to pound him with her fists. He held up his hands and let her until, exhausted, she fell sobbing against him, and he wrapped her in a bear hug and stroked her hair.

Her voice was muffled by his tunic. "Damn you anyway, Jason Nyere!"

"Yeah, I know," he soothed. "Pity the council won't be as easy to persuade! Come on, tough guy. I'm going to put you to bed."

It was the moment Kirk and Mitchell chose to kick in the infirmary door.

"Sorry," Kirk offered lamely. "We thought there might be a problem."

Jason Nyere, still holding Melody, threw back his head and roared.

Humans! T'Lera thought, more with incredulity than with disgust. For them it was over—one crisis averted, a moment of levity before the next—the final—crisis, and its final solution. Did they not understand that in that moment of shared levity the responsibility for that final solution had fallen out of human hands, and into Vulcan, where it should have been from the beginning?

The responsibility was now T'Lera's alone. The methodology would be at her discretion, in the place of privacy that she had asked of Melody Sawyer. She would do what she must—soon, now, before humans could intervene yet again.

"You will inform Captain Nyere that we are returning to our quarters to await his superiors' decision," she instructed her son in her best command tone and, answering his unasked question: "Nothing more."

"Understood, Commander," Sorahl replied, taking her meaning, placing his life once more in her hands. "I am prepared."

His mother/commander acknowledged his fealty with her silence, and departed, that she might also be prepared.

Jason had ordered Kirk and his party to remain in Kirk's quarters while he sorted things out. Dehner, sitting on her bunk in the small cabin, reluctantly made room for Mitchell. Her sharing a cabin with Kirk had required some explaining.

"Lovers, huh?" Mitchell teased her now, scrunching in beside her. "Just for the sake of the mission? You expect me to believe that? Why, old Jim here's got a reputation second only to mine for—"

"Gary, not now!" Kirk snapped. He turned to Dehner, the beginnings of an idea forming in his head. "Did you get what you needed?"

"Fortunately for us," Dehner reported. "One of the station personnel on Agro Four has a form of Parkinson's Disease, and he's under treatment with Neodopamine. *Delphinus* delivers it to him two or three times a year. I managed to get hold of a six-month supply. Far more than we'll need. And there was enough Demerol down there to chill out the entire southern hemisphere. I took as much as I could fit in my pockets."

"Then you're set?" Kirk wanted to know.

"On the supply side, yes. But I'll need a clear head and a quiet place to work before I dare try hypnosis under such primitive conditions."

"We'll see you get everything you need," Kirk said with more assurance than he felt.

"Everything she needs for what, Kirk?" Jason Nyere was beyond the amenities by now, hadn't bothered to knock. "I came to ask you to give Melody a shot of something." He addressed Dehner. "Calm her down, help her sleep, and, frankly, keep her out of my hair for the next couple of hours."

"Of course, Captain," Dehner said.

"I've just come from topside," Nyere said to them all. "The blizzard looks to be letting up some, which means we'll have reporters spewing out of those choppers and swarming up the sides in no time. And it's been half an hour since the last message from Command. That gives me less than that much time to find a way around an order that in conscience I can't obey."

He handed Dehner a key. "I'll show you where we keep the prescription stuff."

"I know where it is, Captain." Dehner took the key from him, thinking wryly of all the skulking around she'd had to do last night. "I won't be long."

"Thank you!" Jason nodded. Nothing this bunch did could surprise him anymore—he thought. He waited until Dehner had left. "Everything she needs for what, Kirk?"

"About your orders, Captain," Kirk stalled, though he already knew what he was going to do. "Are you so sure what they'll be?"

"Kirk, I'm career AeroNav," Nyere said wearily. "That makes me an authority on Murphy's Law. I've also lived long enough to know that it's human nature to solve a small problem by turning it into a bigger one. This Vulcan way of logic begins to sound very appealing after a while."

He shook his head in disbelief. "Why am I telling you this? I've been staring down the barrel of a general court-martial since I first met the lady with the ears. It doesn't matter anymore who you are or if I can trust you; I'm finished."

"What are you going to do?" Jim Kirk asked him quietly.

Jason sighed. "It may be a fate worse than death, but

with the lady's permission I'm going to turn her and her son over to those reporters as soon as the weather clears. I don't know anyone else who could hold up better under the three-ring circus, and once she does not even the PentaKrem can pretend she doesn't exist."

"Captain," Jim Kirk said tightly, "that's the worst thing you can possibly do."

"Oh, is it?" Jason said mildly. "Says who?"

"I guess we still have a lot of explaining to do," Kirk said.

"I'd say that was about right," the captain of the *Delphinus* conceded dryly.

"Well!" Kirk said breezily, rubbing his hands together. Once the decision was made, the rest was easy. Sort of. "Captain, I think you'd better sit down. What we have to tell you is more than a little incredible."

"So if you tell T'Lera what you've just told me . . ." Jason Nyere said after he'd absorbed it all.

"I'm afraid we can't do that, Captain," Kirk said.

"Why not? It would solve everything. If she understood she and her son were interfering with history—"

"We cannot burden T'Lera with certain knowledge of the future, Captain Nyere," Spock explained. Nyere had not been able to take his eyes off this new Vulcan, this confirmation that there really was a planet full of them, and offshoots scattered throughout the galaxy, and who knew what manner of other strange, exotic beings out there to be encountered in a future Jason Nyere would not live long enough to share. The knowledge Kirk had given him was both a joy and great bitterness; he would be glad to be free of it. "Vulcans cannot be made to 'forget' by means of drugs and hypnosis as humans can; therefore whatever information we gave T'Lera, she would have to retain for life. Further, if we are to enable her and Sorahl to return to Vulcan, as I assume we are—"

"Gary may have come up with a solution to that," Kirk interjected, giving Mitchell the floor.

"We may be able to 'borrow' a spacecraft," Mitchell said, ungluing himself from the doorframe where he'd taken to lounging. "There's an abandoned missile installation left over from the Third War dug into the rock under the Western Desert; I flew over it on the way here. PentaKrem records state everything portable's been removed, but there are still three DY-100 sleeper ships unaccounted for, and it's my guess that unless they've been stripped for parts, they're still down there. Not exactly your late-model heavy cruiser, but since I don't think we're likely to scrounge up any antimatter, much less dilithium—"

"Antimatter?" Jason Nyere frowned. "Di-who?"

"Thank you, Mr. Mitchell," Kirk warned. "No need to get too technical. Or to give Captain Nyere too much to forget. What he's saying, Captain, is the same thing you and I discussed a few days ago: if we can get the Vulcans out of here, we can conceivably crank up one of those old sleepers and get them safely off the planet. Granted, it might take them ten years to get back home, but considering the alternatives—"

"You'll have my help, Kirk," Nyere promised. "*Captain* Kirk. Although I don't know how much help that can be without my crew."

"We're—not inexperienced in running a ship, Captain." Kirk eyed Gary thoughtfully. "For the moment, I can at least scare you up a decent navigator. Under duress he's even been known to get his hands dirty."

"Mr. Mitchell," Nyere said, shaking his hand incredulously. "Welcome aboard!"

"Spock, help me!"

This was not a voice Spock had ever heard before. It was not the dispassionate voice of a commander issuing an order, not the sarcasm-tinged tone of the sometime-martinet who had chewed him out on the bridge of the *Enterprise* in a time that had not yet happened, but the voice of a man who had been to the abyss and understood his chances of falling—a man humbled, vulnerable, in need. To fail to respond to such need would be not only illogical, but cruel.

"Help you, Captain? In what way?"

"Instruct me," Kirk said. "Tell me what to say to T'Lera. Because I must go in there, Spock. I must know what to do, what to say to her. And I keep seeing blood on the walls if I fail."

"Captain," Spock hesitated, not wishing to give offense, not knowing how to avoid it. "I do not think it is possible to teach you to fully—understand, to counter T'Lera's reasoning—to think—"

"Like a Vulcan?" Kirk finished, more frustrated than angry. Spock's long hoped-for reappearance had solved nothing. He must speak to T'Lera, but what could he say that he had not said already, and to no avail? He rose from his bunk, all but started out the door. "I have to do something!"

Impatience serves no purpose, Spock thought, and considered what he might have done if Kirk were not here. Had T'Lera come from his own time, a victim of Parneb's tampering as he was, his choices would have been simpler. Nevertheless— "There is an alternative. Logically, I am better able to persuade T'Lera to our ends. If I can do so without revealing my true identity —you must permit me to go alone."

"No!" A clatter of bootheels announced Elizabeth Dehner's return. "You cannot do it alone! Neither of you can! Don't you see? The risk is too great. T'Lera has to know what her actions will do to future history. There is no other way. The way she sees it now, she's caught between a rock and a hard place, and she's fully prepared to sacrifice two lives to what she believes must be done. And you two sit here squandering what little time you have left, perpetuating the myth that humans and Vulcans are so different there can be no common understanding, when—"

"That's enough, Doctor—" Kirk began.

"I don't think so!" she snapped, her pale hair flailing about her face in her intensity. "Haven't you learned anything about trust, Captain? Or you, Mr. Spock? How can you expect to convince T'Lera that humans and Vulcans can work together if you don't believe it yourselves. *You cannot do it alone*," Dehner repeated.

Kirk met Spock's eyes and held them. Both were silent for a moment.

"Do we know where T'Lera is now?" Kirk asked of no one in particular. If what Dehner said was true, every second counted.

"In her cabin," the psychiatrist reported. "Sorahl told Yoshi they would 'await the Council's decision in their own privacy,' unquote."

It was all Kirk needed to hear.

"We go together then, Mr. Spock," he said. The Vulcan was already on his feet. "Together, or not at all."

T'Lera stood alone in the darkness of her cabin, considering the hordes congregating outside the ship.

Some, she thought, would put us on display, and Jason Nyere would permit them, for the sake of the greater good. Others would kill us merely because of our differences, and Melody Sawyer would join them.

They are not ready, she thought. And we must not force them.

Mine is the error, she thought, for not acting sooner. Now mine will be the solution.

"Mother?" Sorahl stood uncertainly in the doorway, framed by the light from the hall.

T'Lera's thoughts had summoned her son. She turned to face him.

"Sorahl-*kam* . . ." she began.

* * *

"She's unarmed," Kirk said as he and Spock hurried down the corridors. "Theoretically she could strangle Sorahl with her bare hands, but—"

"No, Captain. That is not what she would do," Spock said, well aware of what T'Lera would do. *Tal-shaya* for her son, having sought his permission in mind-meld, then a variation on the healing trance for herself—a trance from which no one could waken her—would be T'Lera's choice.

Spock froze in mid-stride, staggered, winced as if in pain. *"Captain!"*

They were just outside T'Lera's door. Kirk grabbed him.

"What is it?"

"I sense—Captain, it has already begun. T'Lera has—"

Kirk crashed through the door, groping for the lights. Spock was right behind him.

Sorahl lay unmoving on the bunk. T'Lera had been seated beside him, her fingers at the reach centers of his face. She was on her feet at once.

"I had forgotten humans lock their doors," she said, her eyes darting from Kirk to his unidentified companion, lingering perhaps overlong on the stranger before fixing on Kirk. "You will leave us."

"No, ma'am," Kirk said adamantly. "See if Sorahl is all right," he ordered Spock, his eyes never leaving T'Lera's.

Spock moved, but T'Lera moved faster, standing between her son and any outside force. Spock realized if he came any closer, if she touched him, she would know what he was.

"I surmise Sorahl is as yet unharmed," he said, "though in deep trance. We have not much time."

His words, his voice, drew T'Lera's attention only for a moment.

"Do not interfere," she said, her eyes still locked on

370

Kirk's. "This is no longer any human thing. Your world is not ready for us. By my logic, there is no other way."

"But there is—!" Kirk said, and stopped himself. Was he out of his mind? Was the only answer to tell T'Lera the truth? Was violating a Prime Directive that did not yet exist the only way to guarantee a future in which it would?

"Commander," he began, feeling his throat tighten around each word. A single wrong one would end everything. "What can I say to persuade you?"

T'Lera studied him, the intensity of her eyes damped down so as not to intimidate him. How vulnerable these humans were! Was it logical, was it ethical, to leave them isolated in a galaxy fraught with unknowns? For the briefest moment she might have relented for this reason alone. But that decision was not for her to make.

"Do not think to persuade me with words, Mr. Kirk," she said slowly. "But if you offer a perspective which outweighs mine . . ."

Jim Kirk hesitated. And in that momentary hesitation, the burden fell to Spock—

—who studied T'Lera, and considered. She looked, he thought, precisely as he had surmised she might, given what she was. Vulcan and commander, dweller in the void of space for more years than he had lived, she would no more be moved by mere dialectic than any Vulcan. Nor was she the only Vulcan caught between a rock and a hard place. Could his human captain possibly understand the moral implications of what they were about to do?

For nothing less than absolute truth, Spock saw, would satisfy T'Lera. Nothing less than certain knowledge of the future would sway her from her present course. And once accepted, that truth, that knowledge would be hers to carry—alone, unrelieved, and in unbroken silence—for all time.

Neither word nor thought, neither mind-touch nor mere slip of tongue could reveal any portion of that truth to any other of her truth-seeking, telepathic kind. Self-exile would be T'Lera's choice—an absolute solitude in which to preserve an absolute truth.

Spock had no doubt T'Lera would consider such death-in-life an equitable exchange for the life of her son and the fate of two species. It was logical. But it was a bitter thing.

T'Lera had been correct; this was no longer any human thing. Only a Vulcan could accept such responsibility. And only one neither human nor Vulcan could make it known to her.

"Commander," Spock began, wondering for the first time in his life which of his worlds he spoke for. "What can I say to persuade you?"

T'Lera now studied him, making no effort to mitigate her gaze. This one, whatever he was, did not fear her. She must know why.

"Who are you?" she asked, slowly approaching him.

Spock hesitated. Since he had entered the room, all his energy had been given to blocking her thoughts from his, preventing her from knowing this very thing. He had only to open his mind . . .

"Who are you?" T'Lera said again, drawing very near. Somehow she sensed that her fate was in his hands, as his future was in hers. Yet she must know.

He is the same as you! Jim Kirk wanted to cry out against the awful silence. As I am, as we all are—more alike than different, stronger together than alone! Dehner's words echoed in his ears, haunted him.

Kirk held his peace. Shouting would not serve. Mere words would not serve.

A perspective which outweighed hers, T'Lera had said. There was no other way.

Kirk looked at Spock, and knew his first officer had reached the same conclusion. Kirk nodded. "Do it," he said.

Slowly Spock removed his hat.

T'Lera's gaze never faltered.

Her far-searching eyes saw in Spock's the future that would form him—halfling, hybrid, offspring of the best of both worlds, bridge between the world presently lost to both of them and the world on which they stood. She whom no planet could contain recognized one kindred soul.

And another. T'Lera's gaze took in Kirk—so obviously human and yet, she saw now, no Earthbound thing. In these two she beheld not one future but two—a future that would give them life, and a future within that future which they themselves could not yet see, which would forge them, at each other's side, into a whole greater than the sum of its parts.

T'Lera saw the future, and accepted the challenge.

The blizzard had let up. The media people, frustrated in their efforts to cut in on *Delphinus*'s silenced radio, had set up a loudspeaker system out of their pooled audio equipment, and mounted a continuous auditory assault upon the battened-down ship.

"Captain Nyere!" boomed out across the ice, penetrating the thick hull to where Nyere and Mitchell labored. *"Captain Nyere! We demand to see the aliens! We demand to know who is responsible for the deaths of four citizens of Earth. We demand—"*

"Citizens of Earth!" Nyere snorted, getting the bugs out of the sonar and checking his fuel consumption ratios.

"Kind of clears your sinuses, doesn't it?" Mitchell mused, working with Yoshi to repair the stress fractures caused by the snowmobile's explosion.

Tatya was manning the radio, jamming everything the media tried to ram through. Jason had drafted the twosome along with Mitchell. After some soul-searching, he'd told them why.

"There's *another* Vulcan on board?" Tatya was overwhelmed by this information; the fact that these were people from another century seemed to have gone right by her. "Can we see him, talk to him?"

"Then what T'Lera and Dr. Bellero—I mean, Dr. Dehner—said was true," Yoshi marveled, staring at Mitchell as if he expected him to glow. "Someday we really will have an alliance with Vulcan."

"And about five hundred other worlds, son," Mitchell assured him. "But not unless you and I get this jury-rigging done right, and fast."

"Gods!" Yoshi said, working faster.

The noise outside was, if possible, growing louder; some of the media types had gotten up the nerve to attempt a physical assault on the great ship, climbing the conning tower and banging on the hatch as if they expected it to open magically for them.

"Hey, Captain!" Mitchell yelled above the loudspeaker, the banging, and Yoshi's welding torch. "How soon before we can put some distance between us and them?"

"Right now!" Jim Kirk announced, striding onto the bridge. T'Lera and Sorahl were with him, and Spock was at his side.

A man couldn't ask for a better crew, Jason Nyere thought, quietly amazed at what he saw happening on his bridge.

The virtually inseparable younger threesome was down in the engine room, the doctor—whatever her real name was—had gone to check on Melody and get some rest herself, and the bridge was still top-heavy with talent. Jason's helmsman, a starship captain in another life, sat at ease beside one of a plethora of navigators, and this new Vulcan, who in his quiet way seemed capable of handling any station, had his ears on, so to speak, at communications. Jason Nyere sat back in his command chair, utterly confident that they would reach their destination, whether it was Fairbanks or Timbuktu.

"A little closer to the latter, I think," Kirk had told him after conferring with Mitchell. "We'll know for sure as soon as we can open communications."

Nyere watched, bemused and utterly calm. He'd used up about a year's worth of adrenaline in the past few days; calm was all he had left. Beside him, essence of calm, stood T'Lera—watchful, certain, as if no ship's bridge were alien to her.

They would be going under the ice.

The racket outside had virtually ceased when a new storm front moved in, first scattering those pounding on the hull, then toppling audio equipment and sending everyone back to the helicopters or to the cold comfort of the complex from where, as Spock reported: "They are tapping our communications, Captain."

It was never clear which captain he addressed; both turned their heads whenever he spoke.

"Let them!" Jason Nyere said. "They'll get an earful in a moment. Engine room: stand by. I'll want full steam in five minutes—mark."

"Affirm, Captain," came Sorahl's crisp response.

I could get used to this, Jason told himself.

The comm screen crackled ominously.

"Message incoming, Captain," Spock reported unnecessarily. The import of the message did not disturb him as much as the fact that: "They are three minutes, fourteen seconds late."

Nyere opened his mouth to say something—he didn't know what—but Jim Kirk had turned from the helm to cut him off.

"Don't mind him, Captain; he does that all the time."

"Understood, Captain," Nyere said conspiratorially. "Transfer to my screen, please, Mr. Spock."

Only the brief flick of his tongue over parched lips

indicated Nyere's nervousness as he prepared to lay his personal future on the line for the sake of a larger one.

" 'The whole world is watching,' " he murmured softly.

It got Kirk's attention. "That's from something, isn't it?"

"Ancient history," was all Jason would say as the bland face of Norfolk Command appeared on his screen.

"Prepare to receive your final orders per disposition of your detainees, Captain."

"Command, stand by, please." Unseen, Nyere motioned to Spock, then leaned into the screen. "Command, we have reason to believe we are under frequency tampering. Repeat: someone is tapping us, Commodore . . ."

Slowly, methodically, Spock began to manipulate a series of dials in the order Nyere had shown him. The commodore's face began to jiggle and blur on the screen.

"We have been under siege by the media since 0830 hours," Nyere continued. "Suggest they may be responsible . . ."

Spock manipulated more dials. The commodore was fairly dancing on the screen now, as well as fluttering in and out. Onscreen at Norfolk Command HQ, Jason Nyere was doing the same thing.

". . . also a storm front moving in, contributing to—"

"Say again, Captain." The commodore seemed to be having difficulty with his voice. Spock's fingers continued to work their magic. "Not—you clearly. Repeat—"

"Sorry, Command, unable to comply," Jason Nyere said in all innocence, and Jim Kirk wondered silently if all ships' captains were blessed with glibness. "Message is breaking up. Repeat—"

At the unseen downsweep of Nyere's hand, Spock broke the connection. T'Lera watching, might have had second thoughts about a future that taught a Vulcan such duplicity.

"Bridge to engine room!" Nyere opened the intership, nodded to Kirk and Mitchell. "Open her up!"

The diving klaxon whooped in time with Jim Kirk's heart as the great ship surged under him, never as smoothly as *Enterprise*, but with a kindred pent-up majesty. The ice surrounding them groaned in protest, as probably did whoever at Byrd could see through the blizzard, as the great ship shrugged them both off simultaneously and lowered away, sounding the depths like some massive version of the creature it was named for.

Jason stepped down from the center seat. "Commander?" he addressed T'Lera formally. "While I ride herd on the sonar, would you care to take the con?"

T'Lera's eyebrows expressed what she could not. "I would be honored, Captain."

Even at this depth, they had to watch out for ice.

"Just treat 'em like asteroids, kid," Mitchell advised Kirk, plotting a course around yet another ominous chunk.

"Give me phaser power and I will!" Kirk retorted, though he was having the time of his life.

Once past the ice and the three-mile limit, they made top speed.

"Captain," Spock announced when they dared break radio silence, "I have reached the mobile transmitter at the coordinates Mr. Mitchell has provided."

"Parneb," Jim Kirk explained from the command chair; it was his turn to play captain. "Gary said to expect a one-word message. Either we're all clear to come ashore where he is, or we'll have to await a new rendezvous."

Spock listened. "The answer is in the affirmative, Captain."

Jim Kirk stopped holding his breath. "Good. Captain Nyere, how much of a safety margin would you say we had?"

"Figure it took them an hour or two to guess we'd bolloxed our own communications," Jason said. "By now they know we've cut and run, but they have no idea where. They'll have deployed whatever they can spare, but they'll be bumping heads in the dark if they're not careful. As long as we stay under, we're maybe an hour ahead of them."

Jim Kirk relaxed in the center seat; it was about what he'd calculated himself.

Bridge personnel had altered somewhat. Sorahl had replaced Mitchell at navigation; beside him, T'Lera had the helm. Spock, of course, remained at communications. The sight of three Vulcans running the ship had given Melody Sawyer a turn.

"What the hell, Captain suh?" she greeted Nyere after her nap. She'd been updated on the situation, not that she believed any of it. She gave the new communications officer a good hard look. "Mr. Spock, is it?"

"Affirmative," he said, returning the look in kind.

Melody sighed. "Well, there goes the neighborhood!"

"Consider the future, Sorahl-*kam*," his mother said so softly human ears could not hear, her eyes upon the hybrid Spock and his human companions.

The young Vulcan had been doing precisely that. "Are we instrumental in this, Mother? Is it because of us?"

"In spite of us, my son . . ."

"Captain suh, are you mad at me?"

"Why? Just because you shot up the chandeliers and damn near busted all my ribs? Why, Melody, think nothing of it . . ."

"Earth will never know!" Jim Kirk mused aloud. "They'll never know what they had in their hands.

What they came so close to missing, what they almost destroyed!"

"Indeed, Captain. But in the fullness of time . . ."

"When they've learned," Jim Kirk said. "Matured, as I had to. Spock, I—"

"Captain, centuries of peace preceded Vulcan's sending T'Lera to Earth. Humans had less time in which to mature. Yet, on the whole, each of us has done remarkably well—together."

The farewells were necessarily brief.

"'Sail forth, steer for the deep waters only . . .'" Jason Nyere rumbled, unsuccessfully banking down his too-human emotions.

"'For we are bound where mariner has not yet dared to go . . .'" T'Lera added. Earth's poetry had been among her many studies.

"'And we will risk the ship, ourselves and all.'" Jason kissed her hand. "I'm going to miss you, lady."

"Live long and prosper, Jason Nyere," T'Lera replied. "I will hold you in my thoughts."

Only she would know for how long.

Yoshi and Sorahl had no words. A simple handshake joined them for the last time.

"So long, Junior," Melody Sawyer blustered. God, but her daughter would hate her for letting this one get away! "Tell your mom I—tell her I'm sorry. Tell her maybe I'll mellow out in about twenty years."

"I shall tell her," Sorahl promised, his velvet-dark eyes betraying some appreciation of Terran humor. "Though I do not believe it."

"Good-bye, Lieutenant Kije!" Tatya whispered through her tears.

Once upon a time, vast pods of dolphins had frolicked along these shores. Indigenous fishermen had noted their migrations and prepared their nets, knowing the fish would come in ahead of them, herded closer to the shore by the playful predators. Man and dolphin had worked in harmony for generations, sharing the largess.

Now the dolphins were gone, the fishermen turned to other trades, and this particular stretch of beach lay dormant in the moonlit night. The conning tower of a great ship breached the surface some kilometers offshore, looking lost and alone, as if seeking its brethren who were no more.

Beside the tower bobbed the small skiff that had in Jason Nyere's capable hands first brought two exiled Vulcans to his ship. A different captain, the one named Kirk, held the tiller now as three Vulcans left *Delphinus* for their journeys home.

"Beautiful night," Gary Mitchell said quietly, scanning the beachfront. "Wish there was a little less moon, though. I read some kind of vehicle up the beach a-ways."

"Just one?" Kirk asked. Mitchell nodded. "We're almost in the clear, then."

Elizabeth Dehner was the last to leave the great ship. She had seen to the "reeducating" of each of the four to be left behind. The experience had drained her. She looked pale, drawn, desperately tired.

"Are you all right?" Jim Kirk asked as Spock helped her into the small boat.

"No, I'm not," she said frankly, pale hair falling over her paler face as she stumbled and Spock caught her, seated her in the last available space beside him in the bow. "I'd like to rest now."

The night was chill. There were blankets in the emergency kit. Spock wrapped one around Dehner's shoulders. Half drugged with weariness, she leaned against him and tumbled into sleep. Spock held her, perhaps only to steady her in the bobbing boat. She woke when they touched ashore.

"I'm sorry!" she murmured, coming to herself with

380

her head against Spock's chest, knowing how Vulcans, and he especially, were disquieted by human touch.

Silently Spock helped her out of the boat.

Sorahl stepped agilely over the gunwale and knelt at the tide line, scooping up two handfuls of sand—one sea-wet, the other dry. His face wore wonderment beneath an alien moon.

"It is this moment, Mother," he said.

T'Lera knew what he meant. They had at last set foot on Earth.

Chapter Eleven

A FAMILIAR ROBED figure stepped out of the overland vehicle parked where moonlit beach met shadowed rain forest.

"All are here and all is well!" Parneb rejoiced as the little entourage straggled up the beach. "I have prepared for all contingencies. The vehicle—is she not a beauty?—will seat you all quite comfortably. I have provided suitable disguises for our guests—turbans and *djellabas* for the gentlemen, a *tobe* and veil for the lady. Ah, if only you had not been born Vulcans, you could have been Egyptians! Oh, and, Captain Kirk," he called to the last member up the beach, busy setting the homing device that would drift the little skiff out to sea and then scuttle her. "I have a small surprise."

Kirk, made melancholy at the thought of sacrificing any ship, no matter how small, to any cause, no matter how large, turned in the direction of the overlander as the "small surprise" uncoiled himself from the driver's side, grinning like a mischievous small boy.

"Lee?" Jim Kirk couldn't believe it. He cleared his throat. "Mr. Kelso, where the devil have you—"

"I got sidetracked for a while," Kelso admitted.

"Little difference of opinion with the authorities about borrowing computer time. They tried to keep me overnight but, a little improv here, a door jimmied there—I've been around."

"I'll just bet he has!" Mitchell remarked. "Bet you he's been lying around in the sun while the rest of us have been where the shooting was. Time we got you to do an honest day's work, Lee."

"On the contrary," Parneb nattered away as they settled themselves into the overlander for the long drive to the Western Desert. "Lee has been a very sorcerer! Wait until he tells you what he has accomplished! Captain Kirk, if you could see your way clear to spare him, what magic I could work with such an apprentice. . . ."

There were indeed two sleeper ships suspended in horizontal berths in the man-made cavern beneath the desert. Beside them, an empty gantry had evidently once held a third.

"Burn marks on the floor," Jim Kirk observed, his voice bouncing off the walls. "Then they can be launched from here, if we're lucky. Go over the two remaining ones carefully," he instructed his augmented crew. "We'll use the one that needs the least refurbishing and strip the other for parts. Let's see how much we can boost these old nuclear engines. I wish Mr. Scott was with us!"

"We'll cope, Jim," Mitchell assured him, tossing a spanner up to Sorahl on the exterior catwalk, boosting Kelso into a crawl space bristling with wires and old-style transistor units.

Spock and T'Lera had already brought up the on-board computer and had their heads together conferring over exterior hull readouts. Kirk rolled up his sleeves and was soon sneezing in the fifty-year-old dust of the reactor room.

* * *

"So you've been censoring the people's right to know, have you, Lee?"

"Well, I wouldn't go *that* far, Mitch. A little judicious cut-and-paste here, an occasional bit of editing there—"

"A little tinfoil here, a couple of tapeworms there—"

Jim Kirk cleared his throat impatiently. The three of them were wedged cheek-to-jowl inside an environmental control conduit; he could live with a little less hot air.

"Mr. Mitchell, get your elbow out of my ribs!" he grunted. "Would one of you mind telling me what you're talking about?"

"You mean Lee hasn't told you what happened after he skipped on the CommPolice?" Mitchell backed out of the conduit to get a spare part for the humidity sensor, called over his shoulder. "Tell him, Lee!"

"Well?" Kirk asked tightly. Kelso's elbow was in his ribs now.

Kelso managed to look sheepish even from this angle. "Well, Ji—Cap—I, um—well, I guess you had to be there. Had to hear the hysteria every time you turned on the vidscreen. You guys were protected from a lot of that. But I couldn't sit there and do nothing, let it get all blown out of proportion."

"I can appreciate that," Kirk conceded, sliding further up the conduit to adjust an oxygen converter valve. "So what did you do?"

"Well, I was afraid someone would get hurt or killed," Kelso went on. "Panic in the streets, riots, mass hysteria. So I—"

"You *what?*" Kirk growled. "Come on, Lee, spit it out!"

"I got into the GlobalNews computers and planted some virus programs," Kelso said all in a rush. "Tapeworms to eat up the inflammatory news stories, new programs to replace them with 'unconfirmed and conflicting reports.' Left them tied up in knots!" he finished, beaming, pleased with himself.

Kirk collapsed against the wall of the conduit. "Lee, you amaze me!"

"I know," Kelso said modestly, not for the first time.

"Maybe I *should* leave you behind with Parneb," Kirk threatened, easing himself out the way Gary had gone. "You still haven't told me how you got away from the CommPolice."

"Maybe that one should wait," Kelso said uneasily. "Remind me to tell you later."

But he never did.

"Logically," Spock explained to Kirk and T'Lera, "Planetary defense systems will be directed outward, in search of incoming hostile vessels. The last Earth system directed against the planet itself, and in essence against its own citizens, was the so-called SDI system of the last century, which was dismantled with the signing of the United Earth Accords. Present systems will not anticipate a vessel containing aliens heading *away* from Earth.

"Consequently, if Sorahl is as skilled a navigator as his commander purports him to be," Spock concluded dryly, studying his paradoxically both younger and elder kinsman, "their vessel should be able to leave the Sol system undetected."

"And that's the best we can do," Kirk said in turn to T'Lera. "I only wish we could give you warp drive."

"It is more than sufficient, Captain," T'Lera replied. "And if my navigator is as skilled as I purport him to be, it will serve."

Kelso had tuned the on-board computer to a nearby radio band to check up on his tapeworm crop.

". . . rumors continue to trickle in from the frozen continent, particularly in light of the discovery of the bodies of four armed individuals, one of them reputedly that of the terrorist leader known as Racher, the Avenging One . . ."

Covered with lubricant and grinning from ear to ear, Lee Kelso slid back under the chassis of the old DY-100 and whistled while he worked.

"In a not-unrelated story, PentaKrem officials have issued a statement confirming that the AeroNav vessel found at anchor off the coast of Mali this morning is in fact the *CSS Delphinus,* the same vessel sent to retrieve an unidentified spacecraft from the South Pacific two weeks ago. Captain Jason Nyere and his first officer, along with two as-yet-unidentified civilians who were the only personnel aboard, were removed from the ship for questioning . . ."

"And if I've done my job right"—Elizabeth Dehner handed off the container of food concentrates Parneb had just unloaded from the overlander to Jim Kirk, who stacked it atop the others in the hold—"they'll find all four of them smiling, cooperative, and totally uninformed about what's happened to them in the past two weeks."

"God willing!" Kirk said.

". . . this just in: security forces in Antarctica report the arrest of four individuals passing themselves off as journalists in an attempt to leave the continent at a point not too far from Byrd Research Complex, the still-unconfirmed site where two alleged extraterrestrials were supposedly being held. One of the four detainees was identified as Aghan, participant in the Twelve November Alliance . . ."

"Optimum launch window at 2300 hours, Commander," Spock informed T'Lera as an automated winch slowly raised the DY-100 to its vertical position beside the waiting gantry.

"Affirm," T'Lera said distantly, her thoughts already on the stars.

". . . further evidence that the body found frozen in

a disabled snowmobile, along with a substantial cache of arms, is in fact that of the ringleader of the group calling themselves the Easter Rebellion. The mystery deepens in conjunction with the death of the survivalist leader Racher and the arrest of four others, suggesting that terrorism in our time has been dealt a serious, possibly fatal blow . . ."

The desert sky was cloudless and abrim with stars. One of this glittering host, a red M-2 sun about which orbited a harsh, demanding world, birthplace of four-teen billion disciplined, logical beings, beckoned two of its number home. A third native of that world, who as yet had no home, began a countdown from the control room beneath the rock. Inside the clumsy Earth ship, T'Lera of Vulcan touched the controls, triangulated off that glinting ruby in the sky, and the lumbering DY-100 lifted off.

Radio telescopes at Arecibo, Puerto Rico, in Khazakstan and the Nevada desert, on Mars and the far side of the moon, scanned the skies outward, unnoticing of a small silver ship slipstreaming under their noses, past Jupiter and beyond.

Sorahl kept Kelso's radio frequency open as long as it was viable.

". . . disease continues to spread unchecked, with unconfirmed reports that the entire South Pacific crop has now been affected. Personnel on Luna and Mars have been advised of possible food shortages and the need to abandon their bases and return to Earth if . . ."

"No sir." Yoshi smiled affably at the intell-agent asking all the questions. "Jason never told us where he was taking us or why. Naturally I wanted to stay with my crops, but pass up a free vacation?"

Other intell-agents, searching his cabin aboard *Delphinus*, puzzled over a book of late-twentieth-century poems entitled *You and I* hidden with his socks.

Yoshi used to read those poems aloud to Tatya on the agrostation, he explained. Love poems, you know. The intell-agents nodded, put the book back, completely missing the crumpled computer printout stuck in it for a bookmark.

"We've done our best," Jim Kirk announced to the remnant of his crew long after the DY-100's trajectory had taken her out of sight. He climbed into the overlander with the others. "Parneb, take us home."

"Leaving Sol system in one hundred seventy-three minutes—mark, Commander," Sorahl reported, reverting to the language and the time measurement of his birth planet, which somehow fitted him not so smoothly after two Earth weeks of speaking Standard.

"Affirm," T'Lera replied, her far-searching eyes containing only the stars.

The transmissions from Earth continued, growing fainter.

". . . begun in 1986 as the World Hunger Year Concerts, in those desperate times when much of the world's people were inadequately fed, this year's sixtieth annual Concert for Peace seems particularly poignant in view of the recent uproar over a possible alien incursion upon Earth . . ."

". . . PentaKrem spokespersons, in a joint statement with the United Earth Council, reiterated yet again today that maneuvers in the South Pacific and on the Antarctic continent, erroneously believed by media infiltrators to be evidence of an alien invasion, were nothing more than a test of Earth's preparedness to cope with any potential invasion. Repeat: rumors of an alien invasion were totally false; the exercises carried on by Combined Services forces were intended to test planetary defense systems and to assess Earth's readiness to deal with life on other worlds. PentaKrem and council officials have stated unequivocally that there were not, and never have been, aliens on Earth. We repeat: the so-called alien invasion . . ."

As the slow-moving sleeper ship passed Pluto, the radio signal continued to fade.

". . . concluding our classical program with the suite from Sergei Prokofiev's 'Lt. Kije.' This comic tale of the imaginary romantic hero created by a stroke of Czar Nicholas's pen—"

Static from the Oort Cloud swallowed the signal. Sorahl, like his commander, turned his thoughts outward to the stars.

Parneb's overlander pulled up in front of his tel in the hour before dawn. Kelso still had the radio on.

"We repeat once again: there were not and never have been—"

"Lee, enough!" Jim Kirk said testily as everyone piled out of the vehicle. "Turn that thing off!"

Kelso did. Everyone but Spock went inside.

"Mr. Spock," Kirk said quietly in the morning stillness. Somehow the relationship between them would never be the same. "Come inside, please. The sooner we get out of here . . ."

The Vulcan seemed lost in thought. "A moment, please, Captain."

He stood in the deserted Theban street beneath a royal-blue sky in the hour before dawn, at the base of a tel of six thousand years' building in this ancient Earth place. He would not have attracted attention had some early riser happened by, dressed as he was in a sky-blue *djellaba,* his stark features enhanced by the turban that did indeed make him look almost Egyptian. Spock gazed for what might be the last in a long time at the sky of Earth, where all but the brightest stars had faded, and reached inside the *djellaba* to remove a thin silver chain from around his neck.

He held the talisman in his gifted hands and considered. This thing belonged to Earth; he had no right to take it with him. Loosening some stones from the base of the tel, Spock buried the talisman in Earth.

The others, back in Starfleet uniform, were waiting

for him in Parneb's ancient cellar. Above and beyond them, as Parneb made his preparations for their departure, an awakening world turned on its vidscreens to the first somber news of the day.

". . . today mourned the death of Professor Jeremy Grayson, who died peacefully in his sleep . . ."

"You're sure this will work?" Kirk asked Parneb, uneasy about the entire process.

"You have worked your magic, Captain," the sorcerer said equably. "Now it is my turn."

He had moved the great crystal down to the ancient room beneath the tel to augment its power; it pulsed and glowed in empathy with the smaller crystal hung about his neck. Jim Kirk found himself wondering if a transporter were any less magical.

He had arrayed his people on the sand-swept floor as if awaiting a transporter beam up, noticed Kelso was out of position. He cleared his throat.

"Mr. Kelso?"

"Just saying good-bye!" Kelso took a last look around, gave Parneb's colossal walls a final loving pat. "I may never find this place again," he pointed out, rejoining the others.

He did not see the look of sorrow on Parneb's face.

"We're ready," Kirk said.

He remembered nothing else.

Parneb's calm had been a sham; he was no more sure of the range of his powers now than when he'd first brought these people here. But he was their only hope for return to their century; how could he possibly tell them that? Clasping the small crystal in both hands, vowing never to tamper with time again if only this worked, he concentrated all of his strength to make wishing make it so. . . .

And overshot the mark. He felt the five of them surge away from him, to a time beyond time. The images in the great crystal sprang out at him, splayed themselves on the walls in images of bloody horror, in montage of betrayal and violence and death, of voices he knew, but voices distorted by urgency, tragedy and fear.

"Above all else a god needs compassion . . ."

"Well, it didn't make any sense that he'd know . . ."

"Spock is right and you're a fool if you can't see it . . ."

"Oh, *dear!*" Parneb lamented, shaking his head as if it could drive the images away, clasping the crystal as if to crush it into submission and pull them back.

"Kill me while you can . . ."

"A god needs compassion . . ."

"Kill Mitchell while you still can . . ."

"I'm sorry . . . You can't know what it's like to be almost a god . . ."

"Pray to me, Captain . . . pray that you die easily . . ."

"Compassion . . ."

"I'm sorry . . ."

"Kill Mitchell . . ."

"Kill me . . ."

"Above all else a god needs compassion, MITCH-ELL!"

Parneb seized the great crystal, wrestled it into submission, his fingers burning into it as if clutching dry ice. The images whirled, assaulted him, fused themselves into him as he pulled them back, back . . .

To a place of swirling blue dust and clouded judgment, where two figures, one standing watch, the other fallen in undignified sprawl in the sand—

"Captain?"

A strong and gentle hand helped Jim Kirk to his feet.

"What happened?" Kirk dusted his trousers, mentally checked for bruises, tried to remember where they were and why. The first was easier than the second.

"Apparently the thinness of the atmosphere is inimical to human lungs, Captain. You lost consciousness. I took the liberty of having the others beamed aboard."

"You did the right thing," Kirk said vaguely. The others. The rest of the landing party, obviously, but who?

"Mr. Mitchell and Mr. Kelso reported some upper respiratory distress," Spock was saying, and Kirk fixed the two names in his memory. Bits of their mission were coming back to him, but why was he so disoriented? "They are reporting to Sickbay."

"Good," Kirk said, beginning to cough from the dust.

"Captain?" The Vulcan appeared concerned. "May I suggest we beam up also? There is nothing further to be learned here."

The details came back to Kirk at last: a landing party, to examine a planet that seemed to disappear. The planet on which they were now standing, and which at any moment—

"You—did not lose consciousness, Mr. Spock?"

The Vulcan shook his head. "I am not aware of having done so, Captain. However, my time sense accounts for a loss of point-five minutes, and somehow I seem to have damaged my uniform." He showed Kirk where the hem of his tunic was torn, his insignia gone.

"And my communicator's missing," Kirk realized, feeling for it, searching the sand at his feet. "If we had more time—you say we lost only half a minute?"

"Affirmative, Captain, however—"

"However, it's not a good idea to stick around and wait for this dustball to take us into oblivion again," Kirk finished for him. "We can continue our research aboard the *Enterprise*. Which, as I seem to recall, is what you recommended in the first place. Remind me, Mr. Spock, to place more confidence in your judgment in future."

The words were said in all seriousness, but a Vulcan

somehow better versed in irony accepted them as they were intended.

"I shall give it first priority, Captain."

～～

Spock terminated the meld, emerging into the realm of light.

And noise. Specifically, McCoy's snoring. The doctor lay sprawled in his chair near the dormant hearth—head thrown back, mouth gaping, hands limp over the chair arms, one booted foot propped like a dead thing on the footrest, the other twisted improbably beneath the chair. He might have been dead, shot through the heart, except for the noise.

He had thundered off to sleep somewhere in the 28.6 hours that the other two had labored down the intricate paths of memory and history. No matter. The tricorder, tumbled out of his insensate hands and upended on the carpet, was still running. Its attentiveness to what had transpired was more important, finally, than McCoy's. No matter what it ultimately recorded, James Kirk's sanity was no longer an issue.

Spock retrieved the tricorder, turned it off, pondered some way to effect a similar result on McCoy. How one could purport to derive any benefit from a state of rest accompanied by such a prodigy of sound . . .

Spock looked at Kirk, who sat slumped forward in his chair, elbows on his knees, face buried in his hands.

"Are you all right, Jim?"

Kirk's shoulders sagged momentarily before that voice restored him. He ran his hands through his hair and looked at his friend.

"Are you?"

Reassured, he too contemplated McCoy, who if anything waxed louder.

"It's a shame he's got no volume control."

"That can be remedied," Spock said solemnly.

Effortlessly he lifted the limp figure from the chair,

intent upon carrying the doctor into the bedroom where he could snore to his heart's content. McCoy responded to the change in position by wrapping his arms around Spock's neck, snuggling into his shoulder, and mumbling something that caused him to smile in his sleep.

"'Rosebud'?" Spock repeated quizzically.

"A girl in the bar he frequents," Kirk said vaguely. "She glows in the dark."

"Indeed."

Wearing an expression of great long-suffering, Spock transported the doctor into the next room. He returned to find Kirk at the window wall, contemplating the twilight. His face, part shadow in the fading light, was set in the human equivalent of a mask, firm of mouth, hard of jaw, but the eyes (windows of the soul, Spock thought; a human metaphor, appropriate to one most human) looked wounded.

Kirk started slightly at the Vulcan's reflection in the glass.

"Spock . . ." The human shuddered, steadied himself against the window frame, passed one hand over his eyes, tried to smile, grew serious. "Parneb must have short-circuited our memories to cover his tampering."

"Precisely." Spock stood close, protective. "So that our memory of the past was forgotten or distorted."

"I'm cold!" Kirk said suddenly, surprised at himself. He set about laying a fire in the barren hearth. Spock remained at his side, to warm his soul.

Kirk stirred the fire, poured himself another brandy, could not speak.

They had had dinner. Kirk had actually slept some, dreamlessly for a change, had awakened in chagrin to find Spock keeping the watch and the dinner dishes cleared away. Spock had permitted himself a single restorative brandy.

Vulcans were for the most part impervious to the effects of ethanol; if they imbibed at all it was largely out of curiosity or for the sake of abiding by human customs when among humans. Spock, more abstemious than most, rarely drank even on such social occasions.

But the long mindjourney had taken its toll on him as well, and if his spirit was beset with thoughts of T'Lera and of Jeremy Grayson, what better way to restore it than to seek a place of warmth and quiet, the companionship of a friend, and the esthetic contemplation of what was essentially a potable work of art?

Nothing that is is unimportant. Spock studied the play of firelight in the amber depths of the vintage Armagnac. There were some things that transcended even the self-imposed discipline of the Vulcan.

"We were wrong!" Kirk said suddenly, poking at the fire. "We spirited T'Lera and Sorahl away from Earth on a totally false premise. Suppose the United Earth Council had decided to welcome them, initiate diplomatic relations? We may have done more harm than good. Spock, did we save the Federation, or set it back twenty years?"

Spock picked up Kirk's bound copy of *Strangers from the Sky*.

"If, as he intended, Captain Nyere had allowed the journalists onto his ship, the stage would have been set for the kind of 'media circus' which, in our shared nightmare, was prelude to the metaphorical blood-on-the-walls scenario," he said carefully. "If, as she intended, T'Lera had by then relieved all human agents of the responsibility for her death by taking Sorahl's life and then her own, our nightmare would have been realized. The means she would have chosen would not have been as violent—the blood-on-the-walls metaphor is yours, Jim—but the end would have been the same."

"Human journalists would have burst in on the bodies of two dead aliens and drawn all the wrong conclusions."

"Precisely."

"Whereas you believe that we, by simply being there, prevented that?"

"So it would seem."

"And our subconscious minds, triggered by my metaphor and unable to keep the secret forever, finished the worst-case scenario we'd journeyed to Antarctica to prevent," Kirk said slowly, piecing it together. "The signposts were there throughout the dreams—my tennis game with Melody, your dream about your mother. Because your memory of Jeremy Grayson was blocked, you dreamed instead about his great-granddaughter."

"Indeed."

"And because we were both needed to tell T'Lera the truth, neither of us could complete the dream alone—any more than we could have completed the job alone. And Elizabeth Dehner became the key, because she alone could galvanize us into forgetting our differences . . ."

"Therefore, Jim, despite our occasionally being cast as buffoons, we were necessary to the outcome."

He handed Kirk the book.

Epilogue

Having been assured that their planet was safe for the moment from talking petunias and little green men, the majority of humans shrugged and returned to the realm of the mundane. Unbeknownst to the majority, however, the continuum had been subtly changed. Life on Earth would never be quite the same.

Yoshi returned to the agrostation to find his entire acreage suffering from advanced kelpwilt. He immediately contacted AgroInternational, submitting "his" formula for an organic cure, and volunteering his station as the test site for Sorahl's synthetic enzyme. Within three days of treatment, the fungus was completely consumed. Patented at Yoshi's insistence under the name "Sorahlaze," the enzyme was made available to all agrostations at cost and eradicated the kelpwilt fungus from the entire planet within a solar year. Sorahlaze is still the specific for kelpwilt on any number of planets Federation-wide.

Did this contribution to Earth's science by an alien who officially did not exist in fact save Earth from famine? The true magnitude of Sorahl's contribution can never be measured. And this was only the beginning.

While terrorism had been virtually eliminated from Earth's political makeup even before the deaths of Racher and Easter, these deaths were in a sense the final blow. The rank and file lacked direction, and soon disappeared into cracks in the society that had spawned them. The arms dealer who had equipped both task forces was exposed and virtually bankrupted. Aghan and the others who were captured were "reeducated" well before the Mind Control Laws would have made this impossible. And while any human society will perforce always have its lunatic fringe, Melody Sawyer's laser rifle ensured that the remainder of Earth's twenty-first century was remarkably free of terrorism.

At the same time other, more positive movements were absorbing human attention and energies. Notable among these was Welcome, a society devoted to preparing humans to accept other intelligent life forms. Begun when *Icarus* left Earth for Alpha Centauri, Welcome did not become a recognized global entity until it included in its membership one Tatiana Bilash.

Tatya returned to the agrostation with Yoshi for a time, but while the two remained deeply affectionate and eventually had a child whom Yoshi raised, their paths had already begun to diverge. Deciding for reasons she could not define that her life required new direction, Tatya threw all her energies into Welcome, becoming its chief spokesperson. She was part of the delegation that welcomed the first Centaurians to Earth, and was one of the elder statespersons to sit at the first Babel Interplanetary Conference in 2087.

How much did Tatya remember of the events that sparked this new career? We will never know. What is known is that for all her travels, the one world she never visited was Vulcan.

Yoshi, however, did journey to Vulcan, as part of an exchange of scientists and agricultural experts in the year 2073. He never returned to Earth, but sought

Vulcan citizenship and was granted a teaching fellowship at ShiKahr, where all trace of him eventually
vanishes into the privacy that is uniquely Vulcan.
Perhaps he simply retired to the desert, perhaps he
became *dVel'nahr,* a Vulcan-by-choice, an honor that
has been granted to few humans. One can only
assume that he at last found the peace he could never
have found on Earth. Whether he and Sorahl ever met
again, whether either retained any memory of the
other, is also lost to their respective privacies.

Back on Earth, all was not order and tranquillity. In
the mop-up operation following the incident, the real
Dr. Bellero was recalled from Marsbase and interro-
gated about her supposed presence in Antarctica. The
true identity of the woman who took her place was
never determined, nor were the identities of the two
strangers—one charismatic, one somber—who succeeded in changing a Vulcan's mind.

Perhaps the key to the entire mystery is Parneb, but
our knowledge of Parneb begins and ends with Sorahl's journals. The young Vulcan made astute observations of the flamboyant human who drove the rescue
party through the Western Desert, chattering all the
way, then sat drinking tea with Dr. Bellero while the
others refitted the sleeper ship. But once that ship
leaves Earth, Sorahl can offer us no further insights on
Parneb or the unnamed strangers. Whoever they were,
their trail conjoins with Parneb's somewhere in the
timelessness of the desert, then vanishes.

Attempts to identify a Mahmoud Gamal al-Parneb
Nezaj result in the discovery of several persons of that
name, including one who married into the vast, extended al Faisal family some years after the Vulcan
incident, though there is evidence that this Parneb was
a much younger man. Whoever he was, he is quickly
lost in the byzantine intricacies of a clan whose roots
extend both to the ruling family of what was once Saudi
Arabia and to the Bedouin tribes extant in the Suez

from ancient times, and whose present descendants include former High Commissioner of United Earth Jasmine al Faisal. The marriage produced no offspring, and that seems to be the end of Parneb.

Controversy continued to plague the captain and first officer of the *Delphinus*. If there were innocent victims of the event other than the Vulcans, these two were among them.

Jason Nyere put in for early retirement from AeroNav not long after the incident he was not permitted to remember. Subsequent hospital records indicate his treatment for repeated bouts of depression in his later years. One can imagine him scanning the night sky from his home near Lagos, uncertain of what he sought, but seeking nevertheless. Jason Nyere died of an unspecified fever in 2064, the year before the Vulcans came to Earth again.

There is no evidence that Melody Sawyer suffered any recollection of the incident. Given her own command of the survey ship *Xeno,* she earned a reputation over the next twenty years as a hard but fair captain. She is recorded as rescuing all hands following an engine-room explosion before going down with her ship. Ironically, an engine design developed by Vulcans and eventually used in Earth vessels could have saved her life.

Sorahl of Vulcan kept a precise record of his ship's voyage home, which in fact took far less time than his human rescuers had estimated. Well beyond the Sol system, he encountered, whether by serendipitous coincidence or simply excellent navigation, a Vulcan robot ship prospecting for antimatter in the interstellar void. He was able to piggyback the adapted Earth vessel onto the robot ship and bring both to his world in under a year. This soon a return, and the account of their rescue as given by Sorahl and his commander, were significant to the Offworld Service's decision to continue its study of Earth.

A curious footnote to the event comes from the transcript of T'Lera's debriefing by the Offworld Service and members of the Vulcan Council, in which she refused to reveal the identities of her two Earthbound saviors. Under questioning, Sorahl was able to state only that "I have no knowledge of them," implying that his mother/commander had for her own reasons removed that knowledge from his mind. Thereafter it is recorded of Sorahl only that he resumed active duty in the Offworld Service, and served on or commanded a variety of exploration craft until his death at the age of 247. His meticulously kept journals were the basis of much of this author's research, for which she is most grateful.

Of T'Lera there is no further record at all. Following her final statement to the Vulcan Council that "It is not a lie to keep the truth to oneself, and some truths are best left unspoken," she simply disappears—from her son's journals, from history, perhaps from the realm of the living. T'Lera herself becomes the final unspoken truth.

Those of us born into a Federation five hundred planets strong may forget how tenuous were its beginnings. Those of us nurtured in a Federation that has kept the peace for a hundred years may forget that history is never simple, never linear, never predetermined, but is in fact the outcome of a tangle of subtext, chance, coincidence, and what-if? No individual reading this can deny that the presence of Vulcans has in some way affected all our lives. . . .

∽∫∽

Spock walked alone through the crowded streets of Thebes. Something drew him inexorably toward a place where he had walked before. He found the tel more by direction than recognition; the entire area surrounding it was now a warren of high-rises, and Parneb's neo-Fathy house was long gone. Perhaps someday the tel itself would be leveled in the name of progress, unearthing all its buried secrets. For now, however, it endured.

Spock did not expect to find that which he had left in this place in a time before he was born. His coming here was motivated more by nostalgia than by logic. He had come to pay homage to his ancestor.

Jeremy Grayson's body had long since gone to dust; his *Katra* lived on in the people of a world who had at last learned the lesson of his small amulet, and in the green blood of his unique offspring. If the amulet itself was lost in Earth, that was as it should be.

"Your pardon, sir Vulcan?" A small boy tugged at the sleeve of Spock's uniform, smiled a Cheshire-cat smile at him. "I believe you have misplaced this?"

He had picked up a fine silver chain from the dust at their feet, offered it to Spock, who studied him carefully. Too tall for his weight or too thin for his height, he was somehow terribly familiar.

"Surely this is yours," Spock answered, attempting to give the chain back to him.

The boy smiled. "But you see, I already have one," he said, showing Spock the milky uncut crystal that hung about his spindly neck. "That one belongs to you!"

He scampered off and vanished in the crowd; Spock could not have found him again if he had tried. Instead he considered the dusty, glinting thing that had been given to him again.

"Fascinating!"

A Vulcan's strong and gentle fingers, touched with the soil of his ancestral Earth, reverently cradled the symbol of peace.

STAR TREK®

STRANGE NEW WORLDS

EDITED BY
DEAN WESLEY SMITH
WITH ELISA J. KASSIN
AND PAULA M. BLOCK

All-new *Star Trek* adventures—by

fans, for fans!

Enter the *Strange New Worlds* short-story contest!
No Purchase Necessary.

Strange New Worlds 10 entries accepted between June 1, 2006 and October 1, 2006.

To see the Contest Rules please visit
www.simonsays.com/st

SNW.03